Susan Parry was born in London, studied chemistry at university and followed an academic career at Imperial College. She was working as a full-time professor with a young family, when she wrote her first crime novel using her experience of forensic and archaeological investigations. It was set in the Yorkshire Dales, an area she knows very well, and it became the first in the Mills Sanderson series.

website: www.susanparry.co.uk

Facebook/Instagram/Threads: susanparryauthor

Also by Susan Parry

MILLS SANDERSON SERIES

Tracks in the Dark

Susan Parry

Viridian Publishing

First published in the United Kingdom in 2024 by
Viridian Publishing

Viridian Publishing
PO Box 594
Dorking
Surrey
RH4 9HU

www.viridian-publishing.co.uk
e-mail: enquiries@viridian-publishing.co.uk

ISBN 978-1-7384149-0-1

For Mark

Chapter 1

The Detective Chief Inspector's words echoed round the bare room.

'These apparently unconnected cases have been investigated by three different police forces. The Major Crime Unit did a very thorough job last year when Amy Hobson's body was found. But even with the resources of two police forces they are no further forward, so I'm not expecting miracles from you. That's why this so called Regional Unsolved Crime Unit is a low-key pilot initiative. You are a very small outfit compared to a Major Crime Unit and we're expecting you to investigate two missing men in addition.' He looked round the room. 'This building is rented for two months, until the end of April. At that point we'll see if you've made any progress. I should warn you that you don't have long, although I'm sure you'll do your best.' He looked at his watch and turned to DI Abbott. 'Is there anywhere that does a decent coffee in Hawes?'

Miriam would describe Charles as overweight to be kind and it was obvious that he didn't take much exercise. She explained that parking in the middle of Hawes might be difficult but he insisted on taking the car anyway. The cold weather and freezing March wind probably explained why the town was quiet, so he proved her wrong by sailing into a parking space almost outside the coffee shop. His uniform turned a few heads when he held the door open for her and she gratefully let him buy her a coffee while she chose a table in the corner.

When he joined her, he was carrying a plate containing a large scone, jam and cream. 'Are you sure you don't want something to eat?' he asked.

She shook her head, wanting to get their meeting over as soon as possible. She was irritated by the very negative way he'd addressed her new team and was expecting their conversation to be even less amicable now it was just between the two of them.

'I know this unit is your special baby, Miriam, but it seems only fair not to raise their expectations. I hope you didn't think I was too downbeat.' He waited for the girl to deliver their coffees, then added, 'Personally I wasn't entirely on board with the project from the start.'

Of course he wasn't keen, thought Miriam. The investigation team he had been responsible for had failed to find the person who strangled Amy Hobson and left her body on the moor. The case was going cold and that would have been the end of the investigation if someone hadn't thought that two apparently unrelated incidents might be connected to her death. Clearly Charles didn't agree.

She knew there would be baggage. She'd been careful to check that her ex-husband hadn't been involved in the original case before taking the job, but Charles had been a friend and mentor of Henry's for most of their married life and without his support Henry would never have made it up the ranks to Chief Inspector. She'd never liked

Charles, he was snobbish, pompous and a misogynist, but she'd done her duty and sat through dinner parties listening to his egotism. Her separation from Henry had created even more difficult relations with her senior officer. However, he seemed oblivious of any awkwardness between them as he bit into the scone and wiped cream from his upper lip.

She just couldn't resist asking if he'd seen Henry recently, just to see his discomfort.

He sipped his coffee, playing for time. 'Yes, actually we had a game of golf last week.'

'Is he well?'

'Yes, I think so.'

'Does he know about my new unit?'

'I don't know. Yes, I think so. We didn't discuss it though.' He put his cup back on its saucer carefully. 'I was sorry to hear you were separated. You were married a long time.'

'Twenty-six years.'

'Really? And so a new start for you.'

That stung. Yes, she'd had to make a new start while Henry carried on as usual, even down to his golf afternoons. Charles was concentrating on finishing his scone. 'So has everyone settled in up here?' he asked, apparently keen to change the subject.

'I would have liked a say in the make-up of the team,' she began. 'Robert may be a reliable bobby with years under his belt and he is familiar with the area, but I'm not sure he's up to acting as sergeant. The others are young and very new to the force.'

'I don't disagree with you. I thought it was being set up too hastily but when the new information came in it was all systems go. You must appreciate this is the first opportunity to set up a special investigation team of this nature and it had to be in place fast to be effective. The selection process was designed to find personnel with specific attributes, of course. The lad, Jack, is a whizz-kid when it comes to digital and the girl was a SOCO before she joined Cumbria CID.'

Miriam knew that Jack's boss had been quite enthusiastic about letting him go as he was on a short-term contract, and Lily had only just finished her training as a DC. 'Hardly an experienced team,' she commented.

He was smiling. 'I'm afraid the office accommodation is rather primitive too.'

Miriam agreed. It was effectively a farmyard barn, one that had originally been turned into a space for martial arts training. 'We'll need to improve the heating and I noticed there was only one phone. We'll need a photocopier and…'

'Steady on, Miriam. We don't have a limitless budget for this. We are already having to fund additional temporary accommodation costs that we didn't anticipate. We can only bankroll this for a couple of months tops, which is why I meant it when I said you and your team have a limited time to find Amy Hobson's killer.'

'And establish whether the two male mispers are also victims,' Miriam added.

'Well, that's pretty unlikely, isn't it? A man who kills a pretty young female isn't going after two men, is he?'

Miriam had learnt that it was important to keep an open mind in police detective work. Patterns, predictions, modus operandi were important but she never failed to be surprised by what people were capable of. It was time to get back to her new team and revive their enthusiasm for the task ahead. She drained her cup and put it down noisily.

'Well I'd best get back and crack on,' she said, grabbing her coat.

Charles was struggling to his feet.

'No, stay where you are and finish your coffee. Just one thing though, next time you see Henry, tell him from me that I hope he'll keep in touch with our daughter – she seems quite upset that he's shacked up with someone young enough to be her sister.'

Damn, she said to herself, immediately regretting her outburst. It wasn't clever or even appropriate.

As the senior rank present while the boss was away, Robert took responsibility for getting the office organised in her absence.

'There are tables piled up in the storeroom. Can you give us a hand carrying them in?'

Lily jumped up immediately, although Robert thought she looked too skinny and frail to heave furniture around. The lad, who was carrying quite a few extra pounds, remained seated, studying his mobile.

'Jack!'

He stood up slowly, tucking his phone into his back pocket. 'Sorry Bob.'

'It's Robert. The sooner we have desks to work at, the sooner we can fire up the computers and access the files.'

'Depending on whether we have any broadband,' Jack muttered. 'I was just checking and it doesn't look promising.'

'Well, that's your department, lad,' replied Robert.

'Making sure we are able to work effectively.'

'No pressure then,' he muttered, following him to the storeroom.

They were discussing how to arrange the furniture in the limited space available when the door swung open and a white-haired woman entered. 'I thought you'd need something hot to drink,' she said, depositing a tray on the nearest table. 'There's coffee here and some biscuits.'

Jack moved forward and grabbed a mug, topping it up from the small jug. 'Biscuit anyone?' he asked offering the plate to Lily.

'That's very kind of you,' said Robert, crossing to push the door shut before turning to the woman. 'I'm Robert by the way.' He added milk to one of the mugs and encouraged Lily to do the same. 'This is Lily and that's Jack.'

'I'm Elizabeth from across the way. My husband didn't tell me you were moving in today or I'd have cleaned around a bit. This place hasn't been used for a while. Although it looks as though you're getting yourselves sorted out.'

Robert smiled at her. 'Yes we'll soon be shipshape.'

Jack took another biscuit. 'But there isn't a broadband signal,' he complained.

She explained that the hub was upstairs and insisted on showing him. He drained his coffee, grinning at Robert as he followed her out of the office.

'He'll be happy now,' said Lily. It was the first bit of conversation she'd offered since they'd met. 'He's some sort of cyber-crime expert, isn't he?'

'I wouldn't go as far as that, Lily. He's only a junior civilian support from the National Crime Agency.'

They listened to the footsteps moving about above them until finally they were coming downstairs again.

Elizabeth looked triumphant.

'Sixty-seven megabits per second,' Jack announced when they reappeared.

'Is that good?' asked Robert.

'Not brilliant.'

'But good enough for what we need,' Lily retorted.

Elizabeth was collecting up their mugs. 'What is it exactly you do, if you don't mind me asking? I knew it was police work because I met your boss this morning but he never explained what you were going to be doing here.'

'We're the Regional...' Jack began.

He was quickly interrupted by Robert. 'Rural Unsolved Crime Unit,' he explained.

'Oh, is that about wildlife and quad bikes going missing?' she asked.

Jack looked at Robert and nodded. 'Yes, it's a low-key thing.'

She picked up the tray. 'If you need anything just give us a knock at the back door.' She pointed across the yard.

It wasn't long before Lily and Jack were arguing about where they should have their desks. Robert had insisted that their boss would want the prime spot by the window and he would be alongside. They would be without a view on the opposite wall. Fed up with their bickering, he went outside for a smoke just as Miriam walked back into the yard. He quickly stubbed out his cigarette and explained that he was letting "the youngsters" get on with it.

'They're arguing over how to arrange the desks,' he explained with a sigh.

'I think we've wasted far too much time already, don't

you?' she asked, stepping past him and through the door. 'The furniture can wait,' she instructed her junior members of staff. 'Come over here so we can start work.'

She threw her coat on the back of her chair and pushed up her sleeves. The others gathered round, dragging chairs into a rough circle. They were eyeing her nervously.

'I'm not going to pretend that our job is going to be easy but, unlike the Chief Inspector, I believe we can do it. But time is of the essence, as they say, because resources are limited. What we do have is the information accrued during the three investigations and we will have to use our wits to establish what hasn't been spotted before. We have the advantage of the recent discovery which points to a possible connection with the geographical area. So I'll start by giving you a brief review of the situation as I see it and then we can work out how to proceed. Ok?'

Everyone nodded solemnly. No-one spoke.

Here we go then, thought Miriam as she picked up her notes. 'Amy Hobson was reported missing last November. She had just turned eighteen and was working in her gap year before going to college. She lived here in Hawes but was doing shifts at a hotel bar in Kirkby Stephen. On the afternoon of Sunday the seventh she didn't return home and her parents rang the police the following day. Her car was found in the town square, Cumbria police investigated but drew a blank.' She looked at Lily, who had been seconded from Cumbrian force. The girl reddened and nodded.

'Two months later she was found on moorland,' Miriam continued, conscious they were hanging on every word. 'She'd been strangled. Her body was located on an estate just beyond Hawes. North Yorkshire Major Crimes Unit did a thorough investigation but it led nowhere and remains on their files. Everyone hopes we can throw some light on what happened to Amy Hobson.'

She looked round. 'Any questions so far?' Silence.

'OK. Next Brian Berry, an eighty-year-old walker doing the Herriot Way. He left Hawes on the seventh of November and was never seen again. His family expected him to call but heard nothing. He rang the B&B in Keld where he planned to stay that night to say he'd be late but never turned up. First of all they searched for him in Swaledale since it was thought he might have got lost in the dark on the last part of his journey, but they also checked the entire route from Hawes in case he'd collapsed somewhere along it. He was never found.'

She asked Robert, who was familiar with the Northern Dales, if he could explain the route Mr Berry would have followed.

'The Herriot Way starts at Aysgarth, then goes to Hawes, Keld, Reeth and back to Aysgarth again. It's fifty-two miles and takes four days. It's named after James Herriot, the chap who wrote "All Creatures Great & Small", the famous vet.'

Jack looked impressed when Robert admitted that he'd completed the walk some years ago.

'Which means,' Miriam continued, getting back to the point, 'that he could have disappeared in this area. Perhaps a coincidence, but at pretty much the same time as Amy Hobson. The possible connection was probably overlooked because the cases were not originally geographically connected.'

Their faces suggested they were busy trying to absorb it all.

'So, to our third case. Greg Nevitt, a keen cyclist from Barnsley. He went on leave in November, no-one knows where he went, and he didn't return to work after two weeks. It was only when his ex-wife couldn't get hold of him, and there was no sign of him at his flat, that he was reported missing several weeks later. No progress was made and West Yorkshire force decided that he was just another misper until his bicycle turned up three weeks ago not far from here.'

Now there was more interest. Lily was writing in a small notebook, Robert was rubbing his chin and frowning, while Jack straightened up in his chair. There were questions. They wanted more details and began talking over each other. Miriam held up her hand.

'Wait! I don't want you to get too involved in all three cases. I'd like each of you to take responsibility for one of them.'

'But they'll all have digital information to process,' objected Jack.

'They will, and I'm sure we'll all need your specialised knowledge, but we're a very small team and the purpose of bringing you together is to think outside the box, look at things from another angle. Lily here is a detective but she has a forensics background, which will be invaluable in interpreting all the evidence we have to trawl through for Amy Hobson. I know you're civilian support staff but this is an opportunity to use your analytical skills.' She took a deep breath. 'So, I would like Robert, who knows the area well and is a keen rambler himself, to concentrate on our missing walker.'

The sergeant nodded.

'Lily, I'd like you to take Amy.'

She was clearly delighted and smiled broadly.

Jack looked disappointed. 'So I'm covering the missing cyclist?'

'Yes.' Miriam raised her eyebrows, indicating that if he wanted to argue, she was ready.

He sank back on his chair with his arms folded.

'Well we'd better get this room sorted so we can work on our laptops,' she said, standing up. 'The tables look fine where they are.' A smile of triumph flickered across Lily's face. 'Jack, we'll need your help getting onto the internet.'

'All done, Ma'am. The hub is upstairs, the old dear from across the way showed us this morning.'

Miriam shook her head. 'We're a small team, we'll use first names. I'm Miriam, but the old dear across the way, as you called her Jack, is Mrs Whitehead to you.'

Chapter 2

Lily approached Miriam while Jack was busy setting up the laptops. 'I thought I'd go to Kirkby Stephen this afternoon to speak to the manager of the bar where Amy worked,' she announced. She expected her boss to be pleased.

There was a pause before she replied. 'It's an idea but perhaps you could consider keeping a lower profile. We've been embedded here in Hawes so we can work as part of the community. We are more likely to gain intelligence by listening quietly rather than rushing in asking direct questions.'

'You mean work undercover?' Lily was surprised but excited.

Her boss smiled. 'Not exactly, just low profile. I suggest you go over in the evening as soon as possible to see who drinks there and get to know the customers.'

Lily nodded, hoping her apprehension wasn't obvious. She returned to her desk, where Jack was working on her laptop.

'Almost done,' he said without looking up as he beat the keyboard with two fingers.

She waited beside him for a couple of minutes, studying his greasy hair brushing the collar of his sweatshirt, thinking he should use a dandruff shampoo, until eventually he asked her to enter a password and she was online.

'Let me know if I can help you with anything else,' he

offered, getting up from her chair. 'And I don't just mean IT stuff. You've got the murder case and I get that, with you being a detective, but I don't think there's much to go on with my missing cyclist so I'll probably have spare time to help you out.'

Lily was about to tell him she was fine, thank you, when she stopped. 'Actually there is something. Are you busy this evening?'

They were interrupted by Robert calling Jack over to get the one available landline connected to the DI's desk, leaving Lily to begin downloading the files relating to Amy Hobson. She studied the girl in the photo which had obviously been taken at a party. She was laughing at the camera. Her lipstick matched her bright red dress and her blonde hair was falling round her face in curls. As Lily began reading her parents' description of their daughter, it built a picture of a girl who knew how to enjoy herself. At first her family had assumed she'd stayed over with a friend, so had not been alarmed when she hadn't arrived home at the end of her shift. She had several good friends in the village who had given statements to the police after she'd disappeared, indicating that it wouldn't have been out of character for her to have gone home with a lad. Lily searched for mention of a boyfriend but there was no-one currently on the scene. She noted down the names of Amy's friends, deciding to find out a bit more about them and spent the next couple of hours trawling through their social media posts, building up a picture of Amy and her contacts.

She looked up when there was a knock on the door and Mrs Whitehead appeared with a kettle. Their DI invited her in and they went into the kitchen together. Lily looked at Jack, who grinned across at her. When they returned after a few minutes, Miriam clapped her hands to attract their attention.

'Mrs Whitehead has kindly offered to provide us with sandwiches, if we would like her to. I said we would certainly appreciate it today, my treat. Is there anything that anyone can't eat?'

There was no reply so the farmer's wife went off to prepare lunch. Lily watched Robert wander outside where he lit a cigarette, while Jack was setting up his computer. She looked over at the DI. She was sure that she would want her to start looking at the forensic evidence since she'd specifically mentioned Lily's background in crime scene investigation. Back in Cumbria she had specialised as a fingerprint expert but her degree had covered many more interesting aspects. Her final year project had been on shoe patterns, which was why Cumbria had been interested in her at the interview. So she was hoping there would be something she could recognise in the forensic pack. As she sorted through the photographs of the crime scene, she realised how very different it was to being present at the time. Now her evaluation was limited to written records and what the photographer had captured, and if evidence wasn't there, it didn't exist. By the time lunch arrived, she'd assumed that any tyre tracks and footprints at the scene were too obfuscating to be useful in the investigation. She made a note to contact the North Yorkshire CSI who had carried out the examination and joined the others, who were already gathered round Mrs Whitehead's tray of sandwiches.

Miriam was asking Robert how he knew the area so well.

'I was brought up in Skipton, my parents still live there, and I joined the local force when I left school. When I married, I got a transfer to West Yorkshire and we moved to Leeds.' He picked up a sausage roll and took a bite.

'So why did you come back here?' Jack asked.

Robert looked up sharply. 'If you must know, my wife died three years ago. I decided a change of scene would be good. Also my folks are not getting any younger so it's an opportunity to spend more time with them.'

It was an awkward moment although Jack seemed unfazed. Lily glanced at the DI, wondering why Robert thought he'd have more time when they would have to work all hours to achieve their goals in the limited time they'd been given.

But Miriam was smiling at him. 'Will you stay with them while you're here?' she asked.

He seemed unsure. 'I was thinking I could cycle up in the better weather but it took me an hour to get here in the car this morning.'

He picked up the box of teabags from the tray, offering to make a brew, then disappeared into the kitchen. Lily felt sorry for him but Jack was grinning as he helped himself to a second sausage roll, despite her pointing out that there were only enough for the four of them to have one each.

Lily was ready to report on what she'd been working on that morning so had her notebook in her pocket, but her boss was more interested in how she was settling in and whether their bed and breakfast accommodation was satisfactory.

'It's nice. The lady who owns it is very friendly and "The Pines" is a lovely house.'

Jack was shaking his head. 'The broadband is slow...' he began.

'It's fine and you enjoyed the big breakfast she served up.'

Miriam was frowning. 'Well, let me know if you have any problems. I requested somewhere within walking distance, Jack, since you don't drive.'

Lily was amused. She'd given him a lift that morning and, looking at the size of him, she guessed he rarely walked anywhere despite having no transport. She carried her mug of tea back to her desk to continue working on the murder investigation. The words gave her a thrill and she couldn't wait to tell her family. Robert was hunched over his laptop and Miriam was asking Jack if he knew how the heating worked. Lily watched him disappear upstairs then opened the evidence file again.

Amy's body had been lying on open moorland for no more than a few weeks. Well that was obvious since she was found three weeks after she went missing. She could have been held somewhere prior to her being strangled but the post-mortem suggested that was unlikely. She was found by a working dog on the estate but Lily couldn't tell whether there had been any pheasant shoots during the previous three weeks, when she might have been found earlier, if the body was there. She made a note to check. The place where Amy was found was marked on a detailed map of the area, only about five miles away from Hawes. The track from the main road went up Cotterdale, past a farm and onto the open moor, presumably to give access to the grouse shooting fraternity, meaning whoever took her up there probably had four-wheel-drive. She made a note to check the vehicles in the car park when she went to Kirkby Stephen. The North Yorkshire police had concentrated on men in the area who were associated with the shoot, on the basis that whoever drove Amy to Cotterdale knew the area. There were numerous statements from keepers, beaters, gun-loaders, dog-handlers, and estate workers. She would go through those later.

The Cumbria police had interviewed staff and customers who were in the hotel bar on the day Amy went missing. Lily planned to spend the rest of the afternoon reading their statements, conscious the boss wanted her to visit the place as soon as possible. The girl had only been working in the hotel for just over a month, so she wasn't particularly well known to most of them. The bar was busy with visitors at the weekend, and it had been impossible to contact everyone who'd been there the day Amy disappeared. However, there were three drinkers who she had chatted to when the bar was quiet. They were local lads who came in for a game of darts or pool during the week.

She hadn't noticed how dull it was getting until Robert got up to switch on the lights and went to make more tea. Lily knew she should offer to do it but she was determined not to end up as the tea-girl. She would talk to Jack about a rota since they were the junior members of the team. She walked down to the cramped cloakroom that housed a WC and wash basin. Someone had left the toilet seat up, presumably Jack, and she wondered if it would be unreasonable to put a notice on the back of the door to remind him. She was sure there were spiders lurking behind the cistern and the water from the hot tap never warmed up. She dried her hands on the rough paper towels, re-tied her ponytail in the foggy mirror and smiled at her reflection. This transfer was turning out to be more exciting than she'd ever imagined.

Back in the office, tea was served. The DI was passing round a packet of digestives, while suggesting her budget might stretch to cover a tea fund for milk and biscuits. Lily said that she and Jack would share tea duty and enjoyed the look of surprise on his face as she presented him with a *fait accompli*. Robert looked pleased with her offer. He told them he'd been familiarising himself with the missing walker, Brian Berry, who apparently came from Northumberland.

'He's a fascinating character,' the sergeant said. 'He was employed by the county council as a road engineer.'

'What, spreading the tarmac?' suggested Jack, dipping a biscuit in his tea.

Robert frowned at him. 'No, far from it. He was a senior engineer, responsible for highway and transport improvement. He retired fifteen years ago. He'd just celebrated his eightieth birthday.'

'What was he doing out walking on his own at that age?' asked Jack. 'That's just irresponsible.'

Robert shut his eyes and shook his head. 'No, lad. Brian Berry was very fit, a good walker, although admittedly he usually went out with a group. This time he decided to do the Herriot Way alone.'

Lily was watching Miriam quietly sipping her tea, listening to the conversation between Robert and Jack. Suddenly she put her mug down.

'I would like you all to become as familiar as possible with the cases you've been assigned before we discuss them in detail. That way we'll pick up more easily on any similarities, common threads etcetera.'

Lily jumped up. 'I'll wash the mugs,' she said, gathering them up.

Robert thanked her and Jack thrust his mug into her free hand. 'I hope you don't expect me to dry,' he said, marching back to his desk.

Never before had Lily felt so close to someone who'd been murdered. As a CSI she'd attended the scene of several attacks, but only when the pathologist had finished and the body had been removed, so examining what was left was quite clinical and remote from the victim. Here there were a series of photos of Amy's body. She was lying on her side, her face turned so it was in the mud. Her blonde hair, as long as Lily's, had been swept back to show the girl's thin, white face. She was wearing a tiny gold earring, her dark eyeliner smudged but still visible. Lily could detect the marks on her neck, evidence that she'd been strangled. Further shots showed that she was wearing jeans and a blouse that had been torn to expose a small tattoo of a butterfly on her shoulder.

Lily sighed. Amy could have been a friend in different circumstances. She seemed like someone who had a bit of get-up-and-go, as her mother would say. One of the lads in the pub had called her "sparkly" and "a laugh", another customer said she smiled a lot. The bar manager was happy with her work, saying that she was polite to customers and was a quick learner when it came to the different beers and lagers. It was her job to serve drinks and take orders for food and, if they weren't busy, she also did a bit of waitressing in the bar area. Lily was reminded that she hadn't told Jack about her plan for the evening.

'Where's Jack?' she asked Robert.

'He went upstairs a while ago. He muttered something about the internet.'

Lily found the wooden stairs off the corridor leading to the kitchen. She was surprised to see how light it was up in roof and found Jack peering out of a large window in the sloping ceiling.

'You get a great view from up here,' he said.

'What are doing?'

'Just checking things, you know, connections... the hub.'

Skiving, you mean, thought Lily.

He opened a door leading off the main room. It contained an old bed. 'Don't you think it's a great space, for offices, I mean,' he said.

Lily agreed then went on to tell him that she planned to visit the hotel in Kirkby Stephen and asked if he would like a lift, adding that they could eat there since they'd made no other arrangements. As she'd predicted, he was up for a bar meal and a pint if she was driving. Relieved, she warned Jack she was going back to the B&B to get changed, so if he wanted a lift, he'd have to be ready in two minutes. Back downstairs, she told her boss of their plans for the evening and by the time she'd cleared her desk Jack was ready to go.

Robert waited until they'd left before commenting that the youngsters seemed to be getting on all right.

Miriam agreed. 'They're very different characters but Lily is already making sure Jack pulls his weight. So how has your first day been, Robert?'

He looked up from packing his laptop into a battered briefcase. 'Not bad. There's not much about the case to go on though. No-one seems to have noticed our Mr

Berry once he started walking. I suppose he won't have passed many people on his route but I thought someone might have remembered him.'

'He spent the first night in a place called Aysgarth?'

'Yes, I'll speak to the owner of the accommodation tomorrow. Her statement is quite brief so I might get a bit more out of her if I have a chat.'

He was pulling on a padded jacket and scarf. 'I'll be off to Skipton then, unless you need me to lock up.'

Miriam told him she'd make sure the place was secure, and watched as his headlights swung past the window, lighting up the farmhouse and then leaving the yard in darkness.

It was time for her to go home too. She laughed out loud; she meant time to go back to the cold, damp cottage that she was renting, just a stone's throw away. She'd bought groceries in town, hoping she could work out how to light the stove and cook herself a hot meal at last. She sighed and shut down her computer. It was always tiring at the start of a new investigation but this was very different without the rush to collect evidence while it was fresh. They had everything that had been secured at the time and it was her job to ensure the team found new evidence if they were to advance any of the three investigations. She just hoped she'd made the right choices when she'd distributed the cases across the team and that they were up to it.

Chapter 3

Robert disliked driving at dusk. The roads back to Skipton were decent enough but they were unlit with bends and narrow parts that meant it would take an hour to travel the thirty miles. He was tired from the early start and his shoulders ached from leaning over the laptop they'd provided him with. That's why he always listened to Classic FM while driving home. They played relaxing music in the early evening when he would be attempting to forget the tensions of the day. Working for West Yorkshire had become even more stressful after Margaret died and he was glad he'd been persuaded to take a break by joining DI Abbott's team. He'd heard good things about Miriam from an ex-colleague in Cleveland, although there was gossip about an embarrassing scene at her section's Christmas party when her husband turned up. Although he'd never met Chief Inspector Henry Abbott, he knew of his reputation as a womaniser and wasn't surprised that Miriam had left him after the harassment claim.

He reflected that his first day had gone quite well, considering the shambolic start. He couldn't understand why they had to have an office in an old cowshed, and the police support lad needed to shape up, but it had been a good start. He'd been through all the documentation on Brian Berry, not that there was a lot, and he had a good picture of the man. He was eighty, a similar age to his old dad, and the similarity didn't end there. They both were retired engineers, played at the local bowls club and were Probus members. They'd both joined the University of the Third Age, although Brian was part of a walking group while Dad was involved with railways. Perhaps, if Mr Berry had stuck with the walking group, he might be alive and well today.

What had happened to the old man was inconclusive, which was why Robert was investigating it, of course. There had been the suggestion that he was so devastated by his wife's death that took his own life but Robert didn't accept that. You go for a long walk on your own to think, or to get away from things, not to kill yourself, you can do that at home without the expense of booking accommodation for four days, surely. No, he understood Brian's motive: he'd wanted time alone after all the fussing and fiddling that happens when your partner of many years dies. It had been like that for him a few months after Margaret passed. He'd told the kids that enough was enough and he was going to Scotland for a few weeks. His daughter wanted to go with him but he'd been adamant, "I want to be by myself for a while," he'd told her. It had been perfect, walking, reading, chatting to a few locals in the pub, it had refreshed him, so to speak. Mr Berry's family hadn't gone along with the suicide theory either. The son thought his father was far too sensible to do anything stupid and, anyway, he'd promised to help build a treehouse for the grandkids. Robert understood that too, his father wouldn't break that sort of promise either.

So far, the road had been quiet but now he was stuck behind a car that was crawling along, with no opportunity to overtake. Robert turned up the radio and leaned back in his seat, taking deep breaths. It wouldn't help to get wound up, although he really didn't want to be late. Mother had insisted they all eat together so he'd promised to be back by seven that evening. But at this rate he'd be lucky to make it in time. Already he was thinking that the decision to live with them for the next two months was a mistake. They had lived in that house for over fifty years, with little changing since he grew up there and Robert admitted to himself that he'd also become set in his ways, in his choice of television programmes, bed-time, breakfast cereal, beer with his dinner, the list was endless. He stamped on the brake pedal as the car in front came to a sudden halt ahead then indicated left. He watched the car turn up a rough track and disappear, then stepped on the accelerator.

'Your mother was getting worried.'

His father had been collecting logs from the shed when Robert finally reached the house. He locked the car and followed him indoors. He automatically checked the thermostat in the hall which was set far too high.

'It's stifling in here,' he muttered, pulling off his jacket and hanging it carefully on the peg that had been cleared for his use.

'I thought you were never coming,' his mother called from the kitchen.

He checked the time. 'It's five past seven. Five minutes, that's all.'

'Well you'd better be quick, I'm dishing up.'

He sighed and went to wash his hands in the downstairs cloakroom. There was an overwhelming smell of lavender from the soap and a candle on the windowsill. He usually liked to have a beer and change out of his work clothes before eating but he had to go straight into the dining room. That was another thing that irritated him, why did their meals have to be so formal when there was a perfectly good table in the kitchen?

'Did you have a good day, dear?' Mother was spooning out some vegetables.

He looked down. It was shepherd's pie again and she was piling cabbage onto the rest of his plate. 'Yes, thank you.'

'What was it like, taking on a sergeant's role?' his father asked.

'Only acting sergeant, Dad.'

'Yes but didn't they say it could be permanent?'

'Only for a year unless I pass the exams.'

'So, it's up to you to show them you can do it, Robert,' his mother said.

He was forty years old and they made him feel like he was wearing short trousers.

His father kept probing until he finally described what his role would be in the investigation.

'So they never found this old feller?' Dad asked.

'No. They lost him somewhere on the Herriot Way.'

That was all he divulged and he didn't tell them about the other two cases. He described their basic office facilities and his parents were soon talking about the last time they'd visited Hawes. After their main course there was apple pie and custard. Robert, who wasn't used to such a large evening meal, feared he would suffer from heart burn later. He moved with his father to the sitting room while his mother cleared up in the kitchen.

'Do you still belong to the University of the Third Age, Dad?' Robert asked when they were seated in front of the coal fire.

Apparently, he had little time for the U3A in the winter. 'They don't organise outings when the weather's poor, son. Easter time they'll start again and I'll be going to visit the York Railway Museum.' Then, as an afterthought, 'You could come with us.'

'No, you're all right.' Robert could see the disappointment on his face. 'I'll probably be busy working on the case,' he added.

'But it's on a Saturday. You won't be working at the weekends, will you?'

'Probably. Time is of the essence. I told you, we've only got two months to close the case.' Robert was beginning to think that working long hours would be the only way he would keep sane if he had to stay with his parents for the duration.

Lily said she'd be waiting outside in the car at seven. It had given her time to shower and change before making a call. Her mother wanted to hear all about her first day in the new job and asked what the people she was working with were like. She was in the middle of describing Jack as immature, arrogant, and not a team player, when he appeared at the side of the car. Lily quickly said her goodbyes as he climbed in, promising to call again the following evening.

'Sorry, I didn't realise you were…' began Jack.

'No, it's fine. It's Mum, she insists I keep in touch.' She was concentrating on getting through the narrow entrance. Once they were out on the road she asked if his parents were the same.

'No. I do call them but not that often. My mum goes on at me about it.'

She asked if he had any brothers or sisters and it turned out he had two older sisters. Lily concluded that he was spoiled, which explained his attitude at work. She wanted to know about his work at the National Crime Agency but the way he described what he was doing, made it sound really boring.

'That's the road!' she exclaimed, checking her mirror before slamming on the brakes.

She'd been looking out for it but had nearly missed it in the dark. The sign said "Cotterdale only". She'd seen on the map that the narrow lane went to the tiny village and then beyond, onto the open moor.

'It's up there where they found Amy Hobson,' she explained. 'I thought I'd go there tomorrow.'

'I can come with you,' suggested Jack.

'You're all right, thanks. I was going to ask Robert because he's got four-wheel-drive. It's a rough track past the village so I can't risk this thing.'

There was an awkward silence for a while until she asked what he'd made of his investigation.

'There's nothing to work with, is there?' he replied. 'A guy disappears without trace…'

'Except for his bike.'

'Yeah, exactly. He hadn't used his phone and there's no CCTV to track his movements. The only thing linking him to the area is his bike.'

Lily had assumed that Kirkby Stephen would be bigger than it was. The main road took them straight through the centre of town and Lily found the hotel. She looked for somewhere to park but as the shops petered out, she had to turn round and pull up in the town square.

As she followed Jack across the road, she noticed he

was wearing jeans, a leather jacket and trainers. She had carefully combined her cord trousers with a cable-knit sweater and leather hiking boots, hoping she looked like a local or at least a walker. As they entered, Jack asked if they could claim expenses. The thought hadn't occurred to her, and she pointed out that if it was official, he would have to have a soft drink, which shut him up. She found a table within sight of the bar and looked round. It was quiet but it was the beginning of the week. A young girl was pouring a pint of lager, a glass of white wine was already on the bar. She watched Jack make his way over slowly and lower the glasses carefully onto the round wooden table, returning to the bar to fetch two menus.

'Cheers,' he said.

The wine was warm but it was dry and she sipped it slowly while she read the menu. She chose a vegetarian curry and Jack decided on the meat pie with chips. She went across to order for them both.

'Hi, can we order some food?' Lily smiled, hoping to start a conversation.

'Sure, what d'you want?'

The girl entered their order on the till and took her payment.

'Quiet tonight isn't it?' Lily commented.

'Always is on a Monday. You should see it later in the week. Rammed on a Friday and at the weekend.'

Lily thought about the day that Amy disappeared. 'And on a Sunday lunchtime?'

'Yes, even at this time of year.'

She thanked the girl and added, 'Will you have a drink yourself?'

She'd heard her father say that to the barman in his local

and thought it was a good way to befriend the girl. She looked surprised but pointed at a beer mug containing a few coins.

'We're not allowed to drink when we're working but if you want to…'

Feeling a bit foolish, she found a five-pound note in her purse and thrust it in the glass.

'Wow, thanks!' the girl called as Lily turned left. 'I'm Trish, by the way.'

'Lily,' she replied, turning to face her.

'Does your boyfriend play pool?' she asked, looking in Jack's direction. 'There's a knockout every Thursday, just locals.'

'That sounds like fun. He's not my boyfriend though, but I'm sure he'd like a game,' she replied and headed back to their table.

'Jack, do you play pool?' she asked quietly.

He nodded. 'Is there a table?'

'I don't mean now. There's some sort of competition on Thursday night. I thought you could enter.'

He looked confused. 'I haven't played for a while, I might be a bit rusty.'

'It doesn't matter. The problem is, I can't play, and, anyway, I expect it's a men's thing.'

She explained that it was a good opportunity to meet the lads that played pool here, the ones who were friendly with Amy. Her colleague was clearly pleased with the chance to muscle in on her investigation. It wasn't her choice but needs must, she thought. She changed the subject to ask him about his plans for the missing cyclist case. He continued to moan about the lack of intelligence, as the case had only been revived with the discovery of the bike.

'How am I supposed to find out where he was cycling to and how far he'd got?' he demanded.

'By detecting, Jack. Not everything is on the internet. Sometimes you have to get out and ask questions.'

'Like what?'

'If he was in the area, where was he staying? B&Bs, campsites, youth hostels, bunkhouses, you need to ask around. Presumably you've got a recent photo of him?'

'Yes.'

'Anything distinctive?'

'Like what?'

'Tattoos or a funny haircut, strange accent or a stutter, I don't know. Use your imagination.'

'It's all very well to say get out and ask questions but without transport it's not easy round here, is it?'

'Then get a bike.'

His attitude irritated Lily and she was relieved to see Trish coming over with their meals. She was smiling at Jack as she placed the pie and chips in front of him.

'So has she told you about pool night on Thursday?' she asked.

'Yeah, I'm up for it.'

'It starts at seven-thirty. There's an entrance fee of three pounds but the winner gets a voucher for thirty-five pounds to spend in here. OK?'

'Will you be on the bar?'

She blushed. 'Yes. I'll see you then.'

As soon as she'd disappeared, Lily burst out laughing. 'She thought you were chatting her up. You'd better be careful.'

He looked at her seriously. 'I thought you wanted me

to work undercover. I was just making connections.'

Lily couldn't decide if he was just pretending to like Trish or he was interested in her. It didn't matter, they would come back later in the week and meet the local lads, which was a result. The place remained empty so they left as soon as they'd eaten, but not before saying goodbye to Trish, who was sitting behind the bar looking at her mobile.

'Don't forget, Thursday at seven-thirty,' she called to Jack, as they left.

Chapter 4

Miriam was alone in the office when Lily and Jack arrived next morning. She told them she was going to visit Amy's parents and left.

As soon as Robert came through the door, Lily fetched him a coffee before asking, 'Does your car have four-wheel-drive?'

'Well, technically it's an all-wheel-drive or AWD car, although they call it a four-by-four, Lily.'

He proceeded to describe in detail the way the different wheels were driven. She listened until he'd finished his explanation then asked, with what she hoped was a winning smile. 'So it could be driven up a rough track in Cotterdale?'

He appeared to be considering the question. 'Are you asking if I would drive you up to the crime scene?'

Jack was watching from his desk.

'Yes, please. Would you?'

The sergeant laughed. 'It's a grand day to be out and about. Are you thinking of going today?'

'Now, if that's all right with you.'

'I was going to Aysgarth but it can wait.' He reached for his jacket and pulled his car keys from his pocket. 'Is Jack coming with us?'

She looked across at him and shook her head. 'Someone will have to stay here, won't they?'

The car was still warm inside. It was spotless and smelt of fabric cleaner. Lily settled into the passenger seat, expecting to have to direct Robert to where the road turned off to Cotterdale.

'I know where to go,' he insisted. 'I was looking at the Herriot Way on the large-scale Ordnance Survey map and noticed Cotterdale over to the west. If I remember correctly, we go right in about another mile.'

The turning was obvious in daylight. It was a good tarmac road, opening onto the hills and the sun was shining. A supermarket van driver was parked on the side, presumably waiting for the allotted time to make a delivery. Lily reminded herself that Amy's journey on that Sunday afternoon would have been no different. Was it possible that she was a willing passenger until something happened to change the situation, or was she already dead?

Robert finally broke the silence. 'How did you come to join our little team, Lily? Did you volunteer or were you pushed?' he asked with a laugh.

It was an odd question. 'I asked to be considered. I thought... I think it's a great opportunity. Ever since I became a DC, I've been hoping to have the chance to do something like this.'

'But weren't you a crime scene investigator before that? Surely that was pretty interesting.'

Was it a comment or a question? 'You'd think so but it can be quite repetitive: burglaries and break-ins, mainly fingerprints.'

'No murders in Cumbria then?'

'That's different. I was occasionally on a team doing a sweep of the scene afterwards but you didn't get involved in the investigation, not like this.'

She was scanning the view as the surroundings became more isolated. She wished Robert would slow down so she could absorb it in detail. There was a forest track going off to the left as they swung round and down into the village, more of a hamlet really, just a few cottages lining the narrow lane.

'Through here is it?' Robert asked, slowing down.

'The track just goes straight on, according to the map.'

He took a deep breath and drove through the narrow opening onto a rough track. Robert was driving more slowly now and to Lily's surprise they soon came to a halt.

'Which way now?' asked Robert.

Ahead the road petered out. There was a gated track leading away to their left. On their right was a bridge over the river.

'We follow the track over the river.'

He drove onto the bridge and stopped in front of another gate.

'It's locked,' he said.

Lily got out to examine the padlock while Robert reversed the car, then consulted the sketch map which hadn't mentioned a locked gate. Robert was looking at his phone.

'There's a bridleway through that wood that joins the track further up. We'll have to walk.'

She strode ahead to a footbridge across the river then into a narrow woodland path uphill beside a stream that spilled into a waterfall. Checking Robert was behind her, she hurried uphill until she came out onto a gravel road.

'Is this the track we saw through the gate?' she asked when he caught her up.

'Yes. Do you know where she was found?'

She pulled out the sketch map again. It showed the last part of the track in detail, not to scale but with distances carefully marked. It indicated where Amy's body had been dumped several hundred metres off the track, dragged through the pine trees to a shallow dip. Approximately seven hundred metres further on was a building of some sort. They soon came to a track leading off to the left, once again gated and marked as private. They walked round the locked gate and into the woodland.

It was a cold and desolate place to be in March and Lily reminded herself that on a November afternoon it would have been just as cold or colder. She led the way up through the trees in the direction of the cross on the map. It was soggy underfoot and her ankles kept turning in the ruts. She almost tripped as a root caught her foot and Robert grabbed her elbow.

'Steady girl, you need some sturdier footwear.'

She looked at her shoes, now covered in mud, and laughed. He was wearing leather brogues but they had fared no better. The bottom of his beige trousers were dark with damp.

'Never mind, they'll clean up,' Robert said, striding ahead.

He reached the dip first. 'Is this it?' he asked.

It was a fair question. There was nothing to indicate there had ever been a crime scene here. There was no point looking for forensic evidence now, that was for sure. Lily stared at the spot. There had been no attempt to bury the body so there was no sign of digging but perhaps a little less vegetation than on the surrounding area. She had learnt not to use her imagination at a crime scene but to stick to the facts. Here there were none. They stood in silence for a minute until they were disturbed by a rustling sound behind them. As she turned, Lily saw a movement in the trees below.

'There's someone down there,' she called out, then laughed when a deer suddenly bounded away, followed by another.

'Phew, that made me jump,' she admitted to Robert, who was still laughing at her reaction.

She covered her embarrassment by taking some photos on her phone to remind her of the scene.

'Enough?' Robert asked when she put her phone away.

'Yes thanks, although I'd like to carry on for a bit if you're all right with that.'

The wind strengthened as they re-joined the track. Below them to the left in a clearing was a stone building.

'This is a pheasant shoot, you can see the posts,' said Robert. He pointed at a series of numbered sticks, placed at regular intervals along the track. 'And that building will be where they have refreshments I expect.'

Lily took more photographs then they carried on for another ten minutes until Robert consulted his phone again.

'This path joins the Pennine Way eventually. It's also part of the route of the Herriot Way between Hawes and Keld so I'll be heading over there later this week. I plan to walk the section between Aysgarth and Keld at least. Following in Brian Berry's footsteps so to speak.'

Lily stopped. 'I guess we can go back now. I just wanted to get a feel for the area.'

'You've got access to all the old files, haven't you?'

'Yes but I wanted to see it for myself first.'

She had thought there was nothing to link Amy Hobson and Brian Berry except that they disappeared at roughly the same time. But standing on the track close to where

Amy was found, they were able to see the route of the Herriot Way.

'So that's why we're here. Good old-fashioned policing. But have we finished now? This wind is perishing.'

They retraced their route back down through the wood to the car in silence. It was a relief to get out of the biting wind but before she left, Lily took a photo of the padlocked gate on the other side of the bridge. She tried to wipe the mud off her shoes before getting into the car but Robert told her not to fuss, he would be cleaning it at the weekend, after he'd finished his walk.

'It'll be even muddier over Great Shunner Fell,' he commented.

She asked where he'd be staying when he did the Herriot Way and he replied that he had booked the same B&Bs that Brian Berry used.

'I told Jack he should check local places in case his cyclist stayed in the area.'

'Is he capable of doing that sort of groundwork?' Robert asked. 'Seems to me he's got his head in the clouds with all this internet business.'

'He doesn't drive. I said he'd have to get a bike.'

Robert laughed. 'Do him good to get out on the road. He's got to get into his chap's head. That's what I'm doing, retracing the old man's steps, to see who or what he might've met on the route.'

When they were back in the tiny village. Lily asked if he could stop for her to take more photos.

'Is this what you did when you were a crime scene investigator?' asked Robert. 'Taking pictures?'

'Sometimes. It helps set out the scene. Where would I be in Amy's case if there weren't photos taken at the time?'

'You're fortunate. The rest of us are working blind. In actual fact I've got less to go on than Jack; at least he has a bicycle.'

'Not yet he hasn't.'

'I expect Forensics are busy working on it.'

'That's all finished. They gave it a quick dusting and did DNA on the blood, which was the cyclists own. And that doesn't prove foul play, he may have come off it and injured himself.'

Miriam sat down opposite Amy's parents and placed her handbag on the floor beside her. She wouldn't be needing to take notes, that wasn't why she was here. So she began by explaining why she had come.

'Thank you for agreeing to see me at such short notice. We've only just got set up and I wanted to inform you about our investigation team in Hawes before the rumours started.'

Mr and Mrs Hobson were sitting together on the sofa in silence, viewing her with curiosity.

'It will help our investigation if we can keep a low profile, so we won't be advertising our presence.' She waited but there was no response from the couple. 'But I wanted you to know that we will be working on Amy's death, along with other investigations connected to the area.'

'Is there some new information about our daughter's…' Amy's father stopped abruptly as his wife put her hand on his arm.

'Not at this stage, I'm afraid. It's what we're here to investigate. However, I would really appreciate it if you could keep that to yourselves. As far as anyone is concerned, we are a Rural Crime Unit working in the area. Is that all right with you?' They both nodded. 'I have a young DC concentrating on your daughter's investigation; she will probably need to talk to you at some stage. Otherwise you won't notice us.'

She reached for her bag and stood up. Mr Hobson rose, leading her to the door. His eyes were moist.

'Do you think this new investigation will find who did it?' he asked.

'That is the intention, Mr Hobson. We don't have long to pursue the case but I can assure you we will be doing everything we can to get justice for your daughter.'

She breathed in the cold air as she walked back to what they laughingly called the office. It was easy to trot those trite phrases to the bereaved relatives but she was hopelessly under-resourced with a team of relatively inexperienced staff. She'd been up until two in the morning reading the files relating to Amy Hobson's murder without finding any gaps in the original investigation. And there was hardly anything in the files of the missing men, which made the situation hopeless in her eyes. She'd been given the impression that failure to make progress after two months would reflect on her ability to lead the team. She would have to take responsibility and any prospect of promotion would be down the pan.

Robert's Skoda passed her as she walked into the yard. The passenger door opened and Lily climbed out as Miriam approached the car.

'We've been up to Cotterdale,' the girl explained. 'To see where Amy's body was found.'

'I'd like to catch up with you now. Robert has his own investigation to attend to.'

When Lily joined her, Miriam emphasised that she must let the others get on with their own work. She listened as the girl explained why she'd persuaded Robert to take his four-by-four. Then she apologised for taking Jack along to Kirkby Stephen when she visited the hotel. Miriam couldn't help but smile at her enthusiasm; she had really hit the road running.

Throughout their conversation, Miriam was aware that Jack was listening. When they'd finished, she went over and perched on his desk.

'How's it going Jack. Have you manged to download Greg Nevitt's files?' He nodded. 'Everything all right?'

He scowled. 'Not really. There's nothing to work on, is there?'

Miriam began listing the intel for him. 'We have his damaged bicycle, and his blood on it.'

'Yes but my area of expertise is cyber-crime and there's not even a phone record available.'

'That's often the way with missing persons, Jack. I agree there's little to go on but I'm depending on you to dig deeper and find out what's been missed.' She stood up. 'Perhaps you could start by talking to the cycling fraternity round here. I understand from the notes that his bike was quite distinctive. Someone may have noticed him if he was passing through,' she added as she left him.

He sighed. 'OK.'

Lily, who had been making coffee, placed a mug down in front of him. She handed him a cupcake in a fancy paper wrapper. 'Robert's mum sent us these,' she said. 'Isn't that nice?'

'Wonderful,' he said grumpily. 'Everything will be fine so long as we have cake.'

'Come on, Jack,' she said, impatiently. 'What about visiting the local bike shops?' No response. 'Look, I can give you a lift tomorrow. You could even hire one, like I said.'

'Yeah, right!' he replied sarcastically. 'I just want to know if they've seen my guy, that's all.'

'OK, but you'll have to wait until tomorrow if you need a lift anywhere,' she snapped.

Jack peeled the paper off his cupcake while he considered what to do next. In his opinion, the bicycle proved nothing. His guy could have fallen off it, dragged it into the side of the road, wandered off with concussion and disappeared into the hills, never to be seen again. He bit into the cake, it had lemon icing. Nice. Whether it was the sugar or the caffeine he wasn't sure but he definitely felt more positive as he wiped his fingers on his jeans. He went on the internet to make a list of all the bike-related businesses in the area, only to discover there was a hire shop in Hawes. It advertised mountain bikes and electric bikes, as well as gravel bikes like Greg's. Now he was interested.

'I'm just off to the bike shop,' he announced loudly as he pulled on his wind-proof jacket.

He was sure they would be sniggering once he was outside. Robert with his outdoor man attitude would be suggesting that he could do with losing the weight. Lily would be smiling condescendingly because he was following her suggestion. Wait until they need some help with their digital intel, he thought, then he'd be the one laughing.

Chapter 5

The hire shop was in Station Yard, which puzzled Jack because he knew there was no railway, having looked for a train when working out how to travel to Hawes from home. The directions on his phone took him through the town and almost out again but eventually he spotted a railway carriage and a sign for the Dales Museum. There was a café at the end of the old station platform where he was told he would find the cycle hub.

Jack introduced himself, saying he was working for the Rural Crime Unit, as instructed. He felt rather foolish when he explained he was interested in someone who was in the Dales last year riding a Trek gravel bike. Particularly when they asked if the man had stopped for repairs or to buy anything, and he couldn't give them an answer. He didn't give a reason for his questions but they assumed the bike had been stolen. Was it security marked, they'd asked. Yes, he replied, it was, because that was how the police knew it belonged to Greg Nevitt, although he didn't tell them that. He was about to leave when, on a whim, he asked about their bikes for hire. They recommended an electric as he'd find it easier to get up the hills on one of those, although apparently you still had to pedal. He said he'd think about it. So the visit would have been a waste of time had it not been for the café. But even after a toasted sandwich followed by a piece of flapjack, washed down with a mug of tea, he felt no more positive about the next day, when Lily was offering to drive him round the dale to discover if anyone had seen Greg Nevitt.

Miriam looked up from her desk. 'Can you give me an update on where you are with the Berry case?' she asked.

Lily and Jack had already gone back to their accommodation and Robert wanted to avoid being late for the family meal again. 'Yes, it's challenging but interesting. I thought I'd cover his route from Aysgarth to here in Hawes to start with. The forecast isn't too bad towards the end of the week.'

Miriam looked surprised. 'Do you mean to walk it?'

'I thought it was the best way to approach my investigation.'

Robert could see that she was puzzled, so added, 'I plan to stop overnight in Hawes and then walk to Keld.'

'He disappeared before reaching Keld, is that right?'

'Yes.'

'Well, rather you than me. How far is it?'

'Each stage is around thirteen miles, it's fifty-two miles in total.'

'So will you be passing places where he might have been seen?'

'Absolutely. There are villages, hamlets, and farms on the way. He probably picked up refreshments during his walk. Of course I could just drive to those spots but I want to do a thorough job.'

'Of course, good for you. So when will you do this trip?'

'I thought Thursday and Friday would give me time to book accommodation, I need an early start from Aysgarth.'

Miriam watched him pack his laptop in his leather briefcase and buckle the straps. He wound his scarf round his neck before putting on his jacket. Finally he pulled a pair of leather gloves from his pocket.

'Goodnight, Robert,' she called after him. 'Drive carefully.'

She had briefly considered offering the spare room in her rented cottage to her sergeant but decided it wasn't appropriate. The younger members of her team would find it odd and he was beginning to irritate her, the way he went on about his walking and this madcap scheme of retracing the route that Berry took before he disappeared. What was he expecting to find – a body? She smiled to herself and shut down her computer. She was beginning to think that she might need to provide the team with more direction after giving them this week to find their feet.

That evening, over a dinner of lamb stew provided by Eileen, proprietor of "The Pines" B&B, Lily explained to Jack how he needed to become more organised. She asked to see the list of places he was going in his search for information about the missing cyclist. He gave her a puzzled look, explaining that they would tour round the area, stopping at likely locations.

'What about the B&Bs? How will you recognise them?'

'Don't they have signs hanging in the window?'

'Not necessarily. Does this one have anything outside?'

He considered. 'I see what you mean.'

'Have you checked where the nearest Youth Hostels are?'

'OK, don't go on, I hear what you're saying. I'll have a look online.'

When Eileen came in to clear the table, Lily asked her

about local campsites. 'We're looking for places where cyclists might stay if they were touring the area.'

The woman stood, plates in hand, as she considered the request, then nodded. 'Yes, there are quite a few around here, and the Youth Hostel, of course.'

She went on to list the various places nearby that took campers while Jack noted them on his phone. After she'd gone, he protested that he could have looked it all up online and went off to his room. She didn't see him for the rest of the evening. With the comfortable sitting room to herself, she fetched her laptop to look at the Amy Hobson files again. When Eileen came in to check on the fire, Lily told her she'd been to Cotterdale, without mentioning why.

'So you're checking up on poachers, then?'

It was a question but Lily ignored it, going on to say how beautiful the area was.

Eileen beamed. 'One of the best shoots in the country.'

'Pheasants?' Lily hoped she was correct.

'And partridges. My sister worked for the caterer in the past.'

'Caterer?'

'Done their lunches on occasions: posh pies and sandwiches, very swish. She's given up now though.'

'The poachers are a problem.' It was a guess but it would be useful if Eileen thought she was working on rural crime.

'I've not heard of it recently, it's more likely deer poachers round here.'

'Exactly.' Lily hoped she sounded sufficiently knowledgeable to satisfy her.

There was nothing in the file about poaching in the

vicinity of Cotterdale but she made a note to talk to whoever looked after the pheasant shoot to see whether there had been any poaching activity in the summer last year.

By the time she went to bed, she had a list of questions she wanted to ask the estate keeper, including whether the padlocked gate had been broken into last November. There was nothing in the file or in the keeper's statement to say it had, but surely someone must have asked the question.

Miriam had picked up fish and chips in town before driving back to the cottage. The place was in darkness and the smell of damp hit her as she opened the door. In the kitchen, the Rayburn had gone out again. It was freezing cold but she wasn't going to relight it until she'd eaten. She poured herself a glass of the Rioja she'd brought with her from Middlesbrough and sat down at the kitchen table, still in her coat. It was strange drinking wine out of a tumbler but the cottage was not well equipped. The holiday let had looked idyllic when she'd booked it online but she hadn't noticed that all the heating and cooking was provided by a solid fuel stove. There was plenty of fuel provided but she obviously hadn't added enough to keep it going all day.

She relit the stove on her third attempt, got a fire going in the sitting room, and finally sank down on the lumpy sofa with her glass and bottle at nine o'clock. She checked her phone but there were no messages. That was no surprise since her daughter was travelling abroad, her son rarely contacted her and most of her friends were the wives of Henry's buddies, so they'd drifted away one by one after the separation. Those she considered to be her own friends who were in the force had become distant, possibly embarrassed by her situation. Which left just a couple of old college friends who lived such a long way away that she rarely caught up with them. She stretched out on the sofa, pulled a throw up to her chin and shut her eyes.

She woke with cramp in her leg, jumped up and knocked over her empty bottle. The fire had died and she checked her watch to find it was just after three in the morning. Staggering into the kitchen, she was hit by the warmth of the room. The stove was roaring away, heating not only the kitchen but the water in the radiators. She topped it up with fuel before dragging herself upstairs to the tiny bedroom which was gratifyingly warm.

It seemed only minutes when her alarm woke her again. She used to enjoy an early start, going for a walk in the park, some yoga or just to have time to plan her activities for the day. This morning the water was hot enough to have a shower, followed by a leisurely breakfast of coffee and toast. It was remarkable how much better things appear in the morning, she thought as she dried her hair and selected a favourite tweed skirt and mustard sweater. The mirror was rather small but she managed to apply the combination of creams and coverings that hopefully disguised the inevitable lines that fifty years of wear and tear generated. She considered she had worn well. Since the separation her hair was being coloured and cut by a very expensive stylist and she'd recently bought new spectacles that she considered rather trendy.

She listened to the eight o'clock news on her phone then put on her coat. The windows were covered in condensation so she assumed it was going to be yet another cold day. The stove had been fed with sufficient fuel to keep it going all day, hopefully. Over breakfast she'd decided to have a serious talk with Jack who seemed to be floundering under the responsibilities she'd given him. That was the most important activity for today, she told herself, as she scraped frost from the windscreen: giving guidance to the junior members of the team.

Miriam found Robert at his desk already. He told her, over coffee, that he'd booked places to stay on the Herriot Way and would be off the next day.

'You must take some pictures and give us a presentation when you get back,' she said.

He seemed unsure if she was being serious but keeping a straight face, she looked at her watch and expressed surprise that Lily and Jack were not in yet.

'They popped in for a minute earlier. Jack forgot to print a photograph of the cyclist,' he replied. 'Lily is taking him round a list of places where he may have stayed.'

'Really.'

'He doesn't have transport, you see.'

'No.' Miriam was irritated by this dependence on private transport to get about but could hardly insist he use a bus. 'Couldn't he have phoned them?' He didn't answer. 'So what have you got planned for today, Robert?' she asked, keeping her tone upbeat.

'I'm going to contact the search and rescue teams who looked for Brian when he went missing. There were mountain rescue teams from Swaledale and Kirkby Stephen, as well as the North Yorkshire force and the RAF.'

'Quite a thorough search then.'

'Oh aye, they spent a long time looking for him.'

For the rest of the morning she tried to ignore Robert's telephone conversations. It was hard not to follow his slow progress on each call as he chatted like an old friend to whoever responded, discussing in detail the search for Brian Berry. No-one appeared to query why he was asking, presumably assuming it was simply another police officer tying up loose ends. When Mrs Whitehead appeared with their sandwiches, Robert leaned back in his chair and stretched his arms above his head.

'That was a good morning's work. I think I deserve a break.'

With that he picked up his jacket and went outside, cigarette packet in his hand.

'Smoker is he?' the farmer's wife asked.

'Yes. Surprising since he's a keen walker. He's doing the Herriot Way tomorrow.'

'Rather him than me; the forecast's not good. We're expecting rain.'

Miriam thought he'd probably relish the additional hardship but said nothing. While she was alone, she took the opportunity to make a few notes regarding progress. She was interrupted by Lily bursting through the door.

'It's freezing out there. I've come back to get warmed up.'

'Is Jack with you?'

She raised her eyebrows. 'No, he's in town, well at the bike café actually. I wanted to get on. I've left him to it this afternoon, he's got loads of places close enough to town that he can walk.'

Miriam was curious. 'Is he making any progress?'

Lily shrugged and went towards the kitchen. 'Tea?'

'Yes please.'

When she reappeared, Miriam tried again. 'I know Jack isn't exactly trained for door-to-door enquiries but presumably he's all right with it?' Lily was sipping her tea in silence. 'You must tell me if there's a problem.'

She put her mug down. 'He means well but he is rather clueless, and disorganised, if you know what I mean?'

'But you were able to help him?'

'I tried but he didn't want me to. He said I was interfering.'

'Slow progress then?'

'Absolutely. Do you think I should go back to help him?'

'No Lily, definitely not. I've said it before, I want to keep the three cases running parallel, at least in the first week or so. Once everyone is up to speed, we can start making connections – if there are any to make.'

Robert came back in, rubbing his hands. 'Is that tea?' he asked, disappearing into the kitchen. When he returned, he told Miriam he wanted to show her something. He had a map on his laptop.

'Fifty search and rescue volunteers with three dog handlers covered the area from Hardraw to Thwaite,' he said. 'These lines criss-crossing the map track the search area. It was a very extensive operation.'

'Very thorough. You'd think they would have found him if he'd collapsed on the route.'

'Or wandered off it,' Robert added.

'So will you still set off tomorrow? They say it's going to rain.'

As she'd predicted he wasn't put off by the weather.

'It's even more important I cover the Herriot Way from the start now I know how well the latter part was searched.'

'So where are you staying tonight?' she asked.

'Aysgarth. I'm making an early start. I've decided to complete the whole route. I can do the last two legs from Keld to Reeth and back to Aysgarth over the weekend and pick my car up again there.'

Miriam felt compelled to suggest they meet for a meal that evening but to her relief he refused rather ungraciously, pointing out he wanted to eat in the village pub alone so he could chat to the locals, in case anyone had met Brian.

'Good idea, Robert.' Then to cover her embarrassment, 'I thought I'd try somewhere in town this evening, saves cooking. What about you Lily? Have you tried any of the local places yet?'

'No, we get a meal in the "The Pines", although Jack says the Indian restaurant gets good reviews.'

'D'you fancy an Indian?'

The girl looked uncomfortable. 'Sorry, I've arranged to go to a Zumba class in Leyburn this evening. Amy used to go and according to Facebook, two of her school friends still do.'

Chapter 6

Eileen was surprised to see Jack back so early and offered him tea with a large piece of fruit cake. When she asked how his day had been, he said it had been bad, really bad. He avoided telling her why he'd been visiting all the places he could think of where a cyclist might stay in the area, but he did explain at length how rude some people were.

'I gave up in the end because everyone was too busy to speak to me.'

She suggested perhaps folk were getting their tea ready, and maybe once the kids were home from school, they would be too preoccupied.

'If it's bed and breakfast accommodation you're looking at, the morning is the best time, after nine if they've got visitors staying.' She asked to look at his list. 'Right then.' She pulled a pen from her apron pocket and put a cross beside several of the names. 'These won't be very obliging. So I suggest you tell them I sent you, that might help. Now, your colleague told me she won't be eating tonight, so I got you a pork chop. Would you like chips?'

Jack said he certainly would and went to his room to write up a report of his progress, or rather lack of it. The addresses were already in the form of a table on his computer and he simply added a column for whether cyclists had stayed last year, yes or no, plus one for comments such as "aggressive dog so didn't stay" or "was too busy to speak to me". In summary, there were just ten addresses in Hawes that accommodated cyclists last

November and none of them remembered Greg Nevitt's name or recognised his photograph. Lily hadn't been much help once she'd lectured him on how to approach his task. She'd asked if he needed a standard questionnaire. Of course he didn't, there was only one question he wanted answered: did this man stay with you last November? Tomorrow he would contact the rest of his list by phone and email, it would be a lot more efficient, particularly as he wasn't going to beg a lift off Lily again.

His colleague arrived just as he was sitting down to his tea.

'I'm off to Leyburn,' she announced when she came downstairs. She was wearing trainers, track suit bottoms and a thick sweater, carrying a towel and a bottle of water.

'I've got a Zumba class tonight. Tell Eileen I might be back late, will you?'

She left before he could ask what a Zumba was.

The journey to Leyburn took half an hour but it was another ten minutes before Lily found the church hall. Inside there were perhaps twenty women, mostly her age or younger. They were standing in small groups and Lily looked round carefully, hoping to find Amy's friends.

A young woman in Lycra was approaching her. 'You must be Lily.'

The instructor introduced herself, asking if she was familiar with Zumba. Lily was, and understood the need to take it steady and, no, she didn't have any underlying health problems.

'OK, ladies!' the instructor called, clapping her hands to gain their attention. 'Are we ready?'

They all shouted that they were and the class began. It

was energetic but no more than Lily was used to. She wasn't familiar with the routine but muddled along as best she could and soon was working up a sweat. There was a short break in the middle for them to have a drink of water. As she stood at the side, Lily was pretty sure she identified one of Amy's friends from her Facebook page and sought an excuse to talk to her.

'I love your leggings. Can I ask where you got them?'

The girl spun round, looking down at her legs. 'These? They're old ones. To be honest I can't remember.'

It was time to start again but when the class finished and everyone was pulling on their outdoor clothes, Lily tried again.

'Sorry, but the reason I asked is because I'm new to the area so I wasn't sure where to go to buy leggings. I'll need some, I'm sweltering in these tracky bottoms.'

The girl laughed. 'You'll have to go to Northallerton or Leeds for something like these. Where are you from?'

It had worked like a charm. 'Hawes.'

'Really? That's where I live!'

After that she told Lily she was Di, short for Diana, and introduced her friend Kirsty. Lily explained she was staying at "The Pines". They both knew Eileen because her son had gone to their school, although he was several years above them.

'Look, it's so nice to have met you. Can I get us a drink before you go home?' asked Lily.

They looked at each other, and Di shrugged.

'Why not.'

Outside, it was like climbing into a cold bath after the heat of the class. The girls ran to the pub, tumbling through the door and causing the other customers to stare.

The girls asked for cider and Lily ordered a pint of cola for herself. Once they were settled at a table, Lily asked the girls if they were working or at college. As she expected, they told her they'd finished school last year. Di, who was the more gregarious of the pair, worked in the family business, a large farm with sheep and cows, and Kirsty was on reception in a hotel in Darlington. Lily asked Di about the farm. It was not the time to mention their friend Amy yet, there was plenty of time for that.

She ordered chips and more drinks, although this time Kirsty wanted an orange juice because she was driving. Lily asked her what it was like working at the hotel but she seemed embarrassed to talk about it and eventually, after looking at her phone, declared it was time to leave.

'Thanks for this evening,' Lily said, before they left. 'It's been nice to have some company. I'll see you next week at the class?' She hesitated. 'Although, I was going to the Indian in Hawes on Saturday, with my friend, Jack. I don't suppose you'd be interested – my treat?'

She wasn't sure whether it was the opportunity to meet Jack that appealed but after the girls had conferred, Di said they were up for it. She had the impression Kirsty was less sure.

'Seven-thirty on Saturday, at the Indian then!' she called as they rushed off up the street.

Lily suddenly realised that she would have to persuade Jack to stay around at the weekend.

Robert had booked into the guest house used by Brian Berry when he attempted the Herriot Way. Clearly, he and the old man had similar tastes because the place was cheap but comfortable, with the bonus that it was situated just a short walk from the pub. The lady of the house made him feel welcome from the moment he went through the door, insisting he had a cup of tea when she heard that he'd walked from Aysgarth. As they chatted, he decided to mention Brian Berry's name to see how she reacted.

'That poor man!' she exclaimed. 'It ruined last year for me, it really did.'

'You remember him then?'

'Remember him? Of course I did. The police arrived a couple of days after he left here, not that he disappeared on the way to Hawes. But they were trying to find out what state he was in.' She shrugged. 'He seemed as fit as a flea but I suppose he was quite elderly.'

'Eighty,' said Robert.

She was suddenly interested in him. 'Did you know Mr Berry?'

Quickly, he responded that they had a mutual friend. 'He told me about what happened when I said I was going to walk the Herriot Way.'

'So you're doing the same as him?'

'Yes.'

'Well you'd better be careful then.'

She asked what he was doing about an evening meal, suggesting the local pub. 'It's where poor Mr Berry went when he was here. I remember him telling me how good the fish pie was.'

So Robert went to fetch his head torch and set off in the dusk. It had turned cold once the sun was gone and now there was a strong wind blowing from the west. Robert was glad to get into the pub, where a log fire was blazing. He was deliberately early, planning to linger in the bar area for an hour or so before ordering any food. With a bit of luck the locals would also have a good recollection of "poor Mr Berry". There was an old man sitting in the corner, a small dog at his feet, so Robert carried his pint over to the adjacent table, nodded to the man and sat down. It never took long for Robert to engage in conversation with other lone drinkers. Pleasant as it was to chat about his walk from Aysgarth, the weather and the flooding that destroyed walls in the dale, the old man hadn't heard about Brian Berry's disappearance. An hour later, when Robert had exhausted all sources of local information from several different customers, and after he'd been told his table was free a couple of times, he headed into the restaurant for his dinner.

Robert would have liked to have lingered for longer over his breakfast in Aysgarth. He'd had a good night's sleep after several pints of Black Sheep, in a bed that was far more comfortable than the old divan at his parents' house. The smell of bacon cooking had greeted him as he came downstairs into the guest lounge, where the table was set for one. Soon he was enjoying a third cup of tea with toast and marmalade after a full English breakfast. He joked that he would need a good long walk after that feast, as he waited for his thermos to be filled with hot water before leaving.

It was on the dot of nine when he set his watch to track his route and took the lane out of the village, heading down the steep hill to the falls. His route would take him along the river to Askrigg where Robert had been told there was a bakery where he could get a pie for his lunch. Perhaps Brian had done the same, he thought. Once he'd left the road, he was following the general direction of the river, crossing fields and stiles, without meeting another soul. He wasn't in a hurry and arrived in Askrigg by half-past ten, just in time for a coffee.

This was his excuse for a chat with the owner. He began by commenting on the weather, then spent a long time deciding what to buy. He allowed a woman to go in front of him while he chose between a sausage roll or a pork pie, then took them both.

'A friend of mine recommended the pies,' he began. 'He was here last November.'

The woman behind the counter listened politely as she bagged up his lunch.

'Yes,' he continued, 'a nice old guy doing the Herriot Way, like me. You might remember him.'

He pulled out the photograph he'd printed on A4 paper and unfolded it, smoothing it out and placing it on the counter.

The woman looked down at it and shook her head slowly. 'Last November you say?'

Robert waited but she couldn't help, so he paid for his picnic lunch and packed it away in his rucksack. He allowed himself fifteen minutes to enjoy a coffee then went on his way. The route out of Askrigg climbed steadily through woodland beside a beck in full flow. He guessed that in the summer it would be a popular spot for visitors, judging by signs asking people to stay on the footpath, but on a weekday morning in March he had it to himself. It was something he would normally enjoy but since the purpose was to talk to people, he felt a little frustrated.

His mood brightened, however, when he reached the open fell and as he strode along with the wind in his face, he began to feel quite exhilarated. It was a great feeling to be free from his mother's oppressive fussing for a few days. He had plans if this secondment went well: he could return to Leeds in his temporary role of sergeant for a limited term but he would consider taking the exam again. He admitted that it had taken a long time to get over Margaret's death but now it was time to take stock and move on.

When it was time for lunch, he found a spot out of the wind behind a wall but it wasn't the weather for a long break, so he was soon off again. The route gave a good view across Wensleydale, in an area he was unfamiliar with and suddenly he was in Sedbusk, a tiny village in the middle of nowhere, with just a few houses and no-one about as he passed through. It began to rain and he was tempted to go straight down into Hawes without visiting Hardraw, but then he wouldn't be able to say that he'd completed the Herriot Way and, more importantly, Brian might have fancied a pint in the Green Dragon before the end of the day. However, it turned out he was far too early for a drink, the pub was shut and so was access to the waterfall. Resisting the desire to drop in to the office to see his colleagues in Hawes, he searched out the bed and breakfast that Brian Berry had described to his son as an extremely comfortable little place on the edge of town.

The owner of the B&B offered to put the kettle on, after showing him to his room to dry off. Soon, over tea and scones in front of a log fire, he encouraged Babs, as she was called, to tell him about Brian's disappearance. Most of what she related had been in her statement to the police, including the fact that the old man had asked her about how they celebrated Remembrance Sunday in

Hawes, as it was on the following day.

'I told him about the service at the Parish Church with the Silver Band. I thought he might like that.' Unfortunately she didn't know for sure if he attended it because he went off with his rucksack at about nine-thirty.

'If he did attend the service, what time would he have left Hawes?' Robert asked casually.

Babs thought for a moment. 'About mid-day, but later if he stopped for something to eat, of course. I offered to make him a sandwich but he said he'd pick something up on the way.'

It would have been helpful to know what time he finally set out. Robert calculated it would take a man of Brian's age close to seven hours to walk to Keld, which meant he would be doing the last section in the dark. When Robert asked her to recommend somewhere for dinner, she replied that all the pubs did good food, so he enquired if she knew where Mr Berry had eaten.

'It was "The Crown",' she replied confidently. 'The police wanted to know so they could question the staff, on account of him going missing the next day. But it was a Saturday night so no-one could remember him particularly.' She sniffed as she picked up the tray. 'They checked the street CCTV too. Turned out I was the only one who had anything to do with him when he stayed in Hawes.'

Chapter 7

It was raining heavily when Lily and Jack left for Kirkby Stephen. It had been a rush to set off with enough time to grab something to eat in the bar before the pool evening began and Lily wanted to ensure that Jack understood why they were there.

'Listen hard but say as little as possible,' she instructed as they set off. 'I want you to find out who the lads are that knew Amy, their names and where they come from.'

'Is that all?' Jack asked, sarcastically. 'Are you sure you don't want to play pool instead of me?'

Lily didn't answer. She knew it wouldn't work if she tried to join in with the lads. She planned to make friends with the bar staff, who she hoped knew Amy and might be able to point out her friends.

'How did you get on today?' she asked Jack. 'You were making plenty of calls.'

It had been a second day of dead ends, although slightly less humiliating when the negative response was at the other end of the phone rather than face to face. He'd given up by mid-afternoon and concentrated on the slim evidence file to see if he could glean anything, now he was more familiar with the area. Initially the bike had been of no significance to him except for the blood, which was Greg's own, but when he spoke to his new friend at the bike hub about the Trek gravel bike, he'd given a low whistle.

'Can you guess how much my guy's bike cost,' Jack

asked Lily.

'I don't know. Quite a few hundred pounds I expect.'

Jack laughed loudly. 'More like ten thousand!'

She didn't believe him because her car hadn't cost that much. 'Who would spend that sort of money on a bike? Was he really loaded?'

'Apparently not but he was a very keen cyclist. It was his life after his divorce.'

'Quite literally it turned out,' she commented.

The hotel bar was deserted at six-thirty except for Trish, who was busy fiddling with one of the beer pumps. She looked up as they approached and gave Jack a big smile.

'You're early!'

'Can we eat now?' Lily asked, not wanting to waste time.

They scanned the menu, chose quickly and Trish disappeared to the kitchen.

'She seemed pleased to see you,' Lily commented in a low voice.

Jack gave her a smug grin. 'I told you, it's all to do with making connections.'

When Trish returned, they remained at the bar, chatting about her work. It emerged she was at college studying design and only worked behind the bar to pay for her studies.

'So have you been here long?' Lily asked.

'Just over a year now.'

Jack and Lily exchanged glances.

'So you must have known Amy Hobson,' Jack said, to Lily's dismay.

The smile left Trish's face and she stopped polishing glasses. 'Was she a friend of yours?' she asked.

Lily gave Jack a warning look before responding. 'No,

just a friend of a friend really. But we heard about what happened.'

Trish put down the glass she was holding. 'We did different shifts, she worked lunchtimes and I do evenings, so we only met in passing. It was a horrible time but the worst thing was that no-one knew who did that to her. We all thought she must have been kidnapped because otherwise why was her car still parked outside?'

She picked up the glass and began polishing it vigorously. The atmosphere had killed conversation so they moved to a table. When Trish went to collect their meals, Jack asked Lily what time Amy had left work that day.

'Between three-thirty and four they reckon. Her family expected her home by half-four, maybe five at the latest. Certainly well before Sunday dinner at six.'

They fell silent as Trish brought their plates over.

Once she was out of earshot, Jack asked, 'Was there something wrong with the car?'

'No. It started first time when they took it away for examination.'

'There could have been a temporary fault,' he said.

'Jack, what do you know about cars? You haven't even got a car.'

'I may not drive but I do know they can refuse to start then later start first time.'

'When?' she challenged him.

'My father's old VW beetle did it when he kept revving it to start. It was something to do with the fuel, it's called….'

'…flooding. It's when the carburettor is flooded.'

He grinned. 'Get you!'

He stopped talking and started eating.

People, mainly young lads, began to appear in the bar area, keeping Trish busy pulling pints of lager. Jack went to the gents then wandered back to the table.

'I'm going to pay my entrance fee,' he said, as he made for the bar with his empty glass.

Lily watched him hand over his money before chatting with two guys who were carrying their own cues. She'd finished her apple juice but waited until the crowd had drifted into an adjacent room before going over to Trish.

'Is your friend any good at pool?' the girl asked.

'I have no idea. But I doubt it,' she added.

She ordered another juice, perching on a stool at the bar so she could chat to Trish. Although the girl wasn't a friend of Amy's, she knew the other members of staff and the customers who frequented the bar. Lily used all her skills to subtly gain as much information as she could about them all. She could hardly be seen taking notes, so she tried to memorise as much as possible. There were three other girls who worked part-time as well as a couple of older men who managed the bar. Sunday lunchtime in November would have been busy in the dining room but less so in the bar. One of the managers, Pete, had been in charge on the afternoon Amy disappeared. Trish saw him when she came on duty at six, by which time Amy's parents had been ringing to find out where she was.

'He was really upset. We all were. We thought she'd had an accident on the way home until one of the kitchen staff spotted her car outside.'

'Did you think that she might have left with someone voluntarily?'

Trish looked at her with her head on one side. 'Do you

mean a customer?'

'Possibly.'

She laughed. 'I don't think it crossed our minds. She was very sociable and popular with the customers but I was told she never got involved with any of them.'

'I wonder if she had a steady boyfriend,' Lily mused.

'I don't know but it's unlikely isn't it because she was saving to spend the rest of her gap year travelling on her own. That's what I heard.'

Someone had come into the bar to order drinks and food so Lily went back to the table to make notes on her phone. She needed to check manager Pete's statement. She jotted down the names of the three part-timers, realising that she'd only recognised one from the file. Occasionally a pool player would emerge to order a round of drinks, taking them back in with him. Eventually Jack appeared, making for the bar, accompanied by three lads of a similar age. From the noise they were making, she guessed they had been knocked out of the competition. He called from the bar to ask if she wanted another drink but she shook her head. He came over carrying a pint glass and soon the others joined them. Someone asked Jack quietly if she was his girlfriend, to which he laughed loudly, saying they were like brother and sister. Lily could tell they misunderstood his remark by the way they were looking first at Jack and then at her, as if seeking a family resemblance. They were discussing football now so she didn't comment but took out her phone to note down their names before she forgot. Soon the three friends were chatting amongst themselves about a girl one of them fancied and Jack was giving her a questioning look.

'Does Trish have a boyfriend?' Lily asked the lad nearest

to her.

They all turned to look at her. She explained how Trish had seemed keen to get Jack to attend the pool match. They looked over at the bar, where she was busy serving. Lily listened uncomfortably as they discussed whether she was good looking or not. When Jack said that she was all right but he wasn't interested, Lily frowned at him but he winked at her and went on, 'Not like Amy Hobson. She used to work here didn't she?'

The three lads froze.

'Did you know her?' the one called Alan asked.

Jack hesitated, then said casually, 'We went to the same school although she was four years below me.'

Lily didn't like the deceit but it was done now.

'She was a looker then,' he went on. 'I hadn't seen her since but I heard about what happened.'

'She was a laugh, wasn't she?' Rick asked his mates. 'Brightened this place up.'

'I bet she had plenty of blokes after her,' Jack encouraged them.

Alan went to say something, looked at Lily then stopped.

She quickly picked up her handbag, edging out from her seat past the table. 'Just going to the loo,' she said and left them to it.

She took as long as she could in the cloakroom, combing her hair and fixing her make-up. When she made her way back to the table, everyone was laughing. She took out her phone to take a picture of the group and they all grinned obediently for her.

'It's ten o'clock, Jack,' she prompted.

Rick laughed. 'Time to go home, little brother.'

Jack went to say something but Lily shook her head. He struggled into his jacket, thanked the guys for the games and agreed to meet up the following week for another session of pool. Lily began questioning him as soon as they left the bar.

'What was the third guy's name, the one with the stubble on his chin? What did they say about Amy? How well did they know her? Did they have any views on what happened to her?'

'Steady on, let's get in the car first.'

On the drive back to Hawes he related what had transpired while she was away from the table. He said he was modifying the language a bit for her benefit though. The guy with the stubble, called Steve, had been out with her a few times but she didn't do steady boyfriends, she liked to play the field. To quote him, "she was quite hot". She liked the banter across the bar and flirted with the customers, according to Alan. Reading between the lines he was a bit jealous of Steve. The general feeling was that she probably went off with a bloke and it ended badly.

'There was no sign of recent sexual activity,' said Lily.

'Perhaps that's what went wrong,' offered Jack.

'That would explain the evidence of a struggle. Unfortunately she was fully clothed and wearing gloves so there was no forensics on the skin or under her nails.'

'The way they spoke, I'm convinced none of those lads had anything to do with it anyway.'

'You sound very sure. At least I have their names now so I can check if they gave statements at the time. It's good that you plan to meet them again, thanks for that.' Then added, 'Little brother.'

'Sorry about that.'

Chapter 8

Miriam had spent the previous evening alone, reheating the remains of a pasta bake and drinking too much Rioja. She promised herself that she would finish work early today to travel to the supermarket in Leyburn and purchase healthy food. She'd heard they had a good wine department too and her stocks were running dangerously low. But this morning she was taking the opportunity to have a team talk with the youngsters while Robert was out of the way. He'd sent a text saying there was nothing to report yet. It was raining hard as she drove to the office and she couldn't help smiling at the thought of him ploughing resolutely through the countryside in his waterproofs.

When Lily and Jack arrived, she asked them to bring their chairs over to her desk for a briefing. She knew Jack had been looking for places where the cyclist might have stayed and wanted to know if he'd had any success. He had not.

'So what are your plans for today?' she asked, looking out of the window.

'More phone calls I suppose,' he replied without enthusiasm.

Miriam turned to Lily, hoping she would be more positive. The girl talked excitedly as she described their visit to the pool night in Kirkby Stephen.

'…and so we'll be going back next week. Meanwhile I'll

check out Steve, Alan and Rick's statements.'

Miriam nodded approvingly. Lily then described how she'd met two of Amy's schoolfriends at the Zumba class and had invited them to a meal.

'Jack's coming too, aren't you?'

He looked surprised. 'When?'

'Tomorrow night.'

He protested that he was thinking of going home for the weekend.

Miriam brought their bickering to a stop by asking exactly what they were telling these friends and associates of the dead girl. 'Do they know that we're investigating her death?' she asked anxiously.

Lily looked at Jack before responding. 'You did say to keep a low profile, didn't you?'

'But I said it was not undercover work, didn't I?'

'Yes,' she replied.

Miriam tried lowering her voice to ask gently, 'So who do they think you are?'

Lily, who answered for them both, had told the schoolfriends that she'd just moved to Hawes. It was Jack who'd pretended that he'd been at school with Amy when talking to the pool players.

'…and he said I was his sister.'

'I did not!' shouted Jack. 'I said "like brother and sister".'

'Well they think we're related.'

Miriam tried not to show her frustration. It had been a mistake to let them loose without direction. Giving them a week to settle in had been a foolish idea that she needed to rectify immediately. Thank goodness Robert couldn't hear this.

'Misleading the public is not something we do here,' she began. 'We are trying to gain their trust and co-operation, aren't we? What happens when these schoolfriends hear that Jack was supposed to have been at their school?' They sat in front of her like naughty children: Jack red in the face, Lily close to tears. She took a deep breath before proposing a way forward. 'Let's start at the beginning, by stating the hypothesis. Any suggestions as to what it is?' They looked at her blankly. 'It's that the crimes are linked, isn't it? Our eventual aim is to establish whether they are connected. However, for now we're looking at Amy Hobson's death and Greg Nevitt's disappearance separately. I want you to come up with possible scenarios to explain the evidence you have. I suggest we have a brainstorming session after coffee to discuss the possibilities.'

She left it there, deliberately. She didn't ask if they had any questions but waved her hand at them to show they were dismissed. She had already worked through the possibilities several nights ago, so it would be interesting to see if their ideas matched her list. The Chief Inspector thought the investigations were unconnected, and she wouldn't have wanted to bet on it, but she was sure there could be possible explanations that linked all three.

When the time came, it was Jack's turn to make coffee, which was disappointing because, once again, he'd made it too strong. Lily pointed out that there was a table and chairs upstairs if they were having a discussion, so she followed them into the roof area.

'This is quite cosy,' she remarked cheerfully, but the atmosphere was formal and when she sat down, the other two took chairs on the other side of the table.

'Fire away,' said Miriam.

Lily opened a large file and began. 'I've looked at the evidence in here.' She indicated the paperwork in front of her. 'From the additional intel about Amy we obtained last night, she was outgoing, she liked to flirt with the customers in the bar and didn't have a steady boyfriend. She was supposed to be driving home for her Sunday dinner so there are only two possible scenarios: she met someone she knew and went off with them; or she met someone she didn't know and left with them. In either case it could have been voluntarily or not.'

'And that's it?' Miriam asked. It was all she'd come up with herself.

Lily looked at Jack before answering. 'There is another possibility if she'd had trouble starting her car.'

'But there was nothing wrong with the car,' she argued.

When Lily explained Jack's theory about the carburettor flooding, Miriam saw a flash of inspiration brightening up the investigation and asked Lily to continue.

'So the third possibility is that her car wouldn't start and she got a lift with someone, who she knew or didn't know.'

Miriam made a note and waited but Lily had finished so she asked Jack for his scenarios. He referred to his laptop.

'Greg Nevitt owned an extremely expensive bicycle that he rode all over the country. No-one knows what route he planned for his holiday and there's no phone evidence, but the bike was found on the route out of Hawes towards Stalling Busk, so he was cycling in the area. There are signs it had been in a road accident. I found four scenarios: first, he ran into an object like a tree and was concussed, leaving the bike in a ditch, and stumbling off into the countryside.'

'Didn't they search the area when they found the bike?' Lily asked, but Miriam held her finger to her lips.

He gave her a hard stare before continuing. 'Second, he was involved in a hit and run, thrown into the ditch then wandered off to die somewhere.'

Lily looked as if she was going to object again but Miriam held up her hand to stop her.

Jack clicked his keyboard. 'The third possibility is that he was in a road accident but his body removed to hide the evidence and the fourth is that he was deliberately run down and his body hidden.'

Miriam summarised, then asked for their opinions. They agreed that Greg's body would have been found close to his bike if he'd simply come off it by himself. Therefore the likely scenario was a road accident, deliberate or otherwise, that had not been reported. Miriam ticked her own list. But she was far more interested in the theory that Amy's car failed to start.

'It was Jack that suggested it,' admitted Lily. 'It didn't occur to me because the file said the car started first time when it was recovered for forensics.'

Miriam smiled encouragingly at Jack and was rewarded with a grin. She suggested they worked individually on their scenarios to come up with the ones that were most probable, not to exclude the others but to put them on the back burner for now. 'We'll gather up here again after lunch and hear what conclusions you've come to.'

She went back to her desk to consider the implications of Jack's theory. Her first car had been an old Ford Escort that was difficult to get going in the winter and she remembered the problem of flooding the engine with too much throttle. Amy's car was registered ten years ago, so it could have been unreliable too. She would wait to hear what Lily had to say but there was a chance that Amy had accepted a lift with her killer.

The atmosphere was positive when they gathered round the table in the attic after lunch. Jack was more alert and Lily looked flushed with excitement when Miriam asked her to start.

'I've two scenarios to explain what we know about Amy Hobson's death,' she began, rather formally. 'She's too confident to be grabbed off the street or to be lured away by a stranger. I think she would have gone willingly with whoever killed her, which means she probably knew him.'

'Definitely a "him"?' Miriam asked her.

'Yes,' she replied. 'I think she might go off with someone for a while before driving home if she fancied him. But I also think she would cadge a lift with anyone if she couldn't start her car, even if she didn't know them. If you look at this map...' Lily pushed it across the table towards her, '...you will see that the road to Cotterdale turns off the route home from Kirkby Stephen just here.'

Miriam had already considered that connection and said, 'That's a really good interpretation of the intel, Lily. What do you think, Jack?'

'It ties in with what the lads were saying about her last night.'

'Really?'

He blushed.

Miriam couldn't help smiling. 'She was a flirt, is that right?'

Jack nodded. 'Yes, that was the general opinion.'

When Miriam asked him to go through his favourite

explanations for the missing cyclist, he turned his laptop round and proceeded to give a presentation. The key intel, he explained, was that a wide area had been searched where his cycle was found but there was no sign of him. That ruled out the idea that he'd had an accident and wandered off injured, so he suggested that Greg was knocked off his bike by a car and his body disposed of elsewhere. Lily argued that the search might not have been wide enough and he might have travelled some distance on foot before collapsing.

'That was my second scenario, if you let me finish,' he snapped.

He pressed the keyboard and the second scenario appeared, just as Lily had described. They discussed whether a new search was feasible but Miriam concluded the area was too vast. Jack seemed disappointed. They needed to move on, Miriam decided.

'Well done, both of you. We have two possible scenarios which you need to consider for potential evidence. She suggested a brainstorming session to come up with what to do next and after an hour, they had a list of actions.

'Let me summarise,' Miriam said, referring to her notes. 'Lily is going to find out if Amy's car has ever failed to start in cold weather and whether she would accept a lift home with a stranger. I'll ask for further forensics on Nevitt's bike, including fingerprints, paint from a vehicle and DNA. Was that all, Jack?'

'I suppose we can't ask for the wider search as well?'

'Not at this stage, no.' Miriam was thinking of her meagre budget. 'Although you could make a list of the most likely locations where a body could remain undiscovered, I suppose.'

She looked at her watch. 'I think that's enough for today. If we can get something to support your hypotheses, we can move forward and start to look at what might link the two. Otherwise it's back to the drawing board.'

They left the building together. Miriam set off back to her flat in Middlesbrough for the weekend., without much enthusiasm. Lily and Jack went into town to collect the fish and chip supper they had promised themselves.

'She's keen on her hypotheses, isn't she?' Jack was laughing.

'It's a good way to approach an investigation,' Lily told him. 'We did it as part of the National Investigators' exam.'

'You went to training college to be a detective?'

'I was a trainee for two years, some of the time was doing college work, yes. For what it's worth, I really like her approach.'

'I didn't say I didn't like her approach; it's just all this is mumbo jumbo to me. For example, how are you going to find out about the car not starting?'

'We'll be talking to her friends tomorrow night and if that fails, Miriam has given me the contact details for Amy's parents.'

'All I can do is wait for forensics on the bike.'

'That could take a while.'

'What am I supposed to do until then?'

'Identify places the body might lie undiscovered, like she said.'

'That's a needle in a haystack scenario.'

'Well, carry on ringing guest houses then. A lot of

detective work is routine and tedious.'

'Did they teach you that in college as well?'

Lily laughed. 'No, in Detective Academy, actually!'

Chapter 9

Robert was regretting starting out from Hawes so late that morning but something that his hostess, Babs, had said was niggling away at him all evening in "The Crown". His enquiries in the bar regarding Brian Berry fell on deaf ears but he did find an old boy sitting alone who knew someone in the Hawes Silver Band, and gave him a phone number. So that morning he'd called to find out whether there might be any photographs of the previous year's Remembrance Sunday service.

'Well that's a strange question indeed,' the voice had said when Robert called. 'I've no idea but I know someone who can tell me.'

He said he would call his friend and get back to him straight away so Robert found a café, ordered a coffee and waited. Ten minutes went by, then twenty. He didn't dare strike out along the Herriot Way in case he lost phone signal so he ordered another coffee and waited. He rang the man back but his phone was engaged. Finally after fifty minutes he was rewarded with the news that there were some pictures taken at the memorial if he was interested. Was he interested? He certainly was. He gave the man his personal email address and was promised they would arrive at the weekend.

'As a matter of interest,' he asked. 'What time did the service finish.'

There was a pause. 'Around twelve-thirty I reckon, maybe later. Definitely not before.'

If Robert's hunch was right and old man Berry remained in Hawes on the Sunday morning to attend the remembrance service for Armistice Day, perhaps a photograph could prove it. It was now just before eleven and he needed to get moving if he was going to reach Keld before dusk. The path to Hardraw was well-trodden by the visitors who walked across to Hardraw Force. He reached "The Green Dragon Inn" in less than half-an-hour, kept going past the cottages and turned onto the track marked "The Pennine Way". He felt the stress of the last couple of hours melting away as he left civilisation behind. At first the walk was pleasant but when the sun disappeared behind a large black cloud the air became chilly and he could sense a fine drizzle as he began to climb Great Shunner Fell.

Finding it quite hard going, Robert decided to stop for lunch, discovering it was already two o'clock. Babs had given him a beef sandwich in a brown paper bag plus an apple. He ate it looking across the dale, suddenly spotting the tiny village of Cotterdale where he'd been earlier in the week. From his position, he could see how isolated it was. He'd covered just six miles and was halfway. He reckoned on it taking about six hours plus stops so that was right, but now it would be five o'clock at the earliest when he arrived in Keld. Brian Berry would have been even later since the service wouldn't have finished until mid-day. He did various calculations while slowly consuming his sandwich. Assuming Brian finally left Hawes by one o'clock, after picking up something to eat, he would be here by four at the earliest and possibly even five. He'd already rung Keld to say he might not be there in time for dinner, which was at seven. That call was made early in the day when he was in Hawes and suggested he'd already made up his mind to attend the service although according to the file, he'd not given a reason at the time.

The rain was falling heavily so Robert packed his thermos away and moved on. The track was easy to follow, even with the rain causing the light to fade early. Robert wasn't concerned because he had a powerful torch in his rucksack, and he always carried spare batteries. But by the time he had cleared the summit of Great Shunner Fell and was descending into Thwaite, the failing light was slowing his progress and the last three miles to Keld seemed endless.

It was an immense relief to arrive at the door of the bed and breakfast that not only served an evening meal but was licensed. Even though the old man had never arrived here, Robert was undeterred and engaged the owner in conversation about Mr Berry. He had apparently rung to give his menu choice for dinner that night.

'With poor mobile signal round here, we ask guests to let us know in advance if they're not arriving before five,' the owner said.

Robert had done the same himself and was looking forward to his shepherd's pie.

'So you were expecting him for dinner?'

'Yes, I said I'd keep it warm if he was after seven.'

'It must have been a worry when he didn't turn up.'

'Guests can be quite late, especially if they're on the Coast to Coast from Kirkby Stephen, it's one of the longer stretches. We didn't worry at first but I did report it when he hadn't shown up by midnight.'

'So they started searching for him straight away?'

'His family were worried when they hadn't heard from

him that evening. The Mountain Rescue Team, dogs, police, and the RAF all turned out. It was difficult because of the short days in November, of course. No-one could understand what had happened to him, so they began the search in this part of the dale as far as Thwaite but then extended it to Great Shunner Fell and High Abbotside. But unfortunately they didn't find him.'

Brian asked for another pint and stared at the fire. He was beginning to feel weary. Struggling through the dusk over stony paths carrying a heavy rucksack had exhausted him, so perhaps Brian, at thirty years older, had found it too much and collapsed. The file said he was fit for his age but what did that mean? The most likely explanation, Robert decided, was that he'd had a heart attack and died alone out on the fell. But if so, he must have wandered off the track because he'd not been found after a very thorough search of the area.

'So what are you doing today?' Jack asked Lily when they'd finished breakfast.

Her normal Saturday would consist of an early trip to the gym, followed by coffee in town with a friend before going home to help Mum with the household chores. In the summer she might wander down to the stables in the afternoon to help with the children's classes if she wasn't going out. Returning to Cumbria after her training had meant she'd fallen back into her old routine, living at home, and meeting old school mates. It was a dull existence but even worse since she'd broken up with Roy. She hoped that by volunteering for this secondment for a couple of months would put her in good stead for a transfer to Manchester or Birmingham or even London, and a complete break from her old life.

'I might have a drive round, get to know the area. It's not a bad day for it.' She hesitated, trying to decide whether it would seem rude not to invite him to join her.

To her relief, before she opened her mouth, he told her he was going to walk into town. She made him promise to be back by six-thirty at the latest, to get ready to go to the Indian restaurant before seven-thirty. He saluted and disappeared to his room. She selected leaflets describing local attractions from the pile in the hallway and put them in her large bag that already contained a map of the area and a guidebook her mother had found for her. She knew the road to Kirkby Stephen well now, so she would travel in the opposite direction and make her way to Leyburn, stopping to explore on the way.

Jack waited until Lily left before coming downstairs because he didn't want any awkward questions. He had changed into his track suit bottoms and trainers, with a waterproof jacket over his sweatshirt. He wanted to get down to the bike hub early, because it was a Saturday morning, and weekend visitors would be queuing up to hire bicycles. It turned out that he needn't have worried.

'Our first customer of the day,' said the owner, looking him up and down. 'What can we do for you?'

Jack explained that he would like to hire a bike.

'Mountain bike?'

'Electric bike.'

Jack was given an explanation of how the electric bike worked before paying for a full day. It had been a long time since he'd been on a bicycle so he took it out onto the roadway before mounting and pedalled shakily away, hoping he wasn't being watched. At the junction he turned left, because it was easiest, and followed the road for a bit, slowing down every time a car came up behind him. He nearly fell off when a lorry went past and, deciding he'd feel safer practising on a quiet lane, he looked for the next opportunity to turn off the road. A minute later he spotted a signpost to Burtersett, a name he recognised. It was close to where Greg's cycle was found, although he had no idea of the exact spot. All he could remember was that it was on the way to a lake called Semerwater. He was concentrating on the road as it narrowed, hardly noticing the village as he rode through it, and then it was up an incline and he was pedalling hard. Soon he had to switch up the boost as the hill became steeper. The road went on and on, always climbing. The hardest part came just before he caught sight of the lake, which meant he'd already cycled well past where the blood-stained bike had been discovered.

Jack stopped at the top to catch his breath and looked down on Semerwater. He was pleased to see that the road was downhill all the way to its shore. There were bends to manoeuvre and he frightened himself a couple of times on the descent. A single car was parked by the edge of the water but there was no sign of the occupants. It was a bleak spot with the cold wind blowing waves across the surface and he wondered where Greg was aiming for when he cycled in this direction. He carried on, leaving the lake and ending up in a place called Stalling Busk. The road ended abruptly in the tiny village but he had just passed a rough track and Greg's cycle was called a gravel bike, which the man at the bike hub said was useful for road and tracks. Jack assumed his cyclist could go "off road". He stopped for a while, considering whether to attempt the track but chickened out and turned back towards the lake, telling himself he'd do it another day. He was so busy looking at the lake below him as he pedalled back that he nearly missed the narrow lane leading off to the right. Without knowing where it led, he followed it between stone walls for miles without seeing a soul. He much preferred this empty lane to the main route out of Hawes but inevitably it led to a busy main road. He took the left turn and descended into Bainbridge, where he spotted a tearoom sign and realised that the exercise had given him an appetite.

Eileen made Lily a cup of tea when she arrived back and offered to light the fire in the sitting room.

'No it's fine. We'll be going out in a couple of hours.' She was planning a nice hot shower before that.

'So did you have a nice day, love?' she asked.

Lily described her route along the dale to Leyburn then back up Swaledale, coming over the road past the Buttertubs. When she told her about visiting the little church in Wensley, Eileen said she'd not been inside, or seen the candle-making workshop. She had visited Hardraw Force once but she declared she was too busy for sight-seeing. Lily was embarrassed and said it must be hard work looking after guests, before excusing herself to go and get changed.

She had a shower, washed her hair, and dried it. She took time to carefully apply her makeup, wondering why she was bothering. She chose her cashmere sweater, the one that went best with her jeans, and pulled on her boots. She heard the grandfather clock chime six times as she left her room. Eileen was in the hall below talking to Jack. She was telling him that it would be safe in the shed and, as Lily moved quietly to the top of the stairs, she thought she saw her handing him something. When Jack heard her coming down, he disappeared out of the front door. Eileen had gone back into the kitchen before Lily reached the bottom of the stairs.

Chapter 10

Lily insisted they walk down to the Indian restaurant because she was certain she would need alcohol to get through the evening. As they approached the restaurant, she warned Jack to be on his best behaviour, and not to start concocting stories again.

'Remember, if we have to say what we do, we're the Rural Crime Unit, OK?' she instructed him before stopping to point out that the building they were about to enter originated in the seventeenth century.

It was the weekend so most tables were already occupied. Lily was pleased to see the girls hadn't arrived yet and suggested a drink to calm her nerves.

'No stories about school friends, remember Jack. In fact, avoid any mention of Amy Hobson please.'

He was already studying the menu and was still engrossed when Kirsty came through the door, followed by Di. Lily hadn't noticed the young man until he joined them at the table. While the girls were taking off their coats, she introduced Jack to them, then waited.

'Oh sorry,' said Di, seeing that Lily was staring at the young man. 'This is my big brother, Karl.'

They shuffled along to make space for him while the waiter laid another place at the table. It was an awkward start, particularly when Kirsty insisted that they would pay their own shares of the bill. But once they had decided what they were going to eat, and they all had a drink in front of them, everyone appeared to relax. Lily thought

Jack looked pleased he wasn't the only male in the group. She started the conversation by asking Di if their sheep were lambing yet. It was too early, she began, but was interrupted by her brother who also worked on the family farm. He'd taken a degree in agricultural science so Di was planning to do the same next year. Kirsty sat quietly, listening but not joining in, so Lily told them how she'd spent her day sight-seeing. Di laughed and called her a "right tourist". When she asked Jack if he'd gone on the tour with Lily, he said no but was vague about what he'd been doing.

Jack and Karl began discussing football while Di described her recent shopping trip to Leeds. Kirsty looked deep in thought, still not saying a word. The topic changed to television programmes, each in turn picking their favourite, but when they asked Kirsty she just shrugged. They shared various dishes when the food arrived, Jack declaring it was a wonderful change from the meals provided at "The Pines" while taking more than his fair share. Lily noticed Kirsty was hardly eating anything, she just picked at it, pushing the food round her plate. She could see Di, who was sitting next to her, glance down then up at her friend's face. So it continued. The two lads were too busy eating to notice but Lily and Di exchanged glances.

'You OK, Kirsty?' Di asked quietly.

Her friend looked up from where she was pushing rice into a pile. 'I'm not really hungry.'

A single tear ran down her right cheek and dripped onto the tablecloth. Her friend went to put her arm round her but Kirsty pushed back her chair and ran to the Ladies cloakroom.

Karl looked alarmed. 'Is she all right?'

'Does she look it?' Di replied sarcastically, as she got up to follow her friend.

He watched his sister go before turning to them. 'She thought that might happen. It's the first time we've been back here since... well, for a while.'

'May we ask why she's so upset?' Lily tried to appear sympathetic without sounding nosy.

Karl rubbed his chin. 'It's just that we used come here with a friend. She's not around anymore, that's all.'

It was an awkward wait until Di reappeared.

'Sorry, she's not feeling very well. She wants to go home Karl. Can you walk her?'

He nodded and pulled his jacket on before finishing his beer.

'Wait by the door,' his sister instructed as she retrieved Kirsty's coat.

He waved a hand before wandering over to the entrance. Jack raised his eyebrows at Lily but she just shook her head slightly. A minute later, Di emerged from the back with Kirsty, helping her into her coat. She almost ran to Karl, who ushered her out.

Di walked over. 'She only lives up the road.' She pulled her chair away from the table and sat on it sideways, fiddling with a lock of hair. 'He won't be long. I said we'd be here when he gets back.'

Lily suggested coffee but Di said she needed another drink. While Jack was catching the waiter's eye, Lily said she hoped Kirsty would be all right. That she'd wondered if she'd been upset by something they'd said.

Di shook her head. 'No, it's just tonight; she'd built it up in her head. She had the jitters before we came. Karl was dead against it but I said we'd got to face it sometime. We haven't been out together for months.'

'What was she worried about?'

'Not worried, just stressed about us being out enjoying ourselves, I think. She's only just started back at the Zumba classes.'

Lily was conscious that she had Jack's full attention. 'Has she not been well?' she asked.

The drinks arrived and Di took a long swig of lager before answering. 'You could say that. We lost a friend last year. It was a shock. Kirsty was quite bad with it. She was off work for weeks and only went back last month. She seemed to be doing so well when we went for a drink with you after Zumba. It seemed a perfect chance to take the next step and have a proper evening out, you know. I hope it hasn't set her back.'

It was awkward. Jack was taking her instructions too seriously and keeping quiet, which left Lily seeking the best way to keep Di talking without appearing insensitive.

'It's always hard when you lose a friend. I guess this friend was young, your age?'

Di pulled a face, as if she was in physical pain.

Lily apologised for being insensitive but Di assured her she wasn't, that they promised they would always talk about her. Then slowly began to describe their friend. 'She was the life and soul of the party was Amy. She was a right practical joker. When we were at school, she used to get into trouble for what she did to the teachers but it was only a bit of fun.' She smiled as she was talking. 'So this one time she changed the clock in our classroom and no-one noticed so we went home ten minutes early.' She turned to face them, pulling her chair up to the table.

'Don't get me wrong, she wasn't a clown, she was bright, really clever. She could've been at university but she said she wanted to have a gap year. She was saving up by working for six months then she was going to Australia.' She went quiet as she sipped the rest of her lager. 'It was such a waste.'

'She sounds like fun,' Lily said.

They were sitting in silence when Karl reappeared. Di asked how their friend had been when he left her.

'She seemed OK. Her mum was in so I left her there.'

'Thanks bruv,' Di said, rubbing his arm. 'I've explained about Amy.'

You haven't, thought Lily, you haven't told us anything that will help us find her killer. Jack must have been thinking the same because he suggested paying up and going along to the pub for a quick pint before they close. Perhaps in a relaxed environment they would be more forthcoming.

They chose the nearest pub, fighting their way to the bar. It was Saturday night, Karl reminded them. Di and Lily carried their glasses through to a table for four occupied by a middle-aged couple, and took the vacant two seats. The lads propped themselves up at the end of the bar with their third, or was it their fourth, pint of lager.

'Sorry about earlier,' said Karl.

It was Jack's opportunity to help Lily. 'So how did your friend die?' he asked.

He began by explaining that Amy went missing the day after they'd had a meal with her at the Indian: Di, Kirsty, Karl and Amy. 'It's was a regular thing. They only allow me to string along as designated driver so I could give them a lift home safely, which is ironic considering what happened.'

'What did happen?'

'She was working the lunchtime next day in Kirkby Stephen. That was when she disappeared. She wasn't found until weeks later.'

Jack was sipping his pint, waiting to hear him say it.

Karl lowered his voice. 'She'd been strangled, left in woodland to be found by a dog.' His face showed his disgust. He sighed. 'So that was why Kirsty was upset. We all are but we show it in different ways. Even Di is nervous of being out after dark because they haven't found who did it. If I found him…' He shook his head and raised his glass. 'I reckon it must've been someone local, to know where to leave her though. We've been over it so many times and we can't understand what she'd being doing up there in the middle of nowhere.' He stopped talking while he sipped his pint, then continued in a low voice so Jack could hardly catch what he was saying, '…Kirsty is so upset because…' The clatter of glasses from behind the bar muffled his voice. '…but she won't say.'

'Won't say what?'

'Who she thinks Amy's new bloke was, in case she's wrong. Anyway, I need the little boy's room.'

Jack, feeling awkward standing alone, took out his phone and studied it. There were several missed calls and a text from the same number. It was a message from Robert. *Staff at Dales Bike Centre, Reeth, spotted a TREK gravel bike – sounds like it could have been your guy.* Jack looked at his watch, it was too late to call him now. He was still staring at his phone when Karl returned.

'I was just checking the weather,' he lied. 'I thought I might go for a bike ride tomorrow. Do you know how far

Reeth is?'

Before Karl could answer, his sister had signalled it was time to leave and he drained his glass. Lily told Di she hoped she'd see her with Kirsty next week at the Zumba class and they went their separate ways. As they walked back to "The Pines", Jack told Lily what he'd heard from Karl.

'It sounds like Amy was dating someone; is there anything in the notes?'

Lily shook her head. 'No, nothing. Her parents said there was no boyfriend, and her friends corroborated it. You say Kirsty thought she knew who it was? I'll have to check her statement again but I don't recall her saying anything.'

'That's what Karl said. She was too worried she might be wrong.'

Lily was halfway through her breakfast when Jack appeared next morning. He sat opposite her, complaining that he'd never been up so early on a Sunday.

'I want to get down to the stables,' Lily told him. 'I'm hoping to have a ride today. Are you doing anything exciting?'

He shook his head. By the time his bacon and eggs arrived, Lily had finished her breakfast. Eileen had offered them a Sunday roast, if they were back on time. They promised they would be ready and waiting at six on the dot. After Lily had closed the door behind her, Eileen perched on the arm of the sofa.

'Are you off on your bike today then, Jack?' she asked conspiratorially.

He finished a mouthful of toast. 'Yes. Do you know

how far it is to Reeth?'

She shrugged. 'Ten miles, maybe fifteen? I've never had to measure it. Is that where you're going today?

'Yes.'

She described several ways of getting there until Jack was confused. Then she went away and came back with a map.

'Here you are, this has all the roads on. You can take your pick but if it was me, I'd go to Askrigg and over the top.'

'Is there a hill?'

She laughed. 'Whichever way you go there'll be a hill to get from Wensleydale into Swaledale, lad.'

Jack quickly drained his teacup and went to his room to collect his things. He could hear Lily still moving about next door so he crept downstairs and out to where his electric bike was charging in Eileen's shed. It was his for three days and he was going to make use of it to ride to the Dales Bike Centre. He planned to investigate the sighting of the Trek gravel cycle, which was rather exciting.

He felt more confident than when he'd left Hawes on the previous day. The road to Bainbridge was relatively flat compared to his trip to Semerwater and it wasn't long before he was at the junction in the village, where he had to take the left lane to Askrigg. As he hesitated, a car drew up in the right lane alongside him and hooted gently. It was Lily smiling and waving before turning right. Jack sighed, now they'd all be laughing at him.

It took him two hours to get to Reeth. He found the climb from Askrigg really tiring, even with power-assistance and had to rest several times on the way. When he finally reached the top, he stopped to eat the pie he'd bought on the way, while he considered whether he had been over-optimistic in going so far. However, after a short rest he told himself the worst was over. The lane was narrow but there were no cars and he freewheeled most of the way down into Swaledale. At the bottom of the hill there was a road over the river, signposted to his destination. Here the road was wider but now he had to contend with cars coming up behind him on the bends and whizzing past on the straight bits. He was relieved when he finally rode down the hill into Reeth. It turned out to be bigger than Bainbridge, with a few shops, including a little grocery store. He took advantage of the opportunity to stock up with chocolate while asking where the Bike Centre was. It seemed he would have to go a little further down the road.

At last Jack turned in through the gap in the drystone wall, before pushing his bike self-consciously over to the café building and locking it. There was a figure in full cycling gear fiddling with the seat of his machine outside the bike shop as Jack approached. A tall man appeared from inside to join him. He hoped this was the owner.

'Excuse me,' Jack began,

He stopped and smiled. 'Can I help you?'

'Robert... I mean my friend, he's called Robert, was here yesterday. He spoke to you about a man with a gravel bike?'

'The new Trek, red and black, with electronic gears and carbon wheels? You couldn't miss it.'

'So you did see him?'

'You mean the guy with the bike? Yes, he was asking about a room in our bunkhouse.'

Jack tried to hide his excitement. 'He stayed here?'

The man shook his head. 'No, he was just unlucky, we had a group booked in for a long weekend.'

'In November?'

He shrugged. 'You tell me.' He was about to go back inside, then turned. 'Why do you want to know?'

'He disappeared. We're trying to find out where he went.' For good measure, he added, 'He was a friend, of Robert's.'

'So when exactly are you talking about?'

Jack did a quick calculation. Greg's credit card hadn't been used after 7th and he was due back at work on 23rd. 'Between 7th and 23rd of November roughly.'

'I can check.'

He disappeared into the shop, returning a few minutes later. 'Yes, we had large groups booked in over a couple of weekends in November: 7th to 10th and the 21st to 24th. There would have been space the rest of the time.'

'So that doesn't narrow it down much.'

'Well, I know it had been wet and wild for a day or two before, which was why he wanted somewhere to dry off. The forecast wasn't good.'

Jack thanked him and went into the café to grab a snack. He reckoned he deserved a rest before heading back over the hill. While he waited for his mug of tea to arrive, he made a note of the dates when the bunkhouse was full. He was enjoying a cheese and chutney sandwich when the owner joined him.

'I checked back in the diary to see when I was around,' he said. 'I was leading a group off-road for a full day on the 19th and 20th, so I couldn't have seen him then.' He got up. 'I hope that helps you trace him.' He looked out of the window. 'I've a vague recollection that he went off towards Wensleydale.'

He was pointing at the hill behind him, describing the route that went over the river and eventually joined up with the route Jack had taken from Askrigg. 'Don't worry mate, it's a much steadier climb on the way back. It won't be a problem on that electric bike of yours,' he assured Jack.

Chapter 11

Robert was outside smoking when Lily arrived for work on foot.

'No Jack this morning?' he asked.

'He said he didn't need a lift so I decided to get some exercise. I guess he's still got the bike,' she replied with a laugh, explaining how he'd hidden it in the shed but she'd spotted him out on the road.

She went inside and began work but before long she was distracted by the door flying open and Jack wheeling his bicycle through the office towards the kitchen.

'Where are you taking that?' she called but there was no reply.

He came back in, removing his helmet and gloves. 'It's not in the way in the corridor,' he said.

She was about to respond but they were interrupted by their boss arriving. Lily noticed that she'd had her hair cut shorter and recoloured, and thought it suited her. Once Robert was back at his desk, Miriam said she had arranged to visit Greg Nevitt's ex-wife.

'Jack, you'll come with me to take notes.'

He turned to grin at Lily. While he was getting back into his jacket, Robert was trying to attract his attention.

'Did you get my message about the bike?' he asked.

'Yes, thanks. I'll tell you later,' he muttered as he followed Miriam through the door.

'Don't mention it,' called Robert irritably. 'Fat lot of thanks you get for doing his job for him.'

Lily asked what he meant and he told her about his discovery at the Bike Centre.

'Hey, that's brilliant. And how did you get on doing the Herriot Way?'

Robert gave her a long and detailed description of his first day's walk, and she was about to ask him to cut to the chase, when he told her about his delayed start on the Friday.

'Actually, that reminds me, the band member promised to send me some photos,' he said, turning to his computer.

Lily waited while he opened his emails, scrolling through until he brought up a series of photographs.

'Anything?' Lily asked, moving nearer.

'They're all of the band,' he replied after a minute or two. 'Nothing of any use.'

'Mrs Nevitt lives in Barnsley,' Miriam explained. 'She's taken the morning off especially so I don't want us to be late. It should only take an hour and a half. Hopefully she can give us a picture of what her ex-husband was like. I would prefer if you just take notes, but if you have any questions, I can ask her.'

Jack had a think before telling her about his trip to the Bike Centre, without bothering to mention Robert's message. He said it was obvious that Greg Nevitt was an outdoor type, setting off into the countryside with his expensive bike. But was he going off road, wild camping, cooking over an open fire, or would he have been looking for B&Bs? He obviously wasn't short of a bob or two but the file said he had a menial job in a small engineering firm, so where did he get the money for his bike from?

'They're all good points, Jack. We'll make a detective of

you yet. I'd like to fill in the details that aren't in his file, such as when he separated from his wife two years ago, was it an amicable divorce, did he keep in touch with her? Did he get on with his work colleagues? How was his mental state?'

The house was a modern semi-detached property on the outskirts of the town, opposite a school. The door was answered by a woman with wispy white hair in a bun, who explained she was Wendy's aunt before leading them into a small sitting room at the back of the house. Greg's wife appeared at the door to ask if they would like coffee, which they agreed they would. Jack decided she was much younger than her husband, who had been thirty-seven when he died. While they waited, the aunt explained that Wendy had moved in with her after she left Greg and they've both found the arrangement beneficial. When Wendy returned, she looked annoyed to find them discussing her financial situation, and asked her aunt if she would leave her to speak to the police alone.

Miriam began by thanking her for seeing them at short notice. She explained that they were reopening the case now that Greg's cycle had been found.

'They told me it was damaged. Was there an accident?' Wendy asked in matter of fact tone.

'That's what we want to find out,' answered Miriam. 'Jack here is helping me discover more about your ex-husband's movements last year but I wanted to fill in some of the background details. For example, how long have you been divorced?'

'I'm not, that is, we weren't. It's two years since we separated, well I walked out, if you want to know. But it took a year to sell the house and sort out the mortgage.

Money was the thing we argued about mostly, even before the end. Greg didn't save anything. Once we did manage to put a bit by each month, he decided we needed a new car and used it for that. We had to sell everything when we split up, and that left peanuts, which is why I have to live here.'

Miriam looked at Jack and nodded.

'It was a really nice bike,' he commented. 'Was he a keen off-roader?'

'Not when we first separated. He bought an ordinary sort of bike to get to work on when he sold the car and that started the bug. The first year he went off to France on it, touring and camping. After that he was obsessed, away at every opportunity. He bought that latest bike brand new with his share of the proceeds from the house sale just before he went off last year. I thought he might have gone abroad, but his passport was in the flat. He could have been anywhere in the country. He went to Cornwall one time.'

'And does he camp when he's away?' Jack asked.

'Probably, we used to camp a lot when we were first married.'

Miriam set her mug down carefully on the coffee table. 'I hope you don't mind me asking, but how did it affect Greg when you left him.'

Again an unemotional response. 'He was upset, there's no denying. He went back to his bachelor days at first, eating takeaways and drinking too much but then he got this interest in cycling and started a fitness regime. A bit obsessive really. I was relieved because he was easier to deal with when we had to sell the house and there was legal stuff to sort out. In the end we worked through it and I think he accepted we were over.'

'Do you know how he got on with the people at work?'

'No, I don't. There was never any trouble when we were together. I don't have anything to do with them now.'

'And finally, Wendy, has anything occurred to you in the months since his disappearance that could give us a clue as to what happened to Greg?'

It was the first time she'd shown any emotion. Her mouth twisted into a grimace before she composed herself and shook her head. 'I thought he was in a good place because he seemed more settled, you know. In a way I was glad when he blew the money on that bike because it meant he was determined to keep fit and eat properly. Silly really.' She looked across at Jack, who was busy taking notes. 'Do you cycle?'

He blushed. 'Er yes, I do actually. Although I'm not a proper cyclist like Greg.'

She smiled at him.

Miriam was standing up. 'Thank you for your time Wendy. May we ring you if any other questions occur to us?'

'Of course,' she replied. 'I do want to find out what happened to Greg. I feel sure he must be dead, and I suppose it shouldn't affect me now we're separated, but I need to know.'

'Do you think it's possible he simply decided to disappear and start a new life?'

'No, he wouldn't do that, I'm certain of it. He'd turned the corner and was getting back on his feet.'

Miriam thanked her for her help and promised to keep in touch.

On the drive back to Hawes, Miriam asked Jack

whether his impression of Greg Nevitt had changed since meeting his ex-partner.

'Not really. It explains where the money came from to buy his bike though.'

'And the fact he camped overnight.'

'Except when it was raining.'

She laughed, 'Yes of course. It wouldn't be my idea of fun either.'

Jack remembered holidays with his dad. They went to Scotland for two weeks once, in the school holidays, just the two of them, while Mum and the girls went to stay with his grandmother. It was the best time, spent fishing and walking, cooking on campfires, and washing in the freezing cold loch. The last time was ten years ago and he hadn't been back since. When Dad died, they'd moved to Milton Keynes to be closer to Nan and that didn't turn out so well after his mother met Vince. His sisters liked him but he didn't. So after university he worked for the police to get away from his family.

'And how did you come to apply for this secondment?' asked Miriam.

Had he really been telling his boss all about his dad dying of cancer and his mother planning to get married again? He covered his embarrassment by replying, with a white lie. He said he asked to join the team, which was sort of true, because when they said he could face suspension if he didn't agree, he applied immediately.

He hadn't guessed that Miriam was already familiar with the facts of his transfer. He would have been mortified to know she was already aware that he'd been caught attempting to access personal information on an innocent citizen called Vince Palmer. In her view, he wasn't the first and she now understood better why he had done it. She suggested they stop at the motorway services for a sandwich so she could find out a bit more about young Jack and what made him tick.

However, lunch provided the perfect opportunity for Jack to ask his boss for a favour.

'...so it's very reasonable to hire the electric bike for a month compared to the cost per day,' he concluded after explaining why he needed the bike for transport.

'It is, but my budget doesn't cater for bike hire, Jack. There's your forensic work to pay for and the accommodation bill is substantial. I don't think we can justify it at the present time. Sorry.'

Lily and Robert had agreed over coffee that the bicycle couldn't stay in the corridor outside the kitchen, where it was in the way. Together, they sorted out the jumble of folding chairs in the cupboard under the stairs and wheeled it in there.

'Perfect,' declared Robert, shutting the door firmly.

Lily smiled, he was a man after her own heart, organised and efficient, if a little boring. They went back to work in a peaceful, congenial atmosphere, something that had been missing when Jack was around. So when he and Miriam returned, she grinned across at Robert, waiting for his reaction when he found his bike was missing. Lily would have allowed him to think it had gone, but Robert was diplomacy itself, pointing out that it was safely hidden away under the stairs, just in case someone spotted it through the kitchen window and broke in while the building was unoccupied.

'Right, Robert,' announced Miriam. 'Let's have your

report on the Herriot Way.'

To Jack's disappointment, she ushered him upstairs to what had now become their conference room.

'Did you have a good morning with the boss?' Lily asked him.

'Yes, very good. Greg's wife was nice. We stopped at Wetherby for lunch on the way back.'

'Teacher's pet, eh?' Then she added, 'And Robert told me how he gave you the lead about the Bike Centre.'

He ignored her mocking tone. 'Yes, I need to check the weather reports for last November.'

It didn't take him long to locate the Met Office database for the previous year. From the 7th to 18th, the weather in the North was mild with wet and windy spells. It continued mostly unsettled and mild until the 25th. Jack did some quick calculations. The heavy rain started around 19th in the North, but the owner of the Bike Centre was out that day and the next. By the time Greg arrived it had been raining at least one night if not two. There was no accommodation available from the 21st so that tied in with when he visited the Bike Centre. The poor guy was wet and wanted somewhere to dry out overnight, so when he set off again in the direction of Wensleydale, he would be looking for another bunkhouse or cheap lodgings. Trawling through the internet for bunkhouses in Yorkshire he spotted a name he recognised. The accommodation was close to Semerwater, the address was Stalling Busk.

Upstairs, Miriam noticed it was getting late. Her rented cottage had been unoccupied since Friday evening and she knew it would take at least a day to warm up again. The sooner she got back to light a fire and get the stove going, the better. Robert had given her a blow by blow account of his visits to the B&Bs on his walk, his conversations with the landladies, descriptions of the pubs he ate in and even the place where Berry was due to stay, if he hadn't disappeared. But amongst all the trivia was a suggestion that Berry had left Hawes very late on the day he vanished, causing him to lose his way in the dark. Unfortunately Robert had no evidence to corroborate his hunch.

She brought their discussion to a close. 'I asked Jack and Lily to work on their preferred scenarios and it sounds as if you have settled on one yourself. Are you happy to pursue it?'

'Definitely. I just need to find some proof that he attended the church service on Remembrance Sunday.'

Chapter 12

What a difference a day makes, Miriam mused, as she drove into work. She'd slept well under the electric blanket she'd brought back from her flat and, to her delight, the radiators were warm. Topping up the stove last thing at night meant it was still hot in the morning, although hungry for another load of solid fuel. She'd warmed the croissants from her favourite bakery and had remembered to bring a pot of Mum's home-made marmalade. The rest of the groceries were still in their bags on the kitchen table, where she'd abandoned them to wrestle with the stove. Peering through the tiny kitchen window as she packed them away, she could see signs of sunlight emerging from behind the hill. She poured a second mug of proper coffee and smiled to herself.

As usual, she was the first to unlock their modest headquarters. She switched on the electric radiators and the water heater in the kitchen before sitting down to consider the next stage in her plan to keep the team on track. Investigations often moved so fast that the focus was lost with people going off at tangents; she had spotted it in the original Amy Hobson investigation. Working with her small team, she wanted them to take an uncluttered view of the evidence, limited as it was, and distil it into a series of simple facts, to develop a hypothesis and plan how to prove it. She based her principles on product design, something she'd touched on at college. The first steps were to ask questions and generate ideas, create a testable hypothesis, conduct the experiment, communicate and prioritise the results. She'd tried it in the past but the principles had usually got lost in the chaos of the investigation. This time she felt it was already working with the team members so as soon as they were all present, she asked them to be ready to discuss their scenarios, as she called the hypotheses.

'But,' she warned, 'I don't want "War and Peace". Keep it brief and to the point. See how few words you can use to summarise.'

After coffee they gathered in the conference room, as they now referred to the area upstairs. Miriam noticed that Lily had brought her laptop with her this time, a sign of the unspoken rivalry that appeared to be developing between her and Jack.

'Who would like to start?' she asked.

'Ladies first,' said Robert amiably.

He was rewarded with a cold stare from Lily but she nodded, turning her laptop so the others could see her presentation, while she read through it.

'The victim, Amy Hobson, aged eighteen, disappeared from Kirkby Stephen after her shift on Sunday afternoon 7th November. Her car was found still parked in the town. Her body was discovered, strangled, on Wednesday 24th November, near Cotterdale. My scenario is that she accepted a lift home from someone because her car wouldn't start. That someone strangled her in Cotterdale, and left her there.'

Lily looked as if she might continue so Miriam stopped her there. 'That's fine, thank you Lily. Questions anyone?'

'Yes,' said Robert, turning to Lily. 'What car did she drive?'

'A VW Polo. It was ten years old so it could have had starting problems.'

Robert nodded as if he accepted her version of events.

Jack had a question. 'Do we have her phone?'

'No. Her handbag was with the body but there's no sign of her phone. They lost the signal just outside Kirkby Stephen.'

Miriam cut any further discussion short and asked Jack to continue with his presentation. He typed vigorously on his laptop before bringing up a map of the surrounding area on the screen.

'Greg Nevitt bought a super bike that's as good off-road as it is on it. He arrived in the Dales last November at some stage during a fortnight's holiday. He was booked off work between the 8th and the 23rd. The weather wasn't bad in the first two weeks but then it rained and I think that's when he tried to book a room in the bunkhouse in Swaledale. Failing that, he carried on to Wensleydale where sometime between 20th and 24th of November he was knocked off his bike by a vehicle and badly injured or killed. Whichever it was, he was left to die somewhere in the area and has never been found.'

There was silence as they considered the cyclist's fate. Then Lily asked if the forensics had come back yet. The answer was no.

'Robert?' asked Miriam.

'I've no questions,' he said irritably.

'In that case, let's hear about Mr Brian Berry.'

He had no digital presentation but handed them each an A4 sheet with just five lines of text each bearing a number.

'I retraced Brian Berry's steps from Aysgarth on the

route of the Herriot Way and made an interesting discovery in Hawes. You'll see number one refers to the fact that it was Remembrance Sunday the day he left Hawes. The second point is that he told Babs that he wanted to attend the service. My assumption is that he went to church and consequently didn't leave town until lunchtime, which is my third point. That leads me to believe it was dark when he was crossing Great Shunner Fell, he got lost, wandered away from the path and was injured or collapsed. That is why, my final point, the search party never found his body.'

'Who's Babs?' asked Jack with a grin.

Robert looked up. 'She owns the B&B where he stayed in Hawes,' he replied sharply.

Miriam thanked everyone for their clear reports. 'So we have your three hypotheses and now we have to test them. How do you suggest we do that?'

There was silence, then Lily put her hand up tentatively. 'Can I ask something? It's just that we haven't talked about how the three investigations… I mean the three hypotheses fit together. Isn't that what we've been asked to do?'

'That's a good question, Lily,' replied Miriam. 'It's one approach and perfectly valid but we have nothing to base it on.' She had thought about this very carefully when first confronted with the problem. 'If we treat all three cases as one investigation, we will only look for evidence that fits that scenario. But what if they aren't connected, we'll miss resolving any of them, won't we?' She looked at them in turn but got the impression that they weren't following her argument. 'Bear with me for now because once we have completed the next stage, we can begin to look for synergies.' She could see that she had lost them. 'Meanwhile can we quickly identify what you each need in order to test your theories?'

She went round the table quickly; conscious it was nearly lunchtime.

'I need to know if Amy had difficulty starting her car,' said Lily. 'I need to talk to her friends, or her parents.'

'OK. Jack?'

'Where did Greg go after he was seen in Swaledale? Is Greg's body near Semerwater where his bike was found?'

'Has there been a thorough search of the area?' Robert asked.

'There's not been a search since they found his bike.'

Miriam made a note to find out whether a search was planned by the North Yorkshire force. 'It was only recovered a few weeks ago,' she pointed out. 'Robert?'

'I'm thinking the same thing. The search for Brian Berry was mainly in Swaledale and only very close to the footpath over Great Shunner Fell. I think they should widen the search area.'

Miriam wrote ditto under her first entry, although the second request seemed much less likely to be approved. 'What evidence do you have that he spent the Sunday morning in Hawes?' she asked, looking for some reason to initiate a second search so long after the man disappeared.

'Ah, that's the problem. I have some photographs of the service but he isn't visible in any of them.'

Miriam closed her notepad. 'It sounds as though you each have some digging to do to find evidence that corroborates your theories. I have a meeting with the Chief Inspector tomorrow, so I suggest we catch up again on Thursday.'

After lunch, they were all hunched over their laptops and the only sound was the tapping of keyboards. But when Lily went to make tea in the afternoon, Jack came in to tell her that he'd put messages on Twitter and Instagram asking people for photographs of the Remembrance Service in Hawes. He said the posts would be seen by thousands of people but, as Lily pointed out, only a handful of them would live in the area and of those, how many would be taking pictures of a church service in Hawes?

'Well, don't tell Robert,' Jack warned. 'I want to surprise him.'

You mean you want to appear cleverer than him, thought Lily as he left the kitchen.

Back at her desk, she was struggling to see how she could prove Amy's car had failed to start on occasions. She could ask the girl's parents but it wasn't a visit she relished. Wishing to avoid the meeting, she decided to see if she could get the information from Kirsty and Di at Zumba the following evening. Meanwhile, she would use the time constructively by searching the local papers for a photograph of the Remembrance Service. Not that she was competing with Jack, just trying to help Robert.

They all worked in silence for the rest of the afternoon. Robert had already left when Miriam announced she would be going straight off to see the Chief Inspector next day, so could they open up the office in the morning.

Lily asked Jack if he wanted a lift back to the B&B.

'Well I haven't got the bike now, have I?' he responded, pointedly.

He'd returned it to the Bike Hub at lunchtime, explaining loudly to everyone, particularly his boss, that he couldn't afford to hire it any longer.

On their way to the "The Pines", Lily asked if he had a driver's licence. He replied that he hadn't taken the test.

'So you never learnt to drive?'

'Don't sound so surprised.' He sounded affronted. 'Not everyone can afford driving lessons and Mum never learnt so we didn't have a car after Dad died.'

Lily apologised.

'Doesn't matter. I could've learnt when I started work, I suppose. Just never got round to it.'

'Well, if you need to go somewhere, I'll take you, provided I'm not busy.' She was parking outside the cottage. 'What d'you think we've got for tea tonight?' she asked.

'Don't mind so long as there's chips.'

Lily sighed. 'There's always chips, except on Sunday.'

Robert had been waiting to be let in when Lily arrived with Jack to unlock the building next morning. He made them both coffee and they sat chatting about what little progress they'd made.

'I know Miriam likes to be methodical,' Robert began, 'but I find her approach very restricting. For example, I can tell she won't be pushing for a new search of the area.'

'But she's right that we need evidence for our theories before we can move forward,' Lily insisted. 'I like the systematic way she works.'

'That's because you're a forensic scientist at heart,' said Jack. 'Very meticulous. I prefer a more holistic approach.'

Lily laughed. 'Do you actually know what that word

means?'

'I do,' he replied indignantly. 'It's a term used a lot in cybersecurity and it means you look at everything, all possibilities. I prefer that, don't you Robert?'

'Yes, to a degree but not to lose sight of the most important things. Take Lily's car conundrum, for example.' Jack smirked but Robert ignored him. 'That car was probably not seen as important in the original investigation because Amy had left it behind. But it could be a significant clue if you are right, Lily.'

She smiled at him. 'Exactly, but we can't ever know if it flooded, can we? Because it started first time when it was recovered for forensics.'

Jack looked puzzled. 'Yes we can. They just need to interrogate the OBD.'

Lily looked at him. 'What?'

'The "On Board Diagnostics". They should've scanned the OBD. That would tell them if the engine had stalled because of flooding, or wouldn't start.'

'I wonder why they didn't look at that?' Lily asked.

'Because,' said Robert, 'like I said, it didn't seem important at the time.'

'And you're lucky, Lily,' said Jack. 'You can call your old mates back in Cumbria to look at it for you.'

'D'you think so? I suppose it's worth a try but I'll have to ask Miriam first.'

Jack shrugged. 'At least find out where the car is now.'

She sent an email to Sylvie, a CSI colleague she'd worked closely with in the past. She spent ages concocting a friendly message about her new post before mentioning the car, almost as an afterthought but adding that it was a significant part of her investigation. She distracted herself while she waited for a response by resuming her search in the November editions of the local papers. By the time Sylvie came back to her, asking her to call her mobile, she'd only found one photograph of Hawes on Remembrance Sunday and that was of people at the war memorial. Not knowing what Brian Berry looked like, she passed it on to Robert, suggesting he might contact the photographer because there could be more where that came from.

'Sylvie? It's Lily, thanks for getting back. How are you?'

They exchanged a few pleasantries before Lily cut to the chase and asked if Sylvie could tell her anything about the car.

'They did a sweep of the car,' she began.

'I know, I've got the report,' Lily replied, trying to keep the irritation out of her voice.

'So you'll know they only did prints. After it came back clean, they returned the car to her parents. Sorry I can't be more helpful. Let me know if you're going to request further forensics, won't you? My Terry did the vehicle search.'

Lily smiled. 'I will but I'm waiting for the boss to come back tomorrow, we're on a tight budget.'

'Keep me in the loop then, I could come down with Terry. I like the Yorkshire Dales, and it would be nice to catch up.'

As soon as she put the phone down Robert was at her desk.

'Thanks for the heads up on the newspaper photographer,' he said quietly. He looked round to see if Jack was listening. 'He's sending over the rest of the pictures he took. You never know, we might be lucky.'

Chapter 13

Amy's parents were aware of the investigation and Miriam had told Lily she could speak to them if she needed to, so why was she so nervous of meeting them? Mrs Hobson had sounded nice on the phone, confirming they would both be home that afternoon. Lily instructed Jack to lock up if she wasn't back by five and set off the short distance to the edge of town. The house was in a row of neat cottages and, as she waited on the doorstep, she noted that someone took good care of the garden. The woman who opened the door looked similar in age and demeanour to her own mother, not homely exactly but a little dowdy, was that the expression?

'Come in, love,' she said, pulling the door open wide. 'It's cold out today, isn't it? In here.' She led her through into a comfortable sitting room with a blazing fire. 'I've made tea. I did some baking this morning.'

There was a tray on the table in front of the sofa. Lily was told to sit in the chair by the fire to warm up while Mrs Hobson poured the tea. Her husband arrived in time to take a cup and saucer and hand it to Lily. She tried to appear professional but it was difficult when balancing a tea plate on her lap. She found herself answering questions about where she was from and how she came to be a detective. It was like having afternoon tea at a friend's house.

She finally began by saying that she was sorry to be visiting them under such sad circumstances, that Amy sounded like a lovely young woman. When she mentioned Amy's two close friends, their reaction was probably predictable in retrospect. Kirsty was such a lovely lass but that Diana, as they called her, was always a handful. The three girls had become inseparable once they got together at school in their early teens. The implication was that Amy had been a model daughter until she met Diana. Once they started, it seemed they wanted to tell her everything about Amy that had caused them worry: the piercings, the tiny tattoos, the unsuitable boyfriends, and the bar work. Lily knew about the boyfriends; their names were listed in her file. They'd all been checked out and none had been in the area the day Amy disappeared.

She took a deep breath as she put her empty plate down on the hearth. 'I really came to ask about her car,' she explained.

They looked at her expectantly and she could feel herself blushing. 'It's rather a peculiar question but I wondered if it ever failed to start?'

They were still staring at her. Mr Hobson scratched his head. 'Why?'

'It might explain why she left her car in Kirkby Stephen.'

'But it started first time when the police took it away. No-one said anything.'

'I know they did forensics at the time but I'd like to have a more detailed examination.'

They looked at her and then at each other.

'Do you still have the car?' she asked, wishing she'd expressed herself better.

Mrs Hobson clasped her hands together, letting her husband explain that it was in a garage at his cousin's farm in Sedbergh. 'I... We couldn't bring ourselves to part with it just yet, could we love?'

Lily hid her excitement. 'Can I send someone down to the farm to examine it?'

He nodded. 'I'd best give you my cousin's number.'

He left the room and Amy's mother looked up at her. 'He says I'm silly to hang on to it but...'

'I understand,' said Lily.

Mr Hobson came back waving a slip of paper. 'I've written his number on here. He's got a set of keys.'

It was time to leave. She went straight back to "The Pines", to get changed for Zumba. As she drove, she wondered if he was referring to the set of keys found in Amy's handbag, because if they were there'd be little forensic evidence left on them now.

Di was chatting to a group of girls when Lily arrived at the hall but there was no sign of Kirsty. She waved, said something to her friends then came over.

'Hi Lily.'

'No Kirsty tonight?'

Di shook her head. 'She said she's not feeling energetic. I don't suppose I could blag a lift back to Hawes with you after. Otherwise I'll have to get Karl out.'

'No problem.'

The class was starting so they took up their places. Lily wasn't paying attention and kept going wrong. She was thinking about Di and the bad influence Amy's parents felt she'd exerted over their daughter. Lily's parents were the same, blaming her friends when she decided to break off the engagement with Roy. She let the rhythmic beat of the music take over as she tried to wipe out the memory of the scenes at home. By the time they stopped for a break, she was feeling more relaxed and joined Di's group.

'This is Lily,' she announced. 'She's just moved in near me, though I can't see why she wants to live in the middle of nowhere!'

One of her friends was more astute. 'So what brought you to Wensleydale?' she asked before taking a swig from her bottle of water.

Five faces were turned to her. 'I… er… I'm with the Rural Crime Unit.'

'What's that?' asked another.

She was saved by the instructor calling them to start the next half of the session. Now she had lost her concentration. What had she told them? Was it the Wildlife Unit or the Rural Crime Unit? Whatever she'd said, she was certain Di would pursue it later.

'I think this class is too hard for me,' she told Di when they were putting their coats on. 'I couldn't keep up towards the end.'

'You'll get used to it. We were all rubbish when we started. The routines come with practice.'

Di didn't suggest stopping for a drink this time and Lily didn't ask. She wanted to leave Di's company as soon as possible to avoid discussing her work. Instead she asked about Kirsty. Was she ill? Her friend thought she was still suffering from depression. She had been the same on and off since last year.

'In fact I'm going to see her when I get back so can you drop me off, I'll show you where.'

Lily put some music on, turning it up loud to make conversation more difficult. Di was in her element, singing along and shouting her opinions of the tracks. Lily asked her what music she liked and she told her about the gigs she'd been to in Newcastle. It kept them going until they reached Hawes.

After she'd dropped Di at Kirsty's, Lily went to the "Chippie" and ordered a cod and chips. She thought it might be a bit cheeky to take them back indoors with her but Eileen rushed to fetch a plate and cutlery.

'Did Jack go with you?' she asked Lily.

'No, why? Has he not been back?'

'I haven't seen him this evening,' she said. 'D'you want any ketchup for your chips, love?'

There was no sign of Jack at breakfast and no answer when she banged on his bedroom door before leaving.

'I'm going now,' she called as she went back downstairs. 'You'll just have to walk!'

When she reached the office, the door was still locked and Jack had the key. As she stared through the glass, there was a movement at the back of the room, a figure running along the corridor from the kitchen to the stairs. It was Jack dressed only in his boxer shorts. She shouted at him and hammered on the door but he didn't respond immediately. Meanwhile Robert's car arrived and by the time he joined her at the door, Jack was unlocking it, fully dressed.

'Sorry, I must've locked it again when I came in this morning,' he said.

Lily glowered at him but said nothing, she would confront him later. She went to the kitchen on the pretext of making coffee but examined the shower room and found it full of condensation. She went upstairs and through the meeting room to the bedroom where she spotted a holdall on the bed. There was a musky smell of deodorant. Had Jack really spent the night here?

Downstairs Miriam was telling Robert about her meeting with the Chief Inspector. She looked up when Lily appeared but continued her conversation. Jack was at his desk apparently engrossed in his computer screen.

'Hi. How did you get on with the Hobsons?' he asked cheerfully.

'Jack, what are you playing at?' she demanded quietly.

'What d'you mean?'

'You slept here last night, didn't you?'

'Shh, I haven't asked her yet. I'm just trying to save money.'

Miriam was calling them. 'You might as well hear this, you two,' she said, standing and moving to the centre of the room.

Lily went back to her desk.

'As you can imagine, the Chief Inspector is pleased with the progress we made last week. But when I raised the possibility of further search effort, in due course when we have more evidence, he pointed out that the budget is fixed. In a nutshell, if we use the money on a search, the time available will reduce accordingly. He was also very concerned about the publicity that a high-profile search would raise. Any questions?'

Her announcement was met with silence, so Miriam returned to her desk. Lily took the opportunity to update her with a report of her visit to the Hobsons. She explained how the OBD could tell them whether Amy's car had failed to start and she'd spoken to Forensics in Cumbria, but now she was worried that the examination would be curtailed for financial reasons.

'I've got the keys to Amy's car,' she began. 'It's being stored in Sedbergh.'

'Good work, Lily. You go ahead.'

Lily grinned at Robert as she finished her call to Sylvie. 'I'm meeting them in Sedbergh tomorrow morning.'

She heard Jack muttering, 'No problem, any time. A thank you would have been nice.'

At coffee time she caught him in the kitchen. 'Have you spoken to Miriam yet?' she asked, knowing that he hadn't.

'Mind your own business,' he replied, just as Robert appeared.

'Hello, what's going on here?' he asked amicably as Jack pushed past him and left the kitchen.

When Lily told him, Robert just laughed. 'Is he entertaining a lady-friend up there?'

'I don't think so. He said it was to save money.'

'But you get an allowance for accommodation, don't you? He can't claim it if he isn't using it. What's he up to?'

Lily picked up her mug to carry it back to her desk but she stopped in the corridor when she heard Jack's voice.

'...but if I don't claim the allowance there'll be enough for the bike hire and more. I'll need something for meals but you'll still be in pocket.'

'It's not that simple, Jack.' It was Miriam. 'Money comes from different allocations. I think it works like that. Have you thought about whether there is insurance cover for someone to live here, there are implications.'

Lily went back into the kitchen. 'He's talking to her now,' she informed Robert.

She waited until they'd finished their drinks before leaving the kitchen. Jack was at his computer; Miriam was on the phone. She couldn't help listening to her boss consult someone about how the finances were allocated. Lily looked round at Jack who pulled a face. She ignored him, returning to her review of the forensics in Amy's file. The girl's handbag and wallet had been examined for prints and DNA, but the conclusion was that the killer had worn gloves. That wasn't surprising as the temperature that afternoon was only 3°C. The car had been examined, using the spare key provided by Mr Hobson to open it and start the engine first time. That was done on the following day and when she consulted the online weather information, it had been sunny, and 9°C, if that was relevant. Lily couldn't understand why the keys hadn't been screened as part of the forensic work. Presumably someone somewhere had decided they were irrelevant.

'So you won't be needing a lift back then?' Lily asked sarcastically when it was time to go. His face was a picture and she burst out laughing. 'Your face!'

He scowled. 'I can walk.'

It was pouring with rain. She told him not to be so silly, making for the door, and he followed her to the car.

'Thanks for telling me about the ODB, by the way,' she said, switching on the windscreen wipers before turning the car round. 'Forensics are going to download it tomorrow.'

Silence.

She waited until they were on the road to ask, 'So what did the boss say?'

'You heard her.'

'So at least she's looking into it.'

'It depends on the finances. I guess I'm stuck relying on lifts.'

'What, like this evening? To be honest, I'm not relishing another boring evening in the bar while you play pool.'

'Actually I asked Karl to come along, so he'll take me.'

You are so transparent, thought Lily. 'You mean you knew you wouldn't be able to ask me for a lift to the pool night if you moved out of "The Pines", so you persuaded Karl instead?'

'Something like that.'

'Well just be careful. First of all, please put them straight about me being your sister and if anyone asks, we are part of the Rural Crime Unit looking for poachers. We'll just have to hope they've forgotten your lies about being at school with Amy.'

Lily was in her room when her mother rang. It had been several days without her calling, which was probably a record. It was obvious she had a particular reason for ringing because, after discussing the weather, she asked if Roy had been in touch. Lily had been ignoring the missed calls because, well it was easier. There was nothing left to say, was there?

'No Mum, but I've been very busy. I'm seeing Sylvie from Forensics tomorrow; do you remember her? She was my boss until I got promotion.'

Her attempt to change the topic was unsuccessful.

'Lily, he's been on to us several times in the last couple of weeks. He wants to talk to you about going to his parents' anniversary dinner. I said I didn't think you would want to upset them by refusing their invitation.'

It would have been nice to see them again under normal circumstances. She liked Roy's mother particularly and she was pretty sure she would understand why Lily couldn't go. She'd been very understanding when she told her that she was breaking off the engagement. It was unfair of Roy to use his parents, and hers, to get her to meet him.

'Sorry, Mum, but I'm far too busy now.'

'But you don't know when it is.'

'No.'

It went so quiet at the other end that Lily thought she'd gone, but then her mother said, 'I think you are being very cruel, avoiding Roy. He's obviously heart-broken and the least you can do is talk to him.'

She wanted to respond honestly, to tell her mother why she broke off the engagement. Poor Roy with his "bit on the side". Mum didn't know about that, did she? No-one did because it was too awful to even think about and she certainly wasn't going to discuss it with her parents. They would want to know the details, which would mean explaining how she'd found them in bed together. It was too embarrassing to describe to another soul.

Chapter 14

Lily was halfway through her breakfast when Jack appeared looking as if he'd only just woken up.

'You had a good night by the look of you,' she said.

'Now you do sound like my sister,' he remarked, filling a bowl with cereal, and pouring milk onto it.

'Anything exciting happen?'

He wiped milk from his chin. 'I won two games before I was knocked out.'

'Is that all?'

'Yes.'

'And how was Karl?'

'I made sure I didn't mention where I went to school or where I work if that's what you mean.'

When she'd finished eating Lily told Jack he would be walking to work because she was off to Sedbergh; she'd arranged to meet Sylvie and Terry at the farm. She scraped ice from the windscreen, inside and out, before setting off along the familiar road, passing the lane to Cotterdale and following the road towards Sedbergh that was still white with frost in places. It began winding beside the river, crossing and turning down a narrow road between stone walls. Finally, the satnav sent her down a tiny lane that had grass growing down the centre. It seemed to go on for ever, although the sign had said just half a mile. Eventually the road ended in a farmyard, where she parked beside a large silver SUV. The door opened and Sylvie emerged with a tall man in a woolly bobble hat.

'This is Terry,' her friend said after giving her a hug.

'I was looking for the van,' said Lily.

Terry shook his head and the bobble waggled jauntily. 'No need, I've brought the scanner. It'll only take five minutes.'

Lily offered to find the owner but Sylvie had already spoken to the farmer, who'd told them where the car was stored.

'I'll show you.' Sylvie was leading the way round the end of the farm buildings to a barn. 'It's in here.'

The double metal doors opened onto a deceptively large interior containing several old-fashioned tractors. At the front was a VW Polo with a 2010 registration plate.

Terry arrived a minute later carrying a small box. 'Have you got the keys?' he asked. 'Let's hope the battery hasn't given up.'

'The farmer says he keeps it charged so he can get his vintage tractors out for the shows,' Sylvie replied.

'We may be lucky then.'

Lily took the keys from her bag and unlocked the car using the electronic fob. There was an audible click.

'Sounds like it's working,' Terry remarked. He opened the box containing a gadget that looked like an overlarge mobile phone. 'Here we go then.'

He opened the driver's door wide and disappeared under the steering wheel. While he worked, Lily took the opportunity to tell Sylvie about her concerns.

'I assume these keys are a spare set. The file says Amy's keys were found in her handbag but there's no forensic report on them.'

'Probably wore gloves.'

'No, I mean they didn't request any forensics on the

keys.'

'Not important then.'

'But don't you see? If the hypothesis is that Amy couldn't start her car, it's possible whoever gave her a lift tried to start it for her first. In fact if it was a man it's inevitable that he would have had a go himself.'

'Well, if that's your *hypothesis* – what kind of word is that anyway, Lily?'

There was a shout of triumph from inside the car and Terry emerged, replacing his bobble hat. 'It's downloaded all right. I'll take it back to analyse it.'

'So what does it say?' Lily asked.

He smiled. 'It's not as easy as that. I'll need to check with VW to ensure I'm interpreting it correctly.' He stopped then grinned at her. 'But if I'm reading it right, there are failures related to starting. I'll know when I've confirmed the output with an expert.'

As she walked back to her car, Lily asked Sylvie if she could check where Amy's handbag and its contents were being stored. She would persuade her boss to have the other set of keys forensically examined as soon as possible.

She watched them leave the farmyard before climbing into her car. She sometimes regretted leaving her job in forensics for detective work but at the time it seemed the more exciting option. She now realised it was a way of putting distance between her and Roy; the beginning of the end of a very long relationship that had started when they were teenagers. Well, forensics loss was CID's gain, she thought as she started the engine and headed into Sedbergh to find a coffee.

She planned to make a detour on her way back to the office. She wanted to visit the place where Amy was found again, but on her own so she could take her time. As soon as she turned onto the road that led to Cotterdale she felt herself relax. It was a sunny morning but she was prepared for the cold wind with hat and gloves. She parked off the road beside a forestry track and went the rest of the way on foot. There was no-one about and she was able to study the handful of cottages as she walked through the village. At the place where Robert had parked, on the bridge over the stream, was a Land Rover and a man in a camouflage jacket was padlocking the gate on the other side.

'The footpath is just up there.' He pointed to where, further upstream, they'd crossed over a small footbridge previously.

She grabbed the moment. 'I'm from the Rural Crime Unit,' she said, waving her warrant card at him. 'Do you look after this area?'

'Yes. Is there a problem?'

'Not at all. I was wondering whether you'd had any issues up here with poaching.'

He shook his head slowly. 'Not recently. Why?'

'Do you keep this gate padlocked?' she asked, ignoring his question.

'Yes.' He showed her the key, as if to prove it.

'And no-one has broken in, say in the last year?'

He hesitated for several seconds before answering carefully, 'No, not on my watch.'

'When someone else was in charge?'

He shook his head. 'I only took over properly in January so I'm not responsible for security before that.' He headed towards his vehicle.

Lily watched him drive slowly towards the other gate

that led onto a track that disappeared into the hills. He jumped out to unlock it and she caught up with him.

'I just need to know if it was tampered with last year,' she demanded, indicating the gate behind them.

He scratched his head, looking bemused. 'Not tampered with, no.' He opened the gate and jumped in the Land Rover. 'My predecessor replaced the chain before he left in November.'

'Why was that?'

'I don't know,' he shouted above the engine as he pulled away.

She watched him disappear up the track while she considered whether a new chain on the gate was significant.

'Where's Lily this morning?' Robert asked when Jack arrived alone.

'She's getting the ODB on Amy Hobson's car scanned, as I suggested,' Jack replied.

'Yes, that was a good call,' Robert observed. 'Credit where credit's due, you youngsters know your way around these new-fangled gadgets.'

Jack laughed. 'You have to move with the times Grandad.'

Robert observed that he didn't know what went on under the bonnet of his car these days and Jack told him how vehicles could tell you a lot about what the driver had been up to, including evidence taken from trackers and recordings from dashcams. 'But unfortunately that doesn't help Lily.'

'It's a pity your chap didn't have a camera on his bicycle,' Robert observed.

It was only later in the morning that Robert, reflecting on their conversation, did a little digging on the internet himself. He waited until lunchtime when Miriam was within earshot to give Jack the benefit of *his* experience.

'I thought I was right but I wanted to check before saying,' he began. 'Bicycle trackers.'

'What?'

'Do you know if your chap's cycle had a tracker? You said it was expensive so I guess he might have fitted one?'

Jack looked confused, much to Robert's satisfaction.

'I can send you some links,' he said airily then went on to explain how a tracker could be hidden in a rear light or the handlebars.

Jack thanked him but pointed out that he knew where the bike was, it was the owner they needed to find.

'Ah but a tracker will tell you where he went before he disappeared,' he replied patiently.

'Only if it stores the route and retains it when the battery dies. His phone records didn't provide any useful information after he started his trip.'

Robert shrugged, 'Only trying to help, son.'

When Lily arrived back from Sedbergh, Miriam invited them to join her in the meeting room. They followed her upstairs, taking their usual seats round the table. She smiled as she waited for them to settle down.

'It's the end of the second week of your investigations so I thought we should have a quick review before we go our separate ways for the weekend. Shall we go round the table? Robert have you spotted Mr Berry at the church yet?'

He cleared his throat. 'I'm waiting for the "Darlington

and Stockton Times" photographer to forward me the pictures he took at the event.' He hesitated. 'Thanks to Lily.'

Miriam nodded, then looked across at Jack. 'Anything to report?'

He reddened. 'Robert mentioned to me that bikes can be fitted with trackers, so I've asked Forensics to check while they're doing their other tests. They've nearly finished with it but they hadn't checked for a tracker.'

'And what will that tell us?' Miriam asked.

'Probably nothing because the batteries don't last long and they won't store much information.'

Robert sighed audibly. Miriam ignored him and asked Lily for her report.

'The VW OBD has been scanned and Terry from Forensics is checking the output. He thinks there could be evidence that the car had starting problems.' She didn't mention her trip to Cotterdale, she was still making sense of a replacement chain on the locked gate.

Miriam thanked them, commenting that they were all playing a waiting game that hopefully would come to fruition early next week. She hid her disappointment as she wished them a good weekend. If there was no photograph of Mr Berry in Hawes, no tracker on the bike and VW's view was that the forensics was wrong, the entire week had been wasted.

Jack had waited at the top of the stairs to ask her about the bike hire again.

'I want to spend time this weekend in Raydale, where they found Greg's bike, and I can only get there if I hire an electric bike for the weekend. It's almost as cheap to have it for the month.'

Miriam was sure it wasn't but she'd considered his dilemma and concluded it was a perfectly reasonable request. She'd just have to find a way of balancing the books.

'All right, Jack. Hire the bike for the month but I don't want you moving in here, it's not appropriate. I'll sign your expenses for the bike if you give me a copy of the receipt.'

His face was a picture. 'It'll be worth it, I promise you. I'm going to get inside the head of Greg Nevitt this way, you'll see.'

Miriam smiled to herself as she followed him downstairs. Everyone was getting ready to leave. Robert went first, hoping he wouldn't be late for his tea. Lily and Jack were off to collect fish and chips to take back to their B&B. She watched them go as she sat back down at her desk. She'd left her report until after the meeting, hoping there would be positive news to replace her series of excuses.

At six-thirty she emailed her best effort and shut down her laptop. She had leftover casserole which she could heat up in the microwave if the Rayburn had gone out. So far this week, touch wood, she'd kept the stove alight and she was even going to try roasting a Sunday dinner for her son. He usually pretended to be too busy to see her, so it was a miracle he'd wanted to come on Mothers Day. But Miriam had concluded he wanted to see where and how she was living, so he could report back to his father.

Chapter 15

'You look exhausted, lass,' Eileen remarked when she came in to lay the table for dinner.

Lily had been dozing in front of the fire after spending much of the day down at the stables. She'd had a wonderful time trekking through the countryside, something she hadn't done for ages. And she didn't realise how much she'd missed it, or how she would ache afterwards. A hot bath had helped, but now she was having difficulty staying awake for her Sunday roast. She looked up when she heard the gate and saw Jack go past the window to the back garden. She guessed he'd hired the bicycle again and was stowing it away in the shed. When the front door was finally opened and closed noisily, he went straight upstairs. She had to wait until he appeared at dinnertime to find out.

'Yes, I've actually got it for a month,' he admitted when questioned.

'Nearly until Easter then.'

He shrugged. 'I suppose.'

'Were you anywhere near Raydale today?' she asked. 'I went up there on horseback, it's beautiful.'

Jack had cycled past Stalling Busk to a bunkhouse he'd discovered at the far end of Semerwater. He thought it might be where Greg Nevitt stayed after he reached Wensleydale. It would explain why his bike was found off the Raydale road. However, the owner had no record of him staying there and didn't recognise his photograph.

132

'It doesn't mean he didn't just wild camp up there,' suggested Lily who could see he was disappointed.

Miriam went back inside the cottage as soon as the taillights of her son's ridiculous sports car had disappeared down the lane. She looked at the dirty dishes on the dining table and reached for the wine bottle, emptying it slowly into her glass. The entire day had been a disaster from the moment she'd come downstairs to find the stove had gone out overnight. Victor said it was something to do with the wind direction but she had no idea why he would know that. He arrived late but that hadn't helped because the oven was still barely warm. He immediately announced that he had to leave at six on the dot. She had imagined them taking a walk across the fields while the lamb roasted gently but he was wearing suede shoes and she didn't have anything that would fit his big flat feet. So they sat looking at the fire and chatted, if you could call it that. Victor told her she was stupid to leave Henry, that his father was willing to patch up everything if she went back to Guisborough. By this time they'd finished one bottle of wine without anything to eat, so things got a bit fraught; in fact very fraught, she would say. She banged around in the kitchen after that, while Victor sulked.

The lamb was very pink when she hauled it out at five-thirty. Victor said he preferred it like that, which was surprising because he'd been such a fussy eater when he was little. The potatoes were still on the hard side but the other vegetables were fine, so dinner wasn't a complete catastrophe. As soon as he'd scraped the last vestige of bought apple pie and ice-cream from his bowl, Victor said he had to go because he was now late. It was five past six.

When asked what he was late for, he wouldn't say so Miriam knew he was going back to Henry to report on his visit. No doubt they would have a bloody good laugh.

The office had a subdued atmosphere on Monday. Heavy rain had been falling all morning, the lights were on and the windows were steamed up. No-one spoke, only the occasional tapping of keyboards, competing with the rattling of rain on the flat roof in the kitchen. Jack offered to make coffee early but even the homemade biscuits from Robert's mother did little to lighten the atmosphere. It was as if everyone was waiting for something to snap them out of it. Lily didn't mind what it was, even if it didn't help progress her case, just something to cheer the team up. She looked round at Jack, who was tilted back in his chair, firing balls of paper into the bin with an elastic band. She turned the other way to see Robert picking his nose. Miriam had her head down over a pile of paperwork.

Suddenly there was a clatter as Jack sat upright and waved an arm. 'Got it!' he shouted. He had everyone's attention. 'Top of the range GPS tracker,' he read off the screen. 'Hidden in the frame under the seat. Long battery life they say.'

He picked up the phone, ignoring their questions, so they listened to his side of the conversation as he repeated the salient points while making notes. He slammed down the receiver at the end of the conversation.

'Minus 165 dBm accuracy, that's pretty amazing,' he said, leaning back in his chair, looking flushed. 'And they think they can download all the history.'

'How long is long battery life?' Robert asked.

'Six months. They wanted to talk to the manufacturer

first. That's why they think they can download the memory. They'll let me know as soon as they've tried.'

They stopped for lunch and the talk was all about Greg Nevitt's bike tracker. There was a buzz as they speculated about what information the tracker would hold, how much detail and for how far back. Robert had looked up the tracker model and was optimistic. Jack even thanked him for pointing him in the right direction.

'No problem, son,' he replied with a benign smile. 'Let's hope it means our luck is changing.'

He'd sent a reminder to the newspaper photographer at the weekend but nothing had appeared and he was now wondering whether the vicar might have seen Brian at the service. The renewed enthusiasm generated by Jack's result prompted him to send an email to the vicarage address, just in case. When he looked up, Lily was standing beside him.

'Can I ask you something?' she said quietly.

'Of course, Lily. Bring your chair over.'

She sat beside him with her hands clasped together while she told him about her meeting with the keeper over in Cotterdale.

'I thought it might help to go over it with you, as you've been there and seen the gate,' she explained. 'He said the chain has been replaced. I've been trying to think why you'd change it and the only reason I can think of is that it was getting thin or rusty.'

Robert considered her question carefully before answering. 'You're right. It would be a sensible precaution before the chain broke... unless it had already broken of course. What condition was the old one in?'

'I don't know but I can try to find out.' She looked

outside at the rain pouring off the roof opposite. There was no point going in this weather, she thought. 'I'll see the keeper tomorrow,' she said.

Robert was unfolding a large-scale map. He carried it upstairs and spread it out on the table. He planned to mark the area where Brian might have strayed if he'd become disoriented in the dark as he crossed Great Shunner Fell. First, he covered the map carefully with a sheet of plastic film. He'd bought a red felt tip pen and with a plastic ruler drew diagonal lines across a rectangular area covering three square kilometres.

Jack had crept upstairs to see what he was doing.

'I could do a digital plot for you,' he offered.

'You could, but have you got a monitor the size of this table? Because I need to see the whole picture, don't I?'

Jack examined the map, turning his head this way and that. 'Is Raydale on here?' he asked eventually.

Robert placed his finger on Hawes then moved it to the patch of blue. 'Semerwater is up there.'

'Miles away,' Jack observed as he made for the stairs. 'Nowhere near.'

He wandered into the kitchen, where Lily was washing up mugs, and leaned on the door frame.

'I reckon there could be a connection between your case and Robert's, but definitely not with mine.'

'Why's that then?' she asked without turning round.

'Come and see.'

Lily dried the mugs before following him up to view Robert's map. It was true, the shaded area almost reached where Amy's body was found, although Robert would have known that, so she wasn't sure if it was significant.

'Geography,' said Jack dejectedly, pointing out the

distance between Semerwater and Cotterdale on the map. 'I never liked geography,' he added before wandering off again.

However, his depression didn't last long. Back at his desk, he found a new message from the forensics team to confirm they would be able send him the digital download from the GPS tracker, tomorrow with luck.

Robert spent the rest of the day studying his map. Lily read through all the witness statements again, particularly those of the casual staff who worked as beaters. It seemed to her that these men, for they were all men, were the most likely people to have regular access to the estate. None had keys according to the records, but she would check that again with the keeper.

When it was time to go home, Robert watched Lily and Jack enviously. Living with his parents had become boring. There was little for him to do around the house and since he knew no-one in the neighbourhood under the age of sixty, there was only his parents to converse with. He had taken to having long solitary walks at the weekend when the weather allowed, but in the evening he had to endure the television programmes that his parents enjoyed, which seemed to centre around food and cooking.

To break the monotony he'd cast around for a society or club to join, and found a notice in the paper advertising a local reading group. He was reticent to contact them but it did encourage him to visit the local library at the weekend to borrow some books on his father's ticket. It gave him an excuse to sit in the dining room, despite its chilliness, or to take himself off to bed early when he was too bored by the television. It was the book on local industrial archaeology that had fired his interest and when he discovered there was a local history group, he made enquiries. There were regular talks, and outings to sites of interest in the better weather, so he was preparing to attend his first meeting that evening. When he told his father of his plan, he listened politely then immediately told him about the U3A group where he was doing the crown green bowling course.

'They're bound to have a class for local history,' he told Robert.

'Dad, I'm forty-one. I don't think they'd even allow me to join if I wanted to – which I don't!'

His mother told him in a conciliatory voice that it was a good thing that he was making the effort to get out and meet people. He knew what she was getting at, because she'd told him a year ago that he should find someone nice and settle down again.

He left in good time, assuming he'd have difficulty finding the place in the dark. Having arrived twenty minutes early, he sat in his car watching dark figures disappearing into the hall. He felt a little nervous as he locked the car and made for the entrance; it was a while since he'd met a load of strangers outside of work. The inner door opened onto a large hall containing around fifty people of all ages. Some were standing in groups, others sat alone waiting for the talk to start. The man sitting at a small table sensing he was a visitor, asked politely for the small fee. He thanked Robert and pointed to a woman wearing an Icelandic sweater.

'That's Dr Jean McGovern,' the man explained. 'She's our secretary. If you want to join, you should talk to her.'

Robert took a seat near the back and was soon joined by an elderly couple who said they hadn't seen him there before and wanted to know where he lived. Soon all the seats were taken and the woman in the jumper rose to make the introductions. She had a very pleasant manner, which Robert was sure would make the guest speaker feel at ease. The lights were dimmed and the talk began, illustrated with some slides. It was about archaeological excavation sites in Chapel-le-Dale, Austwick and Clapham. He had visited the places mentioned so was fascinated as the speaker described how they had found items such as a knife, beads, part of a horse's bridle, and a sheep bell. They had used radiocarbon dating of bone from a female burial to place it in the Anglo-Saxon Period. Much of it went over his head, particularly when members of the audience asked intelligent questions about the excavations.

As he was struggling into his coat, the secretary approached him.

'Robert?'

'Yes.'

She was smiling at him, with her head on one side. 'You don't remember me, do you? I'm Jean McGovern now but it was Curtis when we were at school.'

He looked at her. Was she Jean Curtis? The Jean who was the noisy one in class, the party girl, the girl who everyone fancied.

'I do believe you're blushing, Robert.'

He apologised, remarking on the fact that she now had a doctorate.

'Archaeology. Is it a particular interest of yours? Is that why you're here? I heard you might be joining the group.'

He replied enthusiastically without considering that he would be going back to Leeds in a month or two. She said she would make a note of his contact details and send him further information of their programme for the year. When he gave her his address, she looked up abruptly.

'Of course, I know your mother. She belongs to the WI.'

'Oh yes,' Robert replied with a laugh. 'She's on the committee.'

Jean smiled. 'My mother is in the chair this year.'

They agreed it was a small world.

'In that case I'll ask Mum to pass the paperwork on to your mother.'

Robert was mumbling that he didn't normally live with his mother, when someone came over to speak to her and they parted.

'See you next week!' she called.

Chapter 16

Lily had no clear plan when she set off to Cotterdale, except to ask the keeper a few more questions. She'd eventually found his phone number but it had taken a while, so she arranged to meet him at noon in the same spot where she'd run into him before. As there was no sign of him when she arrived, she wandered over to examine the gate. It was securely locked with a thick chain and a large shiny padlock. It would be difficult to wrench that apart, or cut through it, she thought. She was watching a curlew circling overhead when the sound of an engine alerted her to the keeper's arrival. He looked harassed, so she assured him she wouldn't detain him long.

Taking out her notebook to appear more professional, she began, 'I wanted to ask you about the chain that was replaced last year.' She indicated the gate that led to where Amy was found. 'Do you still have it?'

He looked confused. 'The old one?' Then he laughed. 'I don't think they would have kept it if that's what you mean. You'd have to ask the old keeper, although good luck with that 'cos he's retired to Carlisle and I don't have an address.' With that he climbed back into his vehicle.

'So who *would* have his address?' she called.

'The estate office or one of the other keepers maybe.'

He drove off before she could ask the old keeper's name. Frustrated, she walked quickly to the car and drove straight back to the office, anxious to find the number of the estate office. But her hopes of getting straight onto the task were ruined by a party atmosphere in the office.

'We're celebrating with cake!' Jack announced, crumbs flying from his mouth as he spoke.

'He's received the GPS data from forensics,' Robert clarified. 'It's my mother's fruit cake.'

When Lily asked Jack what the data had told him, it turned out that he'd not had time to look at it yet. He was starting on it that afternoon, in fact right away, and he went off to his desk.

She told Robert what she'd learned at Cotterdale, or rather what she hadn't.

'The guy I spoke to didn't know what happened to the old chain but I need to speak to the person who replaced it, otherwise I won't know if it was broken or just fell apart.'

Miriam had been listening and pointed to a file on her desk. 'The report says the padlocked gate had not been broken into during the period between Amy's disappearance and finding the body. Is that right, Lily?'

'It is but the chain was replaced around that time and I wondered whether it was because it was old. If that was the case maybe it was unreliable.'

'Unreliable?'

'Weak links, malleable, maybe?' Robert suggested.

'Exactly,' said Lily, relieved that he could see her reasoning. 'And no-one would notice if links could be pulled apart. Does that make sense?'

Robert was shaking his head. 'It would be difficult to prize them apart unless you were armed with the right tools, even if they were rusty.'

The conversion ground to a halt and Miriam went back

to her paperwork. Lily rang the estate office but it went to voicemail so she left a message. The usual searches failed to find the name of the retired keeper. She gave an audible sigh and that was when Robert came over.

'It's very long odds, but if I was replacing a chain, I wouldn't necessarily be thinking about what to do with the old one. I might toss it away. I certainly wouldn't keep it if it was rusty. Did you look to see if it had been left there by any chance? Tell me if it's too long a shot.'

Lily took a deep breath, checking the time. 'You know Robert, the way I feel, anything is better than sitting here waiting for a phone call. Would you like to come with me?'

She explained their plan to Miriam, who simply raised her eyebrows and wished them luck. So they jumped in Robert's car and drove to the spot that he christened "Lily's gate".

'I suppose you're an expert in this sort of fingertip search?' he remarked on the way.

It was certainly something she'd experienced when working in forensics. 'And you?'

'Oh yes,' said Robert.

'Our approaches might be different though,' observed Lily. 'I would normally be working inwards to avoid contaminating evidence but I guess today we should start at the gate post and work outwards.'

'Sounds sensible. I don't think it's likely to have travelled far if it was left lying around.'

Robert drove right up to the end of the track and parked the Skoda next to the bridge. They walked to the gate before looking at each other.

'Shall we do this side first?' Lily asked, aware that they would have to either climb over the gate to do the other side or make a long detour through the woods.

'Good idea,' he said.

They worked on opposite sides of the track, Lily at the padlocked end and Robert by the hinges. They crouched uncomfortably working through the grasses, stretching up occasionally and moving out several metres. It didn't take long to establish there was nothing there and soon, to Lily's surprise, Robert was hopping over the gate. She looked round quickly and followed suit. The undergrowth was thicker on that side, stretching away into the woodland beyond. Lily's woollen gloves were getting muddy and caught on thistles, she hoped Robert wasn't ruining his expensive-looking leather gloves. She stood up to stretch her legs, watching her colleague moving along on his haunches like a frog. Was it mean taking a quick photo, she wondered? He didn't notice and she bent down again to continue sweeping through the grass. It was her third trawl in a straight line along the verge, moving further away from the gatepost. There was nothing to see and she was running out of grasses to search in.

She stood up for the last time, pulling off her soggy gloves and stuffing them into her pocket. Robert, who'd had a larger patch of grass, was still working along the verge towards the woods. She didn't want to disturb him, so she stood quietly watching, admiring his meticulous approach; she was sure Jack would not have been such a help. Her gaze wandered over Robert's head and into the trees. Amy's body had lain not far away for two weeks, in the cold and rain. In other circumstances it would be a beautiful place. They'd seen deer on her first visit but there was no sign of them now as she peered through the branches. And that was when she spotted it.

'Robert look!'

Her cry made him jump and he leapt to his feet in alarm. 'What's the matter?' he demanded.

Lily tried to control the excitement in her voice. 'Over there, that tree with the branch sticking out, do you see something?'

She was pointing directly at it but he couldn't see it to begin with. 'There!' she insisted. 'Isn't it a chain?'

He didn't answer but clambered over the fence and tried to reach it using a stick. It took several attempts but finally he knocked it off, catching it deftly in his left hand. Holding it up triumphantly, he climbed back over to her.

'Is this what you're looking for?' he asked with a grin.

Lily wasn't certain. It looked flimsier than she'd imagined but the test would be if it was long enough to fit round the gate and its post. She struggled back into her wet gloves before taking the rusty metal chain from Robert. It felt heavy in her hands. She almost ran down to the gate and was trying it for size by the time Robert caught up.

'Just goes round with a bit to spare,' she announced. 'It could be the one.'

'It's quite a coincidence if it isn't,' Robert commented, climbing back over the gate towards the car.

'I don't believe in coincidences,' muttered Lily, hauling herself over the gate. 'But I do believe in luck.'

Lily held the chain between her gloved fingers on the journey back, anxious to avoid contaminating it in case it held valuable evidence. She carried it proudly into the office, where she was met with congratulatory cheers. Miriam fetched a new plastic food bag from the kitchen and, once the chain was safely inside, they examined it closely one by one. Finally it was handed back to Lily.

'This original chain must have been replaced before Amy's body was found because the photo in the report shows a shiny new one on the gate.' She looked at it again. 'According to the old keeper's statement, no-one had broken in when Amy went missing, but he didn't mention replacing the chain. I really need to find him.'

The excitement of Lily's find had overshadowed Jack's news so it was the following morning before he told the team what he had found so far.

'It's a complete record of his trips from the middle of October. We think that's when he bought the tracker. So it covers the whole of his time in the Dales until it suddenly stops.'

'Is that when the battery died?' asked Robert.

'No, the battery was fine but the bike stopped moving on the 24th of November. I've got to start working on the route now.'

Miriam nodded approvingly and said something about the case moving forward. Jack felt himself blushing as he went back to his desk. He was excited by the prospect of uncovering Greg's route, particularly his movements between Swaledale and Wensleydale, but he was going to approach the task systematically, something that Lily had taught him to do. By six o'clock, when everyone was packing up, he had only covered the first two days of Greg's holiday but he was keen to share what he'd learned with Lily.

'Tell me about it this evening,' she suggested, grabbing her bag, 'or we'll be late for our tea.'

He took her at her word and spent the entire meal

describing in detail the cyclist's movements.

'It's amazing how fast he goes up hills,' Jack said, helping himself to more vegetables. 'I reckon he can go along the flat at twenty miles an hour easily.'

'You can tell that from the tracker?'

'Of course. I've got the route and the time so I can work out the speeds. I'm checking out where he's been in the day and where he stays overnight. I think he must've got the train to Settle, which is at the start of his trip. He stayed in a pub in Horton-in-Ribblesdale and did a circular route down to Ingleton and back the next day.' He looked down at his plate. 'I know that's not round here but I want to get a feel for how he spent his time, does that make sense?'

Lily nodded. 'Yes but how long will it all take?'

'Only a day. It took me a while to get everything onto a spreadsheet in the right format. Now that's done, it will be a lot quicker. I should be finished by the end of the week.'

When the meal was over, Jack went back to his room to collect his laptop. He worked at the table in the sitting room while Lily continued to search for the name of the retired keeper. She could tell how well Jack's work was going by the noises he was making. It was sounding positive until he suddenly declared he was giving up.

'What's the problem?' she asked.

'He's stopped overnight in a spot that can't be right. It's in the middle of nowhere. There aren't any buildings for miles.'

'Camping?'

'No, there isn't a campsite there. It's not even on a road.'

'Haven't you heard of wild camping?' she asked with a

laugh. 'All he needed was a tent. Did he have one?'

'I don't know.'

'It would be cold but if he wanted to save money and the weather was dry...'

Jack ignored her so she continued searching for the keeper's name until she found reference to his retirement in the local paper. With the name she could find his address but it could wait until tomorrow because she had a message to compose, explaining why she had been too busy to go home. In truth she was nervous of bumping into Roy.

'Any more camping stops?' she asked when she'd sent the message.

Jack replied without looking up. 'Yes, that's three in a row, all in different places in Wharfedale. I checked the weather and it was dry then. He must've been cycling in the dark because he doesn't stop at these places until around eight at night.'

'There you are then, the three rules of wild camping: arrive late, leave early and leave no trace.'

After a long silence he stretched his arms and yawned. 'I think I've found a pattern. He goes to the pub for his dinner then cycles off to find a quiet spot for the night. At least that's what happens in the first week when the weather isn't bad.'

He came and sat down in the chair opposite her. 'Are you busy?'

'Not really. Just sending some messages. Mum's badgering me to go home this weekend.'

'I said I'd go on Sunday. It's my little sister's birthday next week.'

'That's nice, how old is she?'

'Sixteen. It's a bit of a family gathering. I won't stay long,' he said, adding, 'My stepfather will be bossing everyone around as usual.'

'Have you got your sister a present?'

'No, I'll give her some money. I've no idea what she wants. Make-up probably or clothes, I suppose.'

'Mine was a long time ago,' said Lily, trying to remember how she spent her sixteenth birthday. 'I think I went out for a meal with my parents. We didn't go in for wild celebrations.'

'I expect Martha's party will be wild for the wrong reasons,' replied Jack. 'My stepfather will drink too much, Mum will tell him off, he'll shout and Martha will cry. Anyway, I'll have gone before then.' He picked up his laptop and left the room.

Lily decided that she wasn't the only member of the team who would prefer to spend the weekend in the Dales.

Chapter 17

'What the hell are you doing?' Robert was shouting from the top of the stairs.

Jack dropped his felt-tip pen in surprise, it rolled across the map before falling to the floor. He crawled under the table to retrieve it and when he stood up Robert was staring at the map.

'What are these black lines?'

'It's Greg's route. I couldn't do the first few days because he was right down in Wharfedale but I thought I'd start plotting once he was on the map.'

Robert was examining his work closely. 'The pen is too thick; it's obscuring the place names.' He turned to go. 'I've got a finer one you can use.'

Jack followed him downstairs and was soon joined by Miriam, who wanted to hear what he'd discovered from the tracker. She seemed pleased by the wild camping angle, encouraging him to carry on while keeping her informed.

'It will be good to have something to report back to the Chief Inspector when I meet him on Friday,' she said with a smile.

Left alone with Miriam at last, Robert told her his news. 'The photos arrived from the newspaper last night. I'm pretty sure I can see Brian Berry in one of them but I'd appreciate a second opinion.' He lowered his voice. 'It's not very good resolution.'

She waited for him to bring the photograph up on the

screen.

'There!' He was pointing at a figure at the back of the crowd standing outside the church. 'He's carrying a rucksack.'

There wasn't much to see, only the face and shoulders of an old man, so Miriam suggested he asked for a better quality photograph. Lily listened to him make a call, asking for a higher resolution version. It sounded as though Robert was in luck because he thanked the person several times before putting the phone down.

Lily was busy searching for the old keeper's address. She'd tried several times to contact his previous employer but no-one could help her.

'I'm just popping out,' she announced, putting her coat on. 'I won't be long.'

She drove straight back to "The Pines", where she found Eileen vacuuming the stairs.

'Forgotten something, love?' she asked, switching off the machine.

'No, I had a question, actually.'

She asked if she knew Mr Mackintosh, the keeper from Cotterdale. Eileen didn't know him, although she'd heard the name, but her sister might. She'd give her a call. Half an hour later, Lily was driving with Eileen to meet her sister in a local café. It was easy for Lily to spot her because she looked so much like Eileen; they even dressed similarly.

'There's Joyce,' Eileen called, making her way over to the table where her sister sat with a large mug in front of her.

Lily went off to order coffees and joined them as Eileen was explaining why they were there.

'You know I told you she was investigating wildlife crime?' she began. 'She needs to talk to the keeper from Cotterdale who retired last year.' She turned to Lily. 'What was his name?'

'Mr Mackintosh.'

'Scottish, was he? There was a keeper from Scotland. Not a friendly sort. Did he retire?'

Lily hid her disappointment as Joyce got up without a word and approached an old gentleman sitting in the corner reading. She sat down and spoke to him while he stared at her. Lily watched the man gradually lower his paper to search in his coat for something.

'Who is she talking to?' she asked Eileen, who shook her head and shrugged.

Finally the man produced a small book, flicking through its pages until he found what he was looking for and Joyce typed something into her mobile phone. Lily and Eileen waited in silence for her to return. When she sat down again, she was smiling.

'I've got a mobile phone number for you,' she announced triumphantly.

'Who was that?' Eileen demanded.

'Don't you recognise him? That's Eric who used to work in the butcher's shop. He knows all the estate managers and breeders round here. He says he used to buy game from your Mr Mackintosh.'

She pushed the phone across the table so Lily could copy the number. When she told Joyce how grateful she was the woman wouldn't hear of it, saying she was delighted to help the police.

Eileen laughed. 'Oh, she isn't the police, Joyce, she's just the wildlife crime people.'

Her sister looked confused but Lily kept quiet, letting the moment pass. She asked Joyce to explain how her catering job with the estate worked.

'The pheasant shoots take place between October and January so the catering staff are casual workers, like the beaters. I'm on the catering team and so is my daughter, while my hubby and son go beating when they can. On a day's shoot they need their lunch in the middle of the day so we set it all up, for the shooters and the beaters. They need hot food inside them with it being the wintertime.'

'Where do they have their lunch? Do they have to come back into town?' asked Lily.

'Oh no, we take it to the lodge. It's quite a trek up there with everything, I can tell you.'

The two sisters began chatting about their plans for Easter, so Lily took the opportunity to send a text to Mr Mackintosh, asking if she could pop over to see him for a chat about the estate, as a wildlife crime investigator. When they parted, she asked Joyce to thank the man in the corner for her. She dropped Eileen home before returning to the office to await a reply from the keeper.

Jack discovered Robert knew the wider area extremely well and they spent the afternoon together mapping the middle section of Greg's cycling holiday. As well as wild camping after a pub supper when the weather was fine, he sought out bunk barns when it rained.

'Probably because they're cheap,' Robert explained. 'If he didn't use his credit card since he left Settle, and he only drew out three hundred pounds for a two-week holiday, he was probably planning to camp.'

'But it wasn't a good time of year for camping, which is

why he sometimes stayed in a pub, I suppose.'

'He would have to be very careful. It's easy to spend quite a bit, even just on a meal and a pint, as I discovered on my trip the other weekend.'

'We don't know how much cash he had on him altogether though, do we?'

'True, it's all supposition. That's why any little thing could help, such as the fact he's a creature of habit. Have you noticed how similar all his wild campsites are?'

'What d'you mean?'

'Look at the map, do you see the features on it, the streams, the trees, the contours? This is a guy who plans carefully, ensures he's got water and shelter, and a slope so it isn't boggy.'

'So what does that mean?' Jack asked.

'I have no idea son, but it could be relevant when we want to find his body, don't you think?'

When Miriam shouted up to say she was wanting to lock up, they had just finished drawing Greg's route across from Swaledale into Wensleydale.

'We'll know where he was staying in Wensleydale by tomorrow morning,' Jack assured Robert. 'Lily goes to her Zumba this evening so I can work undisturbed in the sitting room.'

There was no sign of Kirsty when Lily arrived at the class. Di was already there, busily chatting with her friends as usual. Lily waited until the break to offer her a lift back to Hawes afterwards.

'That would be great,' she said. 'Sorry, I've just got to catch...' and she was off to greet another acquaintance.

Never mind, thought Lily, it's not like I want to be her

friend particularly, so long as she helps me talk to Kirsty. But she did feel left out, hanging around on her own until the class continued. The routines seemed twice as hard in the second half hour and she was relieved when the teacher announced they had to finish. The instructor wished them a happy holiday; classes would start again in a fortnight. She pulled on her coat and waited for Di to stop nattering and get her outdoor clothes on. When at last she was ready, she apologised for holding Lily up.

'No problem, I'm not in a rush.'

On the journey back, Lily asked if Kirsty was ever going to come back to Zumba.

'Well, it doesn't start again until after the Easter holiday so I suppose she might feel better by then.'

'Has she seen a doctor?'

'I don't think so. She said she might leave the hotel and find something else to do nearer home.'

'Is there a problem at work, d'you think?'

Di didn't answer. She was looking at her phone and sending messages. Lily waited until they were nearing Hawes, before casually enquiring whether Di was dropping in to see Kirsty again. She didn't know.

'I could come with you,' she suggested, unsure how else to get an invitation.

'Why?'

It was a fair question and Lily had to think quickly. 'I could offer her some career advice.'

'Are you like a teacher, then?'

'No... but I've changed career recently.'

Damn, thought Lily. Her job was the one topic she had wanted to stay away from.

They drove in silence until she parked outside Kirsty's

house. Di was typing on her phone while Lily waited.

'She says it's OK,' she said, climbing out.

Lily waited, unsure what she meant.

'C'mon, if you're coming,' the girl called and she followed.

Kirsty was wearing an oversized fleece dressing gown and furry slippers when she opened the door. Her lank hair hung like two curtains almost covering her thin, pale face. She led them upstairs to her bedroom, where she lay on her bed while Di perched beside her.

Lily took a small wicker chair that wobbled when she moved. 'I hope you don't mind me coming to see you Kirsty. We've missed you at Zumba, it's a shame you don't feel up to it.' No answer. 'Di says you're thinking of leaving your job. Have you got any plans for what you'll do?'

After a pause she said, 'Not really. Probably work in a café or a hotel round here in the summer.'

'I guess the season starts at Easter,' said Lily.

'There's always vacancies in the summer,' said Di. 'She'll have no problem with her hotel experience, will you Kirsty?'

Di's phone pinged and she laughed, showing the screen to her friend. 'You've got to see this.'

Lily stood up and made for the door. 'I ought to be getting back.'

She was going to offer them both a lift to Zumba next time but realised with a jolt she would be gone by the time the classes restarted after Easter. So she said she hoped Kirsty felt better soon and left the girls alone. As she walked slowly down the stairs, a woman popped out into the hall. She looked quizzically at Lily, probably thinking she was rather old to be a friend of her daughter's.

'Hi, I'm Lily,' she explained. 'I gave Di a lift back from Zumba and I popped in with her to see Kirsty. We've missed her at the class.'

The woman was smiling now. 'Kirsty told me about you. You went to the Indian restaurant, didn't you? It's nice to meet you.'

It was an opportunity Lily didn't want to miss. 'Yes, I was worried when Di said your daughter was ill. What do they think is wrong with her?'

'She won't see a doctor. It's like she was at the back end of last year. I thought she was improving but it's come back. She's so stressed, she's even avoiding going to work if she can.'

'I heard she was thinking of changing her job. Perhaps there's a problem at work?'

Kirsty's mother was looking up the stairs anxiously. 'Come and sit down,' she said in a low voice, leading Lily into a small sitting room, where a middle-aged man was watching television. Ignoring her husband, she told Lily to take a chair close to hers. 'We think it's something to do with work but she won't discuss it. We're worried she might be having problems with a guest. She's an attractive young girl and older men are sometimes a bit, you know... A girl like Di would brush it off but Kirsty is very sensitive.'

'Wouldn't she tell you if she was having that sort of problem though?'

'That's what he says.'

Her husband looked over at her then turned his attention back to the television.

'He thinks she needs to be a bit more assertive.'

As soon as Jack had got in, he'd asked Eileen for an early tea. He set up his laptop once the table was cleared and worked until she returned with coffee at nine o'clock as usual.

'Are you still at it, young man?' she asked. 'I've buttered you a couple of scones. By the way, it's started to snow, I hope it doesn't settle.'

She put more logs on the fire before leaving the room. Jack stood up to stretch his legs and arched his back to release the tension that had built up in his shoulders. He needed to make sense of what he was seeing now that he had come to the end of Greg's journey. He was still calculating speeds between locations when Lily arrived back from Leyburn.

'Would you believe it's snowing?' she asked, lifting the coffee pot and shaking it. 'None left?'

'Don't think so,' Jack muttered without looking up. 'Good class? How are your friends?'

'I went to see Kirsty afterwards.' She paused while she removed her coat. 'She's still very stressed and her parents think it's something to do with work. Anyway, how have you got on? Still working on the tracker data? Have you found out where he was staying?'

'Actually I've just finished. There's something a bit odd about the last trip but I'm getting brain-dead.'

'Best wait until the morning then.'

'I can show you, if you like.' He turned his laptop round so she could see the screen. 'This is my spreadsheet with the journeys in date order. This column is the distance between stopping points, the next one is the time and the one after that gives the speed. What do you see?'

Lily looked at the numbers. 'They're all look very similar. They're all somewhere between fifteen and thirty.'

'Yes, they're the speeds in kilometres per hour. But look at this one.' He scrolled down to the last number.

'Fifty-six?'

'Exactly. I've checked and there's no way a cyclist, even a good one, could cycle through Hawes at thirty-five miles an hour.'

Miriam opened the front door to discover that the snow was settling fast. If it carried on falling during the night she would be stranded and it was imperative for her to be updated by the team before seeing Charles on Friday morning. She checked the time before deciding it was not too late to call Robert. When he answered, she could hear a television or radio in the background.

'Robert? It's Miriam. Is it snowing down there?'

'Miriam?' There was a pause. 'No, no snow, why?'

She explained how she wouldn't be able get out if it settled overnight. 'Even if the road is passable, I won't get down the track. It's getting on for an inch thick already.'

She asked if he could pick her up in his Skoda in the morning, giving him the postcode and explaining exactly how to find the cottage.

'You can't miss it once you turn off the main road because it's the first track you come to on the left. I can wait at the entrance, so you don't have to come down the track.'

Robert offered to get there by eight-thirty and Miriam was about to ring off when he said he had some news.

'I received the high-resolution photograph of Brian Berry at the church this evening. I'm certain it's him.'

'How certain Robert?'

'Ninety-nine percent.'

'We'll catch up tomorrow then.'

Miriam went back to the document she was writing. It was basically her request to continue their investigation beyond the end of the month since that deadline was looming. She was putting her best gloss on what had proved to be a plodding enquiry that had achieved very little so far. She could see her prospects for promotion slipping away with every day she spent on the investigation. Perhaps it would be preferable if the team was disbanded at the end of the month before she was completely forgotten by the bosses. She refilled her wine glass, moving over to sit by the fire. She reflected that she would miss the cottage, admitting that she had enjoyed the challenge of the stove and the sense of isolation when she looked out across the fields. She was certainly experiencing her new life as an independent single woman.

Chapter 18

As soon as she pulled back the curtains, Miriam knew she'd been right to call Robert. The field was pure white, except in the far corner where sheep were gathered round a pile of hay. She skipped breakfast to give herself enough time to load the stove with fuel before pulling on the short wellingtons she'd bought to cope with the muddy track. Wrapped in her thick coat, woolly hat and scarf, she hauled her bag onto her shoulder and slammed the door behind her. Her car was hidden under a layer of white two or three inches thick but the track was deeper. She walked gingerly along the uneven ground, finding potholes that wrenched her ankles, nearly slipping over several times. Snow was getting into her boots and melting, leaving her feet cold and damp. At the end of the track was a gate onto the road which normally opened quite easily but snow had drifted across in front of it and she couldn't drag it open. Looking to check that no-one was watching, she dropped her bag on the other side and was climbing over the gate, just as a green Land Rover appeared at the top of the hill. She quickly jumped down, picked up her bag and turned to face back down the track.

She couldn't tell whether the vehicle was stopping or just travelling very slowly until she heard a man's voice behind her.

'Do you need a lift?'

She turned to see a man with a straggly straw-coloured beard. Sitting beside him in the passenger seat was a black and white collie. They were both staring at her.

'It's not a vehicle for getting about in this weather,' he continued, indicating her sports car parked outside the cottage.

'No, I'm afraid it isn't.'

'So where are you going?'

'Nowhere, I mean I'm getting a lift. My colleague is picking me up in his four-wheel drive.'

'He'll not have any trouble getting up the hill then,' he observed.

She expected him to leave but he turned the engine off and sat looking into the distance.

'I could clear the snow off your track this afternoon if it's not gone,' he offered.

'Oh no, it's too much bother,' she protested, looking back towards the cottage. It would take him all day.

He shrugged and she was about to thank him for the offer when she spotted Robert coming up the hill.

'Is this your colleague?'

'Yes.'

'I'll be off then.'

He started the engine and continued down the hill.

'Was that a neighbour?' he asked when she opened the passenger door.

Robert's car was warm and comfortable. A local radio breakfast programme was playing.

'I don't know. As you can see, I don't really have any neighbours but he might own the farm next door.' Perhaps she should have accepted his offer to clear the snow from the track, to find out more about him, she thought.

When they arrived at the office, the others were waiting

for Miriam to let them in. They'd walked to work although Jack declared the roads weren't too bad. Lily put the kettle on as soon as they were through the door while Miriam removed her boots and put her socks on the radiator to dry. She had spare trainers under her desk but had forgotten about socks. Robert took the opportunity to lobby her for a search of Cotterdale again, pulling up the photograph on his laptop screen to show her the man he was sure was Brian Berry.

'Have you used a facial recognition program?' she asked.

He made excuses about it not being a full-face photo so it wouldn't work properly, which meant he hadn't found a match. When Jack offered to try it on some of the commercial apps, Robert was sceptical. Despite Jack's reassurances, he only grudgingly sent him a copy of the photo to "have a play with".

Miriam was clapping her hands. 'Bring your coffee upstairs everyone,' she called. 'Lily says that Jack has some interesting results to show us.'

Although he was pleased to be asked, Jack was irritated that he'd not had time to produce a proper presentation. He grabbed his laptop and joined the others, who were already hovering over the map.

'I haven't had a chance to draw the last trips on,' he complained, picking up the black pen.

They watched as he carefully followed the line of the road, starting at Hardraw and plotting a route that encircled Hawes until he was back at Hardraw again.

'That was on Friday 22nd.'

He then started out again, describing another circle that went into Swaledale, up to Keld and over to Nateby before circling back to Hawes.

'He was probably staying in the Old School bunkhouse on 22nd but it was dry on 23rd so after eating in Hardraw he went up Bellow Hill a short distance, where there was shelter under the trees and a beck.' He looked at Robert, who nodded.

He drew a black line into the trees on the map then looked up. 'Now, this is the last day, the 24th.'

He was enjoying the silent anticipation as he drew the route of Greg's final ride to Sedbergh and back via Dent. The others were beginning to crowd him, waiting to see where he ate and slept that night. Jack continued his line to Hardraw, stopping to explain that this was around seven o'clock on the 24th.

'After dinner, he cycles in the dark back towards Sedbergh but turns down the road to Cotterdale and stops here at eight-twenty-seven.' He draws a blob by the conifers on the map.

'That's where I parked,' said Lily quietly. 'Just before the village.'

'So he spent the night there?' asked Robert.

'That's what it looks like,' said Jack. 'But the tracker carries on after less than an hour. It travels really fast to arrive at nine-thirty-five in the place where it was found.'

No-one spoke at first, then everyone was talking at once. Jack had to explain again how the speed of the bike on its last journey was too fast for Greg to be riding it.

'Someone must have stolen it,' said Robert. 'They could have driven it away in a van.'

'Why would they dump it straightaway?' asked Lily. 'And Greg had the tracker so he could find out where it went.'

'Only if he had a phone signal.' Jack had been going over and over the possibilities last night.

'I couldn't get a signal there,' offered Lily.

Miriam was staring at the map. 'So we don't hear from Greg after that. Can we say that was the last location we can place him? If he moved after that we can't track him.'

'It's in Cotterdale,' said Lily. 'Close to where Amy was found.'

'And where Brian Berry disappeared if my instinct is correct,' added Robert.

Miriam was the first to break the silence that followed. 'Quite a lot of information to digest. I have a report to finish before tomorrow so I'm going to crack on.'

She was rather hoping that bad weather might prevent her from making the journey but already the snow was turning to slush in the yard and dripping from the roof opposite. Her feet were getting cold and she took her socks from the radiator; they were dry enough.

After she left, the air of excitement upstairs soon dissipated and they wandered down to continue their various tasks. Lily kept trying the phone number that she'd been given for Mr Mackintosh, while Robert was quietly looking at the website for the Swaledale Mountain Rescue Team. Jack needed to call the bunkhouse in Hardraw but he much preferred the digital world and began checking Robert's high-res photograph with some of the more obvious facial recognition apps. However, he was more than happy to break off what he was doing when Mrs Whitehead appeared with a large pan of tomato soup for their lunch. She declared the snow would be completely gone by the morning.

'I thought you might appreciate something hot today,'

she explained as they dipped their mugs into the pan.

While they perched on desks, sipping the hot soup, Miriam asked for any further information she could add to her report, which was still looking very slim.

'Have you received the forensics on the bike yet?' she asked Jack. He shook his head. 'Well, get on to them now please.'

Lily tried to help by saying that she'd arranged to meet the retired keeper at the end of the week. But her boss didn't appear impressed.

'What about you?' Miriam asked, looking at Robert.

He opened his mouth to respond but Jack interrupted. 'I've being testing out the FRT on the photograph with some interesting results,' he began.

Miriam frowned. 'What's FRT?'

'Facial recognition technology,' he explained. 'I've used five commercial apps and three of them gave a positive ID.'

'Only three?'

'That's not bad considering the position of his head and the quality of the picture,' argued Robert, smiling at Jack.

'I'll take your word for it.' Miriam was making notes.

'Enough to warrant a search of the Cotterdale area for Brian's body,' Robert insisted.

'I'm meeting the Chief Inspector tomorrow, as you know, but I can't promise anything.' She looked at her watch. 'I suggest we finish on time today so Lily and Jack can walk back to their digs. Robert, would you drop me off on your way home?'

The afternoon went slowly as she waited to leave. It was barely four-thirty when she began changing her shoes and putting her coat on. The others followed suit without enthusiasm. Her mood had affected everyone.

'I hope your meeting goes all right tomorrow,' ventured Robert as they drove to her cottage.

Miriam tried to sound positive but she couldn't pretend she was expecting it to go smoothly.

'Well, we've given it our best shot,' Robert declared. 'Lily and Jack have worked hard on their cases and they've helped me too.'

Miriam had to agree. It was unfortunate that it wasn't enough.

The road was clear but snow still lay on the surrounding fields as they travelled uphill. The gate had been left open and Robert turned the car into the drive.

'I can take you down to the house. 'Someone's done a good job clearing the track for you.'

'Oh, but I said… How did he…'

'Someone used a tractor to shove this lot out the way.' Robert said as she got out of the car.

She waited to read the note pushed into the letterbox until she was inside the cottage. It was from someone called William, she assumed he was the man she'd met that morning. He hoped she didn't mind but he was clearing round the farm and it didn't take long to do her track as well. There was a mobile phone number. She should thank him, later perhaps, or maybe wait until the weekend.

Her first job, as always, was to top up the stove, then she lit the fire. While she waited for everything to warm up, she moved her car down to the road, leaving the gate open, in case of more snow overnight. Back inside, she opened an email from Henry that she'd been avoiding all day. He was putting the house on the market despite the fact she'd refused to have anything to do with the decision. The estate agent needed her signature. Her instinct was to tell him to go to hell but she was tired of all the arguments and just wanted it all to be over. She didn't reply but made a note of the agent's address, planning to go after her meeting with the boss. She might as well get it all over in one unpleasant visit, stock up with her favourite wine and then return to Wensleydale where no-one could bother her.

Next morning she was up at five and ready to leave before it was light. The meeting was at nine but she wanted time to gather her thoughts and consume several cups of coffee before facing a barrage of questions. She'd been warned by Charles to expect the Detective Superintendent to join them if he was available. She slammed the door behind her, switched on her torch and stumbled along the track to her car. There had been a fresh fall of snow overnight, only lightly covering the track. She wondered how to thank William for clearing it as she scraped her windscreen. To her relief the car started without fuss and she drove onto the road, leaving the gate propped open for when she returned. She had no intention of staying at her flat over the weekend.

Soon all signs of snow and ice were gone, the roads were clear and she made good time. Sadly, her favourite place for coffee, close to headquarters but far enough away to avoid colleagues, didn't open early. Reluctantly she made straight for the café inside the Police Headquarters, or the "Cleveland Community Safety Hub" as the new building was called. She settled in the corner where she wouldn't be spotted and tucked into a Danish pastry, washed down with a flat white, followed swiftly by a second cup. She passed an hour by going through her report, highlighting the points she wanted to emphasise. At ten to nine she packed everything into her bag and made her way up to Charles's floor.

She passed a couple of people she knew by sight but no-one stopped to talk as she climbed the stairs and turned down the corridor where senior staff had their offices. She had almost reached the meeting room when a door flew open and her husband stepped out, almost bumping into her.

'Miriam!'

Had he been watching out for her? Did he know she would be in the building?

Now he was smirking. 'What are you doing here? I thought you were entrenched in the Yorkshire countryside.'

'I've a meeting with Charles.'

'Now? About Operation Pheasant?'

'Operation Pheasant?'

'Isn't that what it's called? I'm sure I heard it called that.'

It was obvious that someone was mocking her investigation. She muttered that she was late and hurried along to the meeting room. In fact she was five minutes early and Charles hadn't arrived yet. She chose a chair at the end of the table, then changed her mind and moved to the side facing the window. She'd brought two spare copies of her report and placed them across the table. There were voices outside then the door opened and Charles entered, followed by Detective Superintendent Barnes, who greeted her cordially. Just as they were settling into their chairs, the door opened again and Henry walked in, announcing that Charles had said he could sit in, to get up to speed. There was an awkward moment when Charles, in his embarrassment, explained to his senior colleague that of course Miriam knew Chief Inspector Abbott. She wanted to tell him to leave, that he had no right to gate-crash her meeting. Did she have to remind her ex-husband that the word detective did not appear in his title? But it would be a mistake to lose her cool before she'd even begun. So she scowled at Henry then shrugged.

Her update took almost twenty minutes because Charles kept interrupting to ask questions, most of which she had answered already. She knew it was only to impress his superior. The Superintendent waited until she'd finished before agreeing that it was an interesting investigation and her team had done well so far – but what was to be done now? It was her chance to ask for a search to find Greg Nevitt's body and after some discussion it was agreed that she could have limited local support, with a handler and his dog, for a day. This minor success gave her confidence to make a further plea on Robert's behalf. 'We also need to find Berry's body,' she added.

'There was an extensive search for him at the time. It lasted a week,' said Charles, looking at the others.

'But not in the right area. Now we know he was walking across the fell in the dark, we need to search Cotterdale.'

Barnes was referring to the map in her report that showed the area of three square kilometres. 'It's up to you Charles, it's your investigation.'

'I'll think about it,' he replied. 'Let's wait until we see what the other search brings up if anything.'

He looked at the Superintendent and Henry, in turn, asking if they agreed. Of course they did.

Barnes closed the report and looked across at her.

'The main problem, Miriam, is time. You don't have long to tie up these cases, do you?'

'I was told two months, until the end of April.' She looked across at Charles, defying him to argue with her.

Barnes sounded surprised. 'Were you?'

Charles coughed. 'Well that depended on progress, didn't it? I'm not sure developments over the past three weeks have been sufficiently significant to warrant the cost of an additional month.'

Miriam was frustrated and angry with him for going back on his word but she wouldn't make a scene, not with Henry sitting like a judge at the end of the table.

Charles was stroking his fat chin. 'Why don't you keep going until Easter, then we'll call it a day. We knew it was unlikely to come to anything.'

The Superintendent pointed out that the Chief Constable had been keen to collaborate with the North Yorkshire Force to form the trial unit. There had been a lot resting on the investigation.

'It's doubtful now that they'll continue such joint initiatives in future,' he remarked looking at his watch. 'I'm going to be late for my next meeting. Are you coming?' He was addressing Charles.

She watched them go. Henry remained seated at the end of the table. She ignored him while she packed her bag.

'Satisfied?' she asked without looking at him. 'I assume you came along to gloat.'

He looked indignant. 'No. Actually I wanted to make sure you got my message about the estate agent.'

Previously she would have screamed at him or thrown something but she felt defeated by her experience in the last half hour.

'Yes, Henry,' she replied quietly, 'I got your email. I'm on my way there now.'

She walked out before he could respond, almost running down the stairs to get out of the building before anyone saw her tears of rage.

Chapter 19

The discussion in Miriam's absence centred on how her meeting with the DCI would go. Jack reckoned he would be impressed with their progress but Robert and Lily were less optimistic.

'Well, if they won't do a search for Greg Nevitt, I'll go and do it myself,' Jack declared.

Robert was certain there would be no help to find Brian Berry and laughed when Jack offered to go with him to Cotterdale.

'Thanks but it's too a large an area for us, son,' he said.

However, the suggestion gave him the impetus he needed to find the contact details for the Swaledale Mountain Rescue Team. Jack, who had put off ringing the School House bunkhouse in Hardraw, finally got through and arranged to see the owner that morning.

'You're not cycling there in the freezing cold, are you?' Lily asked. 'What if the road is icy? We can't afford to have you in hospital when there's so much to do.'

'So how else am I supposed to get there?'

She sighed. 'I can drive you but I've got to go to Carlisle to see Mr Mackintosh later.'

'We could go on the way,' Jack suggested. 'I don't mind visiting Carlisle.'

'No, I'm going to stop off to see my parents while I'm over in Cumbria.'

As soon as the others left the office, Robert rang the secretary of the Mountain Rescue Team and left a message. It was a bit cheeky suggesting they might like to set up an exercise but he was sure they must need scenarios for training purposes. He could provide the perfect set-up for them. Failing that he couldn't see where else he could go to progress the case. The only way he could find out what happened to Brian Berry was by recovering his body for a post-mortem.

It was snowing again and by the time Lily arrived back with Jack, it had begun to settle.

'Doesn't look too good out there,' he remarked as Lily brushed white flakes from her coat.

'It's all right on the roads,' she said, 'but I'll get going now in case it takes longer to get there.'

Robert tried to dissuade her but she was determined to meet the keeper, saying it was too important to leave for another day. As soon as she was gone, Jack produced two packets of sandwiches from his pocket, and offered one to Robert, saying, 'Cheese and pickle, I know it's your favourite.'

'So how did you get on at the bunkhouse?' he asked as he struggled with the wrapper.

Jack sniffed. 'Nothing much to report really. Greg Nevitt stayed there for one night then moved on. He was no trouble, quiet and polite. Not memorable really.'

'Sorry to hear that.' Robert hoped he sounded sympathetic. The lad was trying so hard against all odds to find his cyclist. 'So is that it then?'

'I'm still waiting for the forensics, aren't I?'

'Have you chased them?'

'No, are we allowed to do that?'

'Of course. I can give them a buzz if you like, the word "sergeant" might help.'

But before he could ring the forensics team, he received a call from Swaledale Mountain Rescue. He began by explaining that he was a Detective Sergeant in a Regional Unsolved Crime Unit to ensure that he got their attention. He spoke about the excellent work that the rescue team had done in helping the police search for Brian Berry the previous year. His caller agreed it was a tragic case that had never been resolved. He explained they were still working on the investigation and looking to extend the search to Cotterdale. She sounded interested. He was frank about lack of resources, man-power etcetera and broached his proposal that it might be treated as an exercise by the Rescue Team. The call ended with a promise to get back to him with an answer by Monday morning at the latest.

Jack, who had clearly been listening to Robert's end of his conversation, wandered over.

'I've been looking at the map, and I'm sure Greg planned to wild camp in the woods near Cotterdale.'

Robert agreed. 'It would be a good spot, there's shelter and water.'

'I want to take a look.'

Robert glanced out of the window. 'In this?' Large flakes of snow were settling fast, turning the yard white. 'Best wait until it clears.'

'I heard what you were saying about a search in Cotterdale, could that include the woods?'

'Let's wait to see what they say, shall we? We won't know until Monday whether it's possible.'

Lily was surprised by Mr Mackintosh's honesty when she explained why she was there. It was ironic since she'd told him she was investigating poaching for the Rural Crime

Unit. They were sitting in a tiny flat near the city centre and she was drinking tea from a fine china cup that Mrs Mackintosh has provided before withdrawing discreetly to another room, which Lily guessed was their bedroom. She was tempted to ask why they'd chosen to move from such a beautiful part of the country into a retirement flat for the over fifty-fives, as it was described on the sign over the entrance. Instead, she asked whether the gates to the estate were always locked.

'Always. Never left unlocked.'

'So no-one could get through?'

'They could climb over.'

'Sorry, I was meaning in a vehicle.'

'Not unless they had a key.'

Lily knew that all the keyholders had been interviewed and had solid alibis for the afternoon of the 7th of November.'

'Mr Mackintosh, can I ask about the new chain that you put on the gate last year.'

'Of course, lass.'

He was waiting for the next question. She took a deep breath. 'I wondered why you changed it if it wasn't broken.'

He shrugged. 'I was putting a new padlock on, so I changed the chain.'

His response confirmed the old chain was intact, she noted. 'Were you worried that someone was trying to break in?'

He leaned forward in his chair. 'I was worried someone had got in.'

She could feel her heart rate increasing. 'You thought someone had broken in? When was that?'

'In the summer. I found strange tyre tracks in the woods and I thought someone had got hold of a key, so I ordered a new padlock and chain. Then it turned out it was a vehicle belonging to one of the keepers. But I had the new padlock and thought I'd finish the job.'

'I don't suppose you remember when you changed the padlock and chain?'

'I do. It was my last job before I retired. I thought I would do it before I left. It was the third week in November because I had holiday leave to take after that.'

Lily was calculating the dates. 'So after the 7th but before the 28th?'

He looked at her sharply. 'Yes, it was the week ending the 20th, that's when I retired. Why d'you say that?'

She felt her cheeks redden. 'I've read about Amy Hobson,' she admitted.

He shook his head slowly. 'The police asked me all about security when it happened and I told them, there was no chance that anyone had access with a vehicle.'

'That's exactly what I thought,' she said. 'Thank you for being so helpful.' She gave him her best smile and told him to thank his wife for the tea.

When she stepped out into the street, it had changed. The pavement was covered in snow and large white flakes were settling on her car. Unsure whether to go on to Keswick to see her parents, she decided it was on main roads all the way and the weather would give her a good excuse to leave after an hour or so. She drove carefully down the snow-covered motorway, and even more slowly once she turned off to Keswick. The mountains looked beautiful and she smiled at the thought of the welcome she would get from Sonny, the golden retriever. He was her parents' dog but very attached to her, and she missed him more than anything else back home.

The snowfall had become a blizzard, slowing traffic to a crawl. On the opposite carriageway, a long line of stationary cars queued up beyond a lorry slewed across the two lanes, blocking the road. There was no turning back to Yorkshire now, so she kept going, praying it stayed clear in her direction. Eventually, with a sense of relief, she turned down the familiar road to home. The car was sliding but she was able to keep it under control until she was outside the house, when it skidded into the kerb at a rakish angle. Too exhausted to do anything about it, she grabbed her bag and left the car where it was. The path was cleared, presumably by her father, and scattered with a good helping of grit. Her legs felt like jelly and she was dying for a wee.

After the initial chaos of her unexpected arrival, she settled on the sofa with Sonny's head across her lap. Her father was outside trying to straighten up her car while her mother was making "a nice cup of tea and something to eat".

'I'll get your father to light the fire in the sitting room this afternoon,' she announced as she poured tea into Lily's favourite mug. 'So, you'll be staying the weekend.' It wasn't a question.

'I ought to get back,' she replied half-heartedly.

'You can't drive in this. They say it's in for a few days.'

'I expect the roads will be clear enough by tomorrow. But I'll have to stay tonight.' She didn't mean it to come out like that. 'I'd love to stay longer but we're very busy on the case,' she added.

*

Miriam was surprised she hadn't been even ruder to the estate agent. After waiting three-quarters of an hour she told the stupid girl to post the documents to her in Wensleydale, when she eventually found them. Then she walked out. Because it had been such a horrendous start to the day, she decided to stop for a hot meal on the way back. She spotted a sign indicating that "The Cricketers" was just half a mile off the main road and made a last-minute decision that caused the car behind to hoot its horn. The pub was a solitary building with one car parked outside and no customers inside. Miriam noted the roaring fire with approval.

A woman appeared behind the bar to ask, in a friendly way, what she would like, and Miriam automatically asked for a merlot. She shouldn't drink and drive but she reckoned she deserved a small one. She selected a casserole from the menu and went over to sit by the fire. She was nearly asleep when a girl brought her food over.

'Would you like another drink?' she asked.

'Yes please.'

The woman brought her wine from the bar.

'Looks like it's settled in for the day.' She pointed at the window.

The view was almost obliterated by snowflakes blowing horizontally from left to right. Miriam cursed under her breath as she envisaged the journey back to the cottage. The food was too hot to eat quickly so she became increasingly agitated as time went on. In the end she left half her meal but emptied her glass before settling up at the bar.

'Far to go?' she was asked.

'Wensleydale.'

'Well good luck, my dear.'

'I'll be fine on the main roads,' she replied, forcing a smile.

Her prediction was correct. Once she was on the major roads, everything was fine and she relaxed. Her route was almost clear until she reached Leyburn, where the snow must have been falling for longer. The last part of her journey was on a white road where the tyre tracks were being covered over as soon as they were made. When she finally reached Hawes, she turned onto the lane with a sense of foreboding that turned to panic as she began to climb the hill to the cottage. She thought the car was coping with the fresh snow at first, but every now and then the wheels were spinning. Then the car was sliding and she did exactly what she'd learnt to do, she steered in the direction of travel, and ended up pointing across the road. The only thing that had stopped her crashing into the stone wall was the deep pile of snow that was over the bonnet.

Miriam considered herself a very practical person, good in an emergency, able to look after herself. But at that moment she had had enough and consequently she was in tears when a pair of giant headlights appeared alongside. It was the final humiliation. She rubbed her scarf across her eyes and stepped out into the spotlight made by the tractor. Someone descended from the cab and, to her embarrassment, it was the man called William.

'Oh dear,' he said with a grin. 'D'you need a hand?'

She nodded. He suggested she got back in the car while he sorted out a tow for her. She watched him manoeuvre the tractor back and forth for a while, then he jumped out and began working at the back of the car. She didn't have a tow bar so she hoped he wouldn't cause any damage, not that she had an alternative since she was effectively blocking the road. Eventually he banged on her window and told her to take off the brake and sit tight. That was probably the worst part, as her prized possession was hauled backwards unceremoniously until she was pointing back down the hill. There was worse to come because he then continued to pull the car uphill to her track, where he stopped and told her to make sure the brakes were on before leaving the car.

'I'd offer to take you down to the cottage in the tractor…' he began.

'No, really I'll be fine from here, thanks,' she replied.

'I'll leave the lights for you,' he said.

She trudged through the snow towards the cottage as he swung the tractor round so the headlights illuminated the track. She made slow progress as the snow penetrated her best brogues and soaked into her trouser legs. He waited until she was inside before moving off. Then she realised that, yet again, she hadn't thanked him.

Chapter 20

There had been no change in the weather so Lily agreed to stay for the weekend. The previous evening they had relaxed in front of the television after one of her mother's special curries. Dad found a bottle of wine at the back of the cupboard and, for once, it seemed as if a truce had been called. They even asked how work was going, without the usual questions about why she'd left forensic work with all that training going to waste. Lily was looking forward to taking Sonny for a walk in the park, he loved the snow, and then she would clear out some of the stuff in her bedroom. There were old notebooks from school and curling posters to throw out, CDs and soft toys that could go to charity. But despite her good intentions she wasn't downstairs until ten on Saturday morning.

Lily was hoping for a cooked breakfast. 'Where's Mum?' she asked her father, who was reading the paper.

'She's on the phone.'

He made a comment about how long she'd be chatting once she got going, so Lily decided that cereal and toast would do. She was finishing her breakfast with a second cup of coffee when her mother appeared and insisted that she should have waited for her to make eggs.

'Dad thought you'd be talking until lunchtime so I went ahead,' Lily said, jokingly.

Her mother reddened and turned to busy herself at the sink without reply.

Sonny had been fussing round her since she'd come

downstairs, so she offered to take him to the park. The snow was beginning to thaw and the roads were looking much clearer but there were still icy patches on the pavement. The dog knew where he was going, pulling her along, making the journey quite hazardous and she was relieved when she reached the park gates and was able to let him free on the snow-covered grass. Soon his feet were covered in lumps of ice and his face was white with snow. She threw snowballs for him, his favourite game, until her gloves were soaking wet and he lay down exhausted.

The dog suddenly noticed somebody in the distance and went racing off towards them. She called to him but he took no notice. When he finally stopped, the man made a fuss of him and continued walking towards her. That was when she realised who it was.

'Roy?'

'Hi Lily. Your mother said you'd be walking Sonny this morning.'

At his name the dog jumped up at him again.

'What are you doing here, Roy?'

'I just wanted a chat. Nothing heavy.'

'I told you, I don't want to talk to you ever again!'

She put the lead back on Sonny and pulled him away, heading for the gates as quickly as she could. And she'd thought her mother had stopped meddling. Ignoring Roy's calls to wait, she dragged Sonny back home to confront her. What she hadn't known was that her mother planned to go to the supermarket and had left her husband to explain that she'd be home by one.

'Well, in that case she'll be too late because I'm going back now.'

Her father looked up from his crossword. 'Weren't you

staying until tomorrow?'

She wasn't in the mood to tell him what had happened. 'I was going to but the roads are clearing and I've got work to catch up on.'

Her mother would know exactly why she'd left. Ten minutes later she hugged Sonny, gave her father a peck on the cheek and slammed the door behind her.

It was too cold for sight-seeing so she drove straight back to Hawes, stopping only to grab a sandwich. She hadn't expected to meet Jack when she arrived back at "The Pines".

'Eileen was sure you'd stay over, with the snow being bad,' he said, throwing a log on the fire.

'I was worried it was getting worse,' she lied. 'Anyway, I thought you were seeing your Mum.'

'The trains have been disrupted by the wrong sort of snow. It's bad enough at the weekend but I didn't want to be stuck on a replacement bus all the way from Wakefield tomorrow. She'll understand.'

'You should send her flowers,' Lily suggested.

'What?'

'Send her a nice bouquet. You can do it all online. She'll love it.'

He didn't answer but she was willing to bet he would deal with it later.

Eileen came in to ask if they minded having their tea early, promising she'd made them something extra nice since they were like "two orphans of the storm".

When she left the room, Lily giggled. 'D'you think she knows that's a quote from Brideshead Revisited?' Jack looked at her blankly and she sighed. 'So what are you doing tomorrow?' she asked.

'I'm not going out in the cold, so I thought I'd go into work. Robert gave me the key in case he's late because of the snow.'

'That's not a bad idea. I think I might join you. I need to write up yesterday's visit to Mr Mackintosh.'

She told him about her conversation with the keeper which confirmed there was no access onto the estate for vehicles, except for the keepers, who had all been interviewed at the time and cleared of suspicion.

'…but I'm still convinced that the padlock and chain…'

'…hold the key?' Jack was laughing.

'Very funny.'

He went upstairs to return with two bottles of beer, which he plonked on the table. Not long afterwards, Eileen appeared with two plates bearing giant Yorkshire puddings filled with meat and vegetables. She went back to fetch glasses and a bottle opener.

'There,' she declared. 'A feast fit for a king.'

'Not for orphans of the storm?' asked Jack, winking at Lily.

'That comes from a book we did at school,' she told him.

'Brideshead Revisited?' offered Lily.

Eileen laughed. 'That's right, young lady. Evelyn Waugh. I've read all his books.'

They asked her if she could provide them with a packed lunch the next day, explaining that they'd be working at the office. She promised to make up a nice little picnic and prepare a proper good roast for them when they got back.

The following day, Jack, who had offered to carry the food

in his rucksack, was complaining about the weight of their packed lunch.

'You shouldn't grumble,' said Lily, pointing out that it meant there'd be plenty for him to eat.

They walked slowly along the slippery pavements, chatting about nothing in particular until they reached the yard. Lily hadn't expected it to be so cold in the office and begged Jack to get the heating going, otherwise she'd be going straight out again. He disappeared then returned to report he'd changed the timer and soon she could hear the boiler in the kitchen making its usual comforting noises.

'Well, I'm keeping my coat on for now,' she declared.

Jack admitted sheepishly that he'd received a forensics report on Friday afternoon but he couldn't understand some of the jargon. She was delighted to help him with it and sat quietly going through details before explaining the bits he couldn't follow.

'So does that mean these fingerprints aren't Greg's?' he asked when she'd finished.

'Exactly. But we don't know who they belong to. It could be someone quite innocent who simply moved his bike, or was admiring it. We don't know but it's all intel that could be used to connect our cases.'

'It's the DNA that I found most confusing,' he admitted.

'That's because the results *are* confusing. They found more than one person's DNA but that's not surprising if there are unidentified prints on the bike. The problem is, with Greg's DNA present as well, it will be difficult if not impossible to untangle the patterns.'

'At least the blood only belongs to Greg,' Jack said.

'Yes, and that confirms it was his injury. Do you follow

what they're saying about the paint?'

'The green paint on the bike could have come from collision with another vehicle or a gatepost or similar.'

'Exactly. We don't know when the paint got on the bike. It could have happened at any time.'

'So the report isn't telling us much?'

'No, not until we have other prints or DNA or paint to compare the data with.'

Jack made coffee and they agreed they were a sad pair with nothing better to do than work on a Sunday. Lily assumed he didn't have a girlfriend or anyone special but she asked him outright anyway. He shook his head, muttering that he was fancy free.

'What about you?' he asked. 'Thinking of settling down sometime soon?'

It was a fair question at her age, but rather cheeky, she thought. However, she was in no mood for pretending it hadn't happened. 'Actually I was engaged until a little while ago.'

'Oh.'

Poor lad didn't know how to react to that. 'Yes, he cheated on me with one of my friends.' It felt good to be able to say it out loud. As she pulled off her coat and flung it over her chair, there was a chink of metal.

Jack bent down to pick up the plastic bag containing the old chain and examined it.

'That must have been grim,' he said, without looking up.

'It was. I caught them at it.'

'Gross.'

She watched him fiddling with the chain through the polythene.

'I dumped him, of course,' she continued, 'but I couldn't face telling my parents the exact circumstance, it was too embarrassing, so my mother thinks I was overreacting.' She wanted to scream at him to stop fiddling with the chain and listen. 'Mum rang him to say I was back and he came to meet me in the park. That's why I came back early.' She paused. 'Are you listening?'

Jack looked up. 'What? Er, yes. It's just… look…'

He handed her the plastic bag. Inside were two separate lengths of chain.

Miriam hadn't ventured outside the door on Saturday. Her car remained parked across the gateway at the end of the track, preventing anyone entering or leaving the property in another vehicle, particularly someone in a tractor. She was definitely going to ring William but just not yet. She'd decided that she ought to give him a bottle of wine or whisky as a thank you. Instead she spent the day looking through the files, checking she hadn't missed anything relating to the three cases; they were increasingly looking to be completely unrelated. After a scrappy meal of leftover cottage pie, she watched television without much enthusiasm and went to bed early.

There had been a fresh fall of snow overnight and the fields glistened white in the sunshine. The sky was blue, it looked like a perfect winter morning, except it was two days after the Spring Equinox. It didn't start to thaw until mid-morning when, feeling she had to get out, Miriam decided to take a walk into the village. She bought a paper, deciding to have a leisurely coffee while she sat and read the Sunday supplement.

The coffee was good and she enjoyed reading the paper

but there was only so long that she could sit with an empty cup in front of her. After half an hour she paid and left the warmth of the café. She didn't relish the thought of the empty cottage so found herself drawn in the opposite direction, towards the office. She'd pop in to pick up a couple of files, maybe work on them there for an hour or so before going back.

She was cursing Robert for leaving the light on, until she entered. The door was unlocked, and Lily was sitting at her desk as if it was a weekday. She was surprised to see Jack was also there.

'Have I got the wrong day?' she asked with a laugh. 'What's this then?' They looked as though they'd been caught with their hands in the till. 'Nothing better to do?'

They both nodded sheepishly so she admitted she was at a loose end too. Then she asked Lily whether her visit to the keeper had produced anything new.

'Not really.'

'Have you heard from forensics about the car?'

'Not yet,' she admitted.

Lily realised she hadn't heard back from Sylvie about the key either.

'But you did discover something really interesting,' Jack, reminded her, pointing at the plastic bag.

Lily passed it to Miriam. 'This is the old chain that was on the gate to the estate when Amy went missing. Mr Mackintosh said it was still in good condition and no-one could get in when it was locked, but Jack has found you can ease two of the links over each other to open it.'

'Like a Christmas cracker puzzle,' he said.

He showed Miriam how a small gap in the closure of two adjacent links could be used to separate them if you worked at it carefully.

'It might not be significant,' Jack said, 'but if you knew about it, you could move in and out of the gate without anyone knowing.'

Miriam inspected the chain. 'Do you think the links have been opened up deliberately?' she asked, handing it back to Lily. 'Get it examined for filing marks as soon as possible. It could be an important piece of evidence if it's been tampered with.'

Chapter 21

Robert swung round in his chair and shouted across to Jack, 'Good news! The Mountain Rescue Team are up for a search at the weekend, with dogs.'

'That's great, mate. By the way, thanks for getting in touch with Forensics for me, they sent the results over late on Friday.'

'Any use?'

'I'm not sure. Could be something or nothing apparently.'

As soon as Lily appeared with the coffee, Miriam announced she wanted to report back on her meeting with the DCI. They followed her upstairs with their drinks, and settled round the big table, taking care not to put their mugs down on Robert's map.

Miriam sensed they were all watching her carefully as she spoke. 'So, I met the Chief Inspector and Detective Superintendent Barnes sat in on the meeting.' She dismissed a fleeting memory of Henry observing from the end of the table. 'I gave them a report on our progress so far and they asked a few questions of clarification. It wasn't a long meeting.'

'Did you ask about a search for Berry?' Robert demanded.

'I did, Robert, but the feeling was that it should wait for further supporting evidence.' Before he could retaliate, she continued, 'But they did say we could have one day to search for Greg Nevitt's body.'

Jack grinned. 'Yes!'

'I told them how hard you'd all been working and there were several leads but the upshot is that we have until Easter to complete our task.'

There was silence.

'But that's in less than two weeks,' said Lily.

'I know. It means we must get all the outstanding forensic reports back immediately.'

'Well, I don't know how they expect us to tie everything up by Easter,' complained Robert. 'Anyway, I've made my own arrangements. The Swaledale Mountain Rescue Team have agreed to search the new area for Brian Berry's body, even if our own lot won't bother.'

'Well that's good news, I guess,' said Miriam. 'Perhaps we should discuss the details later.' She turned to Jack. 'I'll contact the local force to ask for the search for Nevitt to be held this week, provided the snow has gone.' Miriam looked round at the team 'Any questions? No? Then let's get every scrap of evidence together by the end of this week to ensure we've done the best job we can in the time available.'

Lily got straight on the phone to Sylvie, demanding to have the results of the ODB check. Her friend responded by asking if she'd got out of bed the wrong side.

'It's not like you to sound so shirty, Lily.'

'We're under a lot of pressure. Please just get Terry to send something official over this morning.'

'I'll try. I was going to call you today anyway because the handbag has arrived.'

'Have you looked for the car keys?'

'Not yet. I'll go down to check and call you back shortly.'

Lily tried to concentrate on her paperwork but kept checking her phone in case she'd missed a message from Sylvie. When the call finally came through, she held her breath.

'Was it just the keys you wanted?' her friend asked.

'Yes, why? Are they there?'

'They were in a side pocket. I couldn't find them at first. Anyway I have them now. I assume you want them fast-tracked?'

'Can you authorise that?'

'Just for you. Prints and DNA?'

'Please.'

'No problem, all part of the service. Bye'

'Wait! What about Terry? Have you spoken to him?'

'Ah, yes. He's out this morning on a job but he said he will definitely send the report today.'

'Can I rely on him?'

'What's the problem? I thought this was a cold case.'

'Lukewarm, yes, but we're on a deadline now. It's all over by Easter.'

'You're kidding.'

'No. We've been given two weeks to wind up the investigation.'

'Harsh.'

'You said it. And there's just one more favour. I've got a metal chain that may have been tampered with. Would you be able to slip that in too, as a job lot?'

'That's a bit cheeky, Lily. Go on then, but you'd better get it over here today because I'm off tomorrow.'

It meant driving back to Carlisle but at least the snow had gone. She hoped there would be time to have a chat with Sylvie. Her friend knew about her breakup and it would be so good to be able to talk to her about what happened with Roy at the weekend.

'See you at the B&B tonight,' she called to Jack as she left.

He didn't mind. He was back on his bike now the roads were clear and he was going to be working late because Miriam had asked him to define the exact search area. She said a team would be there on Wednesday, with a dog handler. He pored over the map upstairs with Robert, who suggested the search was restricted to the wooded area leading from the place where he'd detected a change in the tracker speed.

'If you think the bike was driven away, then Nevitt must have been left there. We might find evidence of his campsite.'

Jack had been through so many possibilities that he wasn't confident they would find anything but Robert told him not to be so pessimistic.

'It's the last chance saloon, isn't it, Jack? There are no other leads left are there?'

He agreed, thanking his colleague for his help yet again.

'No problem. I thought I would come on Wednesday anyway.'

Jack wasn't sure whether he was pleased or not. He'd been looking forward to working with the local force, particularly the dog handler, but Robert would try to take over, he always did. Maybe he'd ask Miriam's advice.

Lily found it strange walking back into her old laboratory. People she knew kept stopping to chat when all she wanted to do was to get the chain to Sylvie as soon as possible. Her friend was in the office, eating a sandwich.

'Want one?' She handed the pack over to Lily. 'I'm on a diet. I buy a pack of sandwiches and give half away. Works every time. So how are things? Are your mum and dad all right?'

Sylvie had met her parents a couple of times at open days and said her father was clever because he understood the chemistry.

'I was there at the weekend,' Lily replied. She waited until she'd finished her sandwich before adding, 'My mother told Roy I was in the park walking the dog so he came to find me.'

'What did he want?'

'To talk. I said I didn't want to see him.'

'Good riddance, that's what I say. Now, if you're ready, we can register that chain of yours.'

Lily knew the process inside out but had to watch obediently as Sylvie entered the chain into the system. She'd already arranged for a technician to have a look at it and within ten minutes he'd arrived back from lunch. They watched through the glass door while he viewed the chain under a huge magnifying mirror. In a surprisingly short time he was back out, confirming that someone had clearly filed the links so they could be undone.

Sylvie looked at Lily with a grin. 'There you are then.'

She arranged to get a report from the technician by the next day. Lily didn't want to leave the chain but it was in the system now.

'What about Terry?' she asked as they walked back to the office.

'He'll be in soon. Meanwhile I've got a preliminary on the key.'

They had found fingerprints on Amy's key and the fob,

so now they were doing the DNA.

'When will the prints go into the database?'

'Today if I get time.'

The door opened and Terry arrived looking dishevelled. 'I've only just got back. Haven't had anything to eat yet.'

'Sorry, I gave the rest of my sandwich to Lily,' said Sylvie with a laugh. 'You can go to the canteen as soon as you've given us the news.'

'Hi Lily,' he said. 'Sorry it's taken longer than I thought but it's good news. The car has a record of failing to start, something to do with the fuel line they think.' He fished around in his pocket and pulled out a creased sheet of paper. 'This is a copy of the download. It probably won't make much sense to you.'

'But you'll send Lily a report?' Sylvie asked.

'Yes, when I get a chance.'

'Not good enough, Terry. As soon as you've had something to eat, you sit down and do it.'

When he'd gone, Lily commented that she'd really got Terry under her thumb.

'He loves it really.'

Robert made sure he left in plenty of time to get home, before going to the history group meeting. He felt that his mother had been rather churlish about the application form, which Jean's mother had given her at WI. It was clear she didn't get on with Mrs Curtis, possibly resenting her role as Chair. He didn't know or care but he did mind his mother making nasty comments about "that Jean Curtis". He had already pointed out that what Jean did and wore during her teens was irrelevant now that she had a doctorate and worked at the university.

Anyway, he'd filled in the form and taken it round to Mrs Curtis to give to her daughter. Tonight he would be seeing her again. The talk was about Neolithic flint axes, which he thought might be popular, so he wanted to get there in good time to get a seat near the front. He didn't wait for pudding but dashed upstairs to change, deciding to wear the corduroy jacket he'd found hanging in the wardrobe in his bedroom. It was probably fifteen years old but it still fitted and he thought it made him look younger.

He left in plenty of time but there were a few people in the hall when he arrived. Jean was at the front talking to a young man in a suit and tie. Robert was about to take a seat behind the front row when Jean caught sight of him and waved him over.

'May I introduce our speaker for this evening,' she said.

It turned out the young man was a student from her department.

Then she said, 'This is Robert an old friend of mine.'

Throughout the talk, Robert kept coming back to her words. "An old friend of mine" could have a whole range of meanings. People used the term affectionately, didn't they? He returned to the talk, which was being delivered in a monotone and was frankly rather boring unless one was obsessed with the finer details of flint axes. Endless pictures of flints filled the screen until Robert felt he was close to nodding off. When it was finally over, Jean came to ask if he fancied a drink.

'It's just that our speaker has suggested going over the road for a quick pint.' She leaned closer, lowering her voice. 'He's such a bore I need moral support.'

It seemed that most of the group used the local pub after the talks and the speaker was very quickly surrounded by members of the audience who wanted to ask more questions. Jean extracted herself to join Robert where he was waiting by the bar.

'Sorry about that. His talk was pretty dire wasn't it? I only asked him as a favour for a colleague. Never again. Mind you, it's sometimes difficult to find interesting speakers. I had to resort to presenting something myself once.'

He realised that he didn't know what she did at the university

'Me? Oh I'm an anthropologist by training but my research is really osteoarchaeology if one wants to be pedantic.'

'Bones?'

'Yes. You look surprised.'

To be honest he was but he wished he hadn't shown it.

'You're remembering how I was at school, aren't you?' she teased. 'Too much makeup and Spice Girls dresses.'

He remembered her reputation for drinking too much and being what his mother would call "available", but he didn't say so. Instead he added, 'And I was the class nerd.'

He filled the awkward silence by attracting the attention of the barman and asked if she'd like another drink.

She looked at her watch. 'Actually I'm driving but if you want to come back to mine I've got a nice single malt that I've been keeping.'

It was almost ten o'clock and he would be getting up at six, the following day. 'Can I take a rain check?' he asked, wondering if he'd got the phrase right.

'You're right. Perhaps we should leave it until the weekend when neither of us have work in the morning.'

They exchanged numbers before making their way back

to the car park. Robert was thinking that he'd be engaged in the search at the weekend and told her that he would be working.

'I suppose I'll see you at the meeting next Monday then,' he said, hoping she could see him pulling a sad face.

'Not next week,' she called as she unlocked her car. 'It's the end of term today, the next meeting isn't until after Easter.' She climbed in and slammed the door.

He was still standing beside her car when she started the engine. Suddenly he stepped over to knock on her window, waiting until it slid down silently.

'You said osteoarchaeology, didn't you? Would you like to come with me to search for a dead body on Saturday?'

Chapter 22

Jack was riding his bike to work, so Lily was already at her desk when he arrived. Sylvie reported that when she ran prints from the car keys through the database, one print was Amy's but the remaining four partial prints were unidentified. Lily and Jack had a lively discussion on the previous evening about the unknown fingerprints from their respective cases. As Lily pointed out, they now needed a detailed comparison of the two sets of unknown prints by a qualified fingerprint examiner, as listed on the National Fingerprint Expert Register, which is exactly what she was before she left the service. She just needed Jack to ask for good quality copies of the bike prints while she got hold of the prints from Amy's keys.

Miriam was surprised they'd been able to lift a number of prints from a single car key but, as Lily explained, the exhibit consisted of an electronic car key fob on a ring with a door key and a small plastic photograph holder containing a picture of Amy with her friends. She was on the phone to the Cumbria science support services asking for copies of the prints when Jack arrived. He had a quick word with Miriam who sent him off to quickly contact the Yorkshire forensic services for Nevitt's prints before they finalised the arrangements for the following day's search in Cotterdale.

Robert had been to a meeting with the Swaledale Mountain Rescue Team leader to discuss their approach to his search at the weekend. When he returned, he was quite energised and spoke excitedly about how it was going to be managed.

'Of course, it will be a much larger scale search than yours tomorrow,' he told Jack. 'It will cover a much wider area, although it will be a smaller team.'

'I'll come along to help,' said Jack, who assumed, since Robert was joining the search for Nevitt, that he would be going as well.

The sergeant shifted his gaze. 'Actually I've got an expert coming to help me, so it'll be a bit awkward.'

'Who's that?'

'It's Dr McGovern,' he said quickly. 'She's an osteoarchaeologist at the university.'

Miriam had been listening. 'How did you manage to get her?'

'She's an old friend. She said she'd be happy to help.'

The prints from Cumbria arrived first, allowing Lily time to examine the contents of the file. The system had made a conclusive identification of just one of the prints on the keys, the one identified as Amy's. She agreed it was a good match, so that went back in the file as completed. Of the four partial prints, one looked close enough to Amy's thumb print that she excluded it too, although she wouldn't stand up in court to defend her decision. After examining the remaining three prints, comparing measurements, and making copious notes, Lily concluded they came from just one finger and a thumb. She was certain she could match up two of them to reconstruct a nearly complete print of a forefinger.

During the lunch break there was a heated debate about what the chances were that the same prints would appear on Greg Nevitt's bike. Robert called it "wishful thinking" while Jack played down the possibility. Lily was irritated by their pessimism, arguing that she'd been involved in many cases where a single print had been the critical evidence in a murder case. Miriam had sat silently throughout the discussion until now.

'Let's hope we do find a match because it's the only connection you'll have between Amy's death and Greg's disappearance,' she said before taking her mug back to the kitchen.

Jack grinned at the others. 'I'd better go and chase them up for the pictures then.'

But they had to wait until mid-afternoon before they arrived. He forwarded them to Lily and hovered as she opened the file, bringing them up on the screen, one by one.

'What d'you think?' he asked.

'They're not bad,' she replied, staring closely. 'I think they'll be clean enough to make a good attempt.' She looked over her shoulder at him. 'But I need to concentrate, so please let me get on. I'll let you know when I've finished.'

There was a tense atmosphere in the office; they seemed to be walking on tiptoes and speaking in whispers around her. She went through the process again with Nevitt's prints: carefully studying the loops, whorls, and arches, noting down points until she had dealt with all the pictures.

'How's it going?' Miriam was standing beside her.

'Ok,' she replied, looking up at her.

'We're very lucky to have your expertise available.'

Lily blushed as her boss went back to her desk. She was

on the last leg of the work now, the part that she'd always enjoyed when she was working in forensics. The moment when suddenly things fall into place. She could feel herself becoming tense as she typed the points into a table. One by one she was putting a cross in the box as she rejected a comparison. She left the best until last; there was a single fingerprint on both pieces of evidence that bore a mark, a small scar perhaps. And, yes, there were more points of similarity. Again, if this was the only evidence in a court case it might not be enough for a prosecution, but as an indication of a connection between the two cases, it was definitely worth pursuing.

She leaned back in her chair, stretching. When she looked round, Jack was watching expectantly. She went over to Miriam first but Jack was already beside her when she reported that she thought she had a match.

'It's an index finger, only partials on the keys, which has a small crescent shaped scar. I'll show you.'

They crowded round to look at the screen where she'd brought up the two relevant pictures.

'How on earth can you work with such poor reproduction?' Jack asked.

'These are quite good. They've taken these pictures from latent prints that have been developed chemically. You get used to working with them, you soon get your eye in.'

She pointed out the similarities in the ridges and the positioning of the mark due to a tiny injury in the skin. They all seemed convinced but once they were congratulating her on making a breakthrough, she was quick to express her reservations regarding how well it would stand up in court.

'As I said this morning,' began Miriam, as she walked back to her desk, 'it's all we have, so we'll take it for now. By the way, before we go off, can we just go over the plan for tomorrow's search for Nevitt's body. It sounds as though you've covered everything Jack, but the forecast is for rain so it's not going to be much fun out there. Do you know how long the local uniformed officers will be there for?'

'Until it gets dark,' Robert replied.

Jack looked at Lily and raised his eyebrows. She knew he was irritated by the way Robert was taking charge. She'd told him not to worry because he was lucky to have someone with Robert's experience helping. Privately she knew that the local force were more likely to respond to Robert than someone as young and naive as Jack.

Miriam was satisfied with the arrangements in place but she took the opportunity to have a quick word with Robert once the others had left for the evening.

'Will you keep an eye on Jack tomorrow?' she asked. 'He's got no experience of this sort of thing. Just make sure he doesn't interfere with the way that uniform work.'

He assured her he would be on top of everything, before dashing off to get home for his tea. Miriam wished someone was waiting for her with a hot meal on the table. She tidied her desk before switching off the lights and locking up. This evening she was determined to do two things that she'd been putting off for several days already. She would sign the documents from the estate agent and call William to thank him for rescuing her from the snow. She had decided she would do both before she allowed herself to prepare a meal or pour her first glass of wine.

A cold wind was whipping across the yard and it began

to rain as she drove the short distance to the cottage. The place was in darkness and uninviting as she travelled slowly along the track. Part of her was pleased that she wouldn't have to stay much longer, although she wasn't exactly thrilled by the prospect of returning to Middlesbrough either.

Once she'd lit the fire, she pulled out the estate agent's paperwork. Her signature on one of the documents had to be witnessed, which meant it would have to wait until she found someone to do it. It wasn't something she wanted to take into work. Sticking the envelope back in her bag, she took a deep breath and dialled William's mobile. It rang and rang. She was about to give up when a breathless voice answered.

'Hello?'

'It's Miriam Abbott.'

'Miriam?'

'Miriam. You rescued my car from the snow. I'm calling to thank you.'

He laughed softly. 'No problem. I couldn't leave you blocking the road, I had the milk collection coming next morning.'

'Oh, sorry.'

'So are you settled in down there? Mum said I should invite you over but I haven't had...'

'No, I should... Look, I've got something I wanted to give you, as a thank you.'

'Well, come on over then.'

'What now?'

'Why not?'

Miriam was put on the spot. Would it seem rude to refuse, since she was the one who had the bottle of wine for him. He gave her directions to the farm at the top of the hill and she said she'd be there in half an hour. She rushed upstairs to change, refreshed her make-up quickly and put a brush through her hair, before grabbing her coat again. She dashed to the car through pouring rain. The wipers went onto top speed and the windscreen was steaming up, so she missed the farm entrance and had to turn round in a gateway before finally reaching the farmhouse. She held her coat over her head as she ran to the door but, by the time it opened, her hair was dripping.

William had the same amused expression he'd worn when they'd first met. He ushered her into a large modern kitchen where he took her coat, telling her to take a seat. She produced the bottle for him, placing it between them on the table. He examined the label before going to a glass-fronted cupboard, returning with two large wine glasses and proceeding to unscrew the bottle.

'No, I didn't mean you to...' she began.

'Don't you want to try it?' he asked, pouring the wine.

She knew what it tasted like, she bought a dozen bottles every month, but she smiled and took the glass he was offering her.

He clinked her glass with his. 'Cheers. So what are you doing in the Dales?'

It was a direct question that she didn't want to answer. 'Just work.'

'What do you do then?'

She sipped the wine before answering. 'I'm in a wildlife crime unit. We're working with the National Park. And you have a dairy farm?' she asked, changing the subject quickly.

'Yes, my grandfather started the herd, my father took

over when he went and now, I'm running it.'

She managed to ask sufficient questions to keep the conversation going until he went to top up her glass.

'No, honestly, no more. I've got to get back. I haven't eaten yet.'

Embarrassingly, William then invited her to stay. He was heating up a casserole and it had been ready half an hour ago. It felt rude to refuse if she'd delayed his dinner. She watched as he took two plates and piled them with a lamb casserole made to his mother's recipe.

'She made this for you?' she asked.

He pulled a face as if he was insulted. 'Certainly not, she gave me the recipe but I made it.'

While they were eating, Miriam told him how difficult she'd found the solid fuel stove. He was impressed that she relied on it for cooking, heating and hot water. He described how he'd modernised the farmhouse when he took it over, installing a biofuel boiler. She remarked how nice the kitchen was and he admitted that the Aga was electric and required no effort at all.

When they'd finished eating and emptied the bottle, Miriam asked a favour. 'Would you mind witnessing my signature on a document? I have it in my bag.'

She explained she was selling her house, without mentioning that it was because she was separating from her husband, but the page had both their names on it and William must have spotted Henry's signature above hers. Neither mentioned it but when he was loading the dishwasher and had his back to her, he asked casually, 'So are you married?'

His directness floored her temporarily. 'Er yes, well no, actually we're in the process of separating.'

'Hence the house sale?' he asked sympathetically.

'Yes.'

'It's a difficult time,' he said. 'I went through it a few years back.'

There was a pause in the conversation, which was getting far too personal for Miriam's comfort. 'Thanks for the meal, it was delicious but I really ought to be getting back,' she said, standing up to leave.

He turned. 'Thanks for the wine, and for the company, it's been most enjoyable.'

'Perhaps I could return the favour some time,' she replied, hoping it sounded sufficiently sincere.

'Just let me know when and I'll be round. I used to play with the lad who lived in your cottage when I was a kid. It doesn't look as though it has changed much since then, judging by the outside?'

'Not at all, I suspect.'

Miriam drove back down the hill carefully. Maybe it was the wine but she felt light-headed. William was good company but he was very direct and she wasn't sure whether she was ready to discuss her separation with anyone yet. She probably wouldn't invite him over. After all, she'd be leaving the Dales very soon.

Chapter 23

'So are you feeling excited about today?' Lily asked Jack at breakfast. 'I wish I was coming.'

'I suppose you can if you want to.'

'No, definitely not. Uniform won't want a lot of hangers-on.'

'That's what Robert said when I asked to go with him at the weekend but he's taking some archaeologist just because she's his friend.'

'I think it's more than that, Jack. She's an expert in bones so if they come across anything, she'll know whether it's relevant or not.'

'But Brian Berry won't have become a skeleton in four months, will he?'

'No, it's extremely unlikely.' She thought about foxes and other animals but decided not to mention them while they were eating. 'Have you ever seen a dead body?'

'No. I suppose you saw loads when you were in forensics.'

'Not a lot but it can be quite unpleasant.' Again she thought about the various stages a decomposing body went through in the first few months. 'I'm just saying.'

She watched Jack devour two more pieces of toast in quick succession and asked if he'd organised a packed lunch. He hadn't and rushed off to find Eileen. Lily poured herself another cup of tea, enjoying the prospect of an exciting day. Much was riding on Jack's search now that she'd made a connection between Greg's bike and

Amy's keys. If they found something in Cotterdale, however small, to prove Greg had camped there, it would be another link in a chain of evidence. She smiled. The chain that had been tampered with was another link. All she needed to know was how they fitted together.

Jack returned fifteen minutes later, dressed in a large waterproof jacket, and carrying a rucksack. 'Robert's waiting outside so I'm off now.'

'I hope it goes all right.'

He grinned. 'So do I. By the way, I told Eileen we were looking for signs of poaching in Cotterdale when she asked where I was off to. Wish me luck.'

He waved cheerfully to hide his anxiety and kept a fixed smile as he climbed into Robert's car.

'Hello, son. All ready?' asked the sergeant as they set off.

'I think so.' He hoped he sounded more confident than he was feeling.

'It was raining on the way up but it seems to have stopped. The forecast is bad though.'

Jack knew there was an eighty percent chance it was going to pour all day. 'Will that affect anything?' he asked.

'Only everyone's mood. Always pleasanter on a nice sunny day. So have you seen the search site yet?'

'No, only on "Google". It's just trees.'

'Just trees?' Robert repeated, shaking his head. 'It'll be hard work getting through the forestry. Still, we'll leave it to uniform to do the searching. We'll just observe. The search manager will have worked out the strategy and passed it on to the lads.'

There was a police van and a patrol car parked at the PLS, as Robert insisted on calling the "place last seen", although Greg Nevitt hadn't exactly been seen there, but his bicycle had been tracked there. They found the senior officer, who was a sergeant so Robert was immediately in his element. He asked where the dog-handler was, to be told that their dogs were trained to find money, drugs or explosives, not dead bodies and they'd been told there was no funding for a cadaver dog to be drafted in. There were six men in total, ready to search the plantation for anything that might suggest Nevitt had been in the area. Jack asked if they would be checking for camping equipment as well as looking for a body, but Robert cut him off.

'It's all in the search plan,' he said laughing.

They watched the team move off, spreading out, each man clutching a map that presumably defined the area they had to cover. A few drops of rain began to fall and Robert suggested they returned to the car.

'I'll just follow behind the guy who went in there,' Jack said, indicating where the last man to leave had gone.

He was disappointed with the low-key nature of his search, particularly without a dog handler. Robert would have the mountain rescue team dog, who presumably would be able to look for bodies. The rain was getting heavier so he hurried into the firs for shelter. Robert was right, it was hard work walking between the trees, so progress was slow. He followed at a distance, keeping his eye on the track to his right that would lead him back to the car and his sandwiches.

The floor of the forest lacked vegetation and there was nothing to see. Lily had explained how it was easy to spot a shallow grave because the soil would sink as the body decomposed. That's what he was looking for, but before long he was convinced the whole venture was a waste of time and made his way onto the track to return to the car.

'You youngsters have no patience,' declared Robert, pouring coffee from a thermos into a small metal cup. 'Cheer yourself up with that. I've got some homemade biscuits here.'

'I suppose you've done this lots of times,' Jack commented.

'I was involved in a few searches when I was in uniform,' he agreed. 'It's not much fun at the best of times, although it's good when you find the missing person safe and sound.'

An hour went by, the rain stopped briefly and Jack went for a stroll to get away from stories of life in the force. Not that he wasn't interested but Robert did go on a bit. If he was so good at policing, why wasn't he a DI by now? Another downpour sent him running back to the car and a further hour of Robert's exploits.

Eventually Jack asked, 'Did you ever want to become a DI?'

Robert smiled. 'I was going for promotion through the ranks but my wife fell ill so I left it. Then she died three years ago and it's not something I've done anything about. For now, I'm focussing on going from acting sergeant to sergeant.'

'Acting sergeant?'

He ignored Jack's reaction. 'Everything rests on my search for Brian Berry. I'm certain he's out there. I just want to find the body to discover what happened to him. I'm sure he died of exposure but I need the post-mortem to prove it.'

When the rain stopped Jack went for another stroll. He

spotted a young officer amongst the trees and called to him, asking if he minded if he tagged along. It was fine if he stayed back and didn't interfere with his work. Jack struggled through the trees, literally following in his footsteps. The forest floor was bare except for fallen pine needles, the trees dripped on him as he brushed against them, no-one spoke. Eventually his companion stopped to stretch his back, commenting that he was too tall for this job.

'Do you do much of this type of thing?' Jack asked.

'What d'you mean? Searches? No.'

'I really hope we find something.'

'What's your interest then?'

'It's my case.'

The officer laughed. 'You're running a murder case? Come on, mate.'

Jack felt himself reddening. 'Well, I'm in charge of the investigation under DI Abbott.'

'Is she here?'

'No, just my sergeant who gave me a lift down.'

'Well, good luck then.'

They continued in single file until their route brought them suddenly out onto the track. As the officer was checking a sketch map of the area, a shout came from their left.

'Someone's got something,' the PC observed. 'Came from over there.' He pointed further up the track.

Jack set off in the direction of the sound, ignoring an instruction from his companion to stay put. The senior officer appeared ahead of him before running into the trees. Jack followed then stopped. A small group had gathered in the clearing ahead.

'Found a rucksack, Guv,' someone shouted.

After that there was a hiatus while they planned what would happen next. The search team was told it was time for their meal break, leaving an officer behind with the rucksack, unopened. Jack asked whether they knew who it belonged to and he said they wouldn't touch it until they had their orders.

'Bit early for lunch, isn't it?' asked Robert when Jack joined him in the car.

'They've found a rucksack.'

'Is it his?'

'They haven't opened it.'

'Waiting for forensics?'

'I don't know.'

Robert got out of the car and went straight over to the police sergeant. They spoke for a while before he returned.

'They're waiting for the green light to open it up. It's just protocol really. He reckons they'll have a look inside after the lunch break. Let's eat while we wait.'

It was unusual for Jack to lose his appetite but he put down the remains of his cheese and pickle sandwich. 'If it belongs to Greg Nevitt, that means there's a good chance he's still here.'

Robert, whose mouth was full, nodded in agreement, before adding, 'They'll resume the search whatever happens but if it is his, I guess they'll focus on the area where they found it.'

Time was passing slowly. Jack watched members of the search team wandering about eating their packed lunches, until another downpour, when they sheltered in their vehicles. Finally they gathered to receive instructions from their leader before disappearing up the track together.

'Right, I'm off,' said Jack, jumping out of the car.

Robert caught up with him as he reached the group. 'Wait for me,' he said, out of breath. 'I don't want to miss the action.'

The senior officer caught sight of them and, once he'd issued his orders, he came over.

'I need you guys to stay on the track. Do not move off it, understood?'

'No problem,' said Robert with a smile that disappeared the moment he turned his back.

There was an awkward silence as they remained fixed to the spot.

'Frustrating, isn't it?' said Jack.

Robert sighed. 'Yes. The rain's getting heavier, I'm going back to the car.'

Jack followed and they sat for the rest of the afternoon, passing the time by going over all the possible ways that Greg Nevitt's rucksack could end up in a clearing in the middle of the pine forest. When another vehicle arrived, they watch a middle-aged woman step out and disappear up the track. She returned half an hour later wearing examination gloves accompanied by a PC carrying the rucksack. He took it into the police van and the woman followed. Jack and Robert looked at each other before making their way over there to watch. She was opening the outside pockets

'She's looking for something to identify the owner,' Robert said in a low voice. 'A wallet or a phone.'

She pulled out a plastic bag and peered at the contents. 'Money,' she said. 'And a cycling club card.'

'What's the name?' the officer asked.

'Greg Nevitt.'

Chapter 24

The CSI left the rucksack in the van with the PC and returned to where the search team was concentrating. Jack and Robert hovered on the track, watching progress through the trees. The men were fanning out from the clearing where the rucksack was found, moving slowly as they examined the ground. Jack was tense with anticipation but after a while it was obvious they were there for the long haul. He sighed.

'Don't give up yet, son,' Robert said, offering him a mint.

'But what if they haven't found him when it gets dark?'

'They'll come back tomorrow.'

'Will they?'

'They can't ignore solid evidence.'

'What if he isn't here, though. What if he was abducted?'

Robert laughed. 'What, by aliens?' He shook his head. 'No, why would anyone want to abduct a middle-aged cyclist? A child, yes, or a woman, even his bike, but not him.'

'What if he was injured and wandered off in a daze. He could be anywhere.'

'Let's hope he's here then.'

The search continued but light was fading by six o'clock and the search was called off. Jack caught up with the leader just as he reached the van.

'Will you be back tomorrow?'

He looked at Jack as if his question was rather impertinent. He addressed his reply to Robert, who was walking over to join them.

'I'm going to talk to my DCI. With a bit of luck we'll be ordered back.'

'Tell him to contact Reg Dyer at West Yorkshire. He was on the original case; he'll want to hear about this.'

'Thanks mate. I'll let him know what's happening, if you give me his number.'

When they were back in the car, Jack asked who Reg Dyer was.

'He's a DI in Leeds. We worked together until he moved into CID. I noticed he was the SIO on the original investigation – that's the senior investigating officer.'

'I know what it is.'

As they reached Hawes, Jack asked Robert to drop him in town, he'd walk the rest of the way.

'Ok, son but I'll pick you up early if they're resuming the search. Are you feeling lucky?'

'Not really.'

Robert cut the engine and turned to him. 'Don't get dejected, they found his rucksack, didn't they?'

'But we weren't allowed to see it. It might have had a clue in it.'

'A clue?'

'Something that explains what happened.'

'It's gone for forensic examination. I'm sure they will be thorough. Finding the rucksack abandoned confirms something untoward has happened to him and they'll want to find out just as much as we do. But, remember, the case is West Yorkshire's.'

'Your friend Reg Dyer's.'

'Exactly. So I'll give him a call this evening.'

Jack didn't know what good it would do if Robert phoned his mate, since there wasn't any more money in the budget for a second day's search.

As he closed the front door of "The Pines" and removed his jacket, he spotted Lily at the top of the stairs.

'I heard you come in,' she explained. 'How did it go?'

'Ok, I suppose.'

She came down and followed him into the sitting room. The table was already laid for dinner and he noticed there were two place settings.

'Aren't you going to Zumba tonight?'

'End of term. Don't change the subject. I want to hear a blow by blow account. Did they find anything?'

He described the day in detail from when they arrived until the rucksack was discovered.

'Why didn't you say that to begin with?' Lily demanded. 'That's brilliant. So you'll be there tomorrow again?'

He shrugged before explaining the situation.

'But they have to continue the search now,' she exclaimed indignantly. 'What did Robert say?'

'He's calling his mate in Leeds who worked on the original case.'

'Well let's hope he persuades him to pursue it,' she said. 'Anyway, my day was not as good as yours; I got the results of the DNA from Amy's keys.'

'And?'

'Unidentified.'

Their silence was finally broken by Eileen, who threw a log on the fire and told them that their meals would be on the table in half an hour.

When Jack had left the room, she asked Lily what was

wrong with him. 'He's got a face like a wet weekend!'

'Just a disappointing day.'

'In Cotterdale?'

Lily nodded. The least said the better.

'Looking for poachers, isn't he?'

She nodded again.

'He should talk to Joyce's husband. He works for the keepers. They know all the locals into illegal activities.'

'Thanks, I'll tell him.'

'Always best to get the local knowledge about these things, isn't it?'

'I suppose so.'

After she'd gone, Lily thought about her meeting with Joyce. Her husband was presumably a beater and she helped with the catering so the estate clearly was an important part of the local economy. While they were eating, Lily told Jack what Eileen had said about her brother-in-law.

'Weren't all the beaters interviewed first time round?'

'Yes, I'll check that he was included. He's married to Eileen's sister, who got me the keeper's phone number. She helps the catering company with the pheasant shoots.'

Jack scraped his plate clean before putting his knife and fork down. 'Did the original investigation interview her too?'

Lily thought for a moment. 'No, I don't think they did.'

There was no message from Robert next morning and no sign of him when Jack arrived at the office with Lily. She'd spent the journey trying to convince him that she should ask for the DNA of anyone who had worked on the estate for the catering company last year. He told her she didn't stand a chance and gave her a knowing look when Miriam confirmed his opinion. The DI's explanation for not approving her request was cut short by Robert bursting through the door.

'Sorry, sorry. Got stuck behind a tractor again. Jack, hurry, we've got to get back down there now. They've started already.'

Miriam looked startled. 'What's going on?'

'Lily will explain,' Jack called, as he grabbed his jacket and ran to catch up with Robert.

'So they're continuing the search?' he asked once they were on the road again.

'Yes. I only heard on the way up here.'

'Did you speak to your mate?'

'As a matter of fact I did but it wasn't really necessary. They're just as keen to close the case as we are. They've sent a couple of extras today. I just hope the rain keeps off.'

As they drew closer to the woodland, Jack could see there were more vehicles than before.

'We'll leave the car here,' said Robert, pulling off the road. 'I don't suppose they'll want us getting in the way.'

They walked down to the police van, where a single uniformed officer was sitting with the side door open. They introduced themselves and he made a note of their names. Jack noticed the woman from forensics seated at the back of the van eating a sandwich.

'All right if we wander up the track, mate?' Robert asked in the chatty voice he used when talking to them.

'If you keep to the path,' the PC instructed.

They could see several of the search team working amongst the trees as they wandered towards the end of the plantation. The clouds were beginning to break up and it was getting brighter.

'You can see Great Shunner Fell over there, Jack.' Robert was pointing at a peak in the distance. 'The search at the weekend will concentrate from there, towards us into the valley.'

'Do you know how many people there will be?'

'Maybe half a dozen if we're lucky.'

'But they'll have a dog?'

'Yes and we can give them a hand.'

Had Robert changed his mind? 'We?'

'Me and Jean. She's used to archaeological digs and suchlike. I think she'll be a real asset.'

'How do you know her?'

'Actually we were at school together but I haven't seen her for years. She's a university professor now.'

'Friends Reunited, eh? Rekindling an old romance?'

'Enough of your cheek, young man,' Robert said but Jack could tell from his tone that he wasn't far off the truth.

They hung around in the sunshine, unwilling to enter the shade of the trees where it was dull and cold, despite the fact it provided shelter from the sharp wind. It was a waiting game that Robert was better suited to than Jack. He felt impatient to be making progress.

'If you're certain about wanting to join the force, you'll have to learn to be patient, willing to play the long game. Things take time to come together,' Robert warned him.

'Yeah, but we don't have time, do we? We've got exactly...' he paused while he did the calculation, '...exactly seven days before Easter and that's including the weekend.'

Eventually figures began appearing from the trees to head back to the vehicles for their lunch break. They followed to catch up with progress but there was nothing so far. Robert tried to calm Jack down by telling him that "everything comes to him who waits" but he'd had enough of Robert's platitudes and took himself off for a walk to look at the village of Cotterdale that he'd only seen online so far. The place was deserted and it struck him that no-one had stopped to enquire what was happening in the woods. He assumed they'd become used to a police presence, following the discovery of Amy's body only a few months previously. The stone cottages pressed up against the narrow lane until he emerged onto a track that led to the estate gate. It was locked, just as Lily had described it, with a shiny padlock glinting in the sun.

There was nothing to see in this deserted spot and he suddenly needed to get back to the search. He practically jogged along the road to the car but Robert wasn't there. He doubled back to the track but it was empty. Walking quickly, he'd almost reached the clearing when someone called his name.

'Jack, over here!'

Robert was standing on the far side of the clearing and when Jack joined him, he pointed further into the trees.

'They've found an area where the earth has been disturbed.'

Soon they were joined by the young PC they'd spoken to the day before. 'Looks like we've found something. They've given the go-ahead to expose the area now.'

Members of the team wandered back and forth, carrying implements. They peered through the trees as men got to work shovelling soil into a neat pile. Jack reckoned it was over an hour before they stopped, stood back and waited.

'What's happening now?' Jack asked quietly.

'No idea. We'll know if they call the forensics lady.'

It wasn't long before they spotted her coming towards them in her white coveralls.

'Have they found something?' Robert asked as she passed.

'Well I'm not wearing this as a fashion statement,' she replied grimly.

Jack laughed at Robert's embarrassment. It was a release of tension that had built up during the day. Now, at last, there might be a good outcome.

'You do understand,' Robert began, 'that if it is his body, it will take some time to get through the formalities, the post-mortem, the inquest and so on.'

'I know, but that doesn't matter. My job was to show that the cases are connected.' He looked towards Cotterdale and across to Great Shunner Fell. 'I think all three are.'

There was a shout from the site where the woman dressed in white was standing and stretching. As she marched back towards them, Jack stepped into her path.

'Have you found him?'

She nodded. 'I reckon so. He's dressed top to toe in Lycra.'

Chapter 25

'I kept it warm for as long as I could but it'll be rock hard if I don't serve yours now,' complained Eileen, holding the plate with an oven glove.

'I don't know why he's so late,' Lily replied. 'I can't get hold of him.'

She assumed Jack was still with the police search but whether that meant things were going well or badly she couldn't guess. She was cutting into a leathery sausage when the bell went and she heard Eileen making her way down the hall. A moment later the door opened and Karl appeared.

'Sorry,' he said. 'She said you were having your tea but told me to wait in here for Jack.'

Lily finished chewing and swallowed before responding. 'He's still at work I'm afraid. Are you off to the pool night?'

'Yes. He didn't say he'd be late.'

'He probably forgot. D'you want to sit and wait? He could arrive any time.'

She finished eating before joining Karl by the fire. It was an unexpected opportunity to quiz him about Kirsty.

But first she asked, 'How's Di? Zumba has finished so we haven't caught up recently.'

'She's fine.'

'And Kirsty? How is she getting on?'

He pulled a face. 'Much the same.'

Lily launched into a soliloquy about how sad it was that

she didn't feel like working and how important it is to have a goal in life. She suggested that perhaps there was something or someone at work that was upsetting her. Perhaps that was why she didn't want to leave the house. She finished by asking about the hotel in Darlington.

'Is it a big posh place?'

'Sort of. It calls itself a boutique hotel, although it's much bigger than their local one.'

'There's more than one?'

'Yes, but the other is more like a guest house really. It's in the grounds of the Grant family estate.'

'Family estate? That sounds grand.'

'Not really. It's not like it's used for shooting or anything. More like a farm but they're a hospitality business really.'

'Do you think there's any reason why Kirsty would be avoiding their hotel?'

'No but I don't really know what it's like.'

'What about the family – the Grants?'

'I've met Rebecca and her brother because they come to Young Farmers events occasionally, or used to until they went to university. But I don't know them well.' He looked at his watch. 'I ought to be off soon.'

'Will you go to Kirkby Stephen anyway?'

'Probably. Tell him I called for him.'

'I will. He'll be sorry he's not got back in time.'

It was eight o'clock when Jack finally appeared. He was flushed with excitement, telling Lily all about it before he'd even taken his jacket off. Eileen plonked a plate down on the table declaring that she hoped he had good strong teeth, before laughing all the way to the door. Lily excused his bad table manners as he continued talking and eating at the same time. She sat through a blow by blow account of the search, culminating in the discovery of Greg Nevitt's body.

'We waited as long as we could but Robert had to get back home at some stage so we left while they were still trying to get hold of a pathologist.'

Lily had questions but Jack was unable to answer most of them. He was told he would have to wait for the post-mortem to find out how Greg died; he would hear if forensics discovered anything at the scene and they would send a report in due course if there were any further developments. 'Basically the case is back with them.'

Lily could see he was disappointed not to be more involved now that something important had emerged.

'They'll have to keep you up to date with developments,' she reassured him. 'But meanwhile, the fact he was buried proves his death wasn't natural and was premeditated, unless the killer normally carried a spade around with him. And he was buried in Cotterdale, about half a mile from where Amy was found. We've proved the deaths are linked.'

'Only geographically.'

'Don't forget the fingerprint from the bike that matches the one on Amy's keys.'

'Yes but Amy disappeared on the 7th of November and Greg didn't go missing until 24th.'

'But they didn't find her body until 28th so it's in the same timeline.'

'Do you think she was still alive until 24th?'

'No. According to the PM she was probably dead for a couple of weeks before they found her. They can do tests with insects and…'

'Whoa! I've just eaten so I don't need a detailed forensic explanation, thank you.'

They were interrupted by Eileen, who had come to offer them a hot drink but Jack yawned loudly, announcing he was going to watch a bit of telly in his room before having an early night. Lily said she would love a cup of tea and soon Eileen was back with a tray.

'He didn't get to his pool tournament, then?' she asked.

'No. Karl had to leave before Jack got back.'

'He's not turned out too bad, Karl, has he? He was a bit of a tearaway before he went to college. But he's settled down a lot now he works for his father.'

Lily grabbed her opportunity. 'He was telling me about his sister's friend, Kirsty.'

'A friend of Diana's?' She considered for a moment. 'Oh, ay. I don't know the lass but I know her mum, she used to work in the creamery.'

'He was telling me about the hotel where Kirsty works.'

'Where's that then?'

'Darlington. It belongs to the Grant family.' Lily waited but there was no sign of recognition. 'They've got another hotel round here somewhere, on their estate,' she continued.

'I know where you mean. My sister was there years ago and she still works on the catering side.' Lily must have looked puzzled because she continued, 'She helps with the shoots in Cotterdale. I told you before.'

'So the Grants own the catering company too?'

'Yes.' She turned to leave.

'Can I ask, does Kirsty help out when there's a shoot?'

Eileen looked bemused. 'I wouldn't know, love.' And

227

with that she was gone.

Jack flushed with pleasure when a cheer greeted him as he stepped through the door. Robert had already given Miriam the news that they'd located Greg Nevitt's body and she congratulated him on identifying where they should search.

'I have to admit, I thought it was a long shot,' she said, 'but I will take great pleasure in informing the DCI when we have our call this morning. Together with the matching print on Amy's keys, I think we can say there is a good possibility we have linked the two deaths, don't you?'

Everyone agreed but Lily pointed out that it didn't explain the connection.

'We'll have to wait for the forensics report and the PM. I'm sure the post-mortem will be done as a priority. I'll make sure they understand we need to hear straightaway when I speak to the DCI.'

Robert and Jack were upstairs drawing a cross in red felt-tip pen on the map, to indicate where Greg Nevitt's body was found. It matched the red cross for Amy's body. They were commenting on how close they both were to the red hatched search area for Brian Berry, when Miriam appeared. She wanted some privacy for her call to the DCI and so they left her to it.

'Is it a convenient time for our chat, Charles?' she began, without giving him a chance to reply, before telling him that Nevitt's body had been found.

'Well, that's something,' was his response.

'And the search team looking for Brian Berry will be out at the weekend.'

'I don't think that's possible, Miriam. We agreed...'

'Don't worry, it won't cost you a penny.'

She explained how the Mountain Rescue Team had risen to the occasion when they heard that the police wouldn't do it.'

'Couldn't, not wouldn't, Miriam,' he replied irritably. 'Any progress on the murdered girl?'

'Yes. A print on her car keys matches prints on Nevitt's bicycle, linking the two.'

He didn't respond so she went on to tell him about the chain used to lock the gate onto the estate, how it had been tampered with so it could be opened without unlocking the padlock. He coughed and pointed out it didn't help unless they knew who had done it.

Miriam sighed. 'You have to agree we are making great progress and I'm sure we only need a few more weeks to find the connections.'

'I think we agreed the deadline is Easter, didn't we?'

When she didn't respond, he said he had another meeting and she was cut off.

She was still sitting with her head in her hands when Lily peered over from the stairs.

'Coffee?'

Miriam looked up. 'Yes please.'

'And may I have a word?'

'Of course. Why don't you bring our coffees up here?'

While she waited, Miriam reviewed the situation. Clearly Charles had no intention of helping so she needed to find an ally elsewhere, and since the cases where centred on North Yorkshire's patch, she would have to look there for support. Unfortunately she might have to ask Robert who to call.

Lily came back carefully balancing two mugs in one

hand and a plate in the other.

'Robert's mother sent some biscuits to celebrate the successful search.'

'That sounds rather macabre.' Miriam took one and examined it. 'So what did you want to discuss?'

'It's about the catering company,' Lily began.

After the last call, Miriam knew there was no way there would be any further funding. 'I'm sorry but there's nothing left in the budget for DNA tests and it would raise too much public interest when we have no guarantee…'

'No! Sorry to interrupt but that's not what I wanted to ask. I just wanted permission to get a list of people who have worked for them in the last year. I know someone who can do that for me. She's my landlady's sister. It was her who got me in contact with Mr Mackintosh. She thinks we're investigating poaching so it won't raise any interest.'

Miriam picked up her mug. It was instant coffee but it was nice and not too strong. She sighed. 'To be honest Lily, anything you can do at this stage is fine by me so long as it doesn't cost anything.'

They sat staring at the map together.

'I should start a timeline,' Lily announced suddenly, 'now we've got a link, because the dates are rather confusing.'

'How do you mean?'

'Amy was reported missing on the 7th of November, and probably died that day, but she wasn't found here until 28th.' She put her finger on the red cross with an A. 'Greg Nevitt's bicycle tracker indicates that he was alive here until 24th.' She pointed to the other red cross, marked with a G.

'Are you saying he could be responsible for her death?'

'I don't think so. The fingerprint match points to the same unknown person helping Amy try to start her car and handling the bike. There is nothing to link Amy and Greg directly.'

Miriam stared at the two red crosses. 'Except the proximity of the bodies.'

'There's one more date I want to include in the timeline,' continued Lily. 'It's about the chain that was tampered with. It was replaced by the keeper in the week he retired, sometime between Monday 16th and Friday 20th.'

'And the relevance is?'

Lily shook her head. 'I don't know but I'm sure it's significant.'

She carried the mugs to the kitchen and Miriam went back to her desk. Jack was hovering by Robert, who was on the phone, listening more than talking. When he'd finished, he turned to Jack with a smile.

'Ok, so he says the PM will be done today and the forensics should be completed by tomorrow morning.'

'Tomorrow? That means I won't see it until Monday,' Jack moaned.

'Not necessarily, they know we need it urgently.'

'Was that West Yorkshire?' Miriam asked. 'Who's your contact? I need to catch up with the investigating officer.'

Robert scribbled on a notepad, tore off the sheet and handed it to her. He'd written a name and mobile number. 'He's an old mate. He said he'd make sure we get the information as soon as they have it.'

'Thanks Robert, we need a friend down there.'

Lily was busy with a large sheet of paper and a felt-tip

pen and when she'd finished, she stuck it on the wall upstairs. She'd used different colours: red for Amy and blue for Greg. Everyone gazed at it until Robert spoke.

'Have you got a green pen for Brian? I need to add his last sighting as well.'

It was the first time that all three cases had been literally drawn together and they continued to stare as Robert added a vertical green arrow to Amy's red timeline on the 7th of November.

Chapter 26

'Thanks for arranging for me to meet your sister again, Eileen.'

Lily was back at the B&B to meet Joyce. Apparently, she went to Leyburn market on a Friday morning but would come straight over when she got back.

'That's all right, pet. She was due to drop some wool in for me anyway. Tuck in,' she ordered. 'I'll make a pot of tea.'

Eileen had promised to 'rustle up a snack', but the table was covered in plates of savouries, sandwiches, crisps, and cake.

Lily took a sausage roll but she wasn't feeling hungry. She wanted her meeting with Joyce to appear a casual enquiry about catering at Cotterdale but the woman was bound to ask why she wanted the information. The poaching story was beginning to wear a bit thin.

Eileen dashed in to deposit a tea tray on the table before going to open the front door. Joyce came in, removed her coat and hung it over the back of a chair.

'Hello again,' she said to Lily. 'Did you find Mr Mackintosh?'

'I did thank you. It was very helpful.'

'Really?' Joyce helped herself to sandwiches before taking a seat. 'How's that?'

Lily could feel herself reddening. 'He was telling me about the security arrangements.' Joyce didn't show any interest. 'Yes,' she continued. 'He told me about the padlock and chain on the gate to the estate.'

Eileen was pouring out the tea and handing a cup to her sister.

Lily decided to keep going. 'I wondered how the catering staff had access during a shoot.'

Joyce looked up, appearing to consider the question. 'I suppose they had a key,' she replied. 'Yes, I'm sure someone must have had a key because we didn't have to wait to be let in.'

Hadn't the old keeper said there were no other keys? Lily let it go and went on to explain why she wanted to speak to Joyce.

'Would you be able to tell me who was involved in catering for the estate last season?'

Joyce looked at her sister then back at Lily. 'Can I ask why? Because it seems to me that you're casting aspersions and I know that not one of them is a poacher.'

Lily apologised. She hadn't meant anything by it, she explained. It was just that she had to make a thorough report to complete the investigation. Eileen poured her sister another cup of tea and she calmed down. Lily pulled out her notebook.

'I understand the company belongs to the Grants?'

'Yes Giles and Yvonne own it. Their son, Alistair, helps when he's not at college.'

Between them, the sisters began a list of names that included Kirsty's mum, Di and her mother.

Lily remarked that they were all women. Joyce and Eileen conferred, finally agreeing that last season, once or twice, a couple of the young lads had helped out with the heavy carrying. Joyce named them, adding, 'And, of course, Karl usually tags along if Diana is working.'

Lily left them to their lunch. There was a name on the list that had grabbed her attention. Karl was the only close friend of Amy's who hadn't been questioned at the time of her death because he hadn't been drinking in the bar at Kirkby Stephen and there was no known link to the estate... until now. As soon as she was back in the office, she told Jack what she'd discovered.

'Do you think he and Amy were more than just friends?' she suggested.

'The others would have known.'

'Not necessarily, although it could explain why Kirsty is in such a state.'

'What? You're not suggesting *he* killed Amy?'

'I'm just thinking aloud. What if he went to Kirkby Stephen to give her a lift when her car wouldn't start and then they had an argument? He might have seen her with someone in the bar or flirting with a customer. Jealousy is a strong motive.'

Jack wasn't willing to believe her.

'It's easily proved,' she said quietly. 'We've got a fingerprint and DNA on Amy's keys.'

'You can't get his prints without arresting him, can you?' he asked in a whisper, looking in Miriam's direction.

She smiled and changed the subject. 'Have you had the PM report yet?'

'Nothing and no forensics either.'

'Would you like me to ring my friend at the Wakefield lab for you?'

Jack groaned. 'Not you as well. Is everything down to who you know?'

'No but it helps speed things up sometimes.'

However, Jack was grateful to Robert for chasing the PM report when it finally arrived later that afternoon. After reading it, he picked out the important sections for the others.

'Injuries pointing to a collision with a vehicle at speed, including a broken pelvis... damage suggesting he was dragged across rough ground... estimated time of death: several months ago, considering the winter temperatures and reduced insect activity. He bled out in the shallow pit where he was buried, so was still alive but probably unconscious when he was placed there.'

The room was silent as they digested the information. Greg Nevitt had developed a personality during the investigation, mainly as a result of Jack's desire to get to the truth of his disappearance. They referred to him as Greg and discussed his obsession with cycling, wondering how he could bear to camp out in the middle of November, and felt sympathy when they learned he chose to spend his meagre funds on a bunk barn to shelter from the worst of the weather.

Miriam cleared her throat. 'So we assume he was hit by a vehicle on the road, then dragged into the woods to be buried in a shallow grave. It sounds premeditated if the driver was carrying a spade.'

Robert pointed out that he always carried one in his boot during the winter. 'I've got one in there now, together with a blanket and a woolly hat.'

Jack grinned at Lily. She ignored him and suggested it explained the green paint found on the bike. She went to the timeline, adding "collision with green vehicle" against 24th November, with the blue pen.

Robert said the vehicle must belong to someone local

to Cotterdale because the road finished in the village. The driver would have no reason to be there unless he was visiting someone, or poaching.

Jack was sceptical. 'At seven in the evening?'

'It was dark by then in November,' Robert snapped back.

'Were there lights on the bicycle?' Miriam asked. 'If not, the collision could have been an accident.'

Everyone looked at Jack. 'I think so. I can check,' he said.

It was left for Jack to find out. Robert briefed Miriam on his plans for the search over the weekend before leaving early to get organised, as he put it. As soon as Jack confirmed the bike was fitted with lights front and rear, Lily said she was leaving so he'd better hurry or he would have to walk back to "The Pines". Miriam was left alone, staring at Lily's timeline, wondering what Robert might add in green pen after the weekend search, if anything.

She drove to the cottage without any plans for the next two days. She would have liked to join the search for Brian Berry but would probably get in the way of the experts from the rescue team. She would get her shopping in the village, maybe go for a walk on Sunday. She parked the car and hurried to the front door before the headlights faded. To her surprise there was a parcel on the doorstep, at least an unsealed cardboard box that obviously hadn't come through the post. Once she was in the kitchen with the lights on, she could see the box had once held dog food. Curious, she opened it up to find a note inside from William. *Enclosed is a nice bit of meat for Sunday lunch (you invited me for a meal so I thought it would be the best time as your busy). Its dexter.* She tutted at his spelling, wondering who dexter was, or had been, as she pulled out a plastic bag containing a large joint of beef.

Lily broached the subject on the way back to "The Pines". 'We need to get prints and DNA from Karl. I think the best way is on a glass. Why don't you invite him out for a drink?'

'What, and walk out of a pub with a glass? No way.'

'Indoors then? You've got a stash of beer in your room, haven't you?'

'I have.' He went quiet for a while. 'I could offer him a bottle, would that do?'

'Perfect but it needs to be clean. You'll have to wash it and dry it carefully. You'd better let me to do that. We can put it on the table pristine. All you need to do is ask him round.'

'For drinks in "The Pines"?'

'No, before you go out. I'll have to take the bottle straight up to Sylvie for analysis.'

'Tomorrow night then?'

'No Jack, tonight!'

He eventually agreed to give Karl a call and was surprised when he accepted straight away. They arranged to meet at the B&B at eight o'clock.

After the usual Friday fish and chips, Lily took the beer bottle to her room and washed it thoroughly, drying it with toilet paper. She carried it downstairs carefully in several sheets of paper and placed it on the table. At her request, Jack produced a second bottle which he opened with his bottle opener.

'Quick give me that,' ordered Lily and rushed upstairs repeating the process to clean it thoroughly.

When she returned with the bottle opener, she explained it would be good for fingerprints. There was an awkward moment when Eileen came to clear the table and nearly picked the bottle up but Lily swooped in to pass her the plates and it was left untouched.

Karl arrived on time and was ushered into the sitting room to wait for Jack, who had disappeared upstairs as planned. He was wearing a quilted jacket and gloves. Lily insisted he remove them to get the benefit when he went outside. He joked that she sounded like his mother.

'Jack's beer is the one that's open. Have one if you like.'

She watched him take the bottle opener, remove the cap from the bottle and put it to his lips. Now she had begun to suspect him of killing Amy, she found it difficult to make small talk. She desperately wanted to ask about the dodgy chain but didn't want to alert him to the fact they knew about it.

'How's Di? I haven't seen her for a while.'

'She's in the car actually.'

'Oh, she's coming as well. In that case I'll get my coat.'

Upstairs she sent a text to Sylvie asking if she would do her a huge favour and test the beer bottle that she planned to secrete in her bedroom before they left the house.

Karl's car was what Lily called a pick-up truck although it probably had a fancier name. It looked black under the streetlight but could have been a dark green. It had four seats with a big open area at the back for carrying stuff, although it was empty when she peered in. Karl drove them to a pub in Leyburn that had Sky Sports so they could watch the football, England were playing Italy. That was fine by Lily as it meant she would have Di to herself once drinks were bought and the lads had gone into the other bar.

'How's Kirsty?' she began.

Di pulled a face. 'No better. She wouldn't come out tonight and she's leaving the hotel. I told her she was daft to hand in her notice but she says she doesn't want to stay on.'

'Do you know why?'

'No idea.'

They sat quietly for a minute or two.

'I hear you help with the catering when there's a shoot in Cotterdale.' There was no point in beating about the bush, as her mother would say.

'The season's over now,' she replied, taking a sip of her vodka and grapefruit juice.

How should Lily express it? She decided to be partially honest. 'I'm investigating poaching and I wondered how vehicles get on and off the estate when the gate is always locked. Do the caterers have a key?'

Di swished the straw round her glass.

Lily pressed her. 'Is there a way to get in without a key?'

The girl sucked on the straw. 'There was. There isn't now.'

'Really?' Lily's heart was racing, she guessed what was coming.

'There's a chain and padlock now.'

'But there was before.'

'Yeah, well it wasn't exactly… secure.'

'What d'you mean?'

'There was a way of undoing it without a key.'

'So you could undo it?'

'I didn't need to because I'd get a lift with Karl.'

Sylvie had replied to her text but Lily didn't read it until she was back at the B&B. Her friend had left a message to say she was working at the weekend and to call her at the lab any time after eight in the morning. Lily wasn't going to wait to have a telephone call, so she told Jack she was taking the bottle to Carlisle first thing tomorrow and to tell Eileen she didn't need breakfast.

Early next morning she put the bottle and opener, in a large brown envelope. She placed the envelope upright in a hessian bag and carried it to her car, where she wedged it carefully in the footwell of the back seat. The roads were quiet and she felt a sense of excitement as she joined the motorway and put her foot down, smiling to herself when she thought of the surprise Sylvie would have when she arrived.

But her friend was busy in the lab so Lily had a long wait before she appeared, looking disgruntled.

'I told you I was working today,' she began. 'You could've called.' She sat behind down and rummaged in the desk drawers.

'You might not have wanted to see me.'

She looked up. 'I don't.' Her face broke into a puzzled frown as Lily pulled the envelope out of her bag. 'What is it this time?'

'A beer bottle and opener.'

'I can see that.'

Lily asked if she could get prints and DNA as soon as possible, as a favour. Sylvie wanted to know what sort of favour because it would have to be paid for by someone.

'Have you got a signature?' she asked.

Lily explained she was getting one but time was of the essence. Once she'd convinced her that she had official sanction, it was agreed Sylvie would check the prints and DNA against those found on Amy's keys.

'I can put it on the same batch number as the keys for you.'

'Thanks Sylvie, you're a real friend.'

'Well, don't tell anyone you've skipped the queue. Luckily it won't take long.'

'Can I wait?'

'It won't be that quick! All I can promise is you'll definitely have the results by Monday.'

'Morning?'

'OK, Monday morning.'

'You're a star. Can I get you something? Coffee? Doughnuts? Chocolate?'

'Just go, Lily, please. I've got a load of things to finish by lunchtime. I promise I'll let you know the moment I get the results.'

Chapter 27

Robert had set his alarm for six but was already half-dressed when it went off. When he tiptoed downstairs, he was met with the smell of bacon; his mother was still in her dressing gown but cooking breakfast for him. She ordered him to sit down while she did the eggs. He explained he was in a hurry so could she just put the bacon in some bread. She insisted on making up a thermos and packing a picnic while he ate his bacon sandwich and quickly downed a scalding cup of tea. It was nearly seven o'clock when he left; Jean would be waiting for him.

The forecast was good, it was going to be warmer than usual with outbreaks of sunshine, and Robert had a good feeling about today, partly due to travelling through the Dales with Jean in the passenger seat. She looked very professional in an expensive waterproof jacket. He noticed she was wearing suitable footwear too. When he asked whether she did much fieldwork, she told him about research trips to countries around the world. The journey seemed to take half the usual time and they were parking in Hardraw by just after eight.

'I brought a flask of coffee,' Jean said, reaching for the rucksack she'd thrown in the back. She had thought of everything, including enough food and drink for them both. 'Shall we have it while we wait for the others?'

She raised her cup. 'Here's to a successful day!'

Robert sighed.

'Cheer up,' she said. 'You've done your research, very

thoroughly from what you've told me. If we don't find him, he's probably never meant to be found.'

Robert asked her to give him an idea of what state Brian's body might be in if they were lucky enough to locate him after four months.

'It depends where he's been lying, whether the ground is wet or dry, acid or alkali...'

Robert listened to Jean as she gave him a lecture on the decomposition stages of a body on the ground. Her voice had lost most of its local accent, due to being a lecturer by profession, he supposed. It was a confident voice. He was impressed with her knowledge of the subject and asked whether she'd ever thought of working for the force. She laughed and said she'd always had a suspicion of the police, a sign of a misspent youth perhaps.

Robert smiled. 'My mother still considers you a juvenile delinquent, you know.'

She laughed. 'Really?' She put her hand on his arm. 'Am I leading you astray?'

Robert was about to say that he wouldn't mind but they were interrupted by the arrival of the Mountain Rescue vehicle. Soon they were joining a group of athletic looking men and women, listening to the briefing from the team leader. He made it clear that if they had to attend an emergency call, they would leave straight away. When Robert asked if they had a dog with them, he was told that the handler wasn't available.

The rescue team had been involved in the original search for Brian Berry in Swaledale and so Robert had to describe why he thought the body could be to the west of Great Shunner Fell. He introduced Jean as his bone expert, which drew a sharp look from her. She clarified her role, explaining she was the osteoarchaeologist who could help identify the age of any bones that were found.

The team leader said he was used to receiving a search strategy from the police. Robert reached into his rucksack and produced copies of the area that he had shaded on the big map back in the office.

'I don't know how you want to play it,' he said, 'but this is where he's going to be, if he's here.'

They peered over the leader's shoulder and he divided them into two groups. They set off in the Land Rovers, leaving Robert and Jean to follow on foot. Jean took his arm as they walked quickly up the track signposted to The Pennine Way.

'This would be quite exciting if it wasn't a search for a dead man. Did you say his name was Brian?' Jean asked.

'Yes. He was a nice old boy, walking the Herriot Way alone.'

'How old was he?'

'Eighty, but he was quite fit apparently.'

'And did he have family?'

'His wife died early last year but he had children and grandchildren.' The death of his own wife was not a topic he had talked about so far. It wasn't something he wanted to discuss with Jean.

In the distance the vehicles had finally stopped and they watched the two teams dispersing. When they finally reached the vehicles, they found a young man waiting, radio in hand. They checked it was all right to follow the group heading down into the valley and set off across the rough moorland, through mud, then bog. Jean laughed as she tripped and nearly fell. A curlew cried high above them and she stopped to watch it disappear behind the peak of Great Shunner Fell.

'It's really beautiful up here,' she said, 'but very desolate.'

'There is a village over there but that's where the road stops. They call it a dead-end dale when it goes nowhere.'

'Seems appropriate.'

They walked on in silence until they reached the nearest group, and followed at a distance for several hours, stopping occasionally to watch the team covering the ground. It was getting on for mid-day and Robert was wondering if it would seem crass to mention how hungry he was, when a shout went up. He thought they'd found something as the group turned and made their way towards them, but it was not good news. They'd had a shout out from Coverdale where someone had got separated from a walking group.

'Sorry mate, but we've got to be on standby over there. We'll try to get back tomorrow. I'll call you.'

He watched them make their way back to their vehicles, where they were joined by the other team. Soon the two Land Rovers were moving away down the track. He sighed.

'Never mind,' said Jean with false jollity. 'We've got lunch and it's a nice day for it. We can carry on after we've eaten.'

So they found a patch where the ground didn't feel too damp and perched side by side. Jean unpacked her contribution to the picnic and Robert added his mother's meat paste sandwiches and fruit cake.

'Just one piece?' asked Jean with a laugh. 'You didn't tell her I was coming with you?'

He felt himself reddening. 'I must've forgotten.'

She nudged him so hard he nearly fell sideways. 'Liar!'

Robert was having more fun than he'd had in a long time, so he was delighted when Jean suggested they carry on searching for Mr Berry's remains, as she called them.

She suggested working in a systematic fashion, using GPS and the ordnance survey map she'd downloaded onto her phone in preparation for the search. Robert was impressed with how organised she was. They must have walked miles that afternoon, tramping up and down over streams and bogs, helping each other over the rougher parts. The time went quickly and Robert was surprised and disappointed when the light began to fade.

'Never mind, we'll be back tomorrow, even if the rescue team aren't.'

On the drive back, Jean suggested stopping for a meal. 'I know a really nice place on the road not far from Grassington, if we can go that way.'

Robert would have agreed to anything to extend his time with her. 'I'll just have to ring to let them know I'll be late.'

'Why not stay at mine tonight, to save time?'

His surprise must have been visible because she added, 'Don't worry, Robert, you're quite safe, I have a very spacious spare room.'

'Did you sleep well?' Jean asked as she offered Robert a plate of toast and poured coffee into two mugs.

He nodded, his mouth full of toast.

'Liar! I heard you marching about in the night.'

It was true, he didn't get many hours sleep. It might have been the strange surroundings and not having his pyjamas with him, but he admitted the excitement of the previous day was probably to blame.

They left early, only to discover that the clocks had gone forward overnight and so it was nearly nine when they parked in Hardraw. The sun was trying to emerge from a covering of cloud and there was a light wind but it promised to be another pleasant day weather-wise. They set off up the track, ready to continue their solitary sweep of the area. Robert had heard nothing from the rescue team so he was surprised to see one of their vehicles in the distance.

'They're here. Quick let's see what's happening.' He only realised that he'd left Jean behind when he stopped by the Land Rover. Already he could see a small group heading across the moorland and the lad with the vehicle confirmed they would be joined by the others and they would work unless they were called away again. Robert waited for Jean to catch up then set off towards the group, to let them know where they'd covered yesterday afternoon. It was agreed that he would continue to search that corner of the map with Jean, while they cracked on.

They'd only been walking for around ten minutes when a second Land Rover appeared and the group, including a border collie, emerged from the vehicle. Soon they were marching towards the far end of Robert's search area. He watched the handler let the dog loose to follow his own path.

'That'll speed things up.'

'Are the dogs trained to find dead bodies?' Jean asked.

'Hopefully they're usually looking for living ones but they're trained to sniff out anything human, even property.'

'I guess it's good that the weather is being kind, it must

make it easier.'

They carried on slowly, with Jean checking her phone to mark where they'd been before turning round for the next sweep. She expressed surprise that they'd found nothing so far, not even a cartridge case.

'I don't think the shoot comes out this far, not for pheasants,' replied Robert.

They stopped for a coffee mid-morning and stood watching the collie covering the fellside. It wasn't long after they resumed their work when they heard a shout.

'Not again!' cried Robert. 'Well that's it. Once they've gone, we might as well pack up too.'

Jean grabbed his arm. 'Wait. I think they might have found something.'

As they watched, the groups were gravitating to where the handler was putting his dog on its lead. They stopped, forming a ring a few yards away from him. They weren't hurrying back to the vehicles but Robert still assumed they were being briefed about a call-out. He didn't dare hope they'd actually found something.

'Quick, let's get over there,' called Jean, who was already stumbling across the rough ground, half running to where they were all gathered.

'No wait. It may be nothing,' he called.

But they were drawn towards the team, walking slowly, expecting to be told they were leaving. Finally, when they were within calling distance the leader turned and waved them over.

Chapter 28

Miriam did a big shop on Saturday morning then spent the rest of the day cleaning the cottage. She put off calling William until later because he was probably busy with lambs or calves, or whatever he did on the farm, at least that was her excuse. She was half hoping that the note inviting himself to lunch was a joke but when he answered her call, she knew he was serious. He immediately asked what time he should come round.

'I, er... when do you think?' she replied.

'I'll be free by mid-day.'

'Right. Good. And thank you for the beef, by the way. Is it yours?'

He laughed. 'No, but I do know where it was raised.' There was an awkward silence. 'Right, I'll see you tomorrow then.'

It was a short conversation and, as soon as she was off the phone, she went online to discover how to cook roast beef in her ancient stove. She found numerous Aga recipes that looked wonderful but she assumed they were cooked in an oven that was controllable, not dependent on the wind direction. She spent the evening panicking about the meal and went to bed dreading the following day.

No-one had told her the clocks had gone forward by an hour overnight, so it wasn't until she put on the radio to discover that "The Archers" omnibus had started already, that she realised her mistake. William would appear in one hour and she hadn't even topped up the stove yet. The temperature gauge on the oven indicated she would be hard-pressed to cook even a meringue currently. She collected a bucket of coal from the shed and poured it in, hoping it wouldn't kill the fire completely then began peeling potatoes and carrots, after which she would get changed. But by the time she'd finished, the stove had gone out. A green Land Rover sailed past the window as she was struggling with firelighters and kindling, hands blackened by coal. Cursing, she went to open the door.

William presented her with a bottle of wine on the doorstep. He'd made an effort with his appearance, she thought, looking down at her mucky jeans. She opened the door wide and led the way into the kitchen.

'The stoves gone out,' she announced.

He regarded it with an authoritative air. 'May I help? My mother used to cook on one of these.'

She was going to object but he was already opening the door and poking about inside the firebox. Then he stood up and peered at the knobs on top. He twisted one this way and that.

'Don't get your sweater dirty,' she warned. It was a nice pale beige and looked like lambswool.

He pulled it over his head, handed it to her, and rolled up his sleeves. Miriam went to fetch wine glasses, pouring them both a drink from the bottle she'd bought especially. The kitchen was becoming quite smoky but she could see flames beginning to take hold. Eventually he shut the door and fiddled with the settings.

'Do you know how to use this?' he asked, standing up and accepting the glass from her.

'Yes, I found a booklet in the drawer.'

He fiddled with the knobs again. 'You've got it set wrongly but I'm wondering if this control is doing anything anyway. It might need some maintenance. Does it ever work well?'

'It heats the water all right but the oven depends on which way the wind's blowing.'

He laughed. She was about to suggest she would pop up to get changed when her mobile rang. It was Robert. He had updated her last night to say the search was over without success.

'I'd better take this,' she said. 'Help yourself to more wine.' She went into the hallway. 'Robert?' She had to tell him to repeat what he was saying. He was speaking fast, excitement in his voice. They had found the decomposing remains of a man, a rucksack beside him. They haven't touched anything. North Yorkshire CID were on their way but should she contact Cleveland as it's their case? No, Robert, I won't ring Cleveland, she thought. She wasn't going to let Charles snatch their victory away from them. She told him she would come over so could he arrange for a Land Rover to pick her up at Hardraw.

Back in the kitchen she cleared her throat. 'I've got to go out, it's urgent. I'm sorry. Perhaps another time?'

She went upstairs to get her boots and grabbed her warmest coat. Back downstairs, William was still fiddling with the Rayburn.

'Can you shut the door when you go?' she asked. 'You have to pull it quite hard so please make sure it's locked.'

She drove too fast, nearly colliding with a quad bike coming round the bend as she approached the main road. It took no more than ten minutes to reach Hardraw, where a Swaledale Mountain Rescue vehicle was waiting for her. The driver said the search dog had located the body hidden in a small gill. She imagined that decomposition would be quite advanced if it had been lying in water and wasn't relishing arriving at the crime scene. The driver stopped the Land Rover, pointing to where, in the distance, four figures stood but there was no sign of a dog.

'The others had to leave. We just waited to provide support if the body has to be stretchered out.'

They walked together across the grass and heather, occasionally hopping across boggy patches. Robert was striding across to meet her.

'It definitely looks like Brian Berry,' he said, then corrected himself. 'Well, it doesn't *look* like him but he's got a rucksack with him.'

'Have you examined it?'

'No. I thought it better to wait for you.'

A woman in the group introduced herself as Professor McGovern. She said the deceased has reached a stage of decomposition called adipocere formation, a waxy layer due to the water, which tends to prevent further decomposition. However, there has been animal interference, that's what the professor had called it, which might make cause of death more difficult. Miriam assumed that meant there would be bits missing. She wasn't looking forward to viewing the remains. She stepped nearer and peered into the ditch. Robert was correct, the sight couldn't have looked less like Brian Berry; under the rotting clothes, the skin was white and waxy.

The forensic pathologist contacted by the North Yorkshire force had said there was no point in coming out to the crime scene, he'd do the PM on Monday. They were trying to contact someone from forensics, but after four months there was little chance of finding anything useful. The general view was to get the body out and over to the mortuary as soon as possible. Miriam wasn't sure she could stomach the sight of whatever was in the ditch being pulled out, but Professor McGovern had some helpful suggestions and the rescue team were willing to offer their services. They went off to get their equipment, leaving the three of them alone.

'Well done Robert, and thank you Professor for your expert assistance.'

'Please call me Jean. I wasn't expecting to be much help. Although I have studied decomposition quite extensively, I've never seen an example of adipocere formation in the flesh, so to speak.' She gave a fleeting smile.

Robert asked Miriam if she'd contacted the Cleveland investigating officer, wondering if they would want to send a crime scene manager. She avoided the question by offering to follow the Land Rover to the mortuary to ensure the chain of custody was maintained. The forensic pathologist had asked for the body to go to Harrogate, a three-hour round trip. She would also attend the post-mortem on the following morning and ensure a forensics team visited the crime scene as soon as possible. Meanwhile it might be wise to do a fingertip search of the immediate area in case anything turned up.

It took well over an hour of careful manipulation under instructions from Jean, who had more experience than the others on moving bodies that were in a state of decay, before what remained of Mr Berry was safely transferred to the body bag and onto a stretcher. Miriam was immensely relieved when the manoeuvrings were over and the body was being carried across moorland to the Land Rover.

The change to British Summer Time meant there was an extra hour of daylight, allowing Robert and Jean plenty of time to cover the area on either side of the gill. Their search uncovered nothing out of the ordinary and at seven o' clock, they made their way wearily back down the track, carrying Berry's heavy rucksack between them.

'Drink?' Robert asked, when they arrived back in Hardraw. He wasn't particularly hungry but thought Jean might want something to eat, since she had seemed unaffected by the sight and smell of the grotesque corpse.

'Good idea,' she said brightly.

Miriam swung her car onto the track down to the cottage. It had been a long wait at the hospital, she was tired and looking forward to a large glass of wine. First she noticed the lights on in the cottage then spotted William's Land Rover outside. There was no sound when she opened the door but the kitchen was warm and smelled of cooking. She tiptoed through to the sitting room to find William stretched out on the sofa, with an empty glass on the floor beside him, and "Antiques Roadshow" on the television with the sound down. He was fast asleep.

'You're still here,' she remarked, picking up the glass and placing it next to the empty bottle on the coffee table.

He opened his eyes, staring at her for a couple of seconds before jumping up and rushing into the kitchen. Miriam could hear him opening the oven door.

'Just caught it in time!' he called. 'If you'd been much later it would have been overdone.'

She followed him into the kitchen, where he was transferring the meat onto a plate. She watched him pour fat from the roasting tin before adding stock and putting it on the simmering plate.

'You're very late,' he commented without turning round.

'I didn't expect you'd be waiting,' she mumbled, unsure whether to be pleased or annoyed that he hadn't gone home as she'd asked him to.

'I thought you'd need something to eat when you got back. I had to make a few adjustments to the controls before I fired this beast up again,' he explained. 'You haven't been using it in an optimum way.'

'Really?'

He told her to open the bottle of wine he'd brought and pour herself a glass. 'You look shattered,' he added.

Great, Miriam thought, but she didn't argue. She sat at the table watching him put the finishing touches to the roast dinner. To complete the effect, at the last minute he produced four large Yorkshire puddings from the oven.

'There,' he announced finally, placing a plate in front of her. 'You must be starving.'

She couldn't bring herself to tell him that she really wasn't. 'It looks wonderful.'

'Dexters are excellent beef cattle,' he said. 'This comes from a small village abattoir and the carcass is hung for a month. The marbling of fat maintains the moisture when it's cooking...'

'Lovely,' Miriam snapped, feeling a wave of nausea at the memory of the crime scene. 'Sorry, I mean it's very nice but...'

'Are you all right?'

'It's been a long day.'

'I wondered why you had to rush away but when I saw your name on that file on the table, I guess you're a police detective, DI Abbott.'

She must have looked alarmed because he insisted that he hadn't looked inside the file.

'I didn't know how long you'd be but I thought I'd sort out the stove for you then I carried on cooking the beef because I needed something to eat anyway. I would have washed up before I left.'

Miriam couldn't resist the yorkshires, the roast vegetables, and the gravy. Soon she was enjoying the beef as well.

'So what were you doing today that was so urgent?' he asked casually.

'Oh just a poaching case,' she lied.

He raised his eyebrows. 'Cotterdale?'

'How do you know that?' she asked, thinking about the file.

He shrugged. 'Just heard the police were round there.'

'Yes. We found someone and I had to accompany him down to Harrogate.'

He looked at her with his head on one side, then carried on eating. Perhaps she wasn't a convincing liar.

After dinner William made coffee then offered to wash up but she forbade him to touch the dishes. He had done too much already, she said, hoping it didn't sound ungrateful. They were by the fire in the sitting room and she'd been staring into her coffee mug for a while when he said he really should be going, because she looked all in and needed to rest.

'I'll find my own way out,' he said. 'See you later.' With

that he was gone.

Miriam was going to wash up but instead she headed upstairs for a shower and was in bed by ten o'clock. But she couldn't shake off the image of Brian Berry's body. When she was with Henry they would talk over cases for hours, examining facts, playing devil's advocate. They called it the daily de-brief, over a drink before dinner. Tonight it would have been good to be able to lay out all the pieces, like a jigsaw, and see how they fitted together. She had to admit it was nice to come home to a hot meal but how strange for William to have waited all that time for her. And then there was the Amy Hobson file she'd stupidly left in the kitchen. Had he really not peeked inside? She was sure she would have had a quick look. She went downstairs to flick through the file until she found the relevant list of interviews. There was an entry against a William Hill at his address – he had been a beater on the Cotterdale estate at the time of Amy's death.

Chapter 29

Miriam had attended a number of post-mortems before this one but she still couldn't decide whether it was preferable for the body to look like a human being or not. Dr David Wrench, the forensic pathologist, said he'd seen worse, but the cadaver was in a bad state so it was fortunate he'd had a distinctive dental plate which would make identification easier. She immediately sent a message to Jack to check it out.

The pathologist moved down the body examining it carefully as he went, giving notes and cursing occasionally at the fragility of the skin when it came away.

'What's this?'

Miriam, who had become used to him talking to himself, assumed he wasn't addressing her. She watched him holding something carefully to the light.

'Hair in his... right hand.' He immediately bagged it.

This is it, thought Miriam. 'Dark, light?' she asked.

'Fair hair, longish,' he replied without looking up.

Dr Wrench continued working slowly, occasionally muttering under his breath. She received the impression that the organs were in a bad state.

'Have you come across grave wax,' he suddenly asked, looking up.

'Not until now.'

'It's caused by anaerobic bacterial hydrolysis of fat in the tissue. It acts like a preservative, slowing down decomposition so it makes my job more difficult when it comes to time of death. He could have stayed like this for years.'

'We know when he went missing,' she offered.

'A few months ago?'

'Yes.'

He nodded and resumed his work. After an hour he stopped to stretch his back. 'That said, I don't think I'm going to get much information from the organs, they're so badly decomposed.'

There was a pause while tissue samples were prepared and the body moved very carefully to allow the next stage to begin. Two hours passed, the pathologist was working on the skull when the door opened and a tall young man burst in.

'DI Abbott!' he demanded. 'Can I have a word?'

Dr Wrench looked up crossly. 'Please wait outside. I'll come out to see you when I've finished.' He looked at Miriam. 'You too... and leave your gown in here.'

As soon as they were both out in the corridor the man swung round to confront her. 'Why didn't you let me know that you'd found a body?' he demanded.

'And you are?' She knew exactly who he was.

'DI Parkes, Cleveland CID.'

Parkes was only a DS when she'd known him. Presumably he'd been promoted before taking over the case. 'I'm so sorry. I did try to contact your colleague,' she lied.

'I heard it from the DCI. He's not happy about the protocol.'

'Oh dear, I'll call him. In fact I'll go and do it now.'

She walked quickly along the corridor and down into the main entrance before he could reply. It was still raining so she sheltered under the canopy at the entrance to make her call, not to Charles but to Jack.

'Did you get the dental records?' she asked.

'Yes, I've emailed them to you.'

'Thanks.'

'Although we're sure it's him because the rucksack had his diary in it.'

'You've examined it?'

'Only a very tiny search. Lily said it would be all right if we wore gloves and didn't turn everything out. She can guarantee chain of custody for the evidence.'

'Can she?'

'Robert says the diary confirms he left Hawes late.'

'Does he?'

'How's the PM going?'

'Fine. I'm waiting for it to finish then I'll be back.' She could see Parkes coming towards her. 'Got to go.'

He approached to within a few feet of her. 'The pathologist wants to see you,' he said, before heading towards the car park.

She went back to where Dr Wrench was sitting in his office.

'Coffee?' he asked, pushing a mug towards her.

'Thank you.'

'So who was that rude young man who intruded on my autopsy?'

'DI Parkes, Cleveland CID. He's gone now.'

'I know. I sent him away with a flea in his ear. He didn't have permission to attend and I told him so.'

'He's in charge of the case at the Cleveland end.'

'So he said but as I pointed out, your name was on the referral to the coroner so you're the one with permission to attend, not him.'

Miriam reckoned Parkes would be driving straight back to Middlesbrough, which meant she had an hour and a half before the proverbial hit the fan.

'So,' he continued. 'You missed the best part, unfortunately. The poor chap has a fractured skull. It may not have been immediately terminal but if he was lying in the open for long it would be the end of him. Could he have fallen from height?'

'Not where he was found. It was quite flat.' She pulled up a photo on her phone.

'No, indeed. That confirms my conclusion that he had a severe blow to the head.'

She remembered to show him Berry's dental records and he nodded, saying the plate was definitely a match.

'What about the hair?' she asked.

'Ah, yes, the hair. Several strands gripped in his right hand. Could they be his?'

'He was nearly bald, just a bit of white hair.'

'In that case, they may belong to the assailant.'

Miriam rang Lily before deciding to send the hair to the Cumbria forensic lab, because Amy Hobson was blonde so it could be hers. Lily offered to drive to Carlisle as soon as her boss arrived back with the sample. Miriam waited for Dr Wrench to fetch the paperwork then signed the chain of custody form before receiving the evidence bag in a padded envelope. The pathologist promised to send a copy of his report by the end of the day.

The journey from Harrogate took exactly an hour and a half. So, once Lily had driven off, and aware that Charles would be on the phone as soon as Parkes reported back, she suggested that the rest of them retire to the meeting room upstairs to discuss developments. She began by describing the outcome of the autopsy to Robert and Jack, who sat transfixed until she'd finished.

'Dr Wrench thinks he suffered a trauma to the head that cracked his skull,' she explained.

'Another vehicle collision?' asked Jack.

'We'll get the pathologist's full report by the end of the day, hopefully.'

Robert had delivered Berry's rucksack to Leeds that morning but not before making a copy of the entry in his diary for 7th November. 'One-thirty, he left Hawes!' he exclaimed. 'What was he thinking? He should have known it would be pitch black before he even reached Thwaite.'

Their one piece of forensic evidence was more challenging. If the strands of hair found in his hand belonged to Amy, what was the connection between them, apart from them being in Cotterdale the same afternoon? Did he kill her or vice versa? Neither had transport out there so how did they come across each other? It was a challenging scenario.

Every so often the phone on Miriam's desk would ring before switching to voicemail. When they ran out of rational ideas to explain how the two victims met, they went back downstairs to make tea and Miriam saw three missed calls on her mobile. She went outside to ring Charles.

Thank goodness for British Summer Time, thought Lily, arriving in Carlisle while it was still light. Sylvie, who was waiting in her office, expressed surprise that Lily had brought official documentation for once. She noted down details of the hair sample, including that the DNA was to be compared to Amy Hobson and the unidentified sample on Amy's car keys.

'What about the bottle I gave you?' Lily asked.

Sylvia sighed. 'What are you like? My boss wanted to know all about it. Have you got the request for me?'

'I'll get it to you, don't worry, but what did you find? Is it a match?'

'Sorry, no. Nothing from the DNA or the prints. Definitely not your mystery man.'

Lily hadn't questioned that Amy's attacker would be a man but of course the DNA had confirmed it anyway. It suddenly occurred to her that she should check the mystery man wasn't Brian Berry, despite it being impossible that he was in Kirkby Stephen. As Conan Doyle said, "when you have eliminated the impossible, whatever remains, however improbable, must be the truth". So she asked Sylvie if the DNA from the hair could be checked against her list of possibilities including Amy Hobson, Brian Berry, Greg Nevitt and the unidentified DNA from Amy's keys.

Sylvie was writing down the names. 'That's quite a list, Lily'.

'I know, and the victim's cases are from the three regions so you may have to contact Wakefield and Middlesbrough for the information.'

'Make it difficult, won't you?'

'Sorry.'

She smiled 'I'll let you know if I have problems. It sounds as if you're getting closer to a result.'

'I hope so, we haven't much time left.'

She drove straight back to "The Pines" where Jack was waiting to tell her about Brian Berry's post-mortem.

'…and that's not all. The phone was ringing most of the afternoon and when the boss finally made a call, she took it outside, on her mobile. You could see her marching up and down the yard waving her arms and shouting, although we couldn't hear what she was saying. She was red in the face when she came back in.'

'Perhaps it was personal.'

'But before we left, she said we had to have our reports up to date and ready by close of play tomorrow. She wants to see them before she sends them to the senior officers from the original investigations.'

'Does that mean we're definitely finishing on Thursday?'

He shrugged. 'Dunno. She wasn't in the mood for a chat.'

They fell silent until she remembered what Sylvie had told her about Karl's DNA.

Jack broke into a grin. 'That's a relief.'

'Why?'

'He's a nice guy. I was sure he was kosher,' he replied.

'But he was able to open the chain on the gate, according to Di.'

Jack shrugged. 'So?'

'He might be able to tell us who else knew about it. Eileen's sister gave me a list of people who did the catering jobs. Karl might be able to narrow it down or even tell us if there's anyone missing. Are you due to see him again this week?'

'Nothing planned.' He paused. 'England are playing again tomorrow night. The match will probably be shown at the pub. I could ask him, although he said it's getting close to lambing now.'

'See if he'll meet you so I can have a quick word when he calls for you.'

The weather had deteriorated next morning. Driving rain beat on the windows and the flat roof in the kitchen. It was the only sound apart from the tapping of keyboards. Lily found the heavy-handed vigorous thumping from Jack more irritating than the slow tapping of Robert's one finger style. The atmosphere had been unusually quiet, and it had not gone unnoticed that Miriam had bags under her eyes. Lily waited to see who would crack first and go to make coffee but when it reached eleven o'clock, she couldn't wait any longer. Jack joined her in the kitchen.

'I got a text from Karl. He's up for the pub this evening. He'll be round at seven,' he said quietly.

'Good work. Help me carry these in.'

They drank their coffee while they worked and when Mrs Whitehead brought sandwiches, they ate them at their desks. It's like being in detention, thought Lily. She knew the DI should have received the PM report on Brian Berry by now, but she hadn't mentioned it. Lily kept checking for a message from Sylvie, giving her the DNA results from the hair sample. When it finally came through, Lily's response must have been audible because Robert looked round at her. It wasn't a woman's hair that Mr Berry had grasped in his hand, it belonged to a man and matched the DNA on Amy's car keys.

'Finally!' she shouted.

It broke the spell. Suddenly they were gathered round Lily's screen while she explained the connections without making any wild assumptions.

'The hair from Brian Berry's right hand is a match with

the DNA found on Amy's keys. The prints on her keys match the ones on Greg's bike. Which suggests that whoever helped Amy try to start her car, also handled Greg's bike and had an altercation with Brian.'

There was a small weakness in her argument but she wasn't going to admit it. She was certain that she had found a match between the fingerprints on the keys with those on the bike but it would need to be officially corroborated, now she was no longer on the National Fingerprint Expert Register.

Chapter 30

Karl wouldn't come in when he called for Jack because they were already late for the kick-off. Lily handed Jack the list of catering staff, making him promise to show Karl. She waited impatiently for him to return, knowing they wouldn't leave the pub until the football was over. She was reading in front of the fire when the door burst open and the lads finally appeared. She looked at her watch.

'Shh! Eileen has gone up already.'

Jack made play of tiptoeing across the room to give her the sheet of paper containing the list of names. 'I haven't had a chance to ask him yet.'

Lily invited Karl to come and join her by the fire. Jack took a seat at the dining table. After an awkward start, Lily explained that they were involved in a very sensitive investigation.

'Yes, Jack told me,' he said, taking off his padded jacket.

Lily looked at her colleague who shrugged. 'He asked and I thought it would be all right since we'd proved...'

'Ok, Jack.' She was confused. 'So he told you about the poaching?'

'Yes. He said it was a cover story.'

Lily waited for Jack to explain but he didn't respond.

Karl leaned towards her. 'I know you're looking at Amy's murder. It's cool.'

It took Lily about thirty seconds before she decided that she might as well show him the list, but first she made it clear they were talking to him in confidence. He took the paper and ran his eye down the page while she waited in silence. Finally she asked, 'Is anyone missing?'

He pondered then looked up. 'No, that's all I can think of.'

Disappointed, Lily asked, 'Tell me about the family who run the catering company. They seem to own quite a bit of land near here, and a couple of hotels, including the one where Kirsty works.'

'Yes, not exactly Lord of the Manor, although they act like it. You won't see them handing round the goujons.'

'Is it just Mr and Mrs Grant?'

'You mean the major and his wife? No, they've got a son and daughter. She works at the hotel and so does Alistair on and off but he's at university in York studying something to do with hotel management.'

'You know him then?'

'Yeah, we used to hang out before he went to uni.'

'Did he help with the catering at the shoots?'

He laughed. 'No way. He'd be more likely to be in the shooting party!'

'One last thing, Karl. We know the chain on the gate into the estate had a loose link that could be opened without undoing the padlock. Would everyone on that list have known about it?'

He looked down the page. 'Possibly, but it wasn't something you spoke about. It just made it easier to get in and out with the vehicles when we were delivering stuff.'

Until now, Lily had found her boss inspiring. She dreamed of becoming a DI one day, and hoped she would have the same confidence, determination, and style. But this morning Miriam seemed diminished. Her voice was almost a whisper as she announced that she had sent their reports off but to let her know if there were any developments between now and Thursday afternoon.

Jack was the one to ask what they all wanted to know. 'Is that it, then?'

Miriam looked up. 'Sorry?'

'Are you saying we're finished here? Because I, for one, haven't finished yet.'

Lily glanced over at Robert, who had stopped mid-action with his hand raised to aim a ball of paper into the bin. Jack was well out of order but Miriam didn't seem to notice.

'Apparently we are to pack up on Thursday and return to base,' she replied, fiddling with paperwork on her desk.

Lily went upstairs to complete her timeline, which had become closer to a mind-map. The only other colour pen they had left was black. Quite appropriate, she thought, as she began to draw in the physical evidence that connected the items associated with the victims. She included details of the removable chain and its replacement. Sitting down to contemplate the result she noticed something that might be important, adding a note to the sheet: the chain had been replaced after Amy and Brian died but before Greg was killed. It could perhaps explain why his body was found this side of the locked gate. Whatever the reason, she felt sure the chain was a significant part of the case.

Jack joined her. He perused her efforts for a while before pointing out that they now had some information about the killer, if he was responsible for all three deaths.

'We know he was in Kirkby Stephen on 7th November,

'We know he was in Kirkby Stephen on 7th November,

'We know he was in Kirkby Stephen on 7th November,

because he tried to start Amy's car. He was in Cotterdale the same afternoon, killing Amy and Brian, so he knew how to open and shut the gate. That makes him something to do with the estate. He was back in Cotterdale on 24th when he knocked over Greg, in his green car, and he left the bike on the other side of Hawes.'

'But he couldn't get through the gate to hide him or the bike this time because the chain had been replaced.'

'Ok.'

'And he has fair hair. We've got his DNA so it's only a matter of finding him to prove that he killed them.'

They heard footsteps on the stairs before Robert appeared. 'What are you two plotting?' he asked amiably.

Lily pointed at the board, explaining the information she'd added.

He stroked his chin before taking a seat. He clearly had something on his mind. 'How sure are you that the three attacks are related?' Before they could answer, he continued, 'The MOs are completely different, aren't they? A young woman strangled, an eighty-year-old hit over the head and, weeks later mind, a cyclist knocked off his bike. We should always be asking who, why and how? We've got the how but what are the motives? We should be concentrating on the why, that's the key.'

Lily, who could see Jack was becoming irritated by Robert's lecture, asked if he thought they should be allowed to continue their investigation now they seemed to have found a link between their cases. To her surprise he agreed enthusiastically.

'Yes, Lily, there's enough evidence to justify extending our stay here but I think Miriam is under a lot of pressure from the DCI.'

'Couldn't we talk to her?' Lily urged. 'Tell her we want to continue.'

Neither of them replied so she stood up, announcing that she would go. 'Stay where you are,' she instructed them. 'I'll let you know when you can come down.'

She didn't feel quite so bold once she was downstairs. Her boss was staring at her computer screen, so she coughed to attract her attention.

'Lily,' Miriam said when she looked round.

'Can I say something?' She stumbled over her words, sounding like a petulant child. 'It's unfair,' she said, 'to stop us now we're getting so close to discovering who the killer is.'

'That's a slight exaggeration, isn't it?'

'Well, we've got evidence, DNA and a description.'

Miriam looked at her over her glasses. Lily reddened. She wasn't doing a very good job of this. Robert should have offered.

'The others agree,' she said. 'We all want to carry on. You said this place was rented for two months. That means we've got another few weeks, doesn't it?'

'The orders are to hand everything back to the original Senior Investigating Officers in the regions. And we all go back to our original roles.'

Lily couldn't argue with that, or could she? 'What if I ask the SIO in Cumbria to give me a bit more time on Amy's case?'

Miriam sighed. 'It's a nice idea but...'

'Please let me try,' she pleaded.

She ran to join the others, nearly bumping into Jack, who was standing at the top of the stairs listening.

'Robert, do you think you could persuade West

Yorkshire to keep you up here for another week rather than pulling you back straight away, if you say you'll solve Greg Nevitt's murder for them?'

He'd booked a week's holiday anyway, although he'd assumed he would be spending it with Jean. Reluctantly he agreed.

'But Greg is my case,' objected Jack. 'I can't go back to the Cyber Crime Unit.'

'No-one is asking you to yet, are they?'

'What about Miriam?' asked Robert in a low voice. 'The DCI will want her back in Middlesbrough right away, won't he?'

'Well I'm staying, even if she has to go back,' said Lily defiantly. The others were looking at her dubiously. 'Let's see, shall we?'

They followed her downstairs, where Miriam watched them approach her desk. Lily explained their plan to continue the work over the Easter week at least, then waited for her response.

'If your managers are willing to support your continued secondment up here – and I mean financially – then I see no reason why we couldn't spend another week, if that's all you think it will take. You must realise that there will be no further funding for forensics and, Jack, you'd better get rid of that electric bike. All expenses will have to go back to your own forces from now on.'

Then she made a call to tell the DCI that she was taking a couple of weeks holiday from the end of the week. Lily was certain that Miriam had deliberately made the call so they could all hear what she was saying.

It was that easy. Lily told her boss in Cumbria she would be staying for another week or two and Robert just sent a message to say he was taking leave. Jack wasn't forthcoming about his position, which led Lily to wonder if he still had a job in cyber-crime but didn't like to ask.

Within a couple of hours the mood had changed and Miriam was clapping her hands to attract their attention. 'I think we should go and have a look at Lily's timeline so you can update me on exactly where we are. I think we should review your hypotheses.'

Lily smiled. Her old boss was back. By the end of the day they had developed a theory that fitted the few facts they had. Miriam called him Mr X but soon he became simply X. The man they called X had tried to start Amy's car in Kirkby Stephen, then probably offered her a lift home, which suggested he wasn't a complete stranger. Now they suspected he drove a green car, they could look for CCTV coverage on the route. That would be Jack's job. X drives to Cotterdale because he knows the area and, more importantly, knows how to open the gate without a key. While he is disposing of Amy's body he comes across Brian, who is lost in the dark. They struggle, which is when the old man grabs some of X's hair. Lily will go over the list of workers associated with the estate again, looking for someone with fair hair. X leaves the bodies and drives off. For some reason, he returns two weeks later and accidently or deliberately knocks Greg off his bike. Lily thinks he may have been trying to return to the bodies but the chain has been replaced and he can't access them in his vehicle. He doesn't want to attract attention so he buries Greg's body in the woods. He's brought a spade with him this time so maybe he was planning to bury the other bodies, to finish the job. Finally, for some reason, X takes Greg's bike and dumps it in Raydale. Is it an area familiar to him? Perhaps it's on his way home? Robert will check the area for connections with Cotterdale.

Miriam looks round at her team. They are all grinning at her. She can't help but smile back at them. She'd never had such loyalty before and didn't want them to be disappointed but their resources were almost nil, and more experienced and better trained staff would probably be floored by the challenge ahead of them.

'Right,' she said. 'Tomorrow I want to see progress on all those actions. We'll meet up after lunch to see what we've got.'

'No pressure then,' muttered Jack.

Chapter 31

Lily was keen to get Jack out of the way after their evening meal. Di had sent a message asking to see her and she'd suggested seven o'clock. When Jack asked what Di wanted, Lily said she didn't know but hoped it was about her friend Kirsty. She had guessed right, as soon as she removed her coat and sat down, Di began to express her concerns.

'When Karl told me that you're on Amy's case, I knew I should speak to you. It's been on my mind for ages but I couldn't work out what to do.' She paused to take a deep breath. 'I'm so worried about Kirsty.'

'Yes, she isn't well.'

'It's not just that. Karl and I have gone over it so many times and we're convinced that she's been acting weirdly ever since Amy went missing, even before they found her body. She was fine on bonfire night and at Karl's party, that was on the sixth. But as soon as Amy didn't come home, she went into meltdown.'

'I'm sure you were all upset,' suggested Lily.

'Yes, and it was worse when they found her, but we've gradually we got over it. I mean, we'll always remember her, but Kirsty is getting worse with time rather than better. Of course, she and Amy were very close.' She fiddled with a ring on her middle finger before continuing. 'Karl said we should tell you in case it was significant. It wasn't at the time but now we think Kirsty's behaviour is odd, particularly throwing in her job at the hotel. She used to love it and I don't know about you but if I'm feeling down, I find work is a useful distraction.'

It certainly is, thought Lily. It was the only thing that kept her going when she broke off the engagement. 'So what are you saying?' she asked.

'I don't know exactly but we think it's important to find out why Kirsty is leaving the hotel.'

Jack reappeared as soon as Di had gone and Lily reported what she'd said.

'Wasn't Kirsty questioned at the time?' he asked. 'She would have told them if she knew anything.'

'They did chat to her but it was only to find out if she'd seen her friend the day she disappeared, which she hadn't. She didn't offer anything further at the time.'

'Remember Karl telling me Kirsty thought Amy had a mystery boyfriend but she wasn't sure? I suppose that's why she didn't say anything at the time.'

'Bit odd, unless he was someone she knew and didn't want to make trouble for him.'

'You should talk to her,' said Jack.

'Really? I'm not sure she'll confide in me if she won't talk to Di.'

'But it's the only option, isn't it?'

Lily didn't respond immediately because she didn't want Jack's opinion but there was another possibility.

He was wondering aloud why Amy would keep her boyfriend a secret anyway.

'The usual reason is because your parents wouldn't approve,' she told him.

'And why would that be?'

'Because he's too old or rides a motorbike or has a reputation.'

'A reputation?'

'Come on, you know what I mean. A womaniser.'

The expression made Jack laugh. 'A ladies' man?' he said in a silly voice.

Lily didn't reply, she was busy searching for the location of "The Grant Hotel" in Darlington. She discovered it was several miles outside the town. The website described it as a family run hotel with a cosy informal atmosphere. She noted that they were looking for staff, which would provide the perfect excuse to take a trip over there.

Next morning, Jack announced he was taking his bike back to the shop. The month's hire was over and there was no possibility of extending it. Lily was anxious to be off but agreed to give him a lift back into work. She hadn't mentioned she wouldn't be coming into the office but told him to let the others know she'd be back by lunchtime. She was wearing a skirt and jacket to make a good impression at the hotel, in the hope she could spend a bit of time talking to the staff under the pretext of being interested in the receptionist's job. She assumed the post was vacant because Kirsty had handed in her notice.

The satnav sent her down a narrow lane well before she reached Darlington. She was beginning to think it was a mistake when she spotted a sign at the end of a long drive indicating that "The Grant Hotel" was open to non-residents for lunch and dinner. The lawns were well-maintained with small evergreen shrubs clipped to perfection. The building looked small from a distance but as she approached, she could see it was a perfect Georgian country house.

She parked on the gravel drive in front of the house,

checking her hair before climbing out and locking the car. The front door opened onto a large hallway where a young woman with long blonde hair sat typing at a small table. She looked up and smiled.

'Hi, can I help you?'

Lily explained that she'd heard they were looking for a receptionist and was thinking of applying. The girl was immediately amicable, telling her what a lovely place it was to work in and how the staff was like one big happy family. Her obvious enthusiasm was poles apart from Kirsty's reaction to her job. Puzzled, Lily asked if there were any downsides to the work, like long hours or awkward guests.

'Oh no. The guests are real sweeties. Most of them stay regularly so we know them well. We've only got ten rooms so it's ultra-friendly. You get to know everyone really well. I'm Rebecca, by the way.'

She explained the receptionist's duties to Lily in detail, telling her it would be great if she applied because they were terribly short-staffed with it being the start of the season. 'I've been holding the fort on my own for the last few weeks, so I was relieved when I heard the advert had gone out.'

'Why did the other receptionist leave?' Lily asked innocently.

'Unfortunately she's not been well for a while. I thought it must be ME,' she looked round before lowering her voice to a whisper. 'But I heard she has mental health issues.' She straightened up in her seat. 'Anyway, would you like to have a quick look round? I can show you the public rooms.'

Lily followed her through to the bar and lounge, where they peered at the grounds through the glass doors.

'The gardens are beautiful in the summer,' her guide told her. 'We serve afternoon tea in the rose garden.'

She introduced her to an old lady sitting alone on a sofa, explaining that Lily was looking for a job. The guest thought that would be lovely. When they were back at reception, Rebecca gave Lily an application form, begging her to apply for the post.

'My mother will be doing the interviews,' she explained. 'She's in this afternoon. In fact, if you fill it in now, I can hand her your form straight away.'

'Your mother?' asked Lily. 'It really is a family business.'

'It certainly is. I did a hotel management degree so I can take over the running of the hotel one day.'

'Are there many other members of staff?'

Rebecca considered for a moment. 'Not many. We have outside contractors to take care of the washing and cleaning. Another for the gardening. The kitchen staff are the only permanent members of the team.'

'I heard that there was a catering company as well.'

'Oh that's entirely separate. My brother is doing a management course so he can take over the day to day operation of that side of the business. Yes, he's got all sorts of plans for when he graduates.'

'So he doesn't work here?' Lily asked.

'Occasionally, when he's not at uni, and he's not busy at our wedding venue. He's home for Easter so you might meet him at the interview.'

Lily waved the application form, saying she'd definitely think about applying before returning to her car.

As she drove back towards Hawes, a plan formed but she had to check something first. She parked the car in a lay-by to make the call.

'Di, you haven't told Kirsty about our investigation have you?'

'No, we thought it would freak her out.'

'So she doesn't know what I am doing?'

'No. I'm not sure she's even heard your story about poachers.'

'Good. That's all. No wait!' She suddenly remembered the job she'd been tasked with by Miriam. She was supposed to be reporting the results that afternoon. 'Silly question but I've got a list of names here.' She struggled to reach her bag and pull out the piece of paper. 'They're people who helped with the catering for the shoot in Cotterdale last year.'

'Ok.' Di sounded curious.

'Tell me if any of them have fair hair.' Lily picked out the males, there were only three.

'No, no and no.'

Lily thanked her and put the list away. There was just time to stop off in Hawes before she had to be back in the office. It was a perfect plan. She would ask Kirsty about the hotel staff on the pretext that she was thinking of applying for her old job.

As expected, Kirsty was at home. In fact her mother confided that she hadn't stepped out of the door for nearly a week. She seemed pleased that her daughter had a visitor, leading Lily upstairs before knocking gently on the bedroom door.

'Kirsty, darling, you've got a visitor.'

The door opened slowly and a pale face appeared. Lily, thinking how thin she'd become, gave her brightest smile, and asked if she could spare a few minutes. The girl's response was unenthusiastic but she opened the door wider to allow Lily to enter. She closed the door carefully and stood in front of it.

'It's nothing important, honestly. I noticed that "The Grant Hotel" was advertising for a receptionist and I thought you might be able to give me some tips if I get an interview.'

She was fiddling with the sleeve of her hoodie. 'That's my old job.'

'I thought it might be,' Lily admitted. 'Di said you'd handed in your notice. That's why I thought I should ask you about it before I apply – in case there's something I should know.'

'Like what?'

'Well, I wondered why you wanted to leave. It seems like a really nice place and I met Rebecca...'

'She's all right.'

'And her mother?'

She nodded.

'I suppose the guests can be a bit... you know...'

She shrugged.

Lily took a deep breath. 'So why did you hand in your notice?'

She shrugged again. 'Just wanted a change,' she said quietly.

'Have you got something else then?'

'Not yet, I'm thinking of moving to Leeds.' She looked straight at Lily for the first time. 'Are you really going to apply?'

'Yes. I thought you could give me some pointers. I understand Mrs Grant is doing the interviews although Rebecca said I'd meet her brother so maybe they all get involved. So what is the rest of the family like?'

She didn't respond.

'What is it? What are you worried about?'

Without a word, Kirsty turned to the door. She opened it wide and stood looking at the ground.

Lily tried once more. 'Is it to do with what happened to your friend?'

The poor girl was close to tears. 'Please go.'

Lily wanted to put her arm round her but she kept her distance. 'Kirsty, if you know something about what happened to Amy you should speak to someone.'

As she went downstairs, Lily could hear a door being locked. She assumed Kirsty had hidden in the bathroom. It was not the outcome she'd hoped for but it proved a point. Kirsty's behaviour was associated with Amy's death and she was sure the hotel was involved.

Chapter 32

Miriam woke at five with a headache. She pulled a sweater over her pyjamas and went downstairs in her slippers to find some pain-relief. She boiled the kettle, threw a teabag into a mug then topped up the stove. The tea was stewed and lukewarm by the time she remembered to drink it. She pulled a rug round her on the sofa and closed her eyes. Last night had been an all-time low, she decided. The estate agent wanted to speak to her about the house sale. Apparently, a super young couple had fallen in love with it; they were offering the full asking price. She was lying when she said how pleased she was. It had been their home for twenty years; Victor and Elizabeth had grown up there. Now she could no longer put off going to clear out everything she and Henry had accumulated together.

She tried to take her mind off it by concentrating on work but the description of a killer with a green vehicle and fair hair had set her anxiety off in another direction. Not only did her neighbour drive a green Land Rover and have straw coloured hair, but William was interviewed in the original Amy Hobson enquiry. He'd said he'd been muck-spreading on the day she disappeared. When Miriam left for work later that morning, she sincerely hoped Lily had located a member of the catering team who fitted the profile of their killer because otherwise she might have to make her concerns official.

However, the team's initial confidence had faded a little when they regrouped to report to her on the morning's work. Disappointingly Lily had not located any men with fair hair in the catering team, and Jack was unable to find a CCTV camera covering the road from Kirkby Stephen.

'Robert, I hope you've got something for us.'

He looked apologetic. 'Not really. The only connection I could find with the bicycle being dumped in Raydale is that the Grants have a holiday cottage near Burtersett. It's their catering company that provides food for the shooting parties in Cotterdale.'

When the others looked unimpressed, Lily spoke up. 'It may sound a bit tenuous,' she began, 'but I believe the Grant family are a piece of the jigsaw, so to speak.'

Robert looked at her with mild interest, Jack was grinning and Miriam appeared puzzled. 'What do you mean?' she asked.

'Amy's best friend, Kirsty, has been in a state of anxiety ever since her friend's murder. She hasn't recovered over time; in fact she seems to be getting worse. She used to work as receptionist for the Grants but she's recently handed in her notice. When I spoke to her she wouldn't tell me why she left but I'm sure it's something to do with the hotel.'

'Karl thinks she knows who Amy's secret boyfriend was,' added Jack.

'Hang on a minute,' said Robert, holding up a hand. 'This is news to me. Where are you getting all this from?'

'Just chatting to the locals,' said Jack with a grin.

'But it's all just hearsay,' added Lily.

Robert folded his arms. 'Well perhaps we should have an official chat with this Kirsty, if she really does know something she didn't divulge first time round.'

'I think she's scared,' said Lily. 'She won't leave the

house. May I suggest a different approach?'

Miriam raised her eyebrows as Lily explained how she'd confided to Karl and Di that she and Jack were working for the police. She proposed they ask Di to persuade Kirsty to talk to them. 'Di can tell her she'd be safe because no-one else knows we're police'.

'Do you really think she's in danger?' Miriam asked.

Lily admitted it was possible if Kirsty knew the killer's identity.

'Do you think he's still around then?' asked Jack.

Miriam nodded. 'It has always been a possibility and, if this young girl is scared then, yes, it is quite probable, which is why we have to be careful.'

The DI finally agreed for them to approach Di and Karl but she asked to be present when Lily asked them to speak to Kirsty. She wanted to ensure that the brother and sister understood how important it was that no-one else knew that they were investigating the murders. They needed to maintain the poaching cover story for everyone's safety.

'Let's keep it official and have them meet us here,' she said.

Karl and Di arrived at five o'clock. Miriam had sent Robert and Jack off so she and Lily could talk to them alone. There was a gentle knock and Karl poked his head round the door. Once inside, they stood like children who had been sent to the headteacher's office. Miriam did her best to make them welcome, thanking them for coming to help them with what was a delicate matter. Once they were seated, she repeated what Lily had told her and explained that she would like their help to persuade Kirsty to talk to them.

She addressed Karl. 'I understand you think she may know of a boyfriend that Amy was keeping secret?'

He nodded. 'She didn't exactly speak about it but she implied it, you know?'

His sister kept looking anxiously across at Lily until she felt she had to say something. 'We think Kirsty can help us find who killed Amy but I'm certain she's scared of something or someone. If she can see that we're just trying to help, you might be able to get her to open up to us.'

Lily observed as her boss continued to put the siblings at ease. Finally Miriam smiled at them reassuringly. 'So would you inform her that we're a special unit reviewing Amy's case and anything she tells us will be in the strictest confidence. Lily and I can come to see her at home if she wishes or however she wants to do it.'

It was left that Karl would let Lily know when they'd spoken to Kirsty.

Miriam waited until their pickup had left the yard. 'Thank you, Lily. This could be a useful lead and if you hadn't befriended that young woman, we would never have known about her. However, sometimes these things come to nothing so don't be disappointed if that's the case.' She looked at her watch. 'You'd better get off or you'll be late for your evening meal.'

Lily pulled a face. 'It's the one thing I miss,' she admitted. 'Cooking my own tea.'

Miriam laughed. 'I expect you're looking forward to getting back to Cumbria.'

'Oh no. I love being here. It would just be nice to have my own place.'

Lily drove back to "The Pines", where Jack was waiting to hear her news. When she explained that Karl and Di were going to talk to Kirsty first, he said he hoped it wouldn't interfere with their pool night in Kirkby Stephen and immediately began texting on his phone. They had just started to eat when his mobile pinged.

'Excellent,' he declared. 'Karl is picking me up in half an hour.'

Lily assumed that meant there was no plan to see Kirsty that evening. She was disappointed that they hadn't treated the request as urgent and annoyed with Jack for distracting Karl from the task. She was finishing her dessert of tinned fruit and custard when there was a knock at the door. Jack thundered down the stairs and she heard Karl's voice. The front door slammed and to her surprise, Di appeared.

'Sorry, are you having your tea?' she asked, hovering by the door.

'No, come in and sit down.' Lily pushed her plate aside and joined her by the fire.

'Karl's taken Jack to play pool,' Di explained unnecessarily.

'Yes.'

'We saw Kirsty.'

'Already?' She hadn't expected that. They couldn't have had much time with her. 'You've already spoken to her?'

'Yes. We told her what you said about talking to you and your boss but she doesn't want to.'

Lily tried to hide her irritation. 'Why not?'

'I think she's scared. I mean really scared.'

'Scared of us?'

'No.'

'Who then?'

'Whoever strangled Amy, I guess.'

If Kirsty was that frightened of the killer, she was clearly in danger, thought Lily, and there was no time to lose. 'We'd better go and see her.'

'When?'

'Now.'

She grabbed her coat from upstairs and they walked into town together. Di kept asking her what they were going to do but Lily didn't answer because she wasn't sure. She would talk to Kirsty's parents, demand that their daughter explained what was worrying her, that her life could be in danger if she didn't talk to the police. Whatever it took to get Kirsty to open up to her.

'I don't know, Di,' she answered finally.

'What about your boss? She said she wanted to see her.'

Lily had forgotten about Miriam in her concern for Kirsty's safety. 'She'll understand,' she replied, without conviction. Another few paces and she stopped. 'I'd better call her.'

On the way to Kirkby Stephen, Karl was telling Jack how their visit to Kirsty had been unsuccessful. 'It's obvious she's terrified of speaking out about someone.'

'D'you still think it's Amy's secret affair?'

He sighed. 'Yes. I know it sounds a bit... you know, but she used to almost joke about it before Amy was killed. She teased her about it. Amy used to tell her to shut up but I'm sure there was something in it because after her death Kirsty wouldn't talk about it. We told her to tell the police but she said she'd made it up. I, for one, didn't believe her then and I still don't.'

'Did you have any thoughts at the time about who it might've have been?'

'Not really.'

'Someone she met in Kirkby Stephen?'

'No idea. Although probably more local if Kirsty saw her with him.'

Jack explained that Amy's phone records and social media posts had not indicated evidence of a relationship with anyone who had not been accounted for.

'In that case,' Karl said, 'she must have been very keen to keep him secret. I wonder why?'

'Married?'

'Perhaps or persona non grata for some other reason.'

Miriam arrived just fifteen minutes after Lily called her. The DI was still in the clothes she'd been wearing at work and looked very professional, Lily thought. Kirsty's mother went to let her in and spoke with her quietly in the hall for some time before announcing they were going upstairs. Lily and Di were left with Kirsty's father, who did little to break the awkward silence. They must have been gone twenty minutes, maybe half an hour, when there were footsteps on the stairs and Mrs Watts reappeared alone.

She looked at them anxiously. 'I've left them to it. Does anyone want a cup of tea?'

Lily followed her into the kitchen. The woman leaned on the table with one hand on her forehead. 'Sorry, love. It must be the relief that she's finally talking to someone.' She pulled out a tissue and blew her nose. 'I've been that worried I didn't know what to do.'

Lily sat down opposite her. 'She's talking to Miriam?'

'Is that her name? Miriam? She seems very nice. She has a sympathetic manner, don't you think?'

Lily was desperate to know if Kirsty was finally talking but the woman had jumped up to put the kettle on. 'This won't get the tea made, will it?' she asked with false cheerfulness.

Cups and saucers were removed from cupboards. A biscuit tin was emptied onto a large plate. A milk jug was rinsed out and filled from a large plastic container. She retrieved an enormous teapot from the top of a cupboard. Lily tried to help but was told that she should take the plate of biscuits into the sitting room. When she did as she was instructed, she found Di having a conversation with Mr Watts about the farm.

They had all been served tea and biscuits by the time Miriam reappeared. It was difficult to interpret her expression. 'Di?' she began. 'Would you like to take a tea up to Kirsty? I think she'd like to relax with a friend now.'

Mrs Watts poured her a cup and Di grabbed a handful of biscuits before disappearing.

Miriam accepted her tea and sank onto the sofa. 'Your daughter has been extremely helpful, so thank you for letting me talk to her. She believed she had some important information regarding her friend's death, which has been worrying her ever since.'

'We knew something had upset her,' said her father. 'But we assumed it was losing her friend.'

'We wanted her to see a counsellor,' her mother added.

'Well, she's promised to come and see us tomorrow morning so we can take a proper statement. Perhaps after that you should find her some professional help?'

Di was still upstairs when Lily left the house with Miriam. Her boss hesitated outside before asking if she'd eaten because she hadn't started cooking and she thought she might grab something in the town. Lily said she'd had her tea but was happy to join her, because she was anxious to hear about her chat with Kirsty.

There were a few people in the bar but they found a table in the corner where they could speak without being overheard. Miriam bought drinks at the same time as ordering her meal, asking for salad not chips, Lily noted.

She couldn't wait to find out what had happened. 'Did Kirsty speak to you?'

'She did. How old is she?'

'Eighteen.'

'Really? She seems younger. Anyway, she is clearly very distressed by her friend's death, which is unsurprising, but there is more to it, as you suspected.'

'Did she say what?'

'Not exactly.' The DI was unwrapping her cutlery from a paper serviette. 'She admitted that there was something worrying her, connected to the murder. She couldn't or wouldn't come out with it because she had no proof. Of course, I told her that didn't matter; often enquiries start without concrete evidence.'

'So she wouldn't tell you what was worrying her?'

Miriam sat quietly for a moment. 'Let me put it this way, she intimated that she had information that might be helpful.'

'But she didn't say what it was?'

'Not exactly.'

Her cod goujons arrived and she asked for tartar sauce.

Lily waited until it arrived before speaking. 'Karl thinks she knows the name of Amy's boyfriend.'

'Yes, I know. I did ask her about him.'

'And?'

'She clammed up. That's when I asked her to come in tomorrow to give a statement. I'm hoping that making it more official might convince her to divulge the name. Meanwhile we'll get Jack to go through the digital forensics again, in case something was missed previously.'

Chapter 33

They had stayed chatting over another drink, or was it two? Miriam, who was ordering large glasses of red wine, insisted that she join her. It was after eleven when Lily got to bed but she couldn't sleep. She heard a car stop outside half an hour later, Jack's key in the lock and his bedroom door slamming. She listened to the taps running, lights being switched on and off, and his wardrobe door closing until, finally, it went quiet again. She lay awake staring at the red glow of the curtains, illuminated by the porch light that was always left on overnight. She was thinking about the case, her case. Amy Hobson's murder had been given to her to investigate. Not to Robert or Jack. It was her responsibility to find the man who killed Amy and it felt as though she was close to identifying him.

Lily tried to sleep but after an hour she turned on the bedside lamp and fetched a sweater before climbing back into bed with her notebook. She wrote down any words that came to mind associated with her case and those of her colleagues. Then she tiptoed over to her kettle and made a drink with the packet of hot chocolate tucked behind the teabags. As she sipped the hot, sweet beverage she reviewed the pages of notes, hoping to make sense of the connections but nothing materialised. Giving up finally, she switched off the light and pulled the duvet over her ears.

In the morning, at breakfast, she related the events of the previous evening. When Jack repeated Karl's assertion that the mystery boyfriend was the key, she retorted that it didn't help unless he knew who it was. When Jack replied sullenly that Kirsty was the one to ask, Lily ignored him.

They drove to work in silence. Miriam was expecting to interview Kirsty at ten o'clock and prior to that she wanted to review their progress. Lily pulled out her notebook, offering to start by going through all the relevant facts she had listed late last night. Miriam wrote them on the flipchart with the green felt-tip pen. When she'd finished, they stared at the sheet of paper.

'May I?' Jack asked, taking the red pen to circle a number of the entries before standing back to admire his handywork.

Robert was the first to speak. 'What's that then?'

'Don't you see it?' Jack asked, looking round.

Lily frowned. 'Do they all relate to the Grant family in some way? Kirsty working at the hotel, their holiday cottage near where the bike was left, the catering company working for the estate?'

Jack was grinning. 'Exactly.'

'Seems a bit tenuous,' remarked Robert.

But Miriam was nodding slowly. 'It's an interesting angle,' she admitted. 'One we can explore with Kirsty this morning. Thank you, Jack.' She looked round the group. 'Anything else that occurs to anyone?' Silence. 'In that case, Jack and Robert, please stay here and see if you can make any more connections on the chart, while we're downstairs talking to Kirsty.'

Lily followed her boss with a sense of anticipation. They quickly compiled a list of questions they wanted Kirsty to address if she was in a more co-operative mood. High on the agenda was whether Amy had a boyfriend at the time of her death because there was no indication of one in the original enquiry. By ten o'clock the list was complete but there was no sign of Kirsty and they began to wonder aloud whether she would fail to appear.

It was twenty-past when there was a gentle knock on the door and Lily jumped up to let Kirsty in. Her face was quite rosy, probably due to exertion as she seemed out of breath as she apologised for being late – she hadn't been sure they'd be expecting her, with it being Good Friday and a public holiday. Miriam offered her a hot drink but she just wanted water. By the time Lily fetched a glass from the kitchen, the girl had removed her coat and was sitting down across the desk from Miriam. Lily pulled up a chair beside her. The DI was speaking softly, reassuring Kirsty that she was free to leave at any time but that her help was going to be invaluable.

They began with how she knew Amy, their friendship at school and outside, where they went and who with. Lily thought the girl seemed relatively relaxed. She recorded places they frequented and the names of others in their circle of friends. Gradually the DI introduced the question of a boyfriend. No, said Kirsty, she didn't know about any boyfriend. Lily thought she looked less comfortable now and made a note. Next, they asked about Amy's job at the hotel in Kirkby Stephen but Kirsty hadn't ever been there and didn't know anyone who worked there. When asked if Amy ever spoke about the job or the customers, she shrugged. Lily couldn't tell if she was hiding something or really didn't know. She was ticking the questions off the list as they were addressed or left a question mark beside those she avoided. There was just one last topic: the Grant family. Lily was concerned that Miriam had forgotten until finally she introduced them but in a roundabout way.

'I understand you work at "The Grant Hotel", Kirsty.'

She frowned. 'Not anymore.'

'But you did?'

'Yes.'

'A family-run business by all accounts.'

'Yes.'

'So you know the family?'

'Not really.' She was looking down at her hands.

'What can you tell me about them?'

She didn't look up but mumbled, 'Mrs Grant manages the hotel. Rebecca, her daughter helps on reception.'

'Like you did?'

'Yes.'

'What about the rest of the family?'

She shook her head.

'You never saw them?'

She shook her head again.

'Can I ask why you left their employment?'

No response.

'Kirsty?' Miriam waited for her to look up.

She lifted her chin reluctantly like a petulant child. 'Yes?'

'Is there anything you want to tell us? Something that's occurred to you while we've been talking, maybe?'

Another shake of the head. 'Can I go now?'

Miriam smiled with a sigh. 'Of course. Would you like a lift back home?'

The girl appeared anxious to leave. No, she didn't need a lift. She would be fine, she told them as she struggled into her coat. Lily thought she looked close to tears and said so once she'd gone. Miriam expressed frustration with the girl's lack of co-operation, calling the others down to discuss what little progress they'd made.

'Kirsty didn't want to talk about the Grant family, which is disappointing but that makes it even more important that we check them out. Jack, please use your cyber-skills to find out about the family members and I'll check if we have anything on the database.' She looked questioningly at Robert, who said he was making a list of the owners of green cars in the area. Miriam wanted Lily to question Karl and Di, who probably knew Rebecca Grant and her brother.

But Lily had a better idea. 'I can go back to the hotel to talk to Rebecca,' she said. 'Her mother might be there too.' Miriam looked worried so she quickly reassured her. 'It's Ok, they think I'm interested in Kirsty's job.'

'Just be mindful that there's nothing to link the family to any of the crimes, no motives as far as we're aware, so this is just a fact-finding exercise in order to cross them off the list.'

Lily began completing the job application while Jack did a quick internet search for the Grant family. He came over as she was signing the bottom of the form. She hadn't been exactly honest about her previous employment but it wasn't like she would be taking the job.

'So I've had a quick look at what they say about Major and Mrs Grant,' Jack began. 'They've been running the estate and the hotels since his father died. That's when they set up the catering business. It looks as though the companies are doing well. I haven't found anything on the children yet except this photo from the hotel website. The daughter is quite attractive, isn't she?'

Lily had to admit they were a good-looking family. The brother and sister were similar in appearance with their mother's oval face and father's piercing blue eyes. The Major looked much younger than she'd expected and she asked Jack his age.

'No idea. He left the army five years ago but he must've retired very early. Karl wondered if Amy's feller was a married man. Perhaps the major...'

But Lily wasn't listening. 'If they were an army family, I wonder where the kids went to school.'

'I'm on to it. I'll have a full resumé by the time you get back.'

She copied her application form before placing it carefully in a new white envelope. Before she left, she told Miriam she would be back in the afternoon. Her boss reminded her, yet again, that she was to confine herself to general chat with the Grants about their businesses. 'And don't take the job if they offer it to you – I need you here!' she called with a laugh.

The sun was shining and Lily felt that Spring might finally have arrived as she drove to the hotel. It was April and she had already spotted lambs out in the fields but the fact it was Easter was not significant. They'd all agreed to work over the holiday and she'd warned her mother that she would be too busy to visit. A parcel was apparently on its way containing the easter egg and card that had been purchased in anticipation of her being at home.

She felt excited by the prospect of visiting the hotel again, although as she drew nearer, she began to rehearse how she might approach it. Clearly the holiday weekend bookings had arrived; the car park at the front of the building was full and she had to squeeze in at the back next to the bins. As she walked round to the entrance, she could smell that lunch was being prepared. The large front door was wide open and Rebecca was seated at her table behind a vase of daffodils.

'It's Lily, isn't it?' she asked.

'Yes. I've brought my application form but I guess you're busy with your guests.'

'Sit down while I get Mother. I told her all about you and she wants to meet you.'

Lily took a chair against the wall to wait. She could hear voices in the bar and an elderly couple were coming down the stairs. They dropped a set of keys on the table before walking outside. Rebecca returned, followed by a tall woman in a turquoise suit, who Lily immediately recognised from the photograph.

'This is my mother,' Rebecca explained unnecessarily when Lily introduced herself.

Mrs Grant had a gracious manner, asking Lily how she'd heard about the job and why she was interested in working for them. She replied that she knew the person who was leaving the post. This was despite having pretended she didn't know Kirsty on her first visit. There was an awkward pause and Lily feared she'd made a silly mistake. She quickly tried to rectify it by admitting that she hadn't liked to say she knew Kirsty previously because her friend had let them down badly. With the equilibrium hopefully restored, Mrs Grant confided that they were incredibly busy and were very anxious to take someone on as soon as possible so she would like to have an informal chat with her now.

'It's quite convenient because you can meet my

husband. He's in the office.'

Lily was ushered into a room behind the reception area where a man was seated at a computer monitor on a large antique desk.

'Darling, this is Lily. Do you remember, Becca told us about her? She's popped in with the application form so it seems sensible to have a chat now.'

The piercing blue eyes she'd seen in the photo were staring across the room at her.

'Hi. I'm a friend of Kirsty's,' she said, to judge his reaction.

He appeared startled, eyeing her curiously before moving out from behind the desk in a wheelchair.

Mrs Grant smiled reassuringly at Lily. 'Alistair and I will have a chat with you in the lounge, dear.' She turned to her husband. 'We won't disturb you any longer, darling.'

They filed out past Rebecca and into the lounge, where Lily was told to take a seat. Guests were beginning to drift through into the dining room and the smell of food made her hungry. Eventually Mrs Grant returned with a young man in tow who looked remarkably like his father, introducing him as her son, Alistair.

Lily was careful not to mention Kirsty again. He stood with his hands in the pockets of his jeans while his mother suggested an informal chat, just to get to know each other. So far, so good. Mother and son sat side by side on the sofa opposite her. Mrs Grant explained how important the guests were, that it was their job to make them as comfortable as possible. Lily listened, although she already knew how Rebecca and her mother looked after this hotel while her son and husband took care of the "other little venture", as well as the catering business. Mrs Grant was in the middle of describing their bijou wedding venture when a member of staff approached and whispered something to her.

She jumped up. 'Duty calls. Alistair will look after you.' She walked quickly into the dining room.

Her son was frowning as he checked his expensive-looking watch. 'She didn't tell me you were coming.'

'That's my fault,' Lily explained. 'I just wanted to drop the form in.'

He shrugged. 'Well, if she's happy.' He peered around him. 'Look, I've got to dash but if you want to have a trial run, I could do with some help at a wedding bash tomorrow evening. It's a small ceremony but there are fifty guests for the evening party.'

Lily smiled. 'Yes, of course.'

It was at the hotel in the grounds of the Grants' estate. He gave her directions, telling her to be there between four and five o'clock, then dashed off.

Rebecca was still at her desk. 'You all right?' she asked, staring out the door.

'Yes. Your brother has suggested I help with the wedding tomorrow evening. I forgot to ask what I should wear?'.

'Anything black,' she replied. 'It's not very formal over there at the evening events.'

'Are trousers Ok?'

'No problem. He likes there to be a relaxed atmosphere. You'll need to keep your wits about you though. It can get a bit wild if the guests have been drinking all day. I'm just saying.'

Chapter 34

Lily decided not to mention that she would be working for Alistair Grant at the weekend. She gave her boss a brief report of her visit to the hotel, mentioning that the male members of the family had blond hair, which she thought might be significant. Miriam asked Robert to show Lily the list of green cars with owners living within five miles of Hawes. She ran her fingers down the page until she reached Major Grant's name and nodded.

'A green Range Rover,' she said.

'Jack is trying to narrow the list down,' added Robert, with a smirk. 'But it's not easy to ascertain hair colouring from the internet. It may require some legwork.'

'That will have to come later, if it becomes necessary,' Miriam muttered. 'I'd rather avoid that kind of intrusive policing.'

Robert guessed she really meant it was unlikely they would have the DCI's support for it. 'So what now?' he asked.

'Jack is happy to carry on trawling for intel on the Grant family. Maybe Lily can help him narrow down the car owners by chatting to her landlady or the youngsters she's befriended.'

Lily conferred with Jack over the hair colour issue and they agreed that the best person to ask was Di. She was more likely to notice men's hair colouring than Karl. Lily messaged her, asking if she was free that evening.

When Robert announced he had plans for the weekend

unless he was needed, Miriam agreed there was nothing further for him to do. Hopefully by Monday, with Jack and Lily's help, they'd have reduced the green car owners to a handful of fair-haired men. She paused before deciding to speak out. 'Incidentally, one of the names on that list is a neighbour of mine, William Hill. I can confirm he has blond hair too.'

No-one spoke. Lily looked at Robert and he coughed. 'Should we talk to him?' he asked, as he made a cross against his name.

'No, I will,' she replied.

They finished the day with a report from Jack on what he'd discovered about the Grants. 'The Major was in a medical regiment that doesn't exist anymore. He left when it was reorganised, which coincided with his father dying.'

'Does that mean he's a doctor?' asked Robert.

Jack nodded. 'He was, but he isn't practising now. His wife was a nurse when they met and I'm guessing she was in the army too because the kids went to boarding school.'

'That explains why Karl and Di don't know them well,' said Lily.

'Rebecca left school with three As, got a first-class degree in hotel management and went straight into the family business when she left uni last year. Her interests appear to be horse-riding and fashion, judging by her social media posts. She's twenty-two and so is Alistair.'

Lily was surprised. 'They're twins?'

'Yes. He left the same boarding school before sitting his A-levels. I assume he was expelled after the drugs incident.' He looked across at Miriam.

She nodded. 'Yes, he's the only member of the family with a note on his records. He was involved in an illegal rave in Cumbria aged sixteen and found in possession of ketamine. It was a small amount for personal use and after considerable negotiations he was given a warning. So what happened about his schooling, Jack?'

'His parents sent him to an expensive tutorial college to take his A-levels. I don't know what grades he got but he's studying "Hospitality and Tourism" at a university in York. The entry requirements are not too demanding. Judging by his social media output, he's throwing himself into student life.'

'No mention of a girlfriend?' Lily asked.

'No. There doesn't seem to be anyone that he hangs around with particularly.'

Lily told them that Alistair was back from York for the Easter holidays now. If it was possible to check when he was home in November last year, it might remove him from suspicion.

'I was thinking about Greg Nevitt's bike being dumped in Raydale,' said Robert. 'It would be useful to check whether the Grants' holiday cottage was used around the 24th of November.'

Jack offered to find out whether they took bookings on the internet, in which case he might be able to extract the information. On the way home that evening, he commented to Lily that they'd been left with everything to do over the weekend while Robert and Miriam took it easy.

'I don't mind,' said Lily. 'In fact I'm going to be busy tomorrow evening. Alistair Grant asked me to help out with a wedding reception at their small hotel in the estate grounds.'

'What did Miriam say?' he asked.

'I haven't told her.' She was ready to defend her decision but Jack wasn't drawn. 'By the way, Di said she'd be down later but she had to get a lift with Karl. I guess we'll be talking to them both.'

As was usual on a Friday evening, they went down to collect fish and chips from town. It was surprisingly busy, perhaps because visitors had arrived for the Easter break, and the queue was out of the door. Lily instructed Jack to get their supper while she waited in the car. She was irritated because she wanted to put her smart black trousers in the wash before they went out, otherwise they wouldn't dry in time to wear to the wedding reception.

They'd only just finished eating when Di knocked for them. Karl was waiting in the car with plans to drive to a pub in Coverdale. Lily could tell it was going to be a long evening.

'Jack,' she whispered, 'I'm staying here. I've got to get my outfit washed for tomorrow night.' She pulled out her phone. 'Let me take a copy of the list so I can show it to Eileen.' It had occurred to her that Di might know the youngsters but not necessarily the older inhabitants of Hawes. 'But please remember to show them the list, Jack. And see if they can tell you anything about Alistair Grant.'

When they'd left, she tapped on the kitchen door and asked Eileen if she could do some washing. The woman had been relaxed about her using the machine and the dryer so Lily had got into a habit of doing her laundry in the utility room off the large kitchen. Eileen was busy baking so, once she'd put the clothes on to wash, Lily lingered.

'I've got a list of people here,' she began, waving her phone. 'It may seem a bit off the wall but I just wondered if you knew what they looked like. You know, things like hair colour, for example.'

''What's that for then?' she asked without looking up.

'Just work. It's to eliminate them.' She was deliberately vague in the hope that Eileen assumed it concerned her poaching story. 'A green car has been spotted,' she added.

'Go on then.'

Lily read out the thirty names. Eileen knew many of the names and could recognise the majority by sight. Lily ensured that hair colouring was included in her description. She specifically asked about offspring aged seventeen and over because they could have been driving the car.

'So, did that help?' Eileen asked when they'd finished. She washed her hands and dried them carefully.

'Yes, thanks.'

'Tea?' she asked, putting the kettle on.

Lily waited until she'd joined her at the table before asking Eileen about the Grant family. She said she supposed they were well known in the area.

'I haven't had anything to do with them personally but my sister has. What d'you want to know about them?'

Lily explained that she'd offered to help Alistair Grant with the wedding reception.

'So that's why you're staying on instead of going home for the holiday. I did wonder. Is Jack going too?'

'No, he's got a lot of work to do.' She excused herself before Eileen asked what was so important that he had to work over the holiday weekend.

'And don't worry, I'll get your things out of the washer when they're done,' Eileen called after her.

Lily spent an hour trawling through the Facebook posts

of Rebecca and Alistair Grant. They didn't tell her much new, except that they took exotic holidays with their parents, and their friends appeared to be scattered far and wide. Giving up hope of learning anything useful, she wandered through to the utility room to check that Eileen had hung her trousers up straight so she wouldn't have to iron them. The washing machine was empty but they weren't on the clothes horse. When the dryer suddenly made a whirring noise, she pulled the door open in a panic and removed her trousers, still hot from the dryer. As she held them up to straighten the legs, she was sure they looked at least one size smaller.

Jack arrived back earlier than expected, explaining that it was lambing time and Karl had been called back to the farm.

'Don't worry, we did the list,' said Jack, 'and I've only got a few missing.'

They compared notes and were able to cover all thirty names between them, some in duplicate. By narrowing it down to just men with light-coloured hair, they had reduced the possibilities to just seven, including the male members of the Grant family. Lily asked if he'd learnt anything new about them.

'Not really. Karl and Di don't mix with the Grants, they say the family are too posh to bother with the likes of them. By the way, they wanted to know why you didn't come with us. I think they thought the washing was just an excuse.'

'Seriously, I had to wash my black clothes so they'd dry overnight but Eileen put them in the tumble dryer so they've shrunk. I can hardly get them on.'

*

Miriam had spent the evening completing her weekly report for the DCI. It should have been sent that morning but she wanted to work without interruption. She finally had a coherent story to work with, connections between the three cases, linked by forensic evidence pointing to someone with fair hair driving a green car. She just wished she could stop imagining William in his Land Rover. She took another sip of wine and began a covering email for Charles, stating that they now had a clear line of enquiry and would need resources for questioning suspects and covering forensic tests. After all, once they had narrowed down the list of suspects, they would only need to carry out DNA testing on the remainder.

She was about to send the email when her mobile rang. The number was unknown but she recognised William's voice immediately. He was pleased she was around because he wanted to invite her over for a meal tomorrow. She began to think of excuses but he was already explaining that his sister and her husband were coming so he needed moral support. She supposed it would be all right. Once the call ended, she was almost relieved. After all, he knew she was a DI so he wouldn't want her snooping around if he had a guilty secret, would he? She was sure he must have had an alibi for the day Amy had been taken. She scrolled through the files to find the relevant entry. William Hill had been interviewed along with the other beaters who worked on the estate. He stated that he had been muck spreading all day and not left the farm. Asked if anyone could vouch for that he'd suggested that unless they ask his dog, he couldn't say whether anyone else had seen him. It wasn't ideal but Miriam supposed there had been no reason to pursue it further at the time. It occurred to her that when she saw him the following evening, she might even find a way to eliminate him from suspicion.

Chapter 35

Lily offered Jack a lift into work on Saturday morning, as neither of them had anything better to do. She would check the files to see if any of their blond suspects had given a statement during the original investigation into Amy's murder. Jack was supposed to be following up the Grants' holiday cottage in Raydale. He soon discovered that it was offered as part of the wedding package to accommodate guests, so he busied himself checking for any bookings for November.

By lunchtime, Lily had managed to delete two more names from the list. One was a long-distance lorry driver who was in France at the time, the other was an old man who'd had a hip operation and wasn't mobile. Now the list contained just five names. Jack had drawn a blank with the holiday cottage, so he sent a text to Robert to let him know.

'I'm going back to wash my hair and get ready for this evening,' Lily announced after they'd had the picnic lunch that Eileen had prepared for them. 'I'll have to leave by about four.'

'In that case I'll carry on. We've got background on the Grants, so I'll look for what intel I can find on the other men on the list, including the boss's neighbour, William Hill.'

As she left, Jack told her to take care.

'I think I can look after myself,' she replied but she smiled to herself as she went to the car.

311

The afternoon went quickly. At four o'clock she was staring at herself in the bedroom mirror. As she'd suspected, her best black outfit was at least one size smaller, so her appearance was more casual than smart. The trousers were tight-fitting now and the top exposed her midriff if she raised her arms. If she pulled it down, it revealed more cleavage than she felt comfortable with. She pulled on her jacket and grabbed her handbag. Downstairs she knocked gently on the kitchen door to warn Eileen she would be back late.

The satnav took her close to the estate but she was glad Alistair had given her directions because it was another half-mile before she reached the turning down to "Grant House", as it was called. The building was even smaller than "The Grant Hotel" but she'd been told the reception was being held in the barn next door. It looked as though it had been built recently, presumably to accommodate the wedding business. As instructed, she parked beside the barn and made her way to the entrance. Inside there were fairy lights, candles, tables with white cloths, tasteful flower arrangements, and a platform at the end with large speakers set on straw bales, presumably for a live band. It looked rustic and she liked it. She was thinking about how she and Roy had argued over the venue when they began planning their wedding. She should have realised they weren't compatible from the start.

'Are you looking for someone?'

Lily turned round. A teenage girl, dressed in black, was holding a pile of napkins.

'Yes, Alistair told me to arrive between four and five.'

'You're working here tonight?' she asked, looking her up and down.

'Yes, is he around?'

The girl laughed. 'No. You need to see Naomi. I'll show you when I've done these.' She indicated the napkins.

'I can help, unless you're going to fold them into swans.'

She laughed. 'No, they just go four to a table like this.'

It didn't take long. Lily counted twelve tables, so that was less than fifty guests. 'A small wedding then.'

'There's not enough space for more than that. We had thirty for the ceremony and that was a squeeze. I'm Grace, by the way.'

'Hi, I'm Lily. What about cutlery?' Lily asked.

'No need, it's just a buffet. The plates and forks are over there.' She indicated a long table at the side. 'Once we've brought the dishes in, they help themselves. They get their drinks from the bar in the house. Good thing too because you and me, Lily, are the only ones working in here tonight.'

Grace led her into the house where they found Naomi behind the bar shifting bottles.

'This is Lily,' Grace said. 'She's helping me tonight apparently. Good of Alistair to inform us.'

Naomi looked at her watch. 'You best start shipping the food into the barn then.'

The next hour was spent transporting the cold buffet on a rickety trolley, from the house across the rough courtyard to the barn. Inside a trio of musicians had arrived and were setting up their equipment.

'It's a ceilidh band,' Grace explained. 'They're really good. They get everyone dancing, you'll see. It gets a bit mad later when everyone's had a few.'

Alistair appeared when they had almost finished setting up the buffet. He went straight over to the platform where the band was doing a sound-check. It looked as though he was paying them in cash. He spotted her as he made for the door and gave her a friendly wave.

'Ok? Know what you've got to do?'

She went towards him. 'Actually, I've not been given any instructions. I'm just helping Grace.'

'That's fine. When the guests come in just tell them to sit anywhere and help themselves to food. They can come and get drinks from the bar inside.' Then he left in the direction of the house.

'Does he work on the bar?' asked Lily.

Grace laughed. 'You could say that. More like he works his way through the bar!'

At seven o'clock they took up positions either side of the big double doors to welcome the guests. Most of them wandered from the house but a few arrived by car and had to be given directions to the bar and the toilets. The band started to play quietly as people mingled or filled their plates.

'The food will be gone in an hour or so then we can start to clear away,' explained Grace. 'This is the quiet time for the next hour. You stay here while I go and grab something to eat, I've been on the go since this morning.'

Lily watched the bride and groom wandering from table to table, happily chatting to their guests. The band had gone to take their break in the kitchen but the level of noise had risen dramatically as the alcohol flowed. Grace appeared when the band returned and Lily began helping her clear the tables. Once the tables were cleared, they were moved to the side for the dancing to begin. The caller was shouting instructions for something called an "Eightsome Reel".

'What happens now?' asked Lily when they were back in the kitchen. Despite loading the dishwasher there were some wine glasses on the side. 'What about these?' It was only nine-thirty but she was feeling tired already.

Grace laughed. 'No, don't worry. I'll just go to see if Naomi needs a hand.'

Lily thought she'd make a start on the glasses anyway and was at the sink when Alistair came in waving a beer bottle.

'Want some?'

His voice was slurred, presumably he'd been drinking, although she thought she detected something else, recalling the report of his drug-taking.

'No thanks.'

'Why not? You've nearly finished your shift, haven't you?'

His words aggravated Lily. He'd asked her to help out as some sort of trial for the job of receptionist and here she was washing up. He moved closer, lounging beside her as she balanced the glasses on the draining board.

'So what d'you think of our bijou hotel?' he asked, waving his arm so wildly that he knocked two of the glasses onto the stone floor, smashing them.

'I don't know, Alistair. I've only seen the kitchen.' She dried her hands to look for a dustpan.

Grace appeared. 'What was that?'

'Just a couple of glasses, nothing important.' Alistair moved away while Grace swept up the pieces, throwing them in a bin under the sink.

'I'll finish those, if you like,' she said to Lily.

'Yes,' said Alistair. 'Lily hasn't seen the house yet. Come on.'

But Lily insisted that she had to tidy up so he left reluctantly.

'Wise choice,' said Grace when he'd gone.

'What d'you mean?'

She didn't answer immediately but after a gap in the conversation she asked Lily if she was looking for a permanent job. Lily explained that she'd been interviewed for the post of receptionist at the big hotel and the girl nodded solemnly.

'Alistair said he'd seen you there.' She had been drying the same glass for several minutes.

'What?' asked Lily.

'Just watch him. I make sure I'm not left on my own with him, if you know what I mean.'

Lily thought she did. 'Thanks for the advice.'

'It was better when the Major ran the weddings but he had a stroke last year and was in hospital for three months before Christmas so Alistair took over. The wedding season's only just beginning but I don't think I'll do it for much longer.'

When they'd finished clearing up, Grace said they should find Naomi because she would pay them in cash. They went to the bar together, where a crowd of guests were gathered round Alistair.

'Lily and Grace!' he called. 'Over here!'

When they didn't obey, he detached himself from the group to join them, placing his hand on Grace's shoulder to steady himself. 'What are you two lovely ladies drinking?' he asked.

Grace gave Lily a knowing look. 'We've come for our wages,' she said, shrugging him off and making for the bar.

He caught Lily's arm as she made to follow. 'I'm having

316

a bit of an after-party up at my place with a few of the guests.' He indicated the people he was with. 'It'll be fun. I've got some booze and some stuff that will liven things up.'

'Sorry, I've got to get back,' she said politely before joining Grace at the bar. She was stuffing notes into her pocket as Naomi counted out thirty pounds for Lily.

'That was a lucky escape,' Grace murmured as they left the building.

The sound of the ceilidh band drifted across the courtyard.

'Don't they need anyone on duty in the barn now?' asked Lily.

'No. Naomi will run the bar until midnight and Alistair will no doubt disappear with his new friends for the rest of the night.'

'So he doesn't know those people?'

'Not until today. He looks out for guests to party with. Like the tall guy I spotted coming out of the toilets rubbing his nose earlier.'

A pair of car headlights flashed and she waved. 'That's my dad. See you later!'

Lily walked into the shadows beside the barn where she'd left her car. She was struggling to get her car keys out of her back pocket when she heard someone approaching and saw the glow of a cigarette.

'Are you going already?' She recognised Alistair's voice. He was slurring even more badly now. 'I thought we could have a drink. Get to know each other better, if you're going to work for us.'

He was supporting himself against the stone wall with one hand while making a grab for her with the other. He put his arm round her neck, preventing her from opening the car door.

'Could you let go please?' she asked politely while peeling his fingers off her.

As he lurched towards her again, she pulled the door open with such a force that knocked him off balance. A series of expletives followed as she climbed into the driver's seat, slamming the door shut and locking it. He was banging on her window with the flat of his hand as she reversed out of the courtyard and sped off.

Chapter 36

Miriam arrived at the farmhouse just after eight. A bright security light came on as she approached and she noted that the only other vehicle was William's Land Rover. She was having a surreptitious look at the front of the vehicle for evidence of damage when there was a shout from across the yard. She turned to see a figure standing in the barn doorway.

'Won't be long,' he called. 'Just got to give this ewe a hand.'

She went across to join him but he told her to go into the house and help herself to a drink; he wouldn't be long. Collecting the wine she'd brought from the car, she made her way into the kitchen, expecting to meet William's sister. The place was empty but on the table was a bottle of red with two glasses. She took off her coat and hung it over the back of a chair before sitting down to wait. Five minutes went by. Then ten. After fifteen minutes she ventured into the hall. There was no downstairs cloakroom so she had a perfect excuse to climb the stairs. There were four doors on the landing. She found the bathroom and checked the cabinet over the basin for something that would have William's DNA on it. She found the brush head for an electric toothbrush but she could hardly remove that without him noticing. She crept into the front bedroom, which was clearly the one he used. It was very masculine with plain bedding and a small wardrobe. She found his brush and comb, and carefully removed the hair using a tissue, which she folded before placing it in her pocket. Her heart was beating fast as she crept along the landing but she nearly cried out when William called her name. She quickly headed for the bathroom to flush the toilet before heading downstairs.

'Sorry, I just needed the...'

'No problem. Drink?' He filled his glass and took a large swig. 'Wow, I needed that.'

His collie came over to her, sniffing at her pocket until William told it to settle in its bed.

'Is the lamb all right?' she asked.

'Lambs. There were two. I thought I was going to lose one but they're both fine.'

Miriam took a sip of wine. 'Your sister hasn't arrived yet?'

'Ah, sorry, I should've said. Their baby has a temperature so they can't make it.' He sounded very matter of fact.

'Oh, in that case perhaps I should...'

'No, no. Absolutely not. You must stay for dinner but it might be a little late.' He explained he'd not yet had the chance to make a start on the preparations for the curry because of the lambing problem. 'There are two options here,' he said. 'We can make it from scratch or we can get one out that I made earlier.'

'I suggest we do that if you're sure you don't want me to go.'

He drained his glass and topped them both up before rummaging in the freezer. Miriam watched him busying himself at the stove, finding it hard to place him on the list of suspects. That is, until they were sitting down with large bowls of brown rice and a chicken bhuna.

'So how is your investigation going?' he began, handing her a naan bread.

She wasn't sure how to respond and simply said it was fine.

'Did you say you were looking for poachers? Only they haven't had a problem on the estate for a year now.' He was looking across the table at her. 'In fact, I was talking to the keeper, who reckons you're looking at the murder of the Hobson's girl. Is that right?'

Why did Miriam feel threatened by his tone? 'I really can't discuss it,' she replied.

They ate in silence for a few minutes until he put his fork down. 'You know I was interviewed at the time.'

'Really?'

'You must know that, you've got the file.'

Miriam was losing her appetite. She tried to make light of it. 'I'm sure everyone was questioned at the time.'

He looked at her. 'It wasn't very nice being under suspicion.' Then he broke into a smile. 'I assume you're not treating me as a suspect?'

'Of course not,' she lied.

'Well that's good. Have you finished?' he added, looking at her dish.

She said he'd given her too much to eat so he cleared the plates away. They stayed sitting at the table finishing their wine.

He then started again, asking her whether she had any new lines of enquiry. 'I suppose you have to go over the old ground but you'll be looking for new information too?'

He pushed until she began to feel very uncomfortable, and, in the end, she had to insist that she really couldn't discuss it with him. It was annoying because she'd hoped to ask him about his work as a beater, without him knowing about the investigation.

'So you know the keeper well?' she asked, casually.

'Yes, he's my brother-in-law, or was before the divorce.'

'Oh.'

'Yes, we stayed friends after my wife left. It wasn't his fault, after all.'

Miriam thought about Henry's family and said she'd be happy never to see any of them again. It made William laugh. The atmosphere was almost back on an even keel so it seemed like a good time to call it a night. As she was leaving, she said she hoped the baby would be all right.

'What?' He looked so puzzled for a second that it made Miriam wonder if he'd planned for her to be the only guest.

'Oh, yes, thanks,' he said, recovering himself.

She left, no more certain in her own mind about whether William should be on the list of suspects than she had been when she arrived.

Robert had told his parents that he was popping back to Leeds for the weekend. Jean had laughed when he admitted he hadn't told them he was staying with her. They were eating breakfast in the kitchen; he was fully dressed but she'd come down in her dressing gown. He watched her make them bacon sandwiches and coffee, admiring her relaxed attitude to their situation. Did she often entertain men friends this way, he wondered.

'So, what do you want to do today?' she asked, handing him a loaded plate. 'The forecast is good. We could go for a long walk.'

'Actually, would you mind if we went up to Wensleydale again?'

She shrugged. 'Not at all. I like it up there. We could walk along the river and have a pub lunch.'

'Yes, that sounds good.' He hesitated, worried about what he wanted to propose. 'But first, could we pop into Raydale to check up on something.'

Jean was wiping grease from her chin. 'Is this work, Robert?'

He admitted it was.

She smiled. 'Even better. What are we looking for this time? More bodies?'

'No, it's more prosaic than that. There's a cottage up there I want to check out.'

'Fine. I'll just go and shower.' She grinned at him.

'What?'

'Nothing, Robert. I won't be long.'

He poured himself another cup of coffee while he waited. It was a perfect Sunday morning. He reflected that Jean was a breath of fresh air, someone who didn't ask why but just went along with whatever came her way. He hoped that their friendship would continue once he had to return to Leeds.

They left the house by ten and were in Wensleydale in less than an hour. They listened to "The Archers" omnibus on the way, despite them both insisting they didn't really follow it. The satnav sent them left into Raydale, through Burtersett, to a row of cottages in the middle of nowhere with several cars in front of them. Robert parked at the end of the line before turning off the engine.

'The Grants' holiday cottage is number five,' he said as

they walked back.

'The one with the grey paintwork?' asked Jean. 'Very trendy. I like the lamp over the door.'

They peered at the frontage.

'What now?' Jean asked.

Robert had to admit he wasn't sure.

'Do we knock?' she asked.

She was about to do exactly that when the door of the adjacent cottage opened and an old man appeared. Robert reckoned he was in his eighties. He had wispy white hair and a weather-beaten face which was screwed into a scowl.

'You won't get any sense out of them,' he called. 'Made a bloody racket 'til three in the morning and now they're probably asleep while we're up and about.'

He was about to shut his door again when Jean called for him to wait. She chatted to him about how hard it must be. Was it a holiday cottage? People coming and going? Very irritating. While she was talking, Robert noticed something above his window.

'Is that a camera?' he asked.

'What if it is? It's not illegal. I've had damage to my car before now, I'll have you know.'

Robert asked how long the camera kept the recordings.

The man shrugged. 'You'll have to ask my son, he installed it. I don't switch it on, it wastes electricity. I can note down any nuisance noise or damage when it happens in a diary, like my solicitor told me to.'

Robert had to control his excitement. 'You keep a diary of when there's a commotion next door?'

'Yes, I do.' He came out further to peer at them. 'Why d'you want to know? Who are you? What do you want?'

Robert hurriedly produced his ID, saying he had a very specific request. 'Do you know if anyone was staying next door on 24th of November last year?'

The old man looked at him curiously then went inside, closing the front door after him. Jean grinned. A few minutes later he emerged with a small hardbound notebook.

'November the 24th? Grant's Range Rover parked in front of my cottage overnight. Banging and crashing from next door until after midnight.'

'Thank you,' said Robert. 'You don't happen to know who was driving the vehicle?'

The reply was a shrug. Robert thanked him, saying he might need to speak to him again. The old man seemed unconcerned and returned to his cottage muttering that it wouldn't make his life any easier.

'So did you get what you needed?' Jean asked, as they settled back in the car.

'Yes, thank you. It's a lovely day. How about a walk round Semerwater?'

Lily was woken by the sound of the shower in Jack's room. She rolled over to look at the clock and quickly got out of bed. Breakfast at "The Pines" was at nine o'clock on a Sunday so she had just ten minutes to get ready. She was dressed and brushing her hair when Jack's door slammed and she heard him on the stairs. When she joined him, he had already started on the breakfast cereal. She normally gave it a miss but this morning she was hungry.

'How did it go last night?' Jack asked between mouthfuls. 'Did you have a good time?'

'Good time? You must be joking. I was washing glasses

until nearly ten o'clock.' She described the set-up and how there were only two of them working plus Naomi behind the bar. 'Alistair was there but he just hung around drinking.'

'What's he like?'

'Creepy. He chats to the wedding guests in the bar then at the end of the evening invites them back for a party.'

'Shame he didn't invite you.'

'He did!'

Jack looked up from his bowl. 'Did you go?'

'No way. It was obvious they were snorting coke at the reception. He was paralytic. He followed me out when I was leaving. There was no way I would've stayed to party with him.'

'So it was a wasted evening.'

Sometimes Jack could be really irritating. 'No,' Lily retorted. 'I didn't waste the evening despite acting as a dogsbody, actually.'

'Did they pay you?'

'Yes but that's not the point. I now know exactly what Alistair Grant is like. He's a creepy, heavy drinking, drug-taking womaniser.'

The door opened and Eileen backed in carrying two plates. For once, Lily was looking forward to her bacon, sausage and egg.

'It's a lovely day,' she said as she handed them their breakfast. 'You two should get out into the sunshine this morning. We're going out for a drive but I'll be back in time to make dinner later.'

Once they were alone again, Lily told Jack what she planned to do. 'I'm going to see the Hobsons to find out if Amy ever worked for the Grants. The girl who was working with me last night couldn't have been more than sixteen. And she warned me to keep clear of Alistair. I might walk as it's so nice.'

It went quiet while they enjoyed their "full English breakfast". Jack was buttering his toast when he asked if he could join her. '…not to go into the Hobsons with you but just for the exercise.'

Lily shrugged. 'Of course, if you don't mind waiting outside.'

Since it was a Sunday, they waited until eleven before making their way to the Hobson's cottage. Jack said he'd probably wander into town so she should call him when she was done. Lily took a deep breath before knocking on the door, hoping they wouldn't mind her unannounced arrival. However, Amy's mother seemed pleased to see her, ushering her into the kitchen and offering her coffee, which she accepted gratefully.

'Have you got some news?' Mrs Hobson asked. She'd called her husband and they were seated together at the table.

'No, not exactly,' Lily replied. 'But I had a question that might help our investigation.' Their eyes were fixed on her, which was quite unnerving. 'We wondered whether Amy ever worked for the Grant family, in either of their hotels?'

Mrs Hobson shook her head. 'No, definitely not.'

'You're sure? I know her friend Kirsty has been working at "The Grant Hotel" and they take casual staff for weddings at "Grant House".'

Mr Hobson's mouth was twitching. 'We didn't let her work for them,' he said severely.

His wife put her hand on his arm. She spoke softly. 'We

didn't want her mixing with Alistair Grant if truth be told. We heard about his behaviour, the parties and worse. Amy's father put his foot down when Amy asked.'

Lily wanted to know if Amy knew Alistair but she was aware that to concentrate her questioning on him would suggest he was a suspect. She shouldn't give Mr Hobson any ideas, should she? She drew the focus away by asking if she'd had any other casual work apart from the pub in Kirkby Stephen.

'No, none,' Amy's mother answered. 'To be honest we weren't happy with her working there.' She paused before adding quietly, 'And look what happened.'

'So, you've made no progress at all?' Mr Hobson asked coldly.

Lily felt she should answer truthfully. 'We do have new lines of enquiry. We believe we are getting closer to finding out what happened to Amy and why.' She knew it was just the usual jargon but it was all she could offer.

Chapter 37

Jack was waiting in the café. He was impatient to hear how Lily had got on but she made him wait until she'd fetched a drink.

'It didn't go very well, to be honest,' she said as she sat down with her mug of hot chocolate. 'According to her parents, she was never allowed to work with Alistair because they'd heard bad reports of his wild parties and lifestyle.'

'You mean she didn't tell them if she had been seeing him.'

'You could be right.'

'So maybe Alistair Grant *was* the secret boyfriend that Karl talked about; the one you wouldn't want your folks to know about.'

Lily stirred her chocolate. 'I suppose I should talk to Kirsty again. Hopefully she'll answer truthfully if she's asked outright about Alistair.'

'You think? Her lips have been sealed so far.'

'Until now she's been worried that she might say something that would make us jump to the wrong conclusion.'

'When she's been right all along, you mean?'

'We don't know that. Alistair Grant isn't the only name on the list, is he?'

Lily wasn't in a hurry to confront Kirsty and persuaded Jack they should have some lunch first. The café was serving hot food now so she chose a bowl of soup while he tucked into a beefburger. The tables around them were filling up so while they waited for their order, they chatted about the fact that neither of them were visiting their family over the holiday.

'My Mum is disappointed,' Jack admitted, 'but I told her I might be back for a while when this is over. Who knows where I'll end up?'

'I thought you were seconded from the Cyber Crime Unit.'

'Not seconded, just moved.'

'Oh, I see.' She didn't really understand. 'So you won't have a job when we finish the case?'

'Not really.'

He confessed that he rather fancied training as a detective but he knew that would be difficult. Lily expressed surprise that he wanted to give up what he'd been trained to do.

'You're so good at the digital stuff. We wouldn't have been able to do half the things you've covered for us.'

She was surprised to see Jack blushing. 'You think so?'

'I do.'

The soup was so hot when it arrived that Lily was still eating when Jack wiped his mouth and fingers with a paper serviette and grinned.

'That was an excellent burger!' He drained his second cup of coffee, leaning back with a satisfied look on his face. 'So what will *you* do after this?' he asked.

Lily put her spoon back down. It was a good question. She assumed she would return to Cumbria to complete her probationary period. One thing was for sure, she wouldn't have as much responsibility once she was there.

'Back to the old routine, I suppose. It won't be as much

fun though.'

They paid and went their separate ways, arranging to meet back at "The Pines" later. Lily hadn't admitted her nervousness to Jack but she felt increasingly anxious as she approached Kirsty's address. She was almost wishing to find no-one home but Mrs Watts opened the door with a smile and welcomed her in. She led her into the kitchen, where her daughter was slicing carrots.

'Shall I leave you and Kirsty to it? She can make you a cup of tea, can't you love?' She left, closing the door quietly.

'Don't worry about tea,' Lily said. 'I won't stay long. I just want to ask you a simple yes or no question.'

The girl had put down her knife and taken a seat at the table. Lily joined her.

'Kirsty, did Amy ever work for the Grants at the hotel or at "Grant House"?'

'Why?'

'Just answer yes or no please.'

'No.'

'Are you sure?'

'Yes.'

'Ok. So just one more question then: did Amy know Alistair Grant?'

'What d'you mean?'

'Well, you presumably know Alistair from working at the hotel, yes?'

She nodded. Her hands were clenched together on the table.

'Did you ever work with him at "Grant House"?'

'Sometimes.'

'What about Amy?'

'No.'

Lily could see she was struggling to retain her composure but she didn't know the cause of the girl's increasing anxiety. 'I'm sorry if this is upsetting you, Kirsty. I just want to get answers to these simple questions, ok?'

The girl sighed with a shudder. Her nod was almost imperceptible.

'Just two more questions then. Did you ever attend any of Alistair Grant's parties?'

She looked up with a frightened expression but didn't reply. It spoke volumes.

'All right, Kirsty. So did Amy attend any of these parties with you?'

Her reply was a mere whisper. 'Once, we only went once. I didn't work at "Grant House" again.' She wiped away tears with her sleeve.

Lily was considering what to do next. She was poised on discovering something important and was conscious of her inexperience, but it was now or maybe never. 'Kirsty, we've been told that you knew Amy was seeing someone in secret. Was it Alistair Grant?'

She waited, letting Kirsty decide whether she would give a response. Eventually she straightened up in her chair, wiping her face again and sniffing.

'I honestly don't know.' She chewed her lip. 'But I thought it was.'

'So why didn't you tell the police?'

She was struggling to hold back the tears now. 'It doesn't mean he killed her, does it?' She was looking at Lily, willing her to agree. When she didn't respond, Kirsty suddenly stood up, making for the door. 'Can I go now?'

Without waiting for an answer, she was gone.

Lily was still at the table, trying to make sense of it all, when Kirsty's mother appeared.

'Everything all right?' she asked.

'I'm afraid I've upset her.'

'I'm sure it wasn't you, dear. She's very emotional at the moment.'

'May I ask you something, Mrs Watts?'

'Of course, dear.'

'Did Kirsty's work mean she had much to do with Alistair Grant?'

She shook her head. 'No, I don't think so. I heard he was at the university now. No, I tell a lie, he did look after the weddings last year, with his dad being ill. I think Kirsty helped out with one or two at the weekends but it stopped well before Christmas. Perhaps they don't do winter weddings.'

Miriam had spent most of Sunday walking. She discovered that she rather enjoyed being alone in the sunshine, taking time to admire the view above Askrigg. She'd found the Herriot Way that Robert had been banging on about on the map and had taken a circular route along part of it. She wasn't used to the exercise, and returned exhausted with aching muscles. After soaking in the bath when she got back, she'd microwaved a frozen meal and spent the evening lying on the sofa in front of the television.

Next morning her legs were still reminding her of the exertions. It looked as though the good weather was continuing, so she chose her linen trousers and matched them with the only summery blouse she'd brought with her. When she checked her hair in the mirror, she was pleased to see that her face had a healthy glow where she'd caught the sun. The last thing she did before leaving for the office was to transfer the tissue containing William's hair into a freezer bag and place it in her handbag.

The team was gathered upstairs when she arrived, anxious to pass on important information. Lily took up a position by her timeline, armed with the felt-tip pens. Robert went first, describing his visit to the holiday cottage in Raydale.

'I spoke to an old fellow who lives next door to the Grants' cottage. Conveniently, he keeps a diary because of the noise nuisance that the visitors make. He told me that the green Range Rover belonging to Major Grant was parked outside his cottage overnight on 24th November. That was when Greg Nevitt's bike was dumped down the road – in case anyone's forgotten.' He looked very pleased with himself.

Miriam congratulated him. 'So the Major is a prime suspect,' she commented.

'Except he wasn't there,' said Lily. 'He was in hospital recovering from a stroke in November and right up to Christmas.' She looked at the others before deciding she would have to explain. 'I was told by one of their staff.'

She didn't want to repeat everything that happened at "Grant House" on Saturday night but she had to admit to being there.

Her boss looked worried but waited until Lily had finished describing Alistair's state during the evening. 'It does sound as if the son is a more likely candidate,' she agreed.

But Lily hadn't finished. 'I thought he could be Amy's secret boyfriend so I asked her parents. They didn't help but when I asked Kirsty, she admitted that she and Amy had been to one of Alistair's parties and she thinks he was seeing Amy.'

Miriam sat with her arms folded while they waited for her reaction. Robert thought she looked none too pleased with Lily. Finally she leaned forward with her arms on the table.

'An awful lot depends on Kirsty speaking up so we can pursue this Alistair Grant. Don't forget, there are a few others on the list with green cars, although we can cross the Major off now.' She couldn't help thinking about the hair sample in her bag. 'We should go through the other names and eliminate them, if possible. I've spoken to William Hill, so, Robert, could you interview the other two without raising too much curiosity? If you really can't eliminate them, ask for voluntary DNA samples.'

Jack had another suggestion. 'There must have been damage to the car that ran Greg Nevitt over, unless it's been repaired. Either way, we could check the cars, including the Major's Range Rover.'

'Good, you go with Robert then.' She turned to Lily. 'I think the most important intel is going to come from Kirsty. The sooner we have a statement from her, placing Amy and Alistair together, the sooner we'll have grounds to interview him under caution.'

Kirsty arrived with her mother, who remained outside in the car. The girl looked as if she hadn't slept; she had dark rings under her eyes and any movement seemed an effort. Miriam attempted to put her at her ease but, apart from accepting a glass of water, she remained frozen to her chair.

The DI began by repeating what Lily had told her: that Amy knew Alistair and possibly they were an item. 'Is that correct, Kirsty? Was Amy seeing Alistair Grant?'

To Lily's relief, the girl nodded. This was going better than before.

Miriam continued. 'So all I need you to do is sign a statement to that effect. Lily can prepare it for you, saying that Amy had met Alistair at a party and they were seeing each other at the time of her death.'

'What if I don't want to?' she asked quietly. 'I don't have to, do I?'

Miriam spoke gently. 'I can't make you sign a statement. But don't you want to help us find Amy's killer?'

Lily's heart sank. Kirsty was in tears again.

'Just because they were together doesn't mean he killed her.' She was wiping her nose with a tissue.

'Of course not,' replied Miriam. 'But it does make him a suspect.'

Lily watched her boss get up and go round to Kirsty's chair. Kneeling, she put her hand on the girl's arm. 'What are you frightened of, Kirsty? Has he been threatening you? We can protect you and once he's been arrested...'

'He'll know I've spoken to you.'

'But you'll be safe.'

There was an impasse as Miriam continued to crouch beside her. Lily gave her boss a questioning look that she seemed to understand. Smiling, she stood up.

'You dry your eyes,' the DI told Kirsty. 'I'll make us all a nice cup of tea.'

It had occurred to Lily that Alistair might be putting pressure on Kirsty to keep quiet. She had attended one of Alistair's parties, where cocaine was freely available. Did he have something on her? With her boss in the kitchen, it was Lily's opportunity to test if her hunch was correct.

'What did he say he'd do if you told anyone, Kirsty?' Lily asked. 'Is he threatening to tell your Mum about the party?' It was wild guess but it caused the floodgates to open finally. Then Lily realised the truth. 'He's got photos, hasn't he?'

Chapter 38

Miriam spent a long time talking to Kirsty's mother. She'd gone out to ask if she'd like a cuppa but Lily knew she'd be asking her to persuade her daughter to act as a witness and give a statement incriminating Alistair Grant, now they knew he'd been blackmailing her. Kirsty was watching them nervously as she sipped her tea and as soon as she'd finished, she went outside to join them.

Lily watched Miriam staring after the car as it left, deep in thought. When she returned, she closed the door quietly behind her. 'Our best hope of a quick arrest has just left the building,' she announced.

'So what happens now?' Lily asked.

'Get as much of this written down as you can. We'll need every scrap of evidence, regardless of whether it's hearsay or not.'

'But it will be inadmissible in court, won't it?'

'Probably, although there are exceptions for oral evidence if a witness refuses through fear.'

Miriam watched Lily typing busily, absorbed in her work. Her own thoughts were all over the place, so she picked up her notebook and went upstairs to gather a list of the facts they did have. After covering three pages with scribbled notes, she decided they had to have DNA from Alistair Grant. It could indirectly connect him to all three bodies. The only problem was how to obtain it when she had no grounds to arrest him. If they asked him to give a sample voluntarily, he could refuse, and it would alert him to the fact he was a suspect. They couldn't afford for him to make a run for it.

She discussed the dilemma with Lily over a sandwich.

'Shame we can't just sneak in and steal his toothbrush,' bemoaned Lily.

Miriam instinctively looked down at her handbag, which held the hair she'd taken from William, without permission. 'You know that's not an option.'

Lily hesitated. 'What if I already have his fingerprints in my possession?'

Miriam looked at her with interest. 'How come?'

'He left them all over my car window on Saturday night.'

Miriam silently considered the excuses they could use for taking the prints, but decided they were without foundation, unless Lily was accusing him of breaking into her car. It was a thought. 'Are you suggesting someone tried to steal your car at the weekend?' she asked with a smile.

Lily looked puzzled for a moment, then grinned. 'I think so. Perhaps I should check the prints against the database.' She began pulling on her jacket, while trying to use her phone at the same time. 'I won't be too long, I hope,' she called as she left.

Miriam watched Lily through the window. She was talking excitedly on her mobile while examining the car window. Soon she disappeared out of the yard in a cloud of exhaust fumes. Miriam went back to her desk to compile her report for the DCI. Assuming they had a positive ID on the fingerprints, the time had come to bring Grant in for questioning. Although the victims came from three different regions, she wanted to hold the interview under Charles's nose in Middlesbrough. Once they were confident they had the right man, she would question Grant under caution, threatening arrest if he wouldn't provide a DNA sample voluntarily, if necessary. He would have to be a very cool customer to refuse.

She compiled an email telling Charles they had a viable suspect who was going to be asked to help with their enquiries to begin with. They would ask for DNA and prints "to eliminate him" and take it from there. She would have Grant's vehicle examined in due course for paint from Nevitt's bike and for physical evidence of Amy having travelled in the passenger seat. Meanwhile, they would check Grant's movements at the times of the murders. Miriam was still hoping that once they'd arrested Grant, Kirsty would be willing to make a statement. The information that he'd been blackmailing her with photos of her behaviour at the party to keep quiet about his relationship with Amy, would be additional evidence against him. She edited the email several times before she sent it, enhancing the level of confidence she had that Grant was their man.

Robert and Jack arrived back late in the afternoon having found their blond men and eliminated them both. One had gone to Scarborough with his family on Friday the 5th of November, returning on the 8th. The other had spent a long weekend at a shoot in Scotland. Both provided a list of people who could vouch for them all day on Sunday the 7th.

Miriam gave a brief report on their chat with Kirsty, confirming that their main suspect was now definitely Alistair Grant. She glossed over why Lily had gone to Cumbria, saying only that she was confirming some fingerprint evidence. No-one mentioned William Hill.

Sylvie had been intrigued when Lily rang to ask for a really big favour. As usual, they were snowed under, which was why she was working the holiday weekend, but her friend said all she needed was fingerprint dust. So when she arrived, the first thing Sylvie asked was whether it was another of her "under the radar" jobs, because she was already in disgrace over the last one.

'I assume it's unofficial since you're also working on a bank holiday.'

'Only slightly unofficial,' admitted Lily. 'Someone tried to break into my car. I've got the prints on the window. Come and look.'

Sylvie followed her out and gave the pane a dusting, revealing a perfect pair of handprints. 'What were they doing, trying to slide the window down?'

Lily didn't answer. She was watching Sylvie at work, lifting the prints with tape onto a clear plate. She was reminded of the many times they'd worked together at a crime scene, collecting and processing fingerprints. When she'd finished, Lily said she would take them away with her.

'You mean you don't need me to unofficially check the database and unofficially find you a match?' she asked sarcastically.

'No, thanks. I just want to make a comparison with another set.'

Her friend looked sceptical. 'This is something to do with your investigation, isn't it?'

'I couldn't possibly comment. But thanks for this, I really owe you now.'

She laughed. 'You'll have to come back and help me get through a backlog of work if you really want to pay me back.'

Lily drove straight to "The Pines", planning to go into the office as soon as she'd had her evening meal. Jack came bounding down the stairs as soon as she came through the front door, demanding to know what she'd been doing. She ushered him into the sitting room, telling him to keep his voice down.

'The boss said you were checking fingerprints but it was obvious she was hiding something.'

Lily told him where she'd been and why. 'But it's not exactly by the book, so she probably doesn't want it broadcast.'

'So do the prints match?' he demanded excitedly.

'I've got them with me. I'm going in tonight to compare them with the others.'

Eileen interrupted them to lay the table and to ask whether they wanted cabbage or broccoli. Jack, who was standing with his back to her, pulled a face when Lily said to do whichever was easiest. She went up to her room for some peace and quiet before dinner.

Eileen had cooked cabbage to go with their sausages, and Jack spent the meal telling Lily how much he missed having a MacDonald's nearby. It seemed to her that he looked healthier since arriving in the Dales but thought it rude to say so. To her surprise, at the end of the meal he insisted on accompanying her to the office to work on the fingerprints.

'I won't get in your way,' he insisted. 'I can do something while you work. But don't you see, this could be the turning point of all our cases?'

She understood that much was hanging on her surreptitious fingerprinting of Alistair Grant. It couldn't be used in court and it was even possible that another expert might dispute her match between the prints on Amy's key and the bike, since she was no longer on the expert register. But she couldn't curb Jack's enthusiasm and he was waiting impatiently for her in the hall, clutching two bottles of beer and a large bag of crisps, when she was ready to leave.

It was eerie driving into the yard in the dark. Lily pointed the headlights at the door as Jack fumbled with the lock. He waved at Mrs Whitehead, who had opened the farmhouse door, reassuring her it was only the "night-shift".

It felt chilly inside so Lily kept her coat on while she waited for her computer to come to life. She printed copies of the fingerprints from Amy's key and Greg's bike, arranging them on her desk side by side with the plate from her car window. Jack made his usual Sherlock joke when she produced her large magnifying glass but she was too busy to think of a suitable comeback. Her work required more concentration than ever without the additional equipment she had access to back in Cumbria. Here, she simply needed to find as many points of comparison as possible and mark them up on the sheets. Fortunately Grant had left an almost perfect set of prints on her car and she could see they were very similar in size and shape to the prints found on the bicycle frame. Half an hour later she looked up to find Jack staring across at her.

'The prints on Greg's bike are a good match with the ones from Alistair Grant,' she announced, stretching to

343

ease her shoulders.

'Shall we celebrate?' he asked, indicating the bottles lined up on his desk.

'Not yet. I want to check the key sample before having any alcohol. A coffee would be good though,' she hinted.

Jack trotted off to the kitchen obediently.

If Lily was correct, the partial print on Amy's key belonged to an index finger. She checked Grant's right hand and there it was again, the same small scar. She gave Jack the news when he brought her coffee but, happy that she had a match, she carried on marking up the points until she had a water-tight case. Meanwhile Jack had already started a celebratory beer.

Once she'd made a rough draft of her notes, she decided to call it a night. 'Ok, Jack, I'll have that beer now, and a few crisps if you haven't finished the packet.'

Next morning Lily completed her report and handed it to her boss. And as soon as she'd finished reading it, Miriam clapped her hands to get everyone's attention.

'I'm confident we have enough to call Alistair Grant in for questioning.' Everyone was alert. 'I'm contacting Middlesbrough to send uniform over to pick him up. If they find him this morning, Robert and I will interview him over there this afternoon.'

Jack raised his hand, looking puzzled. 'Why are you taking him to Middlesbrough when the crimes were committed here in North Yorkshire?'

Miriam nodded. 'And the original cases belong to Cumbria, West Yorkshire and Cleveland? It's a fair question. Our unit was set up through HQ in Middlesbrough; I'm based there and our DCI is over there. Anything else?'

He shook his head, so she sat back down at her desk. Although Charles hadn't replied to her email, she began making arrangements for Alistair Grant to be picked up to "help them with their enquiries". She just hoped he would go voluntarily. Robert wanted to discuss the interview plan so they retreated upstairs for the next hour, until Miriam was disturbed by a call from Charles.

'Would you give us a few minutes?' she asked Robert, who withdrew downstairs.

Lily made him a coffee while Jack quizzed him about what the interview would entail. When she returned, Robert asked about Alistair Grant.

'You've met him, Lily. How d'you think he'll respond to being invited for an informal chat?'

She considered for a moment. 'He's very confident, arrogant, cocky. He's been threatening poor Kirsty. I think he'll brazen it out. After all, we're short on evidence. Once he's arrested, we'll be able to get the forensics we need, including examination of the car for traces of Amy.'

'What can we do now?' asked Jack. 'I should be working on his phone and computer.'

'Not until he's been arrested,' warned Robert. 'The best thing you can do is find out his movements on the 7th and 24th of November. We already know he was driving the Range Rover in Raydale on 24th but is there any way of showing he was in Cotterdale that same evening? What about Kirkby Stephen on the 7th?'

Jack was explaining he'd already looked for CCTV on the route when they were interrupted by Miriam joining them.

'I think we should be going, Robert. Uniform are on

their way so if they do pick Grant up, we'll only just be ahead of them at this rate.' She turned to Lily and Jack. 'We'll keep you informed and let you know if we need you to follow anything up.' She smiled at them and raised her eyebrows. 'Wish us luck!'

When they'd gone, Jack said, 'It's a bit of an anti-climax, after all the work building up to this, isn't it?'

'It's not finished yet,' warned Lily. 'I think he'll try and bluff his way out. I just hope the boss has sufficient grounds for his arrest.'

Chapter 39

Miriam had heard about Alistair Grant's wild parties with cocaine freely available, so she was taken aback by the figure seated across the table. He was dressed in a light grey suit with a pale blue tie. His hair was short and gelled neatly into place with a slight quiff. He was leaning back in his chair looking relaxed, an empty coffee cup in front of him. He stood up and smiled politely when she introduced herself and Robert, and said he was happy to have their chat recorded. He sat up straighter when she told him that although he was there voluntarily, he was being interviewed under caution, but he assured her he wanted to help in whatever way he could once he understood why he was there.

Miriam had gone over their strategy in the car. Essentially, she'd told Robert to follow her lead. So she began by telling Grant he was there to help them investigate some serious crimes that had happened close to Hawes. He nodded, as if indicating he knew what they were referring to. She had a series of questions she would work through, but she wanted to start with a couple of apparently innocuous ones.

'I'd just like to check a couple of dates with you, Alistair. The 7th and the 24th of November last year. Could you tell me where you were on those dates, starting with the 7th, which was a Sunday?'

He frowned then brought out his phone, appearing to scroll through to find the date. 'There was a wedding that weekend. Dad was in hospital so I came back from uni to look after it. I would've been helping tidy up on the Sunday afternoon.'

Robert noticed he had assumed they were only interested in the afternoon and passed a note to his DI.

'What about Wednesday the 24th of November?' Miriam asked.

More scrolling. 'I would've been at uni. There were no more weddings last year.'

'But we can place you at a cottage in Raydale on the night of that date,' said Miriam firmly.

He shook his head. 'No, you're mistaken. I was definitely in York the whole week.'

Miriam paused. 'Ok. So now I'd like to ask you about Amy Hobson. An eighteen-year-old girl who went missing on the 7th of November and whose body was found in Cotterdale three weeks later.' She looked across and he stared back at her. 'How well did you know Amy?'

He said he hadn't known her, although obviously he'd read about the murder at the time.

'We have a witness who says that Amy Hobson attended one of your parties.'

He stared back, almost defiantly. 'They must have been mistaken. Unless she was there and I didn't notice. That's probably what happened.' He relaxed back.

It was then that Miriam felt confident they would be able to arrest and charge him – it was just a matter of time. That being the case, Kirsty would be safe from his threats.

'We have a witness who knows Amy was at the party, and that you and Amy were seeing each other.'

He put his head on one side and half-closed his eyes, as if considering the options then relaxed. 'It's Kirsty, isn't it?' he asked with a laugh, shaking his head. 'She's still mad at me. We had a bit of a fling last year but I have to study as well as look after the wedding business, so I cooled it. Have you seen her? She's a mess. I feel quite bad about the break-up. Has she been spreading lies about me?'

Miriam ignored him and continued. 'We can easily resolve this by taking your fingerprints and a sample of your DNA, if that's all right with you. It won't take long and we can eliminate you straight away.'

His smile changed to a frown. 'That sounds a bit heavy. Shouldn't I have a solicitor here?'

'You can call one at any time, we told you so before.'

He pulled his phone from his pocket.

Miriam nodded to Robert. 'We'll terminate the interview to give Mr Grant time to get legal advice. I'll be back in an hour.'

HQ was less than ten minutes away and she rang Charles to warn him she wanted to discuss an arrest. He was waiting for her in his office, standing at the window.

'What's the rush?' he asked when she said she didn't have time for coffee.

'We suspect Alistair Grant killed Amy Hobson, Greg Nevitt and Brian Berry. We've questioned him under caution and asked for DNA voluntarily but he's fetching his lawyer. I'm worried he'll try to evade us if we let him go. We'll have to arrest him now if we want to get forensic evidence.'

He turned to survey the view while he kept her waiting for a response. 'Are you confident of a charge?'

'Absolutely. With prints and DNA we can link him to all three victims. He's been threatening a witness who knows he was seeing Amy Hobson. Once he's in custody,

I'm sure she'll provide a written statement.'

He hesitated. 'You know there's a lot riding on this. Your unit is an experiment in joined-up policing and we can't afford for it to go wrong.'

This amused Miriam. She was sure he wanted it to fail but she supposed he would be taking the glory when she succeeded against the odds. She assured him it would be done by the book and Alistair Grant would be in custody by lunchtime the following day.

He laughed. 'If that's the case I'll take you out for a celebratory meal.'

She smiled but knew she would be returning to Hawes to celebrate with her team if all went well. On her way back to the police station, Robert called to tell her that Grant's solicitor had arrived from Darlington.

'As expected, the family solicitor has advised Grant to keep quiet. He's a dapper little man with a comb-over called Mr Gascoigne, who's treating his client like a schoolboy.'

'I don't suppose it's the first time he's been called by the family to sort out the young man's misdemeanours. Tell him why we want samples of DNA and prints and if they're not provided voluntarily, we'll have no choice but to arrest his client. Hopefully he'll refuse, otherwise we might have to let him leave afterwards.'

Jack had been to Raydale to visit the man living next door to Grant's holiday cottage. He returned with a copy of his nuisance diary for the 24th of November, on his phone. He was in the middle of downloading it onto his laptop when Lily received a call.

'That was the boss. Alistair has refused to give a DNA

sample so they're arresting him. She wants me to get a written statement from Kirsty as soon as possible.'

'I thought she refused.'

'That was before. Now he's under arrest she'll feel differently, with luck.'

'You might need it.'

Lily rang Kirsty to give her the news then left straight away, telling Jack she was going to get a statement if she had to stay there all evening. He wished her luck, joking that he'd keep her dinner hot for her. Not wishing to be left out, he sent a text to Robert with the entry from the diary, asking him if he could interrogate Grant's phone yet? Robert replied almost immediately to say that they'd just seized the phone and found the photographs that Kirsty was worried about. Jack passed the text on to Lily. She was reading it when Mrs Watts opened her front door.

Kirsty's parents were finally to learn what had really been going on, because when their daughter came downstairs, she said she would like them present. Lily explained that Alistair Grant had been arrested for Amy's murder and Kirsty was an important witness. Now he'd been arrested, there was no reason why Kirsty should be worried about making a statement. Her parents told her she should help the police convict him and she nodded.

Lily, armed with her laptop, suggested she and Kirsty adjourn to the kitchen table, where she was quick to tell the girl that they'd found the photographs on Alistair's phone. She was still pale but her body language was tougher; she said it didn't matter now, even if her parents found out about the cocaine because it was over. To Lily's surprise, Kirsty revealed that Amy had told her about her affair with Alistair but because of his reputation had sworn her to secrecy. Lily took down all the details about when and where Alistair had threatened to post the photograph of Kirsty snorting a line of cocaine on social media. She also showed Lily messages she'd received from him, telling her to keep quiet about his relationship with Amy. As soon as she'd finished typing her statement, Lily turned the laptop round so Kirsty could read it through. She explained that she would receive a formal copy for signature in due course. Before she shut her laptop, she emailed the statement to Miriam.

Kirsty's parents were waiting in the sitting room for their daughter. She smiled as she sat between them on the sofa and said she would explain what was in her statement. Her father put his arm round her.

'I'll leave you to it,' said Lily. 'No, don't get up, I'll see myself out.' She had a lump in her throat as she pulled the door shut behind her.

When she reached "The Pines", she discovered there was one more thing to do before she finished for the day.

'Robert's been trying to reach you,' Jack announced. 'He's sending you a copy of Alistair Grant's fingerprints that he'd like you to check.'

'You do know I did that yesterday?'

'Unofficially, though. This is official.'

'They'll have to be corroborated by an expert.'

'He knows, but it will hopefully be good enough for the charges.'

'I might be able to get Sylvie to authorise my work tomorrow morning if I do it tonight.'

'Robert said they're taking Grant's Range Rover away for forensics this afternoon. It's a very high-end vehicle so I wondered whether it has an integrated dashcam. If it has,

I was thinking I might see if I can access the data.' Then he added with a grin, 'Seeing as that I am actually officially authorised to do it.'

Alistair Grant wasn't quite so chirpy after spending the night in a cell. He slumped in his chair in the interview room while they waited for Mr Gascoigne, who arrived punctually at nine. He began by confirming his client would not be responding to questions. Miriam put it to Grant that his fingerprints matched those on Amy's keys although he said he'd never met her.

'Did you try to help start her car? Did you offer her a lift home? Did you take her to Cotterdale? We have a written witness statement that you were seeing Amy secretly and that you have been threatening the witness if they divulged the information.'

Miriam didn't want to give too much away, so asked if he knew a man called Greg Nevitt. 'He was found dead in Cotterdale. We have your fingerprints on his bicycle, which had been dumped in Raydale on the 24th of November. You were staying at the family cottage that night, weren't you?'

She wouldn't mention the hair in Brian Berry's hand until they'd processed Grant's DNA, but she did ask him how well he knew Cotterdale. 'Don't you shoot pheasants there as a guest of the estate? Doesn't your family catering company provide the lunches for the shoot? You would need to know how to get in and out of the estate for that, wouldn't you? You must know it well.'

With no response from Grant, there was little more she could do but wait for a response to her request to charge. Lily had come up trumps with the fingerprints, with an expert from Cumbria confirming a link between Grant, Amy's keys and Nevitt's bike. Jack was hoping there might be something from the dashcam of the Range Rover but had nothing yet and the DNA evidence would not be available before the deadline at three-thirty that afternoon. They would have to release Grant after twenty-four hours if they hadn't charged him by then. If their request was refused, Miriam was worried that by the time they had a sufficiently watertight case to satisfy the Prosecution Service, Grant could have fled the country.

Jack had finished his breakfast before Lily appeared and was impatient to get to the office. He'd discovered that the Range Rover app would retain information from a dashcam on cloud storage. But even if Major Grant's Range Rover was fitted with the dashcam, Jack wouldn't be able to access it without making some calls first. When he tried to explain it to Lily, she said it was all gobbledygook to her but told Eileen she would just have a piece of toast as they were keen to be off. She admitted she was as anxious as he was to see what might have been recorded by a camera in the car.

Lily said it was strange to be the only ones in the office yet again but Jack was too busy to notice. He was sending emails and texts to a series of contact names and getting nowhere, when Lily suggested he asked the Grants for permission to access the files.

'Well, that's not going to happen, is it? Their son has just been arrested for murder.'

'Exactly. If it was me, I'd want to prove he was innocent, assuming they both think he is. It's worth a try. After all, it is their car, not Alistair's.'

Jack told Lily she would have to make the call and listened as she explained the situation.

'...so we will be accessing your dashcam records as part of the investigation but it would be quicker if you are able to give us the details.' She grabbed a piece of paper and scribbled something down. 'Thank you, Major Grant and I'm sorry to contact you in such difficult circumstances.' She put the phone down muttering, 'I don't think he recognised my name.' She passed Jack the paper. 'Does this mean anything to you?'

He downloaded the app and typed in the password Lily had given him. It was ridiculously straightforward. Soon he was trawling the dates and locating the relevant days in November. It was going to take a while to extract the important sections but fortunately he knew which times were critical and started copying parts that would be most useful. Lily kept his coffee mug filled and came to sit beside him when he told her he had what they needed.

'This is amazing. It records the locations as well as the dates and times. Unfortunately it's not set to record when it's parked but most of the action is here. I've got him in Kirkby Stephen and Cotterdale on the 7th, back in Cotterdale on the 24th then in Raydale. It will take time to gather it together but it's all here.'

The Crown Prosecution Service response was to ask for more supporting evidence. When Miriam told Robert, they both knew there was nothing more to offer. They had two hours left before they would have to let Grant leave without charge. Miriam was sure that would be the end of their investigation, with her trial unit seen as a waste of time and money. The team would go their separate ways and she would be back in her flat with nothing to show for it.

Robert didn't appear that interested in their plight. He was reading messages on his phone, so she offered to fetch them coffees.

'Sorry, boss?' he said, without looking up. 'I'm trying to follow what Jack is saying here. It's something to do with videos.' She waited. 'I think I'd better call him,' he said.

When she returned, Robert was unusually excited. 'The lad's come up trumps,' he said. 'The Range Rover has a dashcam that stores everything. He's got videos of where it was and at what time for the key dates. He says you can even see images of the victims when they were still alive.'

'We'd better get on to CPS before we run out of time then.'

Chapter 40

'So what happens now?' Jack asked, shutting his laptop. 'I suppose we all just pack up and go home.'

Lily told him not to be so silly, there was plenty of work still to do: forensic evidence to collate, reports to write, witness statements to collect. It could take several weeks.

'But after that? Like you said, everyone will go back to their old jobs, won't they?'

He looked despondent at the prospect of being out of work but Lily couldn't think of anything positive to say. She was nursing a hangover. They'd invited Karl and Di to the pub to let them know that Alistair Grant had been charged with Amy's murder and to thank them for their help. Di immediately went off to see Kirsty but they'd stayed drinking with Karl until closing time. Lily had warned Jack not to tell him about the other two murders because they were still waiting for DNA evidence, and she didn't want to jinx the outcome. She checked her emails once again, in case Sylvie had sent something through, she knew Miriam would be waiting for the results too, wanting to complete the charge sheet before coming back to the office. But her inbox was still empty.

Robert appeared in time for coffee and they gathered round to hear a blow-by-blow account of the interview with Grant. The sergeant kept repeating how impressive the boss had been, despite none of her questions being answered.

'He denied everything at first then clammed up when

the solicitor arrived. He tried to make out that young Kirsty had made it all up, swearing he didn't know Amy. That's why your fingerprint evidence on the keys was so important, Lily.' She beamed. 'Even so, the CPS weren't happy with it being the only piece of evidence because if he *was* Amy's boyfriend, his prints could be on them perfectly innocently. It wouldn't put him at the crime scene.'

'But the dashcam did!' Jack exclaimed, with a broad grin.

Robert hid his irritation for once. 'Yes, Jack, it was what clinched it with the CPS for us to charge him with her murder.'

'And the other two murders,' Jack added.

'The boss wanted to wait for the DNA evidence as well because it makes a watertight case, doesn't it?'

'The only thing that's missing is motive,' observed Lily. 'Is it possible he knew Greg Nevitt or Brian Berry?'

Jack put his hand up. It was a child-like habit that amused Robert. 'I need to work on the dashcam videos but I figure it might piece things together.'

'Well what are we waiting for?' Robert asked.

Lily headed for the stairs. 'Why don't you bring your laptop up and show us what you can see?'

She stood waiting by the timeline with a black marker pen. Mr X had a name now and she wrote ALISTAIR GRANT in large letters on the left-hand side of the sheet. Robert and Jack huddled over the computer screen. Eventually they began giving her the details to transcribe onto the page.

'So, he drives to Kirkby Stephen on the Sunday afternoon at twenty-past four and parks in the square,'

Jack began.

'You can see Amy's car,' said Robert.

Lily asked if the camera showed Amy but Jack explained that it stopped recording as soon as the engine was switched off. 'He sets off again about thirty minutes later, on the route back to Hawes but turns off here...'

Robert pointed at the screen. 'To Cotterdale.'

'Yes, he parks up the track in the wood where Greg was found.'

'What time is that?' asked Lily.

'Five-forty,' Jack replied. 'The car is parked for over an hour then sets off again towards the village and this is where it gets more interesting because he keeps the engine running the whole time.'

'Wait,' called Lily, who was still busy writing. When she'd finished, she instructed him to continue.

'That's the gate into the estate!' exclaimed Robert. 'And look, he's undoing the chain.' He was concentrating on the screen. 'He's driven past where Amy's body was found. Where's he off to?'

'He stops up here,' Jack explained, 'but do you see the figure coming in from the right. You can see him better when he reaches the headlights.'

'Is that Brian Berry?'

'It is. Look, he crosses the path of the car when it stops, so we can't see him now but my guess is he's come round to the passenger door.' The recording stopped abruptly. 'There's a forty-minute gap before it starts recording again.'

'My guess is that's when he killed him,' said Robert. 'It suggests Brian saw Amy in the car and Grant had to shut him up. Poor guy, he was obviously lost in the dark, looking for help and ended up in the wrong place at the wrong time.'

Jack was anxious to proceed. 'Now he turns the car round and drives back round the track... stopping here.'

'It's the wood,' said Lily, 'where Amy was found.'

'This time he turns in and leaves the engine running so he can see by the headlights.'

Lily watched in horror as a dark figure appeared, walking away from the camera. She could see Amy's blonde hair waving free as he carried her in his arms into the woods.

No-one spoke but after a short silence Jack explained that Grant reappears fifteen minutes later, and he fast forwards until they can see him returning to the car.

'What's he doing now?' Lily asked when the figure stops to lean against a tree.

'He's throwing up,' Jack replies.

They watch his journey back through the gate, pausing to replace the chain presumably, although it's not in view, and then travelling to "Grant House". Lily recognised the barn where the wedding reception was held.

They sat in silence until Jack asked if they wanted to see the data for the 24th. They agreed reluctantly and they were off again, this time starting from the family home just as it was getting dark. The journey to Cotterdale was familiar now but when he reached the gate and tried to undo it, he failed.

'Mr Mackintosh put a new chain on before he retired,' observed Lily. 'That's why he can't get through.'

They observed the car turn round and travel back through the village at speed. They were round the bend towards the entrance to the woods when a bicycle suddenly came into view. Lily couldn't stop herself from crying out as the rider disappeared under the car.

'He backs up and gets out to move the bike and the body to the side of the road before moving the car onto the track. Then, unfortunately he turns off the engine so we don't see what he does next.'

'How long before he starts the car again?' asked Robert.

'Over an hour.'

'Burying the body?'

'Presumably. So why didn't he bury the others?'

Lily suggested that he'd returned with a spade intending to bury Amy's body, but he couldn't get back in because the chain had been changed.

'So why did he drag Greg's body to where he buried him but decided to dump the bike somewhere else?' asked Robert.

'He wouldn't have been thinking straight about any of it,' said Lily. 'He planned to hide the other bodies but couldn't, and then accidentally killed or seriously injured a third. He probably forgot all about the bike until he saw it as he was leaving and wanting to get away from Cotterdale as fast as possible.'

'He certainly put his foot down on the way to Raydale,' said Jack.

They watched the final part of the evening play out as the car travelled through Hawes and past Burtersett, stopping briefly at the spot close to where the bike was recovered, before finally reaching the cottage where he spent the night.

Robert called Miriam to relay the evidence from the dashcam while the others made coffee. He talked for nearly half an hour before putting the phone down with a triumphant smile. 'The DNA results have come back, confirming Brian Berry had some of Grant's hair clutched in his hand.'

'...and a match for the DNA on the key?' asked Lily.

'Yes, that too.'

They looked at each other. Everyone was grinning. Robert said Miriam was on her way back and they should have a celebration later. 'Meanwhile, she said, please could everyone get their records up to date?'

There was a contented atmosphere as they typed. Even Jack's loud hammering on his keyboard wasn't as irritating as usual. It was over lunch that he suggested they should all go for a meal at the Indian restaurant to celebrate their success. Robert wasn't keen because he had a long drive and didn't want to get back too late but Jack wasn't taking no for an answer and booked a table for early evening anyway.

Later in the afternoon, Miriam rang to tell Robert she was on her way but had stopped off to visit the Hobsons and was going on to see Major and Mrs Grant before the end of the day. Robert told her of Jack's idea of a celebratory meal and she said she would meet them there. She had some good news she wanted to give them. As soon as Robert had passed the message on, he went outside to use his mobile.

'I bet he's ringing his girlfriend,' Jack told Lily. 'It's that archaeology woman he took with him to search for Brian Berry's body.' He was smirking.

'I think it's nice he's got someone,' said Lily sharply.

It was hardly surprising they were the only customers in the restaurant since it had only just opened and the waiter was still laying tables. Robert had driven Jack and Lily down so they could drink so they were already sipping pints of lager when Miriam arrived. There was a large glass of red wine waiting for her on the table.

'How are Amy's parents?' Lily asked her boss as soon as she was seated.

'Relieved we've arrested someone, of course, and I assured them there was plenty of evidence to convict him, thanks to you guys.'

They clinked glasses. There was little talk while they chose what they wanted to eat but once they'd placed their orders and were left alone, they began discussing the case. Miriam confirmed that Grant was admitting to nothing so everything depended on the forensics, including the dashcam evidence.

'That was amazing,' said Miriam. 'I couldn't believe there would be so much on video. It explains how and why Brian Berry and Greg Nevitt became involved, although I don't understand why Grant returned to Cotterdale the second time.'

'To bury the bodies,' said Lily. 'I think he realised he'd made a mistake by leaving them where they could be discovered. As it was, Amy was found during the pheasant shoot. He would have known it was being held that weekend because his family does the catering. He must have thought he could nip back with a spade and finish the job properly, except the keeper had put a new chain on the gate so he couldn't open it. I think that explains why he buried Greg Nevitt but not the others. We still don't know why he killed Amy though.'

'We may never know,' said Miriam.

They fell silent. Their celebration had taken a serious

note so Miriam stepped in quickly to lighten the mood. 'I have a piece of news which I hope you'll be pleased to hear, I certainly was. As you know, our operation was a pilot scheme. It was a new initiative to see if by bringing a small team together with different skills, we could think outside the box, so to speak. I'm pleased to say, the DCI is very pleased with the outcome and it is quite probable that we will receive a commendation as a result. So well done all of you.'

When everyone had settled down again, she continued. 'Because of the success of the pilot, I plan to put in a proposal to continue with the initiative. I believe it will be looked on favourably because the idea that local knowledge is a powerful tool has definitely worked this time.' She looked round the table to judge their response. 'I'm keen to continue the work so I hope you might want to join me.'

She was uncertain whether they would, and at first no-one spoke. Then there were lots of questions about where they would be located and how would it work.

'I don't know. I haven't written the proposal yet but if you think it's a good idea then we can discuss it in due course. But for now I just wondered whether you'd be interested.'

Jack and Lily didn't hesitate. They both wanted to stay in the team to work on more difficult to solve cases that had become, if not cold, lukewarm. Robert wanted to know where they'd be based before committing.

'The initiative covers Cleveland and North Yorkshire, Robert. I believe we could be asked to work anywhere across the Dales and the North York Moors, perhaps even into Cumbria, if necessary.'

Robert conceded that, in that case, he could cope with the travel because he was planning to move back to Skipton now.

At the end of their meal, Robert rushed off and Miriam offered to give Lily and Jack a lift back to "The Pines". They decided to continue their celebrations in the pub so Miriam paid the bill and left. Once back in the cottage, she changed out of her formal attire, opened a bottle of her favourite rioja and filled the stove with fuel. The action prompted her to take the plastic bag from her handbag, remove the contents and throw it into the stove. She watched with relief as William's hair disappeared, then picked up the phone to call him.

Acknowledgements

The Yorkshire Dales is a constant inspiration for my writing and this book is no exception. I have walked most of the footpaths and bridleways in Wensleydale and Cotterdale and can recommend them. All the places described in the book are real, as are the pubs and tearooms, but, of course, the characters and actions are products of my imagination.

An artist who is equally inspired by the Yorkshire Dales is printmaker Hester Cox, so I was delighted when she agreed to work on the cover illustration for my book. The final choice of this jacket has been a very important decision because it defines the style for the series. Our collaboration has worked perfectly; Hester was able to interpret and distil my half-formed ideas into the striking image that was exactly what I wanted for the book. In fact, I was struggling with versions of the title until I saw her print, when it all fell into place. I think you will agree that the resulting jacket is stunning, thanks to Hester.

I want to thank Kym, at Viridian Publishing, who persuaded me to publish my first crime novel and has continued to support my efforts ever since. I am also grateful to Ian, who translates my book covers into a printable form, to Andrew who ensures they look perfect, and to local independent bookshops for putting them on their shelves. Most of all thank you, loyal readers, for your continued interest in my writing.

Finally, my special thanks go to my family and friends who are so supportive of my crime writing career. To my daughter Alice, for taking the time to check that my police procedures are credible and to my husband, Mark, who is always the first to cast a critical eye over my initial draft, to whom this book is dedicated.